Winds of Graystone Manor

An Emerald Ballad Series
by B.J. Hoff

The St. Clare TRILOGY

Winds of Graystone Manor

B.J. Hoff

BETHANY HOUSE PUBLISHERS
MINNEAPOLIS, MINNESOTA 55438

Published by Bethany House Publishers
A Ministry of Bethany Fellowship, Inc.
11300 Hampshire Avenue South
Minneapolis, Minnesota 55438

ISBN 1–55661–435–7

Printed in the United States of America.

Acknowledgments

A special note of appreciation to Carlotta Defillo, Curatorial Assistant, Library, the Staten Island Historical Society, who graciously provided much helpful information on Staten Island.

To Sara Teeter, Thomasville, Georgia, my very capable and resourceful research assistant, whose patience is excelled only by her love of history and her tenacity. Thank you, Sara, for your attention to detail, your willingness to change gears at a moment's notice, and your tolerance of my erratic ways.

Special thanks to Carol Johnson, Editorial Director; Jeanne Mikkelson, Publicity Manager; and Sharon Madison, Editor, Bethany House Publishers, who first shared the vision for this new venture, and whose enthusiasm, encouragement, and faithful prayer support have made all the difference.

To Anne Severance, dear friend and editor: After waiting more than ten years to work with you again, this experience has been a gift of God, for which I am grateful beyond all measure.

Deepest thanks, again, to Anne and Murray Severance and to Sara and Philip Mitchell—

They know why . . . God bless them.

For years, B.J. Hoff's award-winning novels and poetry have crossed the boundaries of religion, language and culture to capture a worldwide reading audience. Acclaimed for her dramatic, authentic depiction of the Irish immigrant experience in America, as well as her memorable characters, Hoff is the author of the bestselling *An Emerald Ballad* series and numerous other popular novels.

She and her husband are the parents of two daughters and make their home in Ohio.

For Jim . . .

before whom all other heroes pale.

"Even in darkness light dawns for the upright,
for the gracious and compassionate and righteous man."

PSALM 112:4 (NIV)

Prologue

*H*e was trapped in the nightmare again.

He stood in the middle of the same vast room, imprisoned by walls so distant they might have been miles away. Beneath the towering pewter ceiling he felt himself dwarfed, reduced to almost nothing. Midnight shadows as dark as death obscured his vision, but he knew without seeing that something lurked in the gloom. Something malevolent and hostile.

Something that hated him.

His every sense was tortured, alert to the vile presence skulking somewhere in the room. Yet he had no idea whether it was beside him or behind him or all around him. It could be anywhere. He knew only that it was *here*, in this room, and that it was evil.

With great effort, he turned. His legs felt weighted, leaden. His pulse hammered as he listened for a sound . . . a whisper . . . a stirring somewhere.

There was nothing. Nothing but the pounding of his own heart, the rasp of his terrified breathing.

The cold engulfed him, immobilizing him.

And then the shadows began to move. Secretive and silent, they lifted and circled, closing in on him.

The unknown menace drew closer. A stone of dread pressed upon his heart. Panic coursed through him, and for a terrible moment he couldn't breathe. He wheezed, choked, finally pulled in a ragged gulp of air.

Still the shadows swept around him, drawing him into their center. The floor beneath him swayed. His head reeled, and with an instinctive move to protect himself, he ducked, at the same time throwing his arms over his face, squeezing his eyes shut to stop the tilting of the room.

After another instant he felt the air grow still. The room thickened with silence. The smell of his own fear washed over him, but he forced himself to lift his head and open his eyes. He saw nothing but the dark . . . a black, impenetrable abyss.

Unexpectedly, a dim, pulsating light appeared in the opposite corner of the room. Like a faint flush of moonlight struggling to escape the night sky, it trembled, then began to inch its way up the wall until it stopped, illuminating a high, ornately carved bed.

He saw her then. Her body, clad only in a nightdress, was flung across the bed like a broken doll, discarded and forgotten. Her heavy russet hair fanned out like a veil against the pale cream linens. A vivid scarlet stain traced the outline of her body, like a shadow set ablaze in the dying sunset.

"Kathleen!" He lunged forward but found himself frozen in place, like an ice statue. The floor pitched beneath him. Again he screamed her name, straining toward her lifeless body.

But he was paralyzed, unable to move.

He saw something stir beside the bed. As he watched, a dark form emerged from out of the shadows and leaned over Kathleen. He knew then with a dizzying wave of horror that this was the presence he had sensed in the room.

Finally he broke free, stumbling toward the dark shape, toward Kathleen, crying her name over and over, in a desperate litany. He moved with maddening slowness, felt the floor grasping, sucking at his feet to pull him down. Every step was labored. He strained, his heart thundering, his chest burning with the effort.

The hulking figure beside the bed turned, caught in the dim veil of light hovering just overhead. The face turned toward him was void, without features, without expression, as if hidden behind a mask in which no openings had been cut.

Struck dumb, he stopped. His head filled with the foul odor of corruption; his ears rang with the sound of his own silent screaming.

The horror deepened, seizing his mind, threatening his sanity, as he saw Kathleen's body suddenly jerk. Stunned, he watched her lift herself up with agonizing effort, then twist around, her heavy hair falling over her shoulder as she turned and stared directly at him.

Her skin was chalk white, the unrelieved pallor of death. The terror in her eyes struck him like a blow, and he cried aloud, straining toward her.

She opened her mouth and began to scream, a terrible, echoing keen that pierced the last vestige of his sanity.

"Roman . . . help me! Help me!"

His own screams awakened him. As always, he bolted straight up, sheathed in the clammy perspiration of terror, his body shaking so violently the bed rocked beneath him. The immense wolfhound stood close by, studying him intently as if to gauge whether this would be yet another troubled night.

For a long time he sat upright, hugging his arms to himself to try and ease the trembling.

"Oh, God," he groaned into the darkness, "will I never know any peace again?"

Later, when the terror had subsided and his heartbeat had finally slowed, he sank back onto the pillows, turned his face to the wall, and wept.

One

Staten Island
November 1867

*S*omewhere in the hills behind Fort Wadsworth and the place called the *Haunted Swamp*, Roman St.Clare finally admitted he was lost. In truth, he had been lost for hours, but only now did he resign himself to sleeping yet another night in his photography wagon. Though enclosed, the cramped quarters didn't do much more than keep out the elements.

The road had grown steep. He had lost sight of the harbor but could smell the river's brackish odor, borne by the wind. In the fog-obscured distance, deeply wooded hills rose, dull brown and shadowed. The wind came wailing down toward the wagon, evoking a low growl from the wolfhound at Roman's side. He tugged the lap robe a little more snugly about him, at the same time watching for a likely spot to pull the wagon—in reality, a type of photography studio-on-wheels—off the road. It was coming on to dusk, and he wasn't of a mind to go much farther after dark, especially with the thick fog rolling in.

He had seen few houses on this part of the Island. The occasional farm or isolated dwelling they passed looked old and slightly neglected, except for one whitewashed cottage that had brought a fleeting thought of Ireland and home.

He wondered if the peculiar quiet was typical of the locale. Even at this time of evening he would have expected to come across a farmer or other passerby on the road, but he had seen no one. It was a strangely unsettling silence, a forlorn stillness that hinted of abandonment and desolation.

"A bit grim, don't you think, Conor?" The wolfhound made a

puffing sound in reply, then turned back to his own appraisal of their surroundings.

Unexpectedly, the road leveled off. Soon after, it merged with a narrow, secluded lane. Roman slowed the wagon for a moment before going on, following what was little more than a rutted path, almost entirely dark and nearly hidden by the thickening fog and overhanging tree branches on either side. If nothing else, it ought to provide a good out-of-the-way place to spend the night, though he didn't relish the idea.

For another five minutes or so he followed the wooded lane. Now the tree branches—oak and maple mostly, and some beech—groped for one another, in some places intertwining and forming a gnarled canopy overhead. Without warning, the road took a sharp curve, then widened in front of two high iron gates, flanked by weathered stone walls. Above the gates, also in stone, were carved the words "GRAYSTONE MANOR."

Roman stared at the engraved slab for almost a full minute before it finally dawned on him that he was no longer lost. The lodging house—or "resort hotel," as the innkeeper had referred to it in their correspondence—should be waiting just inside those iron gates.

With night descending like a shroud, he knew he'd best be lighting the lanterns on both sides of the wagon if he were to see more than a few feet in front of him. That accomplished, he told Conor to stay and, reaching for his cane, stepped down to inspect the gates. They were unlocked, so he pushed them open, hinges clanging, then went back to the wagon and drove through.

He was almost upon the lodging before he realized it. Dense stands of towering trees shielded most of the stone front, leaving only the immense entrance doors and adjacent windows in view. At the back of the property, a forested hill rose upward. Concealed as it was by trees and the fog-draped gloaming, the structure gave little evidence of life. Three windows were lit, two beside each other on the left corner of the second story and another on the ground level, near the doors.

Roman reined in Hobbs, the bay, and sat studying the place. What he could see was impressive, if slightly forbidding in its austerity. The rambling stone structure was one of those many-turreted, gabled manor houses that at the least would be a hundred years old, possibly much older. The stone was dark, deeply weathered, and in places stamped with ivy. It looked to be wholly surrounded by trees, many of a size that indicated an age even greater than that of the house. In several places, their branches scraped against the stone as if to seek entrance. The shrubbery all about the house had gone wild, springing up carelessly where it would.

Roman stepped down from the driver's bench, wincing at the pain that shot up through his leg. Too many days of sitting in the same position, combined with too many hours of inactivity, had stiffened the muscles and bones to the point that even a negligible movement was painful. He had never felt quite so worn as he had of late, not even at the time of the injury. Often he had to remind himself that he was still a young man, and that he would eventually *feel* young again—or so the surgeons had told him. He would regain his strength, his vigor in time, they said. He wondered.

He stood leaning on the cane, looking about. Finally, when no one came to help, he started to lead the horse and wagon round the side of the house, the wolfhound loping along at his side.

The sound of a booming male voice stopped him before he reached the corner of the house. *"That's far enough! Just stop right there!"*

Startled, Roman turned to see a burly, heavy-chested man with a shock of white hair charging toward him, jacket flapping open, one hand holding a lantern aloft.

Conor growled, then barked. Roman silenced him with a short command.

"What's your business, mister?"

Exhausted and taken aback by this rude welcome, Roman stared at the man with some irritation for a moment. "Would you be Mr. Fairchild?" he asked when he finally recovered.

His challenger had stopped just short of the wagon. Now he walked around to face Roman, who again had to quiet the wolfhound.

Square-jawed and brawny, the man looked to be in his sixties. In the glow of the lantern, his face was ruddy, his eyes hard. He was obviously in a foul temper and seemed bent on making Roman the target of his ire.

15

"I asked you your business, mister."

Pain was spiraling up his leg now with such a vengeance that Roman had to make a deliberate effort just to be civil. "My *business*," he said levelly, "is photography. Actually, it's my *lodgings* I'm interested in. I've taken rooms here"—he paused—"if this is Graystone Manor, that is."

The older man brought the lantern a little closer to Roman's face, peering at him in the flickering light. "This is Graystone Manor, right enough. And who might you be?"

Roman detected a faint rhythmic turn in the gruff voice that hinted of the Irish, though probably from long years past. "Allow me to introduce myself," he said. "I am Roman St.Clare. I made arrangements by the mails with one 'A. Fairchild' for lodgings. I hope there isn't a problem?"

The other's eyes narrowed even more. "You're St.Clare? The photographer?"

The man's gaze was unmistakably skeptical. He glanced from Roman to the cane, glaring briefly at the wolfhound. "You were expected this morning," he said accusingly.

"I had every intention of *arriving* this morning," Roman replied, still groping for patience. "But I seem to have gotten myself lost along the way."

"Lost? On Staten Island?" The words were laced with disbelief.

Roman wondered if the man was being deliberately obtuse. He leaned more heavily on the cane, trying to ignore his throbbing leg. "The thing is, Mr.—ah—"

"Doyle."

"Mr. Doyle, I have never been on Staten Island before, you see. I expect I took a wrong turn somewhere. It was late afternoon before I realized my mistake, and, odd as it may seem, I didn't come upon a single soul who might have given me directions. At any rate, I am here now, and could certainly do with some supper and a night's rest."

"The table's been cleared by now." But in spite of his still surly tone, the man drew the lantern back a little. At the same time the hatchet jaw also seemed to relax, though only a fraction. "Do you have identification to prove you are who you say you are?"

"Ident—" Roman drew a long breath. Under different circumstances he thought he might have found the man's cheek almost amusing. But not now. His stomach was burning, he was bone-tired, and a dull ache had begun at the base of his skull and was quickly working its way upward, over his temples. It would take more than a fractious Irishman to amuse him at the moment. "Yes, of course, I have identification," he said, raking a hand over the back of his neck.

He reached inside his greatcoat and extracted a personal *carte de visite*, one of the wildly popular calling cards of the times, prominently displaying the bearer's name and photograph. Roman had designed literally dozens of them for clients during and after the War.

The white-haired man examined the card closely in the lantern light, his eyes darting back and forth from the card to Roman. Finally, he gave a nod. "All right, then," he said, his tone grudging. "You'll probably be wanting to go inside. You'll find Andy somewhere downstairs, more than likely. I'll see to your horse and your luggage."

He reached toward the mare, then turned, the fierce glare back in place. "Andy said there would be a wagon, but we didn't know about the *dog*."

Roman felt an irrational urge to apologize, then checked himself. He would discuss Conor with the landlord. Hopefully, Fairchild would be more reasonable. "There's a great deal of expensive equipment inside the wagon," he said. "You'll see that it's parked in a safe place?"

Doyle had already started to lead the horse around the side of the house. "There is no safe place on Staten Island these days," he grumbled, with no further explanation.

Roman stared after him for a moment, then ordered Conor to stay before starting toward the front of the house. As he hauled himself up the wide stone steps that led to the massive entrance doors, he found himself hoping that A. Fairchild the innkeeper would turn out to be a sight more hospitable than his man Doyle.

———

The entrance hall was spacious but dimly lighted. Halfway up a broad stairway rising to the right, a young girl was perched on her knees, her skirts gathered about her ankles as she pounded one of the steps with a hammer.

Roman found it peculiar that a servant girl would be hammering on the stairway, more peculiar still that such a task would be employed at this time of evening. He glanced around. An open door to his left revealed a darkened parlor. All the other doors were closed or only slightly ajar.

He turned and stood watching the young woman for another moment. He cleared his throat, but apparently the din of the hammer kept her from hearing. Finally, he moved closer to the stairway. "Begging your pardon, miss, but could you please direct me to Mr. Fairchild?"

The girl snapped a look over her shoulder. Although she appeared startled, she made no effort to get to her feet, instead merely stayed on her knees, staring at Roman.

Her face was heart-shaped, delicate, with a childlike full mouth and a saucy nose. The nose and one cheek were smudged with dirt. A kerchief protected her hair. Between her teeth were two or three nails. She appeared to be very young, and her blank expression made Roman wonder if she might not be slow-witted as well.

"I don't mean to be a bother," he tried again. "I can see you're busy. But perhaps you could show me to Mr. Fairchild? I've taken rooms, you see, and I've only just arrived."

Finally, she put the hammer down and stood to face him. After giving her skirts a vigorous shake, she ran her hands down both sides of the material as if to smooth it, then removed the hardware from her mouth.

With her eyes set on Roman, she started down the stairway. Once she stumbled, and he leaned forward as if to catch her. But she quickly steadied herself, thrusting her chin upward in a look of strained dignity as she descended the rest of the way.

She stopped on the next-to-the-last step and regarded him with a curious stare. Roman saw now that while she was young, she wasn't a mere girl. She *was* quite small, however—petite and almost boyishly slender. In truth, she didn't look all that robust, certainly not strong enough to do much in the way of hard work. He felt a moment of displeasure with A. Fairchild, that he would set such a slight girl to what was clearly a workman's job.

"If you'd be good enough to tell Mr. Fairchild that Roman St.Clare has arrived, miss?" he ventured again, watching for some sign of intelligence in those enormous green eyes.

The girl reached to tug the kerchief from her head, and the riot of thick auburn hair that tumbled free brought a catch to Roman's throat. Kathleen's hair had been almost that same shade—burnished mahogany, with random streaks of gold filtering through it like golden ribbons.

Almost angrily, he reminded himself that this smudge-faced servant girl with her freckled nose and wrinkled dress didn't resemble Kathleen by any stretch of the imagination.

"You . . . are Mr. St.Clare?"

Why did he get the feeling that she was surprised? Roman studied her, then inclined his head in acknowledgment. "I'm expected, I believe."

"Actually," she said, arching an eyebrow, "you were expected this morning."

Even her voice was childlike, with an odd touch of huskiness that seemed to catch at the end of her words.

Annoyed at this second reminder of his late arrival, Roman was also surprised that a girl in service would be so bold. "I *would* like to see Mr. Fairchild," he said, knowing he sounded testy but too tired to really care.

He caught a glint of something in those unsettling green eyes. Mischief?

She was odd, no mistake.

"As a matter of fact, it's *Miss* Fairchild," the girl replied.

Still clutching the nails in one hand, she lifted the other to make a brisk swipe down the side of her dress before extending it to Roman. "I'm Amanda Fairchild, Mr. St.Clare. And I'm relieved to see that you've arrived safe and sound at last."

Two

*A*ndy couldn't help but be amused at her new boarder's surprise. Obviously, Roman St.Clare had expected a man.

But when she met his eyes, her amusement quickly fled. The depth of sorrow reflected in that dark gray gaze struck her like a blow as she remembered the newspaper accounts of the terrible tragedy this man had endured. To lose his wife and his unborn child—his *only* child—in a senseless, violent murder must have nearly devastated him.

Finally, he accepted her outstretched hand. His clasp was strong and warm, and Andy felt an unfamiliar jolt of surprise.

Dipping his dark head, he searched her face with an openly curious expression. She might have found such scrutiny offensive in another man, but something in those finely hewn, ascetic features belied any hint of boldness.

"*Miss* Fairchild," he said now, his dark eyes still studying her. "Ah, yes . . . of course. I had thought . . ." He let his words drift off, unfinished, as he released her hand, though not her gaze.

Andy had almost forgotten that he was Irish. Though his voice was quiet, his words somewhat clipped, there was an intriguing kind of cadence, a lilt to his speech that brought a fleeting thought of a strange, ancient music and muffled drums.

It occurred to Andy that Roman St.Clare might be more of a surprise to *her* than she had been to *him*. He was nothing like she'd expected. In addition to being younger than she would have anticipated—he looked to be in his early to mid-thirties at most, despite the faint silvering of hair at his temples—he was also uncommonly attractive.

Startlingly tall, he wore a dark Union greatcoat that flapped open and black leather boots. His hair—a little longer than fashion prescribed—was an unusual charcoal color, his mustache and beard raven-black, his skin deeply tanned. Another surprise, for she tended to think of the Irish as having red hair and fair complexions. His coat was smudged here and there, as were his boots. Overall, he appeared slightly rumpled, yet his mien was anything but ordinary. He might just as easily have been decked in a cape with white lace at his throat, so courtly, so noble was his bearing.

Taken together, his features weren't classically handsome or aristocratic. His dark hair and skin, along with the high-bridged, rather prominent nose, combined to give him a somewhat hawkish appearance, even a *dangerous* one.

Andy reminded herself that St.Clare was *not* dangerous, in spite of his rather intimidating appearance. A quiet dignity seemed to emanate from the man. Nor was he nobility, for all that he seemed to exude a certain eminence. He was, after all, an Irish immigrant, a photographer—though admittedly one of considerable renown. Even President Lincoln had paid tribute to St.Clare's chronicling of the War, as well as his personal bravery during battle.

Like his mentor, the famed Mathew Brady, St.Clare had earned an illustrious reputation for his unique style of photography. Andy knew both he and Brady had taken their cameras to the battlefields in an attempt to capture, for the first time in history, the many faces of war: its barbarity and bravery, its horror and singular acts of heroism. Newspapers and journals across the country had displayed the grim evidence of their efforts, acknowledging St.Clare in particular for his stark, uncompromising depiction of life in the camps, the misery and despair of the wounded, the abominable conditions of the field hospitals, and the final outrage of young soldiers, many of them only boys, lying dead on the battlefields, their faces forever frozen in astonished protest to such an untimely death.

She suddenly realized she'd been woolgathering again—an annoying habit since childhood—when Roman St.Clare's words jarred her back to her surroundings. "I asked about my dog, Miss Fairchild. If you would allow him indoors?"

22

Andy stared at him. "Your dog?"

He nodded. "Conor is very well trained, I assure you. I apologize for not mentioning him in our correspondence, but I didn't think. I'll see to it that he's quiet and no bother."

"What kind of dog?"

She clenched her teeth, wondering why on earth she had asked—it really didn't *matter* what kind of a dog St.Clare owned, did it? A dog was a dog. And quite possibly a problem.

Andy was beginning to feel a little foolish. Finally, the Manor had attracted its first really notable lodger, only for her to greet him looking like a charwoman and gawking like a schoolgirl. Now she couldn't seem to manage a coherent sentence.

"A wolfhound," St.Clare said, continuing to look at her as if she might be a dim-witted child. "An Irish wolfhound."

"A *wolfhound?*" Andy swallowed, reminding herself that St.Clare's rent money would buy wallpaper for the parlor and perhaps the dining room as well.

Still, wouldn't something called a *wolfhound* be awfully large?

St.Clare seemed anxious to convince her. "Conor is very disciplined," he said. "Naturally, I'd take full responsibility for any damage he might incur. But I can promise you, there won't be a problem."

"Is he very large?"

The man's gaze didn't quite meet hers. "Actually, he is . . . but ever so gentle," he quickly added.

Dear oh dear. "Does he smell?"

"Smell?" St.Clare frowned, whether in puzzlement or displeasure Andy couldn't tell. He tilted his head a little and stared down at her in a most peculiar way. "I take it you have never owned a dog, Miss Fairchild?"

Andy shook her head. "Uncle Magnus doesn't hold with dogs. And neither does Miss Snow. She says they smell."

"Miss Snow?"

"Miss Harriet Snow. She lives here year round."

"Ah. Well, then, it seems I should have inquired about Conor earlier. I apologize."

Andy's mind raced. Dog or not, if he stayed long enough, she might even be able to have the chimney repaired.

She looked at him, again struck by a sense of ambiguity in St.Clare. While he appeared to be a man of good breeding and a quiet nature, there was something else . . . something far less quiet . . . lurking behind those deep-set, sorrowful eyes. Even with the evidence of his grief still so starkly visible, there was also a hint of something like anger, a low-burning coal, which threatened to spark at any instant and flame out of control.

Moreover, there were clear signs of pain: physical pain, no doubt occasioned by the injury he had sustained in the War. The newspapers had trumpeted his courage, describing him with effusive phrases lauding the "brilliant photographer who exchanged his camera for a gun . . . taking up arms on behalf of his newly adopted flag and the freedom for which it stands."

Studying the tall, prepossessing man in front of her, Andy couldn't quite imagine Roman St.Clare with a musket in hand. Despite the contradictions that seemed to mark him, what she saw more clearly than anything else was the face of a man who had suffered . . . was *still* suffering . . . not only physical pain, but an overwhelming, relentless personal grief.

Suddenly the extra money represented by Roman St.Clare's board didn't seem nearly as important as simply making the man feel welcome. At that moment, Andy could not entertain the idea of sending him away . . . because of a *dog*.

"Well . . . if your dog is as well behaved as you say, Mr. St.Clare, I suppose it will be all right—" Andy paused, smiling a little—"although you might want to see that he keeps his distance from Miss Snow."

He smiled at her then, and Andy caught her breath at the transformation. The dark, somber countenance suddenly brightened, the sad eyes warming with what appeared to be a mixture of relief and gratitude. "I appreciate this, Miss Fairchild. I've been looking forward to my stay here, you see."

"Well . . . you'll be wanting some supper, I should think. Would a cold roast beef sandwich do? And some apple cake?"

"Indeed, yes. I'd be most grateful." He paused. "But the chap outside who took my horse seemed to think the table would have been cleared by now."

Andy looked at him. "Uncle Magnus? A big man with white hair?"

The photographer nodded, smiling a little. "Your uncle, is he? He's . . . ah . . . very direct."

Andy winced. "Oh, dear. He wasn't rude, was he? Uncle Magnus comes across as rather gruff sometimes, I'm afraid. But he isn't a bit. He's an old softy, really. It's just that he's so protective of me."

"Then he's to be commended. In that regard, I can't help but wonder what he meant by there being 'no safe place on Staten Island these days'—I believe that's the way he put it?"

"Oh, my . . . did he say that?"

How much should she tell him? She didn't want to frighten him off. Not that a man who had crossed the ocean and survived a cataclysmic war was likely to be frightened by some unexplained disappearances. Still . . .

Andy glanced up to find him watching her. She sighed and tried to explain. "There have been some . . . troubling incidents on the Island in the past few months," she said carefully. "Nothing that should disturb your stay with us, though."

"What sort of incidents would that be?"

Andy was about to give him a reluctant explanation when she suddenly noticed his white-knuckled grasp on the wooden cane. *How could she have been so insensitive as to forget his injury?* She felt a flush of embarrassment creep up her face, hoping he hadn't noticed her lapse in manners.

"Why don't I show you to your room first, Mr. St.Clare? I'll have Ibebe—she's our cook—set out a cold supper for you. And something for your dog, as well. You must be very tired."

His eyes narrowed slightly, as though he might suspect her of deliberately skirting his question. But the truth was, he *did* look exhausted, perhaps even somewhat ill. Still, she wouldn't like him to think she was being evasive.

"If you want," she offered reluctantly, "I'll tell you the little I know about our local mystery later this evening, after you've had a chance to rest and have your supper."

"Yes, I'd like that," he said, holding her gaze.

Andy started to ask if the stairway would present a problem for him, but something in the thrust of his chin made her think better of it. Turning, she took the steps with deliberate slowness, all the while mindful that the ascent did indeed seem to require a great deal of effort on his part.

"Is this a holiday for you, Mr. St.Clare?" she asked as they finally reached the landing and started down the corridor.

"Of a sort," he replied. "I'm hoping for a rest, but I'll be working on an assignment at the same time—" he paused—"and a personal matter as well."

"I see." They had reached the door to his room, and Andy turned to face him. "Well, I hope you find everything to your satisfaction. If there's anything more I can do to help you, you've only to ask."

He stared at her in the most curious way, as if he were debating whether or not to speak his mind about something.

Andy saw the slight trembling of his hand on the cane. But his voice was steady, his gaze piercing, when he finally replied, "I will be direct with you, Miss Fairchild," he said. "It's quite true that I've come here hoping to manage a rest and to work on an assignment. But more importantly—in truth, my primary reason for coming at all—is with the purpose of finding the man who murdered my wife . . . and my unborn child."

————

Roman St.Clare's pronouncement about finding his wife's killer continued to nag at Andy throughout the evening, adding to her confusion. So unsettled was she by the enigmatic photographer that she avoided the dining room for as long as possible, leaving Ibebe to wait upon St.Clare throughout his supper.

She excused her behavior by reasoning that she still had another two or three hours of work to do before bedtime, work that included bringing in wood and stacking it while Magnus was occupied elsewhere. Lately, she'd noticed that he often wheezed and turned red in the face when he exerted himself. It would be futile to say anything to him, of course; he could be ridiculously touchy about his health or his age. But he *was* sixty-nine, and even though he looked younger, he was simply not as vigorous as he had once been. Recently, Andy had begun to take over some of the more strenuous tasks herself, thinking that the least she could do was allow him to slow down a little without losing his dignity.

As she pulled on her coat and started toward the kitchen door, she remembered Niles's recent caution about going outside alone after dark. For an instant, her hand on the latch, she hesitated. Then, impatient with herself, she stepped outside. There had been no new disappearances for over a month now, and only one grave-yard disturbance near the old quarantine hospital in all that time.

Niles didn't believe that the business at the graveyard was re-lated to the missing Negro children, but Andy wasn't so sure. It seemed almost too coincidental—all these strange occurrences going on at virtually the same time. She couldn't help but think there was a connection somehow, although she couldn't imagine what it might be.

With a tired sigh, she stooped and began to fill her arms with wood. She couldn't put the thought of the missing children out of her mind, or for that matter, the disruptions at the quarantine graveyard. Staten Island had once been a quiet, sleepy place, the kind of community where nothing much ever seemed to happen. Except for the rowdy army camps during the War and the draft riots in '63, serious trouble was virtually unheard of. In fact, like many of the other children growing up on the Island, Andy had often bemoaned the lack of excitement.

Over the past few months, however, all that had changed. These days everyone was on edge. Neighbors had grown suspi-cious of one another, and few ventured outside their houses after dark unless it was absolutely necessary.

The authorities had had no success whatsoever in solving the ongoing rash of crimes. For over a year now, the metropolitan police had assumed jurisdiction over the Island, but from all ac-counts the old constable system would have been just as effective in dealing with this unprecedented siege of terror.

As time passed and no progress was made, the rumors circu-lating about the Island only grew more preposterous. Some stories had it that a band of deranged Confederate sympathizers were stealing Negro children and taking them off to Latin America, where a "new South" would be established, complete with the vile institution of slavery. Other tales, more incredible still, attributed the hideous crimes to vengeful spirits, in particular, the spirits of those immigrants who had suffered and died from the inhuman treatment at the old Tompkinsville quarantine hospital.

The children on the Island had their own version of these tall tales, one of which Andy had overheard after Sunday services a few weeks past. Behind the sycamore tree in the back church yard, the little Hatter boy had been holding forth to a captive audience of his peers with a detailed yarn about the "monsters" who inhabited the nearby Haunted Swamp. According to Arthur Hatter, the swamp's ghouls were the ones responsible for the grave robberies *and* the missing Negro children, having taken them off in the night for their own fiendish purposes.

Andy had wasted no time in scolding the little rascal, all the while knowing she might as well save her breath. There would be no stopping the rumors until the crimes themselves came to an end.

In an attempt to turn her attention elsewhere, she stepped up her movements, carrying an enormous load of wood into the kitchen and stacking it in the woodbox before going back for more. Outside, she stood for a moment scanning the night sky. The wind driving down from the hills carried a cold, bitter sting, an unmistakable harbinger of winter. Magnus had predicted sleet or even snow by morning, and he was seldom wrong about the weather. Andy could almost feel the edge of the storm moving in.

She shivered, as much from the thought of winter's approach as from the cutting night chill. November had always seemed such a merciless month, stripping the trees of their blazing autumn leaves, turning the Island from a garden of glorious color into a bleak and barren place. As the days grew shorter, the wind sharper, she could almost feel the warmth and light wane from her spirit even as it faded from the year.

It didn't help that years ago her mother had died in the month of November. Even now Andy could still remember that harsh, frigid night, could feel the numbing wave of desolation that had swept over her, a badly frightened nine-year-old fleeing the house in an attempt to escape her grief. As time passed and the most painful of her memories faded, she had come to endure each November with a kind of grim stoicism, bracing herself right at the beginning for the inevitable days of gloom and bitter cold.

She had scooped up another hefty armful of wood and was on her way back inside when the thought struck her that perhaps Roman St.Clare also dreaded November. After all, his wife had been murdered at this time of year. Andy remembered, because while reading newspaper accounts of the slaying and resulting investigation, she had sometimes felt a peculiar sympathy for the bereaved photographer. They had never met—back then she hadn't even known what St.Clare looked like. Yet in sensing his pain, it was almost as if she also shared his loss.

Her mind was still on her new lodger as she finished stacking the wood and went to hang up her coat. For a long time she stood in front of the sink, staring out the window into the darkness. She cautioned herself that, despite her natural sympathy for Roman St.Clare, she would do well to remember that he was a stranger—and, from all appearances, a troubled one at that.

His somber intensity was perfectly understandable, of course, given all he had suffered. As was his desire to obtain justice for his wife's assailant.

But surely he couldn't expect to find the killer *here*, on Staten Island! He couldn't possibly believe that the local spate of disappearances and grave robberies might somehow be related to his wife's murder.

Yet why else had he been so curious about the Island's trouble, so intent on learning more?

The idea, no matter how unlikely, of a vicious killer loose on Staten Island uncapped a whole new well of uneasiness in Andy. Suddenly, what up until now might have been only a frightening and ominous possibility turned darker, more deadly. Shaken, she resolved to press the photographer for an explanation.

She wondered, too, why St.Clare thought he might succeed where the law had failed. It wasn't as if the authorities hadn't *tried* to find the killer, after all. There had been a huge amount of publicity given to his wife's slaying—the kind of sensational coverage that would usually spur even the most indolent of officials to action. Even in newspapers so far removed from the scene of the crime as here in New York, the story had been emblazoned in great detail, exploiting St.Clare's reputation.

After meeting him, Andy sensed that Roman St.Clare was not the sort of man to court publicity; to the contrary, she thought he might abhor it. Something about the man bespoke not only a preference for privacy, but a genuine need for it, perhaps even an aversion to the notoriety that had been forced upon him.

Even so, he might have tolerated the exploitation if he thought it would help to bring his wife's murderer to justice. But the case had never been solved, and in time the journalists had forgotten St.Clare in their search for more timely events to fill their columns.

Andy realized that her feelings about her new boarder were mixed and sorely confused. On the one hand, she felt a real compassion for St.Clare, was drawn to those stricken eyes, to the soft voice with its rhythmic lilt, the brief, uncertain smile. Yet he stirred a vague disquiet, a faint uneasiness, which, although it defied description, could not be altogether ignored.

Perhaps she was only responding to his magnetism, although the thought that she might actually be that shallow made her recoil in self-disgust. Was she suddenly going to start taking on like one of those simpering females in Miss Valentine's novels, the sort who came down with an attack of the vapors every time an attractive man appeared on the scene?

Still, there was no denying the dark good looks, the refinement and elegance of bearing that gave the photographer a certain compelling appeal.

She reminded herself with some acerbity that there was also no denying his probing stare, his blunt questions and ungentlemanly directness.

Thoroughly annoyed with her own foolishness now, Andy worked the pump and began splashing the wood dust off her hands. Roman St.Clare held no particular appeal or interest for her, she told herself, no matter how attractive some women might find him. Why, even solid, comfortable Niles didn't affect her that way.

Though at times she almost wished he did. . . .

She shook off the disloyal thought along with the water from her hands and reached for a towel. She had wasted enough time. There was still a lot of work waiting to be done.

All things considered, she would have preferred to avoid her new lodger for the rest of the evening. However, she *had* promised him an explanation of the Island's trouble, and he didn't seem the forgetful sort. She might just as well get it over with.

Besides, Mr. St.Clare might just have some explaining of his own to do. For one thing, she fully intended to learn more about his purpose in coming here. If he had a good reason for thinking the man who murdered his wife might be anywhere near Staten Island, Andy proposed to find out just what that reason was.

With no further hesitation, she smoothed a strand of hair away from her face and started toward the dining room door.

───────*Three*───────

*T*he first thought on Andy's mind when she awakened before dawn the next morning was of Roman St.Clare.

As it turned out, she had gone back to the dining room the night before only to find the photographer gone, a good part of his supper left untouched on his plate. According to Ibebe, St.Clare had excused himself midway through his meal and gone upstairs, pleading exhaustion. Relieved that she could delay any explanation of the Island's crime wave, at least for a short time, Andy had gone on about her work until her own exhaustion had finally driven her to bed.

This morning, though, she was wide awake, questions about the enigmatic St.Clare swarming through her mind like bees. The sound of winter rain drumming on the roof made her shiver. As always, the bedroom was bitterly cold, but there was no point in laying a fire; soon she would have to go downstairs. But not yet. She could indulge herself for a few more minutes.

Propping her knees up under her chin, she pulled the bedclothes more snugly around her and tried to concentrate on her morning prayers. But to her dismay, her tangled thoughts soon began clamoring for attention again.

Not since her father's death the past September had her mind been in such turmoil. Uneasy reminders about the mysterious happenings on the Island kept intruding, combined with countless questions about the stranger under her roof. She wondered how much St.Clare had recovered from his war injury. It worried her a little that the man might not be well. What if he fell ill during his stay at the Manor? And what about his *emotional* condition? He had suffered more than a serious physical injury, after all. The brutal murder of his wife was the kind of tragedy that might drive a man to the very edge of despair. There was really no telling how desperate he might be.

Ibebe had been quick to offer her observation about the new lodger the night before. "That man wasn't just tired," she told Andy in the kitchen, clicking her tongue, "he was in *pain*. Pale as a ghost and dragging that poor leg of his like it'd been sunk in lead!"

After agreeing that St.Clare *had* looked somewhat haggard upon his arrival, Andy reminded Ibebe of the photographer's war injury. But the tall black housekeeper had merely waved off the obvious, repeating her own opinion. "Seems to me that man is suffering from heart pain *and* bullet pain, likely more than his share of both. He's hurting real bad, I expect."

More than anyone Andy knew, Ibebe had experienced enough suffering in her own life to recognize it in others. A former slave, Ibebe had come North with her brother on the underground railroad before the War, bearing a map of scars on her back as evidence of what her life had been like before reaching New York. If Ibebe said that Roman St.Clare was in pain, he probably was.

Andy had seen the suffering in St.Clare's eyes for herself. Still, she couldn't afford to let her sympathy for the man color her judgment. It would be altogether foolish to take in someone who might turn out to be infirm and require more care than she had time to give. She already had more than she could manage.

Abruptly, she realized the utter selfishness of her thoughts and pulled a face in self-disgust. Had she really grown so callous that she was more concerned with her own convenience than another's pain?

Yet she *had* to be practical, didn't she? There were too many people who depended on her. She couldn't afford to take unnecessary risks.

But St.Clare was already *here*, she reminded herself. There seemed to be nothing else to do now except make the best of things and hope she hadn't made a grievous mistake.

With an impatient sigh, she flung off the bedclothes, jumped up and hurriedly dressed, deliberately putting any further thought of Roman St.Clare out of her mind.

Before going downstairs, she darted a glance out the window to see a weak, gray light beginning to dawn. The rain that had been falling for some time appeared to be steady and laced with ice. No doubt it would go on throughout the morning.

Andy winced at this unwelcome reminder—as if she needed another—that it was, indeed, November again.

———

By breakfast, only the palest mist of light had managed to squeeze through the dining room windows. Even with the oil lamps glowing, the room was still uncommonly dreary. The rain had intensified to a lashing, wind-driven sleet that, despite the blaze in the fireplace, made Andy shiver.

Ordinarily, she didn't take breakfast in the dining room. If she ate at all, it was usually to toss down a hurried bite in the kitchen with Ibebe or to grab a jam-covered biscuit on the way out the door. But after the second barbed exchange of the morning between Uncle Magnus and Miss Snow, she decided to stay nearby. Uncle Magnus, when grumpy, could be a bear; but he *and* Miss Snow in testy moods might be enough to cause their new lodger to have second thoughts about staying at Graystone Manor.

Roman St.Clare was the last to enter the dining room. At first glimpse, he appeared pale and hollow-eyed. Andy suspected he had not slept well, if at all. She also observed that, even though he was impeccably dressed for the day in a casual gray suit and mulberry silk neckcloth, the suit hung rather loosely on him; apparently, he had once been of sturdier build. His stride also seemed more labored than she remembered from the night before, as if a great deal of effort might be required to traverse the room.

He wasted no time in taking his chair, stopping only long enough for the necessary introductions and a polite nod to the ladies before being seated. Miss Valentine, bless her, immediately attempted to put the photographer at ease. Andy had known she could count on the perky, petite spinster. Miss Valentine liked everyone except absolute scoundrels and slaveholders.

Stylishly turned out in one of her frothiest muslin and lace creations, her silver-blond hair trapped in a coy little knot on top of her head, Miss Valentine brought both hands together under her chin as St.Clare sat down across from her. "We are *delighted* to have you with us, Mr. St.Clare!" she said, giving him one of her most dazzling smiles.

Miss Valentine always seemed to manage the rather remarkable feat of looking both girlish and slightly coquettish at the age of seventy. Andy adored her, and, watching Roman St.Clare, suspected that he, too, would succumb to the merry spinster's considerable charms in no time.

His expression had already brightened noticeably as he exchanged a smile with Miss Valentine. Andy tried not to stare at the same transformation she had witnessed the night before, but she couldn't help but notice the intriguing change in those ascetic features when he smiled.

Predictably, Miss Snow was not about to be left out of the conversation. Harriet Snow and Miss Valentine were year-round lodgers, having come to Graystone Manor several years ago, when Andy had been but a girl. Although they were of like age, in every other way the two spinsters appeared to be direct opposites—even in physical appearance. Miss Snow was a tall, sturdy foil to Miss Valentine's small daintiness, as pragmatic and seemingly severe as her diminutive friend was romantic and softhearted. The no-nonsense Harriet Snow was far more likely to demand than to ask, while Miss Valentine, on the other hand, could coax honey from a rock with one of her smiles and a sweet-spoken word. Andy thought of Miss Valentine as an infinitely graceful arabesque, Miss Snow an imperial march.

Through the years they had bestowed upon her their combined affections and the benefit of their considerable, albeit radically diverse, wisdom. Andy often suspected they had tried in their own way to fill the void left by her mother's death, and she loved them dearly for it.

The two women were the best of friends, and even though they made great show of their differences, they were actually far more alike than either would have admitted. One trait they shared in common was a robust curiosity. While Miss Valentine employed hers with genteel discretion, Miss Snow could not be bothered with subtlety.

Seated at the photographer's right, she now regarded him with an imposing stare. "Tell us, Mr. St.Clare—what exactly brings you to Staten Island?" Never one to waste time with the niceties of social conversation, she added, "I should think November would be a poor month for vacationing."

Andy squirmed on her chair. Beside her, Miss Valentine went on smiling, leaning forward as if she found her friend's question of monumental importance—and the anticipated reply even more so.

The photographer's answer was noncommittal, but polite. "I'm afraid my profession doesn't lend itself to the more traditional seasons. I find it necessary to take time away whenever I can manage."

"So your visit is entirely recreational, then?"

Andy cringed, wondering if Roman St.Clare had detected the faint edge of disapproval in Miss Snow's tone.

If he had, he concealed it well. "No, not entirely," he replied in the voice Andy had admired the night before—a quiet voice, but deep and resonant, his diction precise, the lilt in his speech subtle but charming. "I've an assignment to see to, as well as some other business . . . of a more personal nature."

Unexpectedly, he met Andy's eyes across the table, causing her to recall his words of the night before. She hoped he wouldn't bring up the subject of his wife's assailant. Either Uncle Magnus or Miss Snow would be sure to ask too many questions and thereby risk offending him.

She clenched her hands in her lap as Magnus chose that moment to make his presence known from the head of the table. With a loud clearing of his throat, he paused with fork in hand. "I take it you left the dog outside last night, after all," he said. "Sensible. Dogs don't belong indoors."

At the word *dog*, Miss Snow's head snapped around to St.Clare as if on a swivel. *"Dog?"* she intoned, her dark eyes wide with incredulity. "Surely, sir, you have not brought a dog into the house?"

For a moment the photographer appeared at a loss, but he recovered quickly. The glance he gave Andy over his teacup even held a faint glint of amusement. "Actually," he said after a long sip of tea, "Conor did stay inside through the night . . . with Miss Fairchild's consent, of course," he added. "I'm relieved to learn he didn't disturb anyone."

As if he considered the matter of no further interest, he set his cup down and lifted a bite of biscuit to his mouth.

Miss Snow regarded Andy, who again shifted on her chair. "You allowed a *dog* to stay indoors overnight?" The woman couldn't have sounded more astonished had Andy opened the house to an inmate from Bellevue's Insane Pavilion.

Andy swallowed and tried to compose her face. "Mr. St.Clare's dog is very well behaved, Miss Snow."

Uncle Magnus gave one of his annoying snorts, while Miss Snow went on staring at Andy as if she thought her quite mad.

Andy felt an irrational need to justify herself. "Irish wolfhounds are highly intelligent, I'm told," she said, her words spilling out much too quickly. "And Mr. St.Clare's dog is accustomed to being indoors. I'm sure he'll be no problem at all."

She couldn't help but dart a glance across the table. The photographer was watching her with that same peculiar look, an expression that seemed to hold both amusement and perhaps even a certain admiration.

As if realizing that Andy might need a measure of support, he turned a disarmingly warm smile on Miss Snow and leaned toward her. "Miss Fairchild has agreed to indulge me and give Conor—my dog—a fair trial. But should he cause even the smallest disturbance, I assure you I'll banish him to the wagon without delay."

Searching for a way to diffuse the tension in the room, Andy reminded herself that she was the proprietress of Graystone Manor, after all, and as such was wholly within her rights to allow an elephant on the premises if she so chose. Just as quickly, she sensed that this might not be the best time to assert her proprietary rights.

Although Miss Snow's frown was still skeptical, her expression did soften a little. As for dear Miss Valentine, she hastened to assure St.Clare that she, for one, had always rather fancied the idea of keeping a dog as a pet, but had never been in a position to do so. "The wolfhound sounds like such a noble animal," she said rather dreamily. "I've read about them in novels, of course."

She slanted a somewhat furtive look at Miss Snow, who made no secret of her contempt for such frivolity. The latter lifted an eyebrow as if to confirm her disapproval.

Andy glanced at Uncle Magnus and saw with some relief that, while he still wore a disgruntled expression, he seemed far more interested in his breakfast than the conversation around the table.

After another moment, Roman St.Clare pressed his napkin to his mouth and pushed away from the table, clearly signaling an end to the exchange. "If you'll excuse me," he said, "I believe I should see to a bit of breakfast for the wolfhound. I took him out to the wagon rather early, so he'll be eager, I expect."

St.Clare stood with some difficulty, his chair scraping the floor as he negotiated the cane. "Ladies," he said, managing to include not only Miss Snow and Miss Valentine, but Andy as well in a smile and a small bow that could only be described as courtly. "It has been my pleasure." Then, turning to Magnus, he added, "Mr., ah . . . Doyle, is it?"

"It is," the older man said, not looking up from his sausage cakes.

"The Doyles of Kilkenny, by any chance?"

Now Magnus did look up, his expression surprised but suspicious. "Kilkenny, that's right."

"Did you come across, then?" asked St.Clare.

Magnus shook his head. "No, but the mother and father did." He studied the photographer through narrowed eyes. "How is it that you know Kilkenny? I thought you were an Ulsterman."

His disdain was all too evident in the downward turn of his mouth, and Andy suppressed a groan.

St.Clare appeared not to notice the older man's contempt. "I'm from Antrim, that's true," he replied pleasantly. "But I know Kilkenny as well."

Uncle Magnus opened his mouth, but before he could say anything more, Andy jerked to her feet, blurting out the first thing that came to mind. "Why don't we see if Ibebe has some scraps in the kitchen for your dog, Mr. St.Clare? I confess I'm anxious to meet him."

The photographer eyed her with the hint of a smile. "Thank you, Miss Fairchild. I have food for him, in the wagon, of course, but no doubt he'd enjoy a little something different." He paused. "But are you quite sure you want to go out in this weather? It's awfully nasty."

"Mr. St.Clare is right, Amanda," Miss Snow put in. "You'll catch your death."

"Oh, I'm used to running in and out of the weather, Miss Snow. You know I never take cold."

In her haste to get Roman St.Clare out of the room, Andy banged her knee against the table leg. "Feathers!" she muttered, embarrassed at her clumsiness. Her expletive earned her a sharp look of rebuke from Miss Snow, which made Andy feel even more like an ungainly child.

Roman St.Clare gave her a thoroughly provoking grin, as if amused by her adolescent bumbling. Unreasonably flustered, Andy squared her shoulders and started for the kitchen, leaving him to follow.

On the way, it occurred to her that a man of St.Clare's station was probably accustomed to far more elegant lodgings. More than likely he expected to be waited upon by a highly trained staff who would meet his every need with consummate efficiency. Andy grudgingly conceded that it would behoove her to affect at least a degree of sophistication. After all, *she* was reasonably efficient, too, even if she didn't always manage to convey as much. It wouldn't do for St.Clare to think her a green country innkeeper, unaccustomed to his class of boarder.

Accordingly, she straightened her back and drew herself up to full height. While she had never quite mastered the art of gliding through rooms like a lady of quality, she was determined at least to make her way to the kitchen without stumbling.

Four

Outside, the wind drove the sleet in a relentless fury, glazing the leaf-strewn walkway and lawn with an icy slush. Apparently, the winter storm had set in for the morning.

Without thinking, Andy suggested they make a run for it, then felt her face flame at her thoughtlessness. Roman St.Clare, with his lame leg, could not run.

But the photographer seemed to take no offense. "I'm not quite up to a sprint just yet," he said cheerfully, "but if you don't mind helping me a bit, between you and the cane, I think I can manage."

He pulled his greatcoat more tightly about him while Andy secured her cloak. Then, carrying the tin of breakfast scraps for the dog in one hand, she took the photographer's arm with the other and they started off.

As they rounded the house, she held her breath, fearful that St.Clare might slip and hurt himself. Instead, he surprised her with the relative swiftness at which he took the walkway and the dirt path leading to the barn.

Just outside the barn sat the photographer's wagon, a large, lumbering thing, hooded with black. It occurred to Andy that it looked a little too much like a hearse.

The biggest dog she had ever seen greeted them the moment Roman opened the door at the back of the wagon. Of muted gray and black, the animal had a fine, large head and an almost regal bearing. But the excited whimper and vigorous whipping of his tail as they stepped inside was more that of a puppy. Soon he turned his attention to Andy, his enthusiasm still seemingly at odds with his intimidating size and noble appearance.

"Miss Fairchild," said St.Clare with mock formality, "I'd like you to meet Conor—the terror of Ulster. You will take note of the fact, I hope, that he does not . . . *smell*—" he paused—"at least not at the moment."

The wolfhound looked from Andy to his owner as if slightly offended, then turned back to study Andy with a gaze that was disconcertingly human in its intensity and intelligence. She felt herself measured by this great handsome beast and was curiously pleased when he cocked his head and—there was no other word for it—grinned at her.

"Ah," St.Clare said, "he likes you."

"He knows I am delivering his breakfast."

"Not at all. Why, I believe he'd like to shake your hand, if you'll allow it."

Andy looked at St.Clare, only then realizing that she was still clinging to his arm. Immediately she dropped her hand away. In the meantime the wolfhound had lifted an enormous paw and now sat waiting for her to respond.

Delighted with him, Andy laughed and leaned forward to shake his paw, precariously balancing the tin of scraps in her other hand. "He's very handsome! And such a gentleman."

"In truth, he's a terrible infant, but a good traveling companion, all the same. I shouldn't quite know what to do without him, I confess."

Andy straightened. St.Clare's unmistakable fondness for the wolfhound touched her somehow. She found it strangely boyish, not at all in keeping with her preconceived notion of the man. "How long have you had him?"

"I raised him from a pup, actually. A friend brought him across for me as a gift. He's almost two now."

"He's magnificent," Andy said, meaning it. "And may I assure you again that he is welcome inside the house anytime."

As if he had understood every word of the exchange, the wolfhound grinned even more broadly, whipping his tail back and forth in a circle, bobbing his head with uninhibited pleasure. Andy set his breakfast down in front of him, but the dog showed great restraint, waiting until St.Clare gave a nod of assent.

"Well . . . you've obviously made a conquest," the photographer said, turning back to Andy. "But you may bring down the wrath of your uncle and Miss Snow upon your head. I doubt the wolfhound will win their approval quite so easily as he has yours."

"Oh, feathers, they're all bluff, the both of them! As soon as they see how clever and well-behaved Conor is, they'll adore him. Just see if they don't."

Trying not to appear too curious, Andy scanned the wagon's interior. It was larger than she would have expected, almost resembling a small apartment. Yet in spite of the limited space and diversity of furnishings and equipment, it gave off a surprisingly cozy appearance. At the far front, a neat row of cooking utensils hung overhead. A little farther back, a well-worn but comfortable-looking chair was tucked against the wall. On the floor opposite the chair was an oversized pallet, strewn with plump blankets and pillows.

Andy's embarrassment at coming upon what obviously served as St. Clare's sleeping quarters was quickly dispelled by the sight of an ornately framed portrait resting on a small table nearby. The smile of the beautiful young woman with the thick dark hair defied the sour-faced expressions so common to many photographs of the day. With her hands folded atop a Bible, the woman seemed to be looking directly into the eyes of the beholder.

A great sadness swept through Andy as she stood staring at the photograph. She knew at once that this was St. Clare's deceased wife, and the enormity of his loss fell over the moment like a shroud.

She glanced away, but apparently he had noticed her interest. "My wife, Kathleen," he said matter-of-factly. "I took it myself, shortly after our wedding."

At a loss, Andy merely nodded and kept silent, again looking around the wagon. In the rear, to her left, some sort of partition had been established by the hanging of a heavy, black drapery. "My darkroom," St. Clare said, inclining his head toward the partition. "It's makeshift, but serves the purpose."

On both walls, shelves and compartments had been built in to accommodate an impressive array of photographic equipment. Varying sizes of cameras and other supplies, such as tripods, boxes, and small tanks, which St. Clare identified as chemical containers holding sulfuric acid, silver nitrate, and ether, ran the length of both sides of the wagon, as did numerous books, some heaped on the floor, others crammed onto shelves of their own.

Fascinated, Andy studied the examples of the photographer's art squeezed in among the equipment: tintypes of individual soldiers, looking tragically young and brave; photographs of battlefields; and portraits which she took to be of officers in a variety of groupings. There was also a large, familiar portrait of Abraham Lincoln, one the newspapers had often carried, and individual poses of Generals Grant and Meade, as well as pictures of men Andy surmised to be government officials—certainly, they looked grim with self-importance.

"Did you do all those?" she asked, turning to St.Clare.

He nodded, and she studied him with admiration. "What an exciting life you must lead!"

"Rewarding, perhaps. Not necessarily exciting, though it suits me."

"I'm afraid I really don't understand very much about your work," Andy admitted. "Photography has always seemed such a mystery to me, though a fascinating one. To think of being able to capture people and places in such a way that they'll never be forgotten—I think it's quite wonderful!"

"I do enjoy the work, I'll confess. But it *is* work. I put in rather long hours, actually, when I'm on assignment."

"I should enjoy the travel most of all, I'm sure," Andy said thoughtfully. "That, and meeting so many interesting people—I can't imagine anything more . . . exciting!" she finished feebly. For the life of her, she didn't know why she kept repeating herself.

But she was entirely in earnest. For years she had secretly dreamed of traveling about the country. It was, of course, a wildly fatuous, impossible notion, but one she had never been entirely able to disregard.

St.Clare was smiling at her in a way that suddenly made her feel very young and unsophisticated . . . and slightly foolish. Instantly, she attempted to draw herself up into a more dignified posture.

"Well, Miss Fairchild," he said, his tone light, "as luck would have it, I'm going to be advertising for an assistant soon. I had to leave my associate back in Baltimore—to manage the studio—so before I go back on the road again, I'm hoping to find someone who would like to apprentice. A willingness to travel is, of course, one of the chief requisites of the position." He paused, still smiling. "Perhaps you'd be interested in applying?"

He was joking, of course, but Andy was glad he couldn't know about the funny little skip her heart gave at his words. She hoped she didn't sound too terribly banal as she tried to match his light-hearted tone. "Let's hope you can find someone far less clumsy than I. I'd probably destroy your camera my first day on the job!"

He said nothing, but Andy was unsettled to find him still watching her when she turned around.

"I wouldn't have realized the need for an assistant in your work," she went on, "but then, of course, I really don't know anything *about* your work." She knew she was chattering but couldn't seem to stop. "I suppose I always assumed a photographer did everything on his own."

He shook his head. "As a matter of fact, it's a rather involved process. Oftentimes, it's quite difficult to work *without* an assistant." He stopped, regarding her with a measuring expression. "Perhaps you'd come out with me one day while I'm working. I can show you what I mean."

"Oh, I'd like that!" Andy said with genuine enthusiasm. "You'll be taking pictures here, then—on the Island?"

He nodded. "Here, and in Manhattan, too, I expect, although I've done some work there previously." His searching gray gaze was on her face. "Perhaps I can convince you to sit for a photograph, Miss Fairchild?"

Disarmed by both his question and his scrutiny, Andy felt the blood rush to her cheeks. "Oh—I . . . I don't think so . . ." she stammered.

Still he studied her. "You've never sat for a photograph before?"

Andy shook her head. "I'd feel foolish."

He frowned. "I can't think why. You'd make a fine subject. You have a very . . . lively countenance."

Andy stared at him. "Lively?"

He smiled and nodded, regarding her with such interest that

43

she began to feel ridiculously self-conscious. "Lively, indeed," he said, his gaze steady.

Andy wasn't sure she wanted to know what he meant. She suddenly felt uncomfortable, alone with him in what was beginning to feel like a much too intimate setting. With the storm beating against the snug walls of the wagon, the wolfhound resting comfortably on a woven rug between them, there was a feeling of refuge, a coziness that had caused her, at least temporarily, to forget the fact that she was, after all, alone with a total stranger in what amounted to his private quarters.

Added to that was the demeanor of the man himself. St.Clare seemed far too direct, too casual with her, for the sake of propriety. But then, she allowed, perhaps things were different in Ireland. Perhaps Irish men did not observe the same bounds of correct behavior as did American men. Besides, she sensed there was no cause to feel uncomfortable with Roman St.Clare; the man was obviously devoted to the memory of his wife.

And, just as obviously, he considered *her* with nothing more than simple amusement. No, she told herself dryly, she needn't worry about her new lodger making improper advances, whatever the setting. The worst she might expect from him would be that annoying, albeit appealing, smile.

To conceal her nervousness, Andy began to pace around the floor of the wagon, pretending an excessive interest in her surroundings. The wolfhound looked at her expectantly, and she stooped to scratch behind his ears. When she rose, St.Clare was still watching her.

"I really must be getting back," she said quickly. "I have a great deal to do this morning."

She started for the door of the wagon, only to be blocked by St.Clare's tall frame. "You promised to tell me your mystery," he reminded her.

Andy looked up at him, her eyes wide. "My mystery?"

"The strange happenings on the Island?" he prompted.

She had entirely forgotten. "Gracious, I did, didn't I? But I really shouldn't take any more time right now. At dinner this evening, perhaps?"

Her avoidance was only partially deliberate. The truth was she *had* been away from her work too long and would no doubt pay for it with a frantic afternoon.

But when she would have whisked past him to leave, he moved again, so slightly Andy couldn't be sure it was intentional. "Surely you can take another moment or two." It was a statement, not a suggestion.

They were standing so close to the rear of the wagon they both jumped at the clatter outside, Andy jostling St.Clare's arm with the sudden movement. Someone pounded on the wall of the wagon, and, behind them, the wolfhound shot to his feet and growled. The photographer silenced him with a sharp command.

St.Clare caught Andy's arm to move her out of the way as the door of the wagon flew open.

It took Andy a moment to react. *"Niles?"* She stared at him in disbelief.

Niles looked from her to St.Clare, his expression positively thunderous.

Andy felt her face flame with embarrassment. She was struck by an irrational need to explain herself, having been found alone in a wagon with a man Niles had never met. Instead, she reminded herself that it wasn't up to Niles to dictate her behavior. "Niles . . . why aren't you at the hospital?" she stammered. "What on earth are you doing *here*?"

Niles dragged his gaze away from St.Clare to level an incredulous look on Andy. "I should think that would be obvious, Amanda," he said, his eyes accusing. "I came to see about you. When Magnus told me you'd been gone for well over an hour, I came out here to make sure you were all right."

He virtually stamped inside the wagon, raking Roman St.Clare with a withering look as he came. Then he turned his attention back to Andy. "Well," he demanded, his fists clenched at his sides, *"are* you all right?"

Andy refused to look at Roman St.Clare as she hastened to assure Niles that, yes, of course, she was quite all right and why in the world would he think she *wouldn't* be?

Five

*R*oman took no pleasure in Amanda Fairchild's obvious embarrassment. On the contrary, a rope of anger coiled through him at the stranger's rude behavior. The man's tone was demanding, his eyes suspicious.

"Amanda, what on earth are you doing out here? Are you all right? You shouldn't be out in this weather." His icy stare was fixed on Roman as he spoke.

Clearly, it was not the inclement weather that concerned him, Roman thought. The fellow was obviously in a temper, his thin face flushed, his eyes glinting with an emotion that might have been either anger or anxiety. Roman felt his own face flame in response to the blatant suspicion directed at him.

The wolfhound seemed to share his annoyance with their unexpected visitor. Teeth bared, ears back, the dog appeared ready to lunge at the slightest provocation. In light of the man's proprietary manner toward Amanda Fairchild, however, Roman thought the two might have an understanding, in which case his feisty young landlady would probably not appreciate Conor's interference.

In any event, it was none of his affair. He quieted the wolfhound, calling him to his side. With some interest, he observed that while Amanda Fairchild might indeed be flustered by the man's overbearing behavior, she didn't seem inclined to tolerate it.

"Niles, for goodness' sake, of course, I'm all right." With a quick glance at Roman, she softened her tone only a little as she turned back to the man called *Niles*. "And would you mind lowering your voice?"

Amanda Fairchild's sharp words seemed to have met their mark. The long jaw relaxed a bit, and the man's tone was slightly more civil as he expelled a long breath, then moved to make a semblance of apology. "I'm sorry, Amanda, I didn't mean to be short. It's just that I've come with more bad news, and I suppose I was hoping to find you safe indoors. Instead . . ."

He didn't finish, nor did he need to. His meaning was stingingly clear as he turned to look at Roman.

Was it jealousy that fueled his rudeness? Roman wondered. If so, it seemed excessive in the extreme.

"I am quite safe, Niles." Amanda Fairchild's words were edged with unmistakable impatience. "Mr. St.Clare has been showing me his photographic facilities. Allow me to introduce you, by the way. I'm sure you recall my mentioning Mr. Roman St.Clare, our new lodger?"

The look the slender-framed man turned on Roman seemed to chill the air even more than the windy, sleet-driven morning.

Amanda Fairchild appeared suddenly awkward, even conciliatory, as she completed the introductions. "Dr. Niles Rutherford is . . . a close friend of the family," she said, her smile somewhat thin.

Rutherford's sour look made it clear he had hoped for more by way of an introduction. He didn't offer his hand, but simply made a stiff nod of acknowledgment in Roman's direction.

No doubt it was the hostility bristling from Rutherford that evoked yet another snarl of disapproval from Conor. Even as Roman silenced the wolfhound once again, he empathized with the dog's impatience; he, too, was beginning to find this *Dr. Rutherford* somewhat boorish.

Amanda Fairchild, however, seemed more at ease now. "What did you mean about more bad news?" she asked. "Surely not another disappearance."

"I'm afraid so," Rutherford replied, his lips tightening to a thin line. "It seems they've found a body. A little Negro boy. Murdered, apparently." He paused. "Mutilated as well, I was told," he added, his voice strained.

"Oh, Niles, no!" She shuddered visibly, and Rutherford put a hand to her shoulder.

"I'm sorry, Amanda. I knew you'd be distressed, but I didn't want you to hear about it through Island gossip. That's why I decided to come by before going on to the clinic."

He paused, frowning as he leaned toward her. "Amanda, I want you to promise me you'll be more cautious. You know how I worry about you."

Her expression seemed to hover between genuine fear and confusion. She blinked and looked at Rutherford. "You shouldn't worry, Niles. I'm always careful. Truly, I am."

Rutherford's face softened to a look of affection, and Roman thought for an instant that the man was going to embrace the Fairchild girl right there. He suddenly felt himself to be an intruder in his own wagon and looked away as they went on with their conversation.

"Where did they find the little boy, Niles?"

"Near the Haunted Swamp."

"Has he . . . been identified?"

"No, at least not yet. They think he might have been a runaway—" He paused, giving Roman another long, speculative look. "Amanda, I'll see you back to the house before I leave."

"That's not necessary, Niles. Besides, I'm going to scrape the ice off the walk before I go back inside. I don't want anyone falling."

There was a long sigh. "Couldn't you have Ibebe or Magnus do that?"

"Ibebe already has more than she can handle, and Uncle Magnus worries me to despair these days. I've told you how he wheezes and gasps with the slightest exertion."

"Magnus just needs to lose some weight," Niles said flatly. "Amanda, I do wish you'd show as much concern for yourself as you do for everyone else."

"Niles . . ."

Roman heard the note of exasperation in her voice and suppressed a smile. He rather liked his plucky young landlady by now and would have been disappointed had she *not* found Rutherford's overbearing air a bit annoying.

Rutherford drew another sigh, a prolonged one. "Very well. Perhaps I'll stop by this evening, after I leave the hospital."

Roman turned back to the two of them, meaning to offer a civil word of acknowledgment at the man's departure. But

Amanda Fairchild delayed Rutherford with another question.

"Niles? The little boy they found . . . do they know how old he was?"

"How old?" Rutherford looked at her somewhat blankly for a moment. "Six or seven at most, I believe."

Her face contorted. "Oh, Niles, isn't it ever going to end? Why can't they find the monster who's responsible for this?"

Rutherford shook his head. "I don't know, Amanda. I'm sure the police are doing everything they can."

"Well, it's not enough!" Her hands squeezed to a knot. "There must be *something* more they can do. The entire Island is living in terror. And for good reason."

Roman understood her outburst. He still remembered his frustration and anger when the police had failed to produce Kathleen's killer immediately following her death. He was able now to realize that the authorities had suffered their own sense of helplessness. At the time, however, he had thought them totally ineffective, or, worse, indifferent.

"Just *you* be careful," Rutherford was cautioning Amanda Fairchild again. "Until all this is resolved, *no one* is safe—" he paused and gave a dark frown—"especially as isolated as you are out here, and so close to all the trouble."

"Don't, Niles. Not now," she said, plainly impatient.

He looked at her, then muttered something about being on his way.

She took it up at once, as if suddenly remembering her manners. "It was awfully good of you to come by, Niles. And do stop in this evening, if it isn't too late." Despite her polite smile, Roman heard the note of dismissal in her tone.

Still, Rutherford hesitated, glancing from her to Roman as if he found the idea of leaving them alone together intolerable.

After he had finally gone, Amanda Fairchild turned to Roman. "Please don't think him rude."

That was exactly what Roman *did* think of the good doctor, but he made no reply.

"Niles can be somewhat . . . domineering at times, but he means well."

"Are you betrothed, then—you and the doctor?" Roman asked matter-of-factly, watching her.

50

"Betrothed?" The question seemed to surprise her. "Oh . . . no. Not at all. It's just that we more or less grew up together, you see, and Niles has always taken it upon himself to protect me."

"And do you need protection, then?" It occurred to Roman that this lively young woman could probably take care of herself rather well without any help from the likes of Rutherford, but that, too, was none of his affair.

She smiled a little, an impish smile that brought a glint to her eyes. "I should hope not. But I haven't quite convinced Niles of that fact yet." She paused. "Well . . . I really must be getting back. Mornings are very busy around here. I expect you have things to do as well, Mr. St.Clare."

Clearly, she was trying to contain any anxiety that Rutherford's news had caused her. But her usual quick brightness—the *sunniness* about her to which Roman could not help but respond—had faded.

In a remarkably short time, Amanda Fairchild had stirred a genuine liking in him, as well as a warming of his spirit he wouldn't have thought possible. Now he found himself reluctant to let her go. "This murder of the little black boy—does it have to do with the other incidents you alluded to last evening?"

Her countenance sobered even more, and she nodded. "I need to explain what's been happening here on the Island." She seemed reluctant to speak further, but taking a deep breath, she plunged ahead. "I'm sorry for putting you off, but to tell you the truth . . . I was afraid you might not want to stay if you knew."

Roman was surprised at her candor and warmed to her even more.

"We've had a number of disappearances over the past several months, you see," she went on, not quite meeting his eyes. "All unexplained, and all involving children. Negro children."

Roman frowned. "And none have been found? Until today?"

"None," she said tightly. Suddenly she looked very young. Young, and perhaps a little frightened. "There's more to it than the missing children, though."

She went on then to recount an incredible tale about graves unearthed and left empty near a former quarantine hospital. "What with the missing children and the grave robberies, the Island is awfully close to panic, I'm afraid. The police don't seem

51

to be making any progress whatsoever. And now *this* . . ."

She didn't finish, but Roman understood. He had seen panic before, knew how quickly it could spread and become a threat in itself, victimizing people as much by the fear and suspicion among themselves as by any enemy outside.

"I'm sorry, Mr. St.Clare," she went on. "This is all very ugly, I know. As you can see, Uncle Magnus may not have been exaggerating. Perhaps there really *is* no safe place on the Island these days. I'll understand perfectly if you want to leave, and of course I'll refund the money you paid in advance."

Roman studied her, sensing the effort her words had required. He had already gathered that she might be in financial straits. That might account for her doing all manner of odd jobs about the place herself. It probably also accounted for her willingness to suffer a lame stranger and an immense wolfhound on the premises.

Although Graystone Manor must have been magnificent at some time in the past—even now it still retained a certain grandeur and faded elegance—he had not missed the small economies throughout the house: the draperies mended a few times too often, the carefully patched lampshades, the worn upholstery covered by too many antimacassars.

He would figure Amanda Fairchild to be a clever sort, resourceful and seemingly tireless in her efforts to keep the place in good condition. But she was in need of money, right enough; the signs were all there.

He might have been prudent to do exactly as she'd suggested—recoup his advance rent and leave. Instead, he found himself anxious to reassure her. "I've no inclination to leave the Island, Miss Fairchild. I expect Conor and I can look to ourselves very well. We'll be staying on, at least for now."

Did he only imagine her sigh of relief?

The strong little chin lifted somewhat, and the marvelous green eyes brightened once again. "I'm pleased to hear that, Mr. St.Clare," she said, smiling at him.

"I do wish you'd tell me a bit more about these incidents, though," he prompted. "How long has all this been going on?"

"It started in the spring. More than six months ago, actually. At first, there were several weeks between disappearances. But after the grave robberies began, other children turned up missing, more and more often."

"Are these random occurrences, or confined to a particular area?"

"Most of the missing children were from Stapleton, or nearby. Several Negro families live there, especially around McKeon Street. But the grave robberies have all taken place at Tompkinsville, at the old immigrants' quarantine."

Roman considered her reply. "Why is your friend Dr. Rutherford so concerned for you? You'd seem to be perfectly safe, I should think, given the fact that only black children and immigrant graves are involved."

Only when he saw her bristle did he realize that his words might have sounded insensitive.

"I realize you are from a border state, Mr. St.Clare, but here in the North, many of us feel that colored children are just as important as white children. Their disappearances aren't taken lightly, to say the least. As for the immigrant graves"—her expression turned even more grim—"those poor souls were tortured quite enough when they arrived in the city without suffering the further indignity of a mutilated grave site."

Roman only barely managed to suppress a smile at her scolding. He *did* like this girl!

"I meant no offense, Miss Fairchild," he said quickly with a deferential nod. "I was simply questioning the reason for the doctor's concern."

She eyed him closely for a moment. "Niles just worries too much, I expect. He assumes the role of an older brother toward me, and there's not very much I can do about it."

Roman thought Rutherford's feelings for the girl were probably anything but brotherly, but it was hardly his place to point this out.

Six

*A*fter she left, the wagon seemed colder, the shadows darker. Roman shivered at the sound of sleet driving against the walls and went to toss an afghan about his shoulders. He was always cold of late, could never quite ward off the chill that had hovered about him since Kathleen's death.

For a long time he stood staring at the door through which Amanda Fairchild had made her exit. Somehow it seemed as if all the warmth of moments before had followed her. He was seized with a sudden, irrational desire to put off the cataloging of prints and go after her.

Shaken, he recognized the unacceptable direction his thoughts had followed and tried to call them back. Not since Kathleen had he responded, even in friendship, to another woman. Sometimes it seemed as if all his former capacity for gaiety and lightheartedness, for even the slightest feelings of affection, had been snuffed out when Kathleen died.

It had been Kathleen who had first taught him how to love. He had grown up in a loveless home, with a mother who suffered from one crippling emotional illness after another and an egocentric father who buried himself in his work. Anthony St.Clare had been a highly successful artist, shown both in England and in France, but as a husband and father he was an utter failure. Both Roman and his sister had struggled through their childhood with no one from whom to draw affection except each other. Mary Frances, three years older than he, had married at seventeen and immediately set out to raise a large, boisterous family. As for Roman, he had eventually sought escape from his bleak homelife by going to university in Dublin, then emigrating to the States.

He met Kathleen in a Washington hospital during his convalescence from the injury sustained at Gettysburg. She had opened an entirely new world to him, a world where love was unconditionally given and affection freely shown. Under her tutelage, Roman had become almost a different person. For the first time, he had learned to celebrate life, to live fully without fear of rejection or indifference.

To Kathleen, he owed his first real experience of joy—and his first real experience of God. She had introduced him to a God different from the vengeful, belligerent deity of his mother. Kathleen had led him, slowly, patiently to the God of love and tender mercies, a God who didn't turn His back on His prodigal sons, but opened His arms wide to them with welcome and forgiveness. Because of Kathleen, Roman had finally come to know a God whose love was so vast, so compassionate that He would send His own Son to save the world—the very same world that had broken His heart.

Kathleen had helped him to find the Christ of the Cross, where at last Roman had gained healing for his heart and wholeness for his soul. But when Kathleen died, he lost not only his sweetheart and best friend, but very nearly lost his faith in God as well. The shock had been devastating, the grief almost paralyzing. For months he had turned his back on the God he had only begun to know and trust.

But somehow, in ways that even now he could not begin to comprehend, the Divine Love he had tried to reject refused to let him go, had instead held him fast and reaffirmed a Father's unconditional caring. Eventually that same love had brought him deliverance from the dark abyss of his grief and despair.

Sometimes he could almost imagine Kathleen pleading for him at the very throne of grace, attempting to convince the King of Heaven himself that her "beloved of the sorrowful eyes," as she was fond of calling Roman, was indeed worth the effort of salvation. It would have been just like her.

She had been gone for three years now, and his earlier thought that in all that time he had not once felt even the slightest interest in another woman had been no exaggeration.

There had been no stirring of desire, no response to a pretty face or an inviting smile.

What, then, accounted for his reaction to Amanda Fairchild? What was there about the diminutive, almost childlike, young woman that had, at least momentarily, seemed to thaw the fortress of ice about his heart?

The thought startled him, and immediately he was struck by an overwhelming sense of guilt. He felt as if he had somehow defiled his memories of Kathleen, even betrayed her.

He knew the guilt to be irrational. The last thing Kathleen would have wanted for him was this emptiness, this barrenness of spirit that had plagued him ever since her death.

Once, in what had then seemed a lighthearted moment, she had told him that if anything should ever happen to her, he must not grieve, but must instead find a new love right away. "That dreadful melancholy of yours would be the end of you, darling," she'd teased. "You would absolutely have to take another wife, and soon. Now, it might be best if she's not too awfully attractive, of course. But do choose a girl merry enough to counter that wretched Ulster grimness of yours."

He had not had to pretend indignation at the thought that he could ever love anyone else but Kathleen. Even then, when she had still been alive and vital and sitting next to him on a park bench, he had been unable to bear the thought of losing her, of going through life without her.

Mercifully, he had not known at the time how soon he would have to do just that.

With a weariness far too great for such an early hour, Roman sighed and willed the memories away. Annoyed with himself for giving in to the melancholy, more annoyed still that he had allowed a mere slip of a girl like Amanda Fairchild to so thoroughly divert him, he tossed the afghan from his shoulders, intending to work. But as he crossed to the other side of the wagon, he stopped and picked up the framed portrait of Kathleen.

His hand trembled slightly as he traced the smooth line of her cheek, her slender neck. After a moment he slipped yet another photograph free from its hiding place behind Kathleen's. This, too, he stood studying, even though each minute detail had been committed to memory long ago. Every face in the group, every vague image in the spacious hall, was engraved upon his mind. Most were men he knew or men he had known—members of the same profession, photographers or apprentice-photographers—who in some cases had traversed several states to attend the awards ceremony in Washington that fateful night.

Finally, his eyes came to rest on a face at the very back of the crowd. The blurred features of the figure in the farthest recesses of the room had been captured in the shadows, and appeared little more than a smudge on the photograph. One hand covered the side of his face, almost entirely concealing his identity. But something about the way the man stood looking across the room, some furtive, indefinable tension in the set of his shoulders, the thrust of his chin, had been enough to convince Roman that he hadn't belonged with the others, that he was an intruder. Later, some weeks after Kathleen's death, a number of the other photographers in the same photo confirmed his suspicion, for none of them could identify the stranger in the shadows either.

For three years Roman had lived with the chilling possibility that he might have actually captured the likeness of Kathleen's assailant on film only moments before . . . or after . . . her murder. This worn photograph and a few isolated newspaper accounts of other mindless murders committed in a similar fashion were all he had to lead him to the killer.

Finding the man in the photograph was his primary reason for coming to New York, and he could not—would not—allow anything to distract him. Certainly not a bright, elfin girl with eyes too large for her face, nor by the dark, ugly horror that seemed to be spreading over this small Island.

It wasn't vengeance that drove him, he insisted at those times when his conscience would have questioned his motives. He didn't think of himself as being obsessed with a lust for revenge or a passion for justice.

He *wanted* justice, of course, wanted the monster who had so brutally slain his wife to pay. But more than anything else, he was driven by the need to know *why*. He knew he would never again find peace, not even the poorest kind of peace, until he discovered the truth behind Kathleen's murder.

Had she, as some of the authorities suggested, merely come upon the man by accident? Had she encountered him in the act of burglarizing their hotel room, thereby startling him into an uncalculated act of violence? Or was there something more, something neither the police nor Roman himself had even considered? Something hidden, something so dark that *no one* had thought of it.

It was the *not knowing* that urged Roman on, that kept him following a trail even he had to admit might not exist, except in his own mind. For months he had haunted newspaper offices and police stations wherever he went, asking endless questions, making himself a general nuisance in his quest for something . . . anything . . . that might open a door.

He had so little to go on, that was the thing. Only the newspaper accounts of a chain of robberies and murders that seemed to reach from Richmond to, more recently, New York.

There were always robberies, of course, but two in particular had caught his attention when he'd first learned of them. About a year before Kathleen's death, there had been an odd incident in Richmond, during which a local photographer's residence had been burglarized. No one had been injured, but among the missing items had been a number of the popular *carte de visites*—calling cards—which the photographer had displayed as samples in his waiting room, just as Roman did in his Baltimore studio.

Another burglary, this one in Washington, had seemed even more peculiar. A senator and his wife had been posing for a portrait at the prestigious Alman's Studio, when a masked man with a knife burst in, robbing both the senator and the photographer. In addition to jewelry and money, the burglar had taken a number of sample tintypes from the studio.

Again, no one had been injured, although the victims had described the masked man as being excessively brutish and rough. The resulting publicity, however, had damaged the studio's reputation, causing a rash of canceled sittings and a general decline in business.

In both cases, the burglar was never apprehended.

After Kathleen's death, one particularly agonizing experience marked the first time Roman had begun to sense a kind of pattern emerging from some of the seemingly unrelated crimes. Months ago, a package—unmarked and unaddressed except for the name *St.Clare* scrawled in a nearly illegible hand—was left at the back door of his Baltimore studio.

Inside the package had been a photograph of Kathleen—one of two missing since the night of her murder. There had been no message, no possible means of tracing the sender—only the photograph. Roman's every instinct told him the package had been sent by Kathleen's assailant, perhaps as some sort of hideous taunt.

At the time he couldn't have known that this diabolical act would be repeated elsewhere throughout the coming months—that others who had lost loved ones would have their grief reopened by the same kind of chilling reminder.

In late spring, the newspapers had carried an account of a murder in Philadelphia that made Roman's blood run cold. A prominent photographer and his daughter had been surprised upon their return home by a masked man who forced both of them into the cellar, beat the photographer into unconsciousness, and then murdered the young woman.

She was seventeen years old, an only child.

The ensuing investigation revealed that the house had been burglarized and that among those items stolen had been several photos of the murdered girl.

Another slaying—this one in Newark, New Jersey, during the summer—had caught Roman's attention as soon as he read of it, because of its painful similarity to Kathleen's murder. A newly married photographer had returned home one evening after working late at his studio to find his house ransacked, his wife dead. Unlike Kathleen, this particular victim had also been molested.

Roman had visited the survivors and, with growing dread, learned that both the father of the girl slain in Philadelphia and the husband of the New Jersey victim had received photographs of their loved ones months after the killings, just as he had.

He had not yet spoken with the survivor of an equally vicious murder in Manhattan. The wife of yet another successful photographer, Samuel Harrington, had been savagely beaten and violated before her death. Perhaps it was too soon for Harrington to have received the predictable anonymous package, but Roman intended to contact him, all the same.

He knew with grim certainty that the one who had sent the packages was the same man who had murdered his Kathleen . . .

and the other three women. It was almost as if in some perverse way the attack on Kathleen had opened a tide of bloodlust within the beast that now demanded to be satisfied more and more often.

The killer had to be either mad or a devil. For months now Roman had studied everything he could find about those deranged criminals often referred to as *mass murderers*. He had learned that, throughout history, there had been those who, either caught up in the grip of lunacy or an evil too ghastly to be conceived, went about destroying the lives of the innocent, usually in savage, inhuman ways.

Sometimes the killings appeared to be entirely random, with no method or motivation ever revealed. More often, though, upon closer study, there would appear some common thread, some pattern, no matter how vague, behind each succession of slayings.

Clearly, the man who had murdered Kathleen and the other women harbored some sort of hatred or grudge against photographers. That he apparently made no effort to hide his particular obsession puzzled Roman. Such negligence—or was it a kind of demented arrogance?—must mean something.

Or was the killer simply playing a deadly game, indulging himself in a crazed kind of chase, recklessly dropping clues to leave a trail, daring someone to catch him?

Roman meant to do just that. He knew the police would go on trying, but he had no real hopes for their success. The trail was too far-reaching, the clues too obscure and random. Besides, there were never enough men to solve all the cases demanding their attention.

He was determined to find the killer himself. If he were ever to learn what had happened to Kathleen, ever to find out if her death had been simply a meaningless act of violence or if there had been some secret, malevolent reason for it, he had to find the man who had taken her life.

To live the rest of his years without knowing the truth would somehow add even more torment to his grief. Unless he found the reason for her death, he did not think he would ever really be able to live freely again.

To that end, he was determined that nothing would distract

him, nothing would divert him. No matter how long it might take, no matter how far he had to go, he would find the man in the photograph. Not only for the sake of his wife's memory, or for his own peace of mind . . . but to stop the madness. A blood-beast had been unleashed and would doubtless continue to wage his fiendish acts of savagery until someone hunted him down like the animal he was and put an end to his evil.

This was Roman's purpose for being here, in New York, and he meant to remind himself just as often as necessary that it must remain his *only* purpose.

——————

The man laid his small bundle, wrapped in a tattered blanket, by a gnarled, ghost-white birch tree, then set the lantern down and began to dig.

He wore heavy gloves, but his hands still ached from the cold. The driving sleet had ended earlier, leaving the night fog-shrouded and silent. Although it wasn't likely anyone would be nosing around the graveyard this late, he was grateful for the mist that helped to conceal him as he shoveled the heavy, sodden ground.

As he worked, the fog wound its way up his boots and overcoat, all but veiling him from view. Impatience snaked through him as he plied the shovel. This was time he could ill afford, time he hadn't planned. But it was unavoidable. It wouldn't do for another body to be discovered so soon after the last one. Since this grave had already been unearthed once, only a few days ago, no one would notice that it had been disturbed again. It would probably take several weeks or months before anyone found the body. If they found it at all.

There was an investigation under way, of course, but that was the least of his worries. The police were buffoons for the most part, fools who tended to bungle anything they put their hands to. From what he'd heard, they were no further along now than when they'd first begun to investigate months ago. Still, it wouldn't do to get careless. Even an imbecile could strike gold if someone tossed nuggets into the pan.

For the next few minutes he shoveled with an almost feverish intensity. The frigid night air stung his face above the muffler. His throat and nostrils burned from the acrid smell of salt water carried shoreward.

Finally, when he'd gone deep enough, he set down his spade and went to retrieve the lifeless bundle from under the tree. He looked around the graveyard one more time, then lowered the body, still wrapped in its blanket, into the grave and began to cover it with dirt.

Somewhere in the distance a dog barked. The man's stomach muscles tightened, and he stood listening. When he heard nothing else, he resumed his efforts.

After he had finished, he picked up the lantern and started down the hill. By the time he reached level ground, his next move was already taking shape in his mind. With white tendrils of fog coiling about him, clutching at him, he turned and walked into the woods.

Seven

*T*he next morning brought a startling change from the previous night's winter storm. Sometime in the predawn hours, the sky had cleared to produce a day with plenty of dazzling sunshine.

In his eagerness to take advantage of the good weather, Roman left off breakfast, save for a cup of tea. When Ibebe the cook tried to protest, he assured her that more often than not he delayed eating until the noon hour.

In truth, it had been a long time since food had held any real appeal for him. Even on the infrequent occasions when he actually felt hunger, he was easily satisfied with only a few bites. Consequently, he had never regained all the weight he'd lost after his injury at Gettysburg. And after Kathleen's death, he had shed even more.

Even so, some of his stamina had returned. The bouts of weakness came less frequently these days, and although he still tired far too easily, he could feel himself growing stronger day by day. His leg would always be stiff, of course; the surgeons had been perfectly clear about that. But this morning as he and Conor started out on the wagon, he could almost imagine himself fit again.

The air was crisp and bracing, the sun promising a later warmth. The Island's tranquility held renewed appeal for Roman as he pulled outside the iron gates, slowing to allow Conor to leap from the wagon. The wolfhound had had little chance to burn some of his excess energy of late. Now he bounded off joyously, careening first one way and then the other before turning back to trot just ahead of the wagon.

65

Beneath the low-hanging tree branches, the lane was encrusted with mud and glazed with dead leaves, sliced off by the sleet of the night before. At the juncture where the property line merged with the road, Roman veered off to his right. Conor took off again, running in circles and barking in jubilation at this unexpected taste of freedom.

Roman watched him, laughing at his antics. "Enjoy yourself, chum. I'd join you if I could."

They passed an entire succession of blackhaw bushes, their berries now withered and sparse. Farther on, Roman became increasingly aware of the pungent aroma of the cedar trees that populated the Island, along with a wide variety of others—poplar, elm, and willow, mostly. Amanda Fairchild had mentioned that large quantities of the Island's trees had been destroyed by fire during the draft riots of '63, when angry mobs had burned in rebellion against the President's call for troops to replenish the army. There still seemed an abundance of woodland, however.

He took his time, passing along streets of attractive dwellings, a surprising number built in the Greek Revival style, a design he would have previously associated with the South. Like the Vanderbilt mansion and the Ward-Nixon house, which he'd seen upon arrival, these elegant buildings with their columned porticos and entry porches presented a classical appearance that spoke not only of wealth, but of careful, intelligent design.

Also much in evidence, though not as numerous, were the sprawling Gothic mansions, of which Graystone Manor would definitely be one of the largest and most imposing. These presented a special allure for Roman, for he had always admired the romantic flair of these grand old structures, with their medieval parapets and grouped chimneys, their ornate gables and the occasional widow's walk.

Eventually, the larger, more pretentious homes gave way to friendly-looking farmhouses and whitewashed country cottages. These, too, he noticed, were neatly landscaped and maintained with obvious pride of ownership.

He wondered idly why Amanda Fairchild hadn't had some of the forest cleared away from her property. Certainly the place would give a far more attractive appearance if the jungle of trees and ivy that engulfed the entire grounds were to be thinned out.

Most likely, the neglect was due to a lack of funds. Such an undertaking would require considerable expense, and Roman had already concluded that there was no money to spare at Graystone Manor.

Not for the first time he wondered what a young, unmarried woman like his landlady was doing in her present circumstances. Managing such an establishment seemed a formidable undertaking, more practical for a husband and wife together, perhaps, or even an entire family. Yet there seemed to be no domestic help other than the solitary black cook, a former slave, who apparently doubled as housekeeper, and no one to assist with the heavier work except for the aging uncle. What else but a critical need for money would motivate a young woman like Amanda Fairchild to open her home to guests, thereby consigning herself to a life that must amount to little more than drudgery?

Obviously, her friend Dr. Rutherford was unhappy with the situation. He had been anything but subtle about his feelings during the previous day's exchange in the wagon.

As he reined in the bay, Roman reminded himself that his young landlady's romantic affairs were none of his concern. Still, he couldn't help but be curious about her relationship with Rutherford. Although it was careless to judge a man upon first meeting, his initial impression had been that of a severe, even caustic personality—certainly a personality in stark opposition to Amanda Fairchild's bright, expansive nature. Rutherford's proprietary behavior had seemed to stem less from affection than from a certain presumption on his part, as if the girl were more an object of ownership than a gift to be cherished.

Still, she was quite young. Perhaps she found Rutherford's possessive attention more flattering than annoying. Irritably, Roman told himself that Amanda Fairchild's personal life was her own affair entirely and had nothing to do with him.

His wandering thoughts had drawn his attention away from his surroundings for some time, and Roman now realized he had gone much farther inland than he'd intended. Impatient with himself, he stepped down from the wagon. He had hoped to shoot some of the more rustic sites on the Island, but the sky, which earlier had been so clear and bright, was now showing signs of clouding over. He decided to walk a short way and see if he could find a likely-looking place to set up before he lost the light entirely.

————

Only moments later, the sun seemed to have disappeared, and Roman found himself hemmed in by woodland, dense and dark. An unexpected feeling of confusion and isolation swept over him at this sudden change of scene, and he realized his thoughts had gone wandering again. Irked with his own carelessness, he called Conor back. The wolfhound came at a bound, slipping in next to Roman and nuzzling his great head against his master's side.

Shuddering against the dank chill of the woods, Roman looked about, trying to calculate how far he had come and exactly which way would take him back to the wagon. Finally, with Conor hovering close, he turned back and started off, veering slightly to the east.

Within minutes, he realized that he'd misjudged his direction. Again he turned, and with the wolfhound now trotting ahead of him, he headed west. So intent was he on making his way back that he was completely unprepared for the monstrosity of a house that suddenly loomed in front of him. Like some sort of hulking, primeval beast, it seemed to appear out of nowhere, leering down from a light rise just ahead.

Roman saw now that they had entered a kind of clearing, surrounded by dense foliage. The road leading up to the house could scarcely be made out, obscured as it was by the rank overgrowth of bramble bushes and weeds. Coarse brown grass grew high and out of control all about the house, pushing its way through the openings of a rusted iron fence and gate.

The house itself, reminiscent of Postmedieval English, appeared to be abandoned. The massive central chimney was missing a large chunk, and at the narrow second-story windows, darkness gaped out from behind shattered panes. Several wood shingles were broken off from the siding, perhaps from the gnarled tree branches that pressed in on either side, as if to squeeze the very life from the place. The steeply pitched tin roof, which looked to have been lifted on one side by years of windstorms, was leprous with rust spots.

A flight of ten or more sagging steps mounted up toward the heavy entrance door. Ever fascinated by old houses, Roman was tempted to approach, but thought better of it. Even if the place were deserted, he might be found trespassing. Besides, the steep bank of steps was deterrent enough, especially given the treacherous condition they were in. He wasn't willing to risk a fall merely to satisfy his curiosity.

The low growl from Conor's throat startled him. As he looked from the dog back to the house, a vague feeling of unease spread over him. The wolfhound had the keen instincts characteristic of the breed, and Roman had learned to pay attention to those instincts.

But it was more than that, something he sensed on his own. He had always been excessively sensitive to mood—to the emotional barometer of other persons, as well as to the ambiance of whatever setting in which he happened to find himself. In truth, he thought it might be the very thing that had drawn him to photography. He found a keen satisfaction in attempting to capture the mood of a person or a place—even a house—and conveying it in realistic, oftentimes starkly dramatic ways with his camera.

He was convinced that whatever this indefinable sensitivity was, it had contributed immeasurably to his success as a photographer. Sometimes, however, he questioned whether it was a gift or a curse, for not only could he frequently feel the emotional climate around him, he also tended to absorb it.

At the moment, he sensed an almost oppressive air of malevolence, an impression of some sort of wintry menace out of all proportion to the actual setting. He recognized the feeling as irrational, but undeniable all the same.

Given his own uneasiness as well as the wolfhound's peculiar behavior, Roman knew a growing urgency to return to the wagon. He glanced back at the sinister-looking old house only once, refusing to examine more closely what he had felt in its proximity. Instead, he made a concentrated effort to put the place out of his mind. It was only a house, after all; though admittedly it was ugly enough to set the most dull imagination to fits of fancy.

Perhaps he would ask Amanda Fairchild about the place later. If it had a history at all—and surely any house so hideous would have some sort of a past—no doubt his clever young landlady would know the story in detail.

Eight

When Roman St.Clare hadn't returned by noon, Andy began to worry. She wasn't responsible for him, of course; he was a lodger, not family. But she *felt* responsible all the same, perhaps because he was at such an obvious disadvantage with his lame leg. Still, she supposed it was possible that the river of sorrow that seemed to run through the man might account, at least in part, for her concern.

She stood at the kitchen sink, where she'd been fiddling with the cantankerous hand pump for nearly half an hour. It was stuck again, locked up tight. She'd watched Uncle Magnus fix it often enough so that she ought to be able to do it on her own, but she had just about reached the end of her patience. Finally, she straightened and sighed, looking around the kitchen. At least she had the satisfaction of seeing *some* results of her morning's efforts.

While Ibebe had worked upstairs in the guest rooms, Andy had tidied the kitchen. She was pleased with the sight of the brightly polished, cream-colored earthenware neatly stacked on the cabinet and the blue-and-white china gleaming on the shelves above. The range, newly blacked only last week, had been wiped clean, as had the table. And, earlier, Ibebe had turned out several loaves of bread to rise on the sideboard.

After a moment, Andy glanced out the window over the sink, thinking she might catch a glimpse of St.Clare. But there was nothing to be seen except the steep wooded hills in back. The sun that had shone so brightly only that morning had disappeared behind the clouds; in its absence, the woods had faded to a dull and dreary brown.

71

Andy decided she'd had enough of the kitchen for now. She yanked her coat off the wall peg by the door and went outside. In back, the grounds were swathed in shadows from the hills. Leaves scratched the walk and tumbled across the yard in the light wind that had risen. Andy stepped off the porch and went around the side of the house. It occurred to her that the photographer might have returned without her knowing and gone directly to his work, instead of coming inside. But as the barn came into view, she saw that the wagon wasn't in its place.

She pulled her coat a little more snugly about her and stood looking around. She hoped he hadn't gone too far and exerted himself. Or, worse yet, lost his way.

Chilled, she allowed her thoughts to dwell only a moment on the other possibilities. The horror of the missing children . . . the specter of the recently discovered small corpse . . . were never far from her mind. What if something equally as dreadful had happened to St.Clare?

She shook off the thought. More probable, but almost as disturbing, was the chance that he might have taken a fall and further injured himself. He could have blacked out and be lying unconscious somewhere along the road. Or in the woods. Perhaps she ought to go looking for him.

Even as she stood there worrying, she felt a stab of annoyance with St.Clare. At least he might have had the courtesy to leave word as to when they could expect him. At this rate, he was going to miss lunch as well as breakfast. And from the looks of him, he couldn't afford to skip either.

No doubt he would be expecting Ibebe to set out an extra meal when he finally showed up, Andy thought, feeling increasingly cross with the man. Well, he could just forget *that* notion. It was true they had provided him a late supper the night of his arrival, but he needn't get the idea that he could simply amble in at any old time and expect to be waited on at his leisure.

Magnus came walking out of the barn just then and saw her. "If you're looking for the photographer, he's not back yet," he said sourly. "Haven't seen hide nor hair of him or his ugly dog since early morning."

Irrationally, Andy rushed to St.Clare's defense. "Ibebe said he left before breakfast to take some pictures. I'm getting a little worried about him, Uncle Magnus. He's been gone an awfully long time. Do you think he's all right?"

Magnus twisted his mouth. "He's a sly sort, I'm thinking. Shifty. I can't help wishing you hadn't let him a room, Andy. No telling what the likes of him is up to."

Andy waved away his words. "Now don't start, Uncle Magnus. For goodness' sake, you don't know the man at all, and already you've decided he's devious! That's not like you."

The stubborn jaw jutted forward still more. "The fact that we don't know him is just the point, girl. What with everything that's been going on around here of late, it seems to me we're taking a terrible risk bringing a stranger under roof right now."

"And it seems to *me*," Andy shot back at him, "that we ought to be thanking the good Lord to have *anyone* under our roof right now! We need the money, Uncle Magnus—it's as simple as that."

He shook his head. "We don't know this man, Andy. We don't have any idea what he's doing here."

It was on the tip of Andy's tongue to *tell* him what Roman St.Clare was doing there, but this wasn't the place or time. Besides, even though St.Clare hadn't asked her for her confidence about his wife's murder, she wasn't sure she ought to discuss it without his consent.

She sighed and tried to be patient. "Mr. St.Clare is here to rest and work on an assignment. I'm convinced he's perfectly respectable, Uncle Magnus. I really don't sense anything sly or deceitful about him."

He squinted at her. "You seem to have forgotten, girl, that there were those who thought St.Clare might have had something to do with his wife's murder."

Andy bit back the sharp retort that rose to her lips. She was surprised at the quick surge of anger Magnus's words had triggered. Even so, she couldn't bring herself to be cross with him, irascible as he might be at times.

Magnus Doyle wasn't really her uncle, not by blood. He and her father had become close friends while working in the Brooklyn shipyards as young men. Not long after Andy's family had acquired Graystone Manor and begun to turn it into a resort hotel, Magnus's wife, Betsy, had died. Within a few months, he had taken rooms at the Manor and had never left.

Looking back, Andy couldn't imagine what they would have ever done without him. Throughout the years, he had more or less appointed himself groundskeeper and caretaker of the Manor, as well as a surrogate uncle to Andy. When her father passed away in September, Magnus had set aside his own grief to help Andy deal with hers.

She loved him, she depended on him, and she would always be grateful to him. But there were times when his churlish streak of Irish cynicism did try her patience.

"No one ever took that ugly rumor seriously, Uncle Magnus, and you know it," she pointed out. "From all accounts, Roman St.Clare was absolutely devastated by his wife's death. Surely you can look at him and see that he's not over it *yet!*"

He brushed a stray shock of white hair back under his cap, then shrugged. "Perhaps," was all he said. "But I should hope you'll keep your distance from him, all the same."

Andy watched him as he turned and started back to the barn. "Lunch soon," she called after him.

"Won't be *myself* who's late, I'll wager," he shot back over his shoulder.

Shaking her head, Andy started toward the house. She was tramping along, head down, intent on what she might say to her wandering lodger when he finally showed up—assuming they didn't have to go and rescue him—when the eager bark of a dog halted her.

She whirled around. Roman St.Clare was driving his wagon up the lane, the wolfhound bounding ahead of him, directly toward Andy. She was caught off guard by the wave of relief that washed over her at the sight of them.

The wolfhound reached her and came to an abrupt stop, plopping down on his haunches and looking up at her expectantly. Unable to resist the dog's charm, Andy grinned at him and stroked his ears. "Hello, Conor. Been exploring, have you?"

When she straightened, Roman St.Clare was stepping down from the wagon. She noted the slowness of his gait as he approached. When he drew nearer she saw that his appearance was slightly haggard, and that, though he was smiling, his hand was knotted tightly on the cane. Clearly, he had overtaxed himself.

"I believe you have stolen my wolfhound's heart, Miss Fairchild."

Andy forced herself to ignore his strained features, which upon closer regard appeared even more drawn than she'd first thought. She frowned at him, oddly annoyed that he refused to heed his own limitations. "We have been *quite* concerned about you, Mr. St.Clare."

She was surprised at her tone; she hadn't meant to sound so sharp. Even so, she couldn't seem to stop herself from adding, "You might have left word you were going to be gone so long. Are you all right?"

His look was puzzled, even slightly injured. Andy immediately regretted her tactlessness.

St.Clare dipped his head a little to better meet her gaze. "Am I—why, yes, of course. I'm perfectly fine, thank you." He paused. "Why do you ask?"

Andy stared up at him, suddenly feeling foolish. "Well . . . it's just that you've been gone such a long time, and you really don't seem—"

She had been about to say that he really didn't seem well enough to be gallivanting all over the place on a cold November day. But that would have been incredibly rude and probably embarrassing for both of them.

"I'm sorry," she said instead, not looking at him. "With things as they are on the Island right now, I suppose I tend to worry unnecessarily." She kept her eyes averted, but she could feel him studying her.

"Miss Fairchild?"

Andy looked up. He was smiling in that cryptic, watchful way he had.

"I should apologize," he said. "It was thoughtless of me not to leave word that I might be gone most of the morning."

Not wanting him to think she had actually *missed* him, Andy opened her mouth to interrupt his apology. But he ignored her, going on in the same quiet, precise way. "It was good of you to be concerned," he said. "I'm afraid I simply didn't think. I'm on my own so much of the time, I expect I've grown rather careless of my manners. Next time I'll leave word as to when you can expect me."

Suddenly embarrassed by her behavior, Andy again started to explain. Again he overroad her attempt.

"Perhaps I should have been more precise regarding the state of my health, Miss Fairchild." Andy was surprised that, contrary to what she might have expected, St.Clare didn't seem to find the subject of his physical condition in the least awkward. "While it's true that I'm not exactly . . . strapping . . . I'm actually quite fit. At least most of the time. You're not likely to find me lying at the foot of the stairs or sprawled in the garden. I manage rather well, you see, so you mustn't fret."

Why did the man invariably make her feel as if she hadn't a snippet of sense?

Andy drew herself up, regretting, as she often did, her lack of stature. It was so exasperatingly difficult to achieve any real dignity when one was the size of a moppet. "I'm relieved to hear it, Mr. St.Clare," she replied coolly. "And now I really must go inside and help Ibebe with lunch. I'm sure you must be famished after your excursion, and Miss Valentine and Miss Snow will also be waiting."

She knew he was watching her as she hurried down the walk toward the back of the house. She stubbed her toe once, straightened, and continued at a stiff little run, feeling much like a disjointed marionette as she hobbled on.

———

As he watched her hurry off down the walkway toward the back of the house, Roman wondered why her concern for his well-being should have pleased him so much. And she *had* been concerned. He'd known it instinctively, in spite of her ill-concealed efforts to make him believe otherwise.

It had been a long time since anyone had worried over his welfare. Indeed, since Kathleen's death, there had been no one to even notice his comings and goings.

Before Kathleen, his parents' attention had been erratic at best. More than likely, they would have excused their neglect by insisting that children should be reared to be resourceful and independent. It seemed to Roman that both he and his sister, Mary Frances, had trudged through their childhood as small adults, with a father far too self-consumed to give them much more than a distracted thought, and a mother too emotionally unhealthy to provide any real sanctuary for her children.

One of the many things Roman still missed about his marriage was the wonderfully snug, comforting awareness that someone was *waiting* for him: someone who cared enough to be sensitive to his habits and his routine—someone who would grow concerned, even alarmed, should he depart from his normal behavior. So starved, and thankful, had he been for Kathleen's affection that he would have never taken it for granted, even if they had had an entire lifetime together.

Her love had virtually overwhelmed him . . . and remade him. Their marriage had been a haven to Roman, a sheltering, safe harbor—the first he had ever known—and there were no words to adequately describe the utter loneliness he still endured now that she was gone.

He stood, gripping the cane with both hands to rest his weight, feeling all of a sudden like a pathetic fool. Was he really so lonely, so at odds with himself, that the reprimand of a sharp-tongued slip of a girl could evoke a feeling of *gratitude*?

The low-hanging clouds had turned dark and threatening, and the wind had taken on a nasty edge. Roman pulled his greatcoat more tightly around him. His gaze swept the front of the imposing lodging house, and he realized at that moment that his spirit felt as dark, as bleak and cold as the weathered facade of Graystone Manor.

He shuddered and, after another moment, took Conor to the wagon, then hurried back to the house, where he hoped to find a fire.

Nine

*A*ndy had planned to spend the evening in the library, working on accounts—or, to be more accurate, *juggling* accounts. But no sooner had she settled herself at the desk and opened the register than Niles appeared in the doorway.

"Niles! Surely you aren't just now getting home from the hospital?" For only an instant, Andy almost wished he hadn't come. She still had so much to do, and her back was already aching from fatigue. But then she noticed how tired *he* looked, and she quickly forced a smile of welcome.

"Actually, I am," he said, coming into the room. "There was an emergency at the last minute. One of the inmates in the insane pavilion stabbed another with a piece of broken glass."

Andy pushed the register away with a little shiver of revulsion. "One of these days you're going to get badly hurt in that place. I don't know why you continue to go there."

He shrugged, but his expression was entirely serious. "Someone has to look after the poor wretches."

"I still think you should open a society practice uptown in Manhattan," Andy teased. "Why, as fine a doctor as you are, you'd make a fortune in no time. Certainly, your hours would improve."

She grinned at him, but it seemed to take Niles a minute to realize she was joking. He would never be interested in a posh practice, of course. Even as a boy, he had been intent on helping the underprivileged. Although he did maintain a successful practice here on the Island, he spent much of his time caring for the indigent and critically ill at Bellevue. Andy admired him for his dedication, but she worried about him, too.

She studied him as he stood across the desk from her, hands clasped behind him, his back to the fire. His skin had an unhealthy pallor, Andy noted. He had always been too thin, but she was sure he had lost even more weight recently. "Niles, you look awful," she said bluntly. "I don't think you take care of yourself at all. Now, what kind of an example is that for a doctor to set?"

He flushed, and Andy wondered if she'd been too frank. But she was used to being frank with Niles. He was, after all, her best friend, and over the years had also become something of an older brother figure to her.

The problem was that Niles wanted to be *more* than a brother or a friend, while Andy wasn't willing to deepen the relationship. At least, not yet.

"I think you're working much too hard," she said, striving to keep the conversation on a light note. "Surely you're long overdue for a vacation."

His features cleared and he smiled at her. "I confess that I rather enjoy your fussing over me, Amanda, though I can't help but be amused when *you* worry about *me* working too hard. Why, I don't know anyone who works as hard as you do."

"But you keep such incredibly long hours, Niles! You can't possibly get enough rest."

"You know what my work means to me. I don't mind the long hours."

"Still, a break would do you good," Andy insisted. "That's why Roman St.Clare came to the Island, you know—for a rest. And he seems every bit as absorbed in his work as you are in yours."

Abruptly, Niles's expression darkened. "Is that what he told you? That he's here on holiday?"

"Well, he's also covering an assignment," Andy said, hedging a little. "But mostly he plans to rest. I don't believe you *ever* relax, Niles."

Again he shrugged. "I don't need all that much rest. My work is everything to me, Amanda. You know that." His gaze roamed her face. "Except for you, medicine is the most important thing in my life."

As always, his bringing the conversation around to a personal level made Andy uncomfortable, and she moved to change the subject. "Why don't I ask Ibebe to make some hot tea?" she said.

"You must be chilled through after the ferry ride."

He looked so pleased that Andy felt genuinely ashamed of her earlier impatience with him.

"That would be nice," he said. "But you're obviously busy—"

Andy dismissed his concern with an airy wave of her hand and got to her feet. "I can work on the accounts later. I'm always glad for any excuse to put off paying bills."

She tossed the words off lightly, but apparently he heard the strain in her voice. "Are things still all that difficult for you, Amanda? I meant it when I offered to help, if you'd only allow me—"

"Niles, we've already discussed this, and you know how I feel." She hadn't intended to be caustic, but even though she didn't question his sincerity, she found the idea of accepting financial help from Niles—or from anyone else, for that matter—inconceivable.

Of course, Niles had been helping her in one way or another for years, but not with finances. Sometimes it almost seemed that she had grown up under his watchful eye. Five years older than Andy, he had assumed the role of her "protector" when she was still a little girl. Although they hadn't exactly grown up together—their families had been mere acquaintances, never close—she and Niles had been friends from the time he'd begun working for her father after school as a boy.

Their childhoods had been very different. Andy knew Niles had always thought of her family as "old Island"—not exactly a part of the elite, outrageously wealthy element of the Island's populace, but one of the older, more "respectable" families nonetheless.

Poor Niles. He had always been special—exceptional, really—intelligent, hardworking, dependable, ambitious. He'd gone on to become a brilliant medical student and a diligent, conscientious physician. But the family that had been a constant source of humiliation to him throughout his youth had proved just as much a hindrance in his attempt to achieve success and respectability later on. In spite of his education, his countless patients who were utterly devoted to him, and his self-sacrificing use of his medical skills to charity clinics, Niles had never quite been accepted into the inner circle of the Island's society—or even by

81

his peers among the medical community. As much as she hated to think of it, Andy suspected that his family had cost him the social acceptance to which he had long aspired.

Islanders had speculated that Niles's mother was mentally ill for years before she finally committed suicide. As for his father, Zachary Rutherford, the former steamboat captain had been a cold, severe man, a tyrant of a husband and father, who bitterly resented the aristocratic Islanders and their rejection of him and his family. Andy's own father had been convinced that Zachary Rutherford was every bit as unbalanced as his wife, if not more so.

Andy knew little about the father Niles had so obviously feared, other than the fact that he had badgered his son unmercifully, driving him to fulfill an entire host of impossible expectations. She sometimes wondered just how much of Niles's ambition was his own and how much had been fostered by his domineering father.

Both parents were gone now, Zachary Rutherford having died in a freak fall from his own rooftop only a few years after his wife's suicide. Niles almost never spoke of them. The slightest reference to his parents invariably evoked such a look of abject misery that Andy had learned to avoid the subject. On those rare occasions when Niles happened to mention his mother, he never alluded to the cause of her death, but spoke of her passing as if it had been entirely due to natural causes. As for his father, it was as if the man had never existed.

Andy ached for the lonely, unhappy childhood she knew Niles had suffered, though she was careful to conceal even the slightest hint of pity. He had always been so eager to be her hero that she couldn't bring herself to let him know she felt sorry for him. In later years, she sometimes regretted that she had allowed him to become so important in her life. But she had been an only child and often, after her mother's death, a *lonely* child. Her father had done his best, and they had been close, but there had never been quite enough time for Andy after the demands of the Manor. Niles had always seemed to be there for her, and eventually she had come to assume that he always would be.

Only as they grew older and Andy sensed that his feelings had deepened to something different from her own did she begin to feel uncomfortable with their relationship. He had never tried to take advantage of their friendship, of course; Niles was much too honorable, too decent, to try to manipulate her.

But she knew he lived under the illusion that she was "his girl," and that they would one day marry, when in fact Andy had never promised any such thing. On the contrary, the few times they had actually discussed the subject, she had tried to make him aware of her feelings. But other than showing an occasional streak of disappointment or stubborn resistance to the truth, Niles continued to treat her as he always had, quietly demonstrating his affection while speaking of marriage as if it were a foregone conclusion.

Loath to hurt him, Andy had fallen into the habit of allowing his discreet clasping of her hand when they walked, even his chaste kisses upon parting. Eventually, she had almost begun to believe that they *would* marry someday. It was just that she wasn't ready for a permanent commitment yet, she reasoned. It wasn't the right time for her; she had too many other responsibilities. But one day—when she was ready to be a wife—surely Niles would be the man she would turn to.

His voice pulled her abruptly back to her surroundings. "You're doing it again."

Andy blinked, staring vacantly. "What?"

"Wandering. Going off wherever it is you sometimes go in your thoughts."

Andy started to apologize, but he merely smiled and waved off her attempt. "We're both tired," he said. "And as much as I'd love to stay, I have to admit you're right—I do need to get some rest. It would probably be best if I go on home. Perhaps we can spend some time together over the weekend."

Ignoring the faint sense of relief she felt at his words, Andy walked him to the door. He stood studying her for a moment, one hand on her shoulder. "Amanda—about St.Clare—you will be careful, won't you?"

Andy frowned. "Careful?"

Niles tightened his grip a little. "The man *is* a stranger, Amanda. And you're quite vulnerable, out here as you are, with virtually no one nearby."

"Goodness, Niles, I'm not exactly alone here! I have Uncle

Magnus—and Miss Snow and Miss Valentine. And Ibebe."

"Yes, but we really don't know anything about this fellow, Amanda, or what he's doing here. And there is the matter of his wife's murder. . . ."

Niles left his thought unfinished, but the look he gave her made it clear what he was hinting at. Andy's earlier impatience with him suddenly returned. "Roman St.Clare is perfectly respectable, Niles. I can't believe anything else."

He gave a long sigh of exasperation. "You believe the best of everyone, Amanda. That's your nature and it's admirable. But not everyone is to be trusted. Believe me, I know." He took her hand. "I mean only to protect you. Don't be angry with me."

"I'm not angry with you, Niles. But you must *stop* trying to protect me all the time. I'm not a little girl anymore."

She moved to step back, but he dropped his hand from her shoulder and caught her wrist, holding her firmly. "I'm very aware of that," he said, his eyes exploring her face. "But surely you won't scold me for wanting you safe?"

He brought his face close to hers then, as if to kiss her. For just an instant, Andy hesitated. It occurred to her that at best she was *enduring* Niles's touch, and the thought appalled her. How could she be so cold, so uncaring, when he so obviously adored her?

She closed her eyes, willing herself to respond to him. Yet there was no denying the relief she felt when he merely brushed his lips lightly over her cheek, then let her go.

————

Roman stood poised in the doorway of his room, unnoticed by the couple in the entrance hall below.

In spite of the conflicting emotions boiling up in him, for a moment he was unable to turn away from the scene downstairs. He shouldn't have been surprised to see Amanda Fairchild move into Rutherford's embrace. He had known there was something between the two, hadn't he? Her insistence that she and the taut-faced, trenchant physician were merely "friends" hadn't quite rung true; he had sensed there was something more to the relationship than she had admitted.

Certainly there was no reason why she shouldn't permit Rutherford's caress. They were both young, unmarried, good friends—perhaps in love. That being the case, why shouldn't she let the man kiss her?

Then just why, exactly, did it bother him so much?

Even as he recognized the sudden rush of jealousy for what it was, Roman tried to deny it, recoiling from it. She was nothing to him, after all. A mere girl. A virtual stranger.

Even so, a somewhat spiteful feeling of satisfaction stole over him when he saw the brevity of their embrace. Instantly a stab of self-disgust ripped through him, and he stepped backward into the bedroom, quietly closing the door.

But even there he could not block out the memory of her up-turned face, her closed eyes, the obvious reluctance with which Rutherford had released her.

Roman knew his preoccupation with the girl was absurd. He had no real interest in her, could not *allow* such an interest to deter him from his real purpose in coming here. Yet his emotions continued to war within him. Feelings he had believed long dead had been stirred by Amanda Fairchild's heart-shaped face, the freckles that danced across her nose, the mouth that was at once both childish and disturbingly sweet, the bright green eyes that studied him so intently.

Very well, he was attracted to her. He *was* still a man, after all. And the girl wasn't altogether unattractive. She had a winsome-ness about her, a vibrant charm seldom encountered in one so young and unaffected. But he needn't play the fool simply because his head had been turned for the first time in years.

Instinctively, he withdrew the miniature of Kathleen from inside his suit coat and stood looking at it. The old familiar tightness clamped his chest. His eyes stung at the sight of her loveliness. He was ashamed for even thinking of another face, another smile, dismayed that he could have forgotten, even for a moment, what Kathleen had meant to him.

He was acting like a schoolboy, a fatuous *gorsoon*, smitten by a pretty face. Incensed by his adolescent behavior, he resolved to avoid Amanda Fairchild as much as possible. He would take care not to indulge his foolishness.

Roman stood where he was for a long time, studying the miniature of his dead wife with trembling hands and a guilt-laden heart. Finally, he became aware of the wind blowing up outside and walked to the window. He parted the drapes to look out, but there was nothing to be seen except the black, forbidding hills looming at the back of the house and the gnarled branches of the hulking sentinel trees writhing in the wind.

At last he turned and, with the portrait of Kathleen still in his hand, went to sit at the desk across the room. He propped up the miniature in front of him and sat staring at it in the glow from the single beeswax candle, its flame flickering in the chill draft of the room.

Ten

The next day Roman took the ferry to Manhattan. Upon disembarking, he went first to the police station on Franklin Street, where he was ushered into the presence of a Captain Finnegan, with whom he had corresponded a few weeks past.

Finnegan was an angular man with slate-colored hair and a hatchet jaw. But his eyes were friendly as he motioned Roman to a chair. "Well, now, and how can I help you, Mr. St.Clare?" His accent marked him as Irish, though several years removed from home.

Roman sat down, instinctively preparing himself for the skepticism he was used to encountering from other police officers, in other cities. "You recall my letter?" he began. "I wrote to you about the murder of my wife."

The captain nodded and leaned back in his chair, hands locked behind his head. "We read about it in the papers when it happened. My condolences, of course, but I still don't quite understand how we can help you."

Roman reached inside his coat pocket for the news articles he'd brought with him. "These are accounts of a number of robberies—and murders," he said, handing the envelope across the desk to the policeman. "Including the story on the Harrington murder, here in Manhattan."

Finnegan looked at Roman, then straightened and withdrew the news clippings from the envelope. "I'm afraid we don't have much to go on in the Harrington case. Doubt I'll be of much help to you."

"I understand. But if you'll read the articles, you'll see that there are some rather striking similarities in each case—not only in the slayings themselves, but in the robberies as well. Yet each occurred in a different city."

The policeman sniffed and rubbed his hands together—the office was bitterly cold and damp—then began to scan the clippings.

"You'll also note," Roman went on, "that in each case a photographer—or else a member of a photographer's family—was a victim."

The policeman glanced up, his attention obviously snared.

"There's more," Roman told him. "Apparently the murders were particularly brutal, as if the killer were angry when he struck. Also, in each incident, one or more portraits of the victim were stolen." He leaned forward on his chair. "What you *won't* find in the news articles is the fact that Marcus Greenwood—the photographer whose daughter was murdered in the Philadelphia case—received one of the stolen portraits of his slain daughter quite a long time after her death . . . just as I received a portrait of my wife, months later. Both arrived in plain wrappers—with no return mailing address, of course."

He paused. "I haven't spoken with Samuel Harrington yet, but I plan to do so later this afternoon. If I'm right, he will have received a similar package, if not yet, then eventually."

Finnegan rubbed a hand across his chin, openly scrutinizing Roman. "Are you saying that you believe the same man is responsible for all these?" He glanced at the articles in front of him.

Many times before today, Roman had encountered the same dubious expression he now saw reflected in the captain's features. It was, he suspected, the hard, wary look of policemen everywhere who tended to believe nothing without irrefutable evidence.

"That's exactly what I think, Captain. That's why I'm here."

Finnegan continued to study him. "You're following some sort of trail in search of this fellow, is that it, then?"

Roman sighed. He grew tired of repeating the same explanation. "The authorities say they've done all they can, and perhaps they have. But even if they've exhausted all their leads, I can't simply give up. I'm trying to learn what I can on my own. I thought that since the case here in Manhattan was fairly recent, you would still be investigating. I'd hoped you might fill me in on any information you think would prove helpful in my own efforts."

Finnegan's eyes narrowed. "That would be police business, I'm afraid, sir. Private business."

In spite of Finnegan's guarded reply, Roman sensed a certain interest, perhaps even a willingness to help. "Influenza is medical business, Captain, until it becomes an epidemic. Then it can no longer be kept private. I submit that these killings are becoming epidemic. My only interest is in finding the man responsible. I'm merely looking for information."

Finnegan made no reply, but sat browsing through the clippings on his desk. After a moment he glanced up. "What do you know about the case here in Manhattan?"

"Only what I've read in the papers. As I told you, I plan to talk with Samuel Harrington this afternoon."

"You'll not learn much from him, I'll wager. Poor fellow is devastated."

"I can imagine," Roman said tightly.

The policeman looked at him, then averted his eyes. "Aye, and of course you can." Finally he turned back to Roman. "Harrington doesn't know much at all, don't you see? He returned home after working late at his studio to find his house ransacked, his wife dead in their upstairs bedroom." He paused. "Mrs. Harrington had been beaten to death. But she had also been violated. If I recall correctly, that wasn't the case with your wife."

Roman gripped the cane in front of him more tightly. "No," he said, shaking his head. "Kathleen wasn't assaulted . . . that way." *At least she had been spared that much. . . .*

"Actually, the police believed she surprised her assailant in the act of burglary," he told the captain. "They're not certain he even meant to kill her. The theory was that he must have lost control, struck her—" Roman stopped, swallowing with difficulty before going on—"struck her several times, then hurled her across the room."

As if she were no more than a limp rag doll. . . .

"They said it was most likely the blow to the head that killed her." He lifted a hand to his own head. "There was a terrible gash. And blood . . . a great deal of blood. Apparently she struck her head against the marble hearth when she fell."

That was how he had found her, late that evening after coming upstairs from the hotel banquet hall, where he, among others, had received a presidential award for his photographic chronicling of the War. He had entered the room to find Kathleen sprawled in front of the hearth—bruised, broken, lying dead in her own blood.

Finnegan's voice, quiet with a hint of pity in it, called him back to the present. "You really believe the man who killed these other women is the one who killed your wife?"

Roman saw the doubt in the policeman's eyes. "Was a portrait of the Harrington woman stolen, Captain?"

Finnegan fingered the collar of his blue uniform as if to loosen it. "Aye, now that you mention it, there was. Her husband took the photograph himself after their marriage."

Roman nodded, watching the captain.

After another moment, Finnegan pushed away from the desk and rose to his feet. "We know very little, Mr. St.Clare. But I'll tell you what we do know, for whatever it's worth to you, though I can't think how it will help."

Roman leaned foward, both hands still braced on the cane.

"We know that the man who killed Annabel Harrington is more than likely a big bruiser," Finnegan said, his face as hard as slate. "Mrs. Harrington wasn't a small woman, but he slammed her about as if she were no more than a willow limb. She was badly battered, but—" he stopped, met Roman's gaze with a hard look—"it was a killing blow to the head that took her life."

Roman winced but did not lower his eyes.

"Her husband found her on the floor. At first, we thought perhaps the killing had been unintentional, that the beating just got out of hand, but I'm not so sure. More likely, the brute flew into a rage after the assault and began to knock her about. Aye, I think he knew what he was doing, all right. He meant to kill her. That's what *I'm* thinking."

"What kind of a monster could do this to a woman . . . and continue to do it over and over again?"

Roman hadn't realized he'd spoken aloud until Finnegan startled him with a response. "An animal," the policeman bit out.

"And a fiercely angry one at that."

Roman looked up.

Finnegan clenched his fists at his sides and nodded. "Murderously angry. I'll wager we have ourselves a degenerate who's been hauling his baggage of rage about for years, and has only begun to rid himself of it."

They talked for a few more minutes about the sort of man they might be looking for. Then Roman raised a question he had long sensed might be crucial to locating the killer. "And the connection with photography? What do you make of that?"

The captain shrugged. "Could be nothing more than coincidence."

Roman didn't think so. It was too odd entirely. There had been too many slayings, too many similarities among them to discount the possibility that there was a link. It was peculiar—but not, he was certain, a coincidence.

He glanced at his pocket watch, saw that it was already past two. "I'd best be on my way. I'm to meet with Mr. Harrington within the hour." He stood. "I do want to thank you, Captain."

"Sorry I couldn't be of more help," Finnegan said, coming round the desk to shake Roman's hand. "If you turn up anything you think might be important, wouldn't we be in your debt if you'd let us know? Are you staying nearby?"

"On Staten Island. I thought it might be a bit quieter than Manhattan, more restful."

Finnegan raised an eyebrow. "Not all that quiet on the Island these days. They've a few problems of their own, you know."

"So I've learned. Strange occurrences for such an area, wouldn't you say?"

"More the type of thing you'd expect to find here in the city, 'tis true. But when you've been on the force as long as I have, you learn that evil makes its nest in some unlikely places." The captain paused, regarding Roman with a speculative expression. "The business on Staten Island—you'd not be thinking there's some sort of connection between that and the murders, are you now?"

Roman shook his head. "No, not at all. I only just learned about the incidents on the Island after I arrived, from Miss Fairchild and some of the others at the boardinghouse."

"So you're staying at the Graystone, then?"

"I am. You know of it?"

"I knew Matthew Fairchild," the captain said, walking Roman to the door. "Good man. Fine family all around. I never could figure the store Matthew set by that gloomy old house, but apparently the lass is as taken with it as her daddy was."

He followed Roman out of the office. "You're lodging awfully close to where most of the trouble has taken place. I'd caution you to have a care for your own safety. There's no telling what's going on over there. Our men have turned up virtually nothing as yet."

"Thank you, Captain. And you needn't worry. I have every intention of keeping my distance from the Island's troubles. I've enough of my own."

Roman's assurance was entirely genuine. The last thing he needed was to get caught up in something that had nothing to do with him. That much, at least, he had learned from his father—to tend to his own business and avoid the other man's.

———

Later that night, Roman took Conor with him to the first-floor study that Amanda Fairchild had invited him to use. Apparently, it had been her father's favorite retreat, but, since his death, was seldom occupied.

Roman had quickly come to appreciate Matthew Fairchild's fondness for the small study. Of all the rooms in the rambling old house, this one, though simply furnished and somewhat cluttered, seemed to him the most inviting. The desk was scarred, but expansive; the windows, snug; the sofa, well used and extraordinarily comfortable. It was plainly a male refuge, with its solid colors of brown and gold, the vast stone fireplace, and the heavy furniture given more to comfort than to style.

Someone had laid a fire, to which Roman was immediately drawn, as was the wolfhound, who wasted no time in stretching out on the hearth for a doze. Roman had intended to sort through his notes for the *Harper's* assignment, but found that he was unable to concentrate. Instead, he stood warming himself in front of the fire for several minutes, then began to pace the room, all the while going over the afternoon's meeting with Samuel Harrington.

Although the newly widowed photographer had made every attempt to be hospitable, his grief had been painfully evident throughout their conversation—a constant reminder to Roman of his own anguish during those first numbing weeks after Kathleen's murder. Even now, hours later, he could not shake the memory of the haunted, slightly stunned expression in Harrington's eyes. He had been helpless to offer any real consolation to the man, indeed had found himself tempted to leave soon after his arrival, just to get away from the other's misery.

"I can't imagine ever finding any real peace again," Harrington had said more than once, the tortured look in his eyes begging Roman to disagree.

But to his own shame Roman had been unable to offer anything more than one of the bromides he himself had come to detest after Kathleen's death, something to the effect that "time would make a difference." What was always left unsaid was that while time might indeed make a difference, it was no guarantee against those recurring bouts of almost debilitating grief or the wretched, paralyzing loneliness that, even years later, would strike when least expected.

And there was always the other . . . that numbing, unrelenting fear that he himself, during one of his . . . black and mindless moments . . . might have somehow been responsible for Kathleen's death.

Please, God, no . . .

In the end, Harrington had been unable to offer any new information about the assailant. Like Roman, he had arrived too late to confront the attacker or to save his wife from her violent, untimely death.

Finally, in an attempt to get his mind off Samuel Harrington and his own growing sense of melancholy, Roman stopped his pacing and began to scan some of the books on the shelves. Arranged in no discernible order, most of the volumes appeared well used, although there were newer editions among them: Dickens, travel journals, even a few small works of poetry— mostly about the sea. Apparently Matthew Fairchild had been fond of adventure; his personal collection seemed to range from varied exploits of world explorers and army scouts to tales of ocean adventurers and pirates.

After a moment Roman decided on a worn copy of Melville's *Moby-Dick*, which he had read twice before. Settling himself on the sofa, he slipped his reading glasses from his pocket and put them on, thinking that perhaps Ahab's obsession would distract him from his own, at least for now.

Eleven

*R*oman had been reading for well over an hour when he realized that it had begun to rain, quietly but steadily. He yawned and removed his glasses, about to go upstairs when Amanda Fairchild rapped lightly on the open door and stepped into the room.

Laying the book aside, Roman fumbled for the cane.

"Please, don't," she said, with a halting gesture. "I only came to check the fire."

The wolfhound stirred and began to slam his tail eagerly at her approach. She bent to stroke his ears, and the great beast gave her a besotted grin.

Roman smiled and shook his head at this puppylike enthusiasm. Yet he, too, had felt an unexpected sense of pleasure at the sight of his young landlady. She went to stoke the fire, and as he studied the slender back, the riot of auburn hair only barely confined by a blue hair ribbon, he felt an unaccountable tug of tenderness. Instantly he blinked and looked away, unsettled by an emotion he had thought long dead.

The fire cracked and hissed. He turned back, watching her add a log.

"So it's you I have to thank for the fire," he said, slipping his glasses into his pocket. "I've been enjoying it immensely."

She straightened and faced him, smiling a little. "I thought you might. I know the ferry can be brutally cold on a night like this." She glanced at the book beside him. "*Moby-Dick*? My father must have read it dozens of times."

Roman nodded. "It's a grand story. I'll take it upstairs with me, if you don't mind."

"Of course not. Help yourself to any of the books you like," she said, looking around the room. "My father always kept his favorites in here. He wanted them nearby so he didn't have to go looking for them. His books were like old friends to him."

"You were quite close, the two of you?" Roman was somewhat surprised to find that he was genuinely curious about her—her family, her past, her life.

"My mother died when I was very young," she told him. "My father raised me. So, yes, we were close."

Roman nodded. "You must miss him a great deal."

Her expression sobered still more. "Terribly. I imagine I always will . . . especially at this time of night. We used to sit here, in front of the fire, almost every night, just talking about our day. Even now I sometimes half expect to see him sitting here, waiting for me, when I walk in."

Again Roman gave a nod, knowing all too well what she meant.

Suddenly she looked at him, an expression of dismay pinching her features. "I'm sorry . . . of course, you would understand. . . ."

She broke off, and Roman found himself touched by her awkwardness. She was so refreshingly unaffected, so thoroughly . . . *nice.* He found himself wanting to reassure her.

The idea caught him off guard. How long had it been since he'd had even the vaguest concern for another's feelings? He had been alone for so long, absorbed in his own life, his own emotions; he had almost forgotten what it was like to consider someone else's feelings.

On impulse, he gestured to the sofa cushion next to him. "Obviously, we're both missing someone to talk with by the fire. Please . . . won't you stay and talk with *me* for a while, Amanda—Miss Fairchild?"

She looked startled, and for an instant Roman thought he might have offended her. But then she smiled, uncertainly, and came to sit beside him.

"Actually," she said, perching forward at the farthest end of the sofa and folding her hands primly in her lap, "I prefer 'Andy.' That's what most people call me—'Andy.' "

Roman sensed that she was taking great care to avoid meeting his eyes. "Andy," he said thoughtfully, testing the sound of it. "Yes, it suits you."

———————

Andy definitely liked the sound of her name when he said it, accented with the lilt of his native tongue—"Ahn-dee."

She supposed it might be considered forward, his asking her to sit here alone with him. Aware of his eyes on her, she instinctively edged a little closer to the arm of the sofa.

Somehow, though, she knew there was nothing improper about Roman St.Clare's invitation. He could be unnervingly direct, of course, but she sensed it was merely his way, not an impertinence. Perhaps the Irish were simply more forthright by nature.

Andy made herself turn and look at him. Just as she'd sensed, he was studying her with that faint, cryptic smile of his.

"Is that what your father called you?" he asked. " 'Andy'?"

She nodded, her own smile rueful. "Apparently he thought 'Amanda' was too much name for such a wretchedly small baby. Most everyone on the Island calls me 'Andy' . . . except for Miss Snow and Miss Valentine, that is. They don't think it's a proper name for a lady." She didn't bother adding that Niles, too, found the nickname somewhat demeaning.

As for being a lady—well, she'd never had much success in that area anyway. There was neither the time nor the money to indulge in high fashion and endless social calls, and from what she could tell, that was pretty much what ladies did. It all sounded dreadfully dull to her.

She glanced at Roman St.Clare to find his dark gray eyes glinting as though he knew exactly what she was thinking and found it more than a little amusing.

"What about your family, Mr. St.Clare?" she asked abruptly, thinking to banish that annoying light of humor in his eye. "Do they still live in Ireland?"

He nodded, his smile fading. "My father passed on a number of years ago, but my sister and her family live in Antrim. And my mother as well."

"Do they plan to join you here in the States eventually?"

His eyes took on the shuttered look she had seen before. Andy could almost hear the door close with a resounding thud on that private, solitary part of himself he seemed so reluctant to reveal. "No," he said flatly. "They've no plans to leave Ireland."

Silence hung between them until Conor rose and padded up to Andy, clearly in search of an affectionate hand. When she obliged him, he rested his enormous head on her lap and stared up at her with soulful eyes.

"You certainly have charmed the hound," Roman observed, the warmth returning to his voice. "I've never known him to take to anyone as he has to you."

Andy smiled at the dog, who grinned back at her. "He knows an admirer when he meets one. I think he's quite wonderful."

"Careful. He's already an arrogant beast. Any more flattery, and he'll be insufferable."

Conor went to him then, and Andy watched, enjoying the unmistakable bond between the two. The wolfhound studied his master with a look that was nothing short of adoration. As for St.Clare, his large hands were infinitely gentle as he rubbed the dog's head, his smile one of genuine fondness.

"Seeing the two of you together makes me regret never having had a dog of my own," she said, meaning it. "I think I've missed quite a lot."

St.Clare went on stroking the wolfhound. "Well, this great oaf has more than enough affection to go round," he said, turning toward her. "It's obvious that he's decided to adopt you, so you might just as well enjoy him, if you like."

Apparently satisfied for the time being, the dog gave a great sigh and made his way back to the fire. "Tell me," St.Clare said, inclining his head toward the heavily draped window across the room, "does it always rain this much here?"

What had earlier begun as a sullen drizzle had intensified over the past few minutes until now it threatened to erupt into a full-blown storm. Although the old house was as sturdy as a fortress, the windows rattled under the onslaught of the wind and driving rain.

Andy shuddered at the sound. "I'm afraid we're not at our best this time of year," she admitted. "November can be a little depressing, even to those of us who are used to winter on the Island. But doesn't it rain almost all the time in Ireland? I've always heard that's why the country is so green."

He feigned a look of indignation. "Certainly not. Besides, Irish rain is a lady, gentle-natured and well-mannered. Nothing at all like your bad-tempered harridans here in the States."

Andy was intrigued with this rare lightness from him. Most often he seemed either solemn to the point of grimness or, more unsettling, faintly mocking.

They were silent for a time, each staring into the fire. After a moment, he changed the subject abruptly. "Has there been any further news about the child who was found murdered?"

Another gust of wind lashed the windows. Andy sat forward to absorb more of the fire's warmth. "No," she said. "And I really don't understand why there hasn't by now. You'd think the police could have turned up *some* kind of lead in all this time."

"According to Captain Finnegan, the police are as much in the dark as everyone else."

Andy looked at him in surprise. "You've talked with the police?"

"Not specifically about the business here on the Island, no. I went to inquire about a recent murder in Manhattan. The captain brought up the incidents here."

Andy studied him for a moment, wondering if she should ask. "This murder," she said carefully, "do you think it's somehow related to your wife's death?"

He spoke freely about his meeting with the police that afternoon, telling her about his fruitless talk with Samuel Harrington and, finally, his suspicion that the same man was responsible for killing both his wife and the Harrington woman, as well as others.

Andy didn't take her eyes off Roman during his entire monologue. She was acutely aware of the smudges of fatigue beneath his eyes, the white-knuckled grip of his hands on the cane. She was just as aware of the intense, white-hot emotion that seemed to emanate from him.

For a long time after he had finished, Roman sat staring into the fire. When he spoke again, his voice was hard. "I'm going to find him."

He turned toward her, and Andy shrank inwardly at the mingling of anger and anguish in his gaze.

"He's going to go right on killing if he's not stopped. He's becoming bolder, more brutal. Something has been unleashed in him, some streak of darkness and evil. It will only grow wilder and more dangerous until he's caught."

His eyes seemed to have taken on the heat of the fire in front of them as he leaned toward Andy. "It's very much the same with this business here on your Island, don't you see? Something has been unloosed—something terribly wicked—and it's spreading, growing more savage all the time. That's the nature of evil, I think. Left alone, it will only feed on itself, spread and grow more powerful, until it seems virtually indestructible."

Andy studied him, moved by the obvious depth of conviction that burned within him. "I wish I could help. I wish there were something I could do," she said without thinking.

He gave her a puzzled look. "Help?"

Andy nodded, at a loss to express, or even to understand, her emotions. "I wish I could help you find him . . . the man who murdered your wife. And the monster who's doing the terrible things here on the Island."

He stared at her blankly for a moment. Then his features relaxed, his expression gentled. "That's very good of you. To care, I mean."

Andy knotted her hands together in her lap, groping for words to frame her feelings. "It's just that I think I understand how important it is for you to find him. And I agree with you that he must be stopped. Just as whoever is responsible for the awful incidents here on the Island has to be stopped. If only we could find a way . . ."

Andy let her thoughts drift off, unfinished. St.Clare was still watching her as if he didn't quite know what to make of her.

"Thank you, Miss—*Andy*," he finally said. "It's good of you to want to help."

Andy's attention was drawn then to his hands on the cane; they were trembling. Alarmed, her eyes searched his face, and she saw that even in the firelight he looked pale. "Mr. St.Clare— are you ill?"

He shook his head and gave the ghost of a smile. "No, I'm perfectly fine. A bit tired, perhaps. It's late."

Andy glanced at the clock on the mantel and saw that it was almost ten. "Goodness, it *is*!" Suddenly embarrassed, she scrambled to her feet. "I'm awfully sorry, I didn't mean to monopolize your eve—"

He waved off her apology and, using the cane to support his weight, pushed himself up from the sofa. Andy very nearly put out a hand to steady him, but stopped herself just in time.

"But I'm *glad* you stayed," he said, sounding thoroughly earnest. "You can't imagine how I've enjoyed this." He seemed to hesitate, as if choosing his words with deliberate care. "Miss Fairchild . . . *Andy*—"

Andy watched him, waiting.

"Perhaps you'll think me presumptuous—" He paused, almost as if he expected her to agree with him before he finished. When she didn't, he suddenly seemed at a loss for words. "I would like it very much if we could . . . ah, if we could be friends."

Andy tried to ignore the feeling of elation that spiraled through her. "Why . . . yes, I'd like that, too. But aren't we . . . that is, I thought . . . we already were."

He leaned on the cane, smiling at her. Andy couldn't think why that odd little smile of his should affect her so strangely.

"*Did* you?" He seemed genuinely surprised . . . and pleased. "Well, then," he said, eyeing her with the faint glint of amusement she had come to recognize by now, "that being the case, do you think you could manage to call me 'Roman' from now on . . . *mo chara?*"

Andy's mouth had suddenly gone very dry. "*Mo chara?*"

He studied her face for a moment, then did an astonishing thing, the kind of thing Andy had only read about in books. Bending over her hand, he brought it to his lips with a touch so gentle, so fleeting, she might have imagined it. She was so dumbfounded she almost jerked her hand away as if she'd been scalded!

But she didn't.

"In the Irish," he said softly, his eyes going over her face as he lifted his head, "*mo chara* means 'my friend.'" He paused, then added, "So, then, Andy . . . *mo chara* . . . perhaps we'll talk again tomorrow night?"

Only when she nodded her agreement did he finally release her hand.

Andy stood watching the empty doorway long after Roman and the wolfhound had left the room. She felt ridiculously confused, her emotions as turbulent as the rainstorm battering the house. Once she lifted her hand, looking at it as if the warmth that still lingered from his touch might be visible.

She was loath to go upstairs, not wanting to shatter the moment. Yet she knew she must not make too much of this night. He intended only friendship, she reminded herself sternly. The courtly gesture would more than likely fluster any woman, but she needed to remember that he was of a different world . . . at least, a different country, a different culture. Probably in Ireland such an act meant nothing. Nothing at all.

But as she turned and went to bank the fire, she couldn't quite dispel the memory of his searching gaze when he had lifted his head and looked into her eyes, any more than she could stop herself from silently repeating the strange words he had said to her, words that had sounded almost like music on his lips . . .

Mo chara . . .

My friend.

Twelve

It was very late—he had no idea how late—when the man completed the night's work and prepared to leave the laboratory.

He was tired, but satisfied, for the procedures had gone well tonight. He held the lantern aloft, its light swaying gently as he made a final check of the basement. Small cubicles—cells—had been erected along two of the stone walls, with wooden partitions and doors fitted with iron bars and locks. Each cell contained its own pallet and water jar, a clay bowl—nothing else.

The entire underground basement was windowless. Even the coal chute had been boarded shut. A huge, ugly furnace squatted against the wall adjoining the cells. Ash and a faint chemical odor hung in the air, along with the stench of an ancient, unidentifiable decay.

The silence in the basement was broken only by the shriek of the wind and the slashing of sleet against the walls. Occasionally, a small form stirred in one of the cells and moaned in its sleep. Overhead, the stillness was absolute, the hush of a house long abandoned, uninhabited except by spiders and an errant field mouse.

The figures in the cells were, for the most part, unmoving. They slept through the night and most of the daylight hours as well. Their surroundings were almost in total darkness now, the only light that of the flickering lantern in the man's hand. The shadows revealed the faint outline of a massive desk piled high with journals and reference works, an immense iron sink stacked with boxes and tubing, wooden cabinets secured on the wall above. A large examining table stood in the middle of the room.

The floor was grimy and pitted with crumbled mortar and dried mud, the corners ripe with mold. A menacing cold permeated the entire area.

It was a place too dark for light to enter, an unhallowed place that harbored rustling creatures of the night and terrible secrets of the past. But none of this mattered to the man with the lantern. He was doing something here that he could not accomplish anywhere else—a work of such magnitude, such extraordinary consequence that once he had achieved it, he would be able to work wherever he wanted. He would never again be confined to this dank, underground warren.

But for now it served his purpose quite well—a purpose of such momentous proportion that, for a time, he could almost feel a certain affection for the place, even a reluctance to leave it.

His eyes went to the far wall, to the cell at the very end. For a moment, he stood gazing at it with a kind of fondness. Larger by half again than the other cells, it was furnished with a bed—small, but comfortable—warm blankets, a brightly colored washbowl and some crockery on a nightstand. At first glance, it resembled a guest room in a private home. Except for the bars on the door, of course.

He smiled then and, lifting the lantern to light his way, turned to go, leaving the darkness behind.

Sometime in the night, Andy dreamed of a shadowy, sepulchral gallery where portraits of bleak-faced children rattled in the wind, a wind that roared through tall, stained-glass windows, shattering them into thousands of pieces and hurling the shards inward onto the floor.

The striking of the downstairs clock awakened her. How many chimes? She couldn't be sure. She lay still for a moment, listening to the sound echo in the entrance hall as she tried to sort through the eerie dream. Her eyes were still heavy with sleep, her mind as dull as if she'd been drugged. But the image of the haunted faces and broken glass was disturbingly vivid. When the wind wailed outside the bedroom window, she shivered and pulled the covers up to her chin.

Suddenly, a new sound jarred her out of her drowsiness, and she sat up with a jerk, listening.

Footsteps. Below, in the entrance hall.

A chill rippled through her as the footsteps made their way to the staircase. Then it occurred to her that it was probably just Uncle Magnus on the way back to his room after one of his late-night excursions to the kitchen.

But after a moment, Andy recognized the soft scraping and uneven step of Roman St.Clare, then the frisky padding of his wolfhound. The instant of relief she had felt quickly gave way to a troubling uncertainty. Why would Roman be wandering around the house at this time of night? He had pleaded fatigue earlier in the study, and certainly he had *looked* exhausted.

She got out of bed and tiptoed to the door. The floor was cold to her bare feet as she stepped off the rag rug, and she hugged her arms to herself as she pressed her cheek against the door-frame and stood listening. She tensed as the shuffling sounds grew nearer. The palms of her hands were clammy, her pulse unsteady.

She hated herself for the awful images the scraping rhythm conjured up. Her mind was suddenly filled with grotesque imaginings, no doubt implanted from the reading of too many tales by Mrs. Radcliffe and Mr. Poe. But the unseen thud and scrape of the approaching footsteps sent a glacial shiver up her spine all the same.

The footsteps were just outside her door now. Andy held her breath. A sudden blast of wind and sleet struck the bedroom window, and she jumped, choking down a startled cry.

Irked at her own foolishness, she pulled in a steadying breath and gritted her teeth. She was acting like a silly child! It was Roman, for goodness' sake—Roman and the wolfhound—not some mythical horror from the Haunted Swamp.

"Ninny!" she grumbled under her breath. Obviously, she needed to change her reading habits.

The footsteps went on down the hall. Andy waited another second or two, then cracked the door open just enough to peer out into the dimly lighted corridor.

She swallowed, her heart pounding as she watched the wolfhound and Roman St.Clare, his dark greatcoat slung over his shoulders, disappear into his room at the end of the hall. In their wake could be seen a faint trail of wet imprints on the floor. Ob-

105

viously, they had been outside, in spite of the inclement weather.

For a moment Andy stood absolutely still, staring down the hallway into the shadows. The late-night silence seemed oppressive, the darkened corridor strangely unfamiliar. Again the windows rattled, and she rubbed her upper arms briskly, more from the chill of her imagination than the cold.

Struck by an unexplainable need to retreat from the forbidding silence of the house, Andy stepped back into the bedroom. After a moment she resorted to something she hadn't done for years—she turned the lock on the door.

The act had troubling implications, implications she would rather not consider. Earlier tonight in the study, she had felt a genuine liking for Roman St.Clare, even an excessive pleasure in his bid for her friendship. In the warm comfort and familiarity of her father's study, her feelings had seemed perfectly natural and right. The firelight, the room's snug, safe surroundings had made it all too easy to forget how little she actually knew about the stranger she had taken in.

Now, in the frigid darkness of the night, with the wind wailing and scraping at the window, nothing was the same. She cringed at how easily she had violated her father's caution never to trust another human being too much, too soon. "Trust is something that must be earned," he had told her, "and it usually takes a very long time to earn something so valuable."

The truth of the matter was that her instincts about Roman could be drastically in error. It was entirely possible that she had trusted him "too much, too soon"—the very thing her father had warned her against. Roman was a strange sort of man, after all—remote, taciturn, distracted. A solitary kind of man who did not seem to need or want anyone else in his life. Yet, this very night, he had asked for her friendship as if it were a precious gift.

And she had given it, eagerly. Too eagerly? Again she shrank inwardly to think how quick she had been to take him at his word. A plea for friendship didn't necessarily mean he could be trusted.

On the other hand, she might just be acting foolishly, allowing herself to be caught up in the lateness of the hour, in the aftermath of a troubling dream—not to mention the storm howling outside her window. Why, for all she knew, Roman St.Clare might have the same penchant for raiding the pantry after hours as Magnus did!

There was also the possibility that the wolfhound might simply have had to answer the call of nature at an untimely hour.

Feeling better now, Andy chided herself for acting like one of Miss Valentine's witless romantic heroines. The very thought made her grind her teeth.

With an impatient sigh, she deliberately unlocked the bedroom door, then scurried across the room and dived under the bedclothes.

Inside his bedroom, Roman pressed his hands to his throbbing temples, then pulled them away in surprise. His face was wet, as was his hair, and raindrops . . . like huge tears . . . were falling onto the floor, puddling around his feet.

Conor looked up at him, whining softly, nuzzling his hand. There was a look of pain in the wolfhound's eyes, as if he felt Roman's dismay and bewilderment and longed to convey his understanding.

With a great groan, Roman flung his greatcoat from his shoulders and sank down onto the side of the bed, burying his face in his hands. Where had he been *this* time, and . . . oh, dear God . . . *what had he done?*

Exhausted, drained, he fell back across the bed and lay staring into the darkness of the room. Pain crept up the back of his neck and clutched his skull. He closed his eyes, grasping at sleep, if only to numb the pain and quell the sick fear gripping him.

But sleep came late and brought no peace. Instead, he writhed and thrashed as the old, familiar nightmare slowly surfaced, clawing at his mind, tearing at his sanity. With a despair that even sleep could not diminish, he saw Kathleen's slender body outlined in scarlet upon the pale linens . . . her russet hair, a flaming veil . . . her chalk-white face, a death mask. He watched in horror as the dark, unknown form emerged from the shadows, at the same time felt the stirring, the cold, menacing presence of an evil he could not name . . . an evil he dared not confront, for fear of losing his mind . . . and perhaps his very soul.

Thirteen

*F*or three days various accounts of the discovery of the murdered Negro child appeared on the front page of all the area newspapers. Almost as evident as the feature articles were those letters to the editor demanding immediate police action. As was to be expected, the public was outraged—and badly frightened.

Both the white and Negro population had become more and more suspicious over the passing months, hurrying home before dark, and once there, staying safely behind their locked doors until morning. Many social functions and political gatherings were put off indefinitely. Neighbors had taken to studying one another with furtive looks, while strangers had become anathema. Even the ferryboats were suffering, with no one using their services except for businessmen and those residents who couldn't avoid a trip across the river.

Despite all this, and even taking into consideration her own growing uneasiness, Andy wasn't prepared for the way certain members of her congregation behaved toward Roman St.Clare at services on Sunday morning. At first, she hadn't thought to invite her new lodger to worship with her, assuming that, since he was Irish, he would also be Roman Catholic. Later she had convinced Uncle Magnus to suggest that St.Clare might like to attend worship at St. Patrick's with him. Magnus had invited him readily enough, only to inform Andy later that *"himself* is of the Protestant conviction." This was volunteered with a slightly caustic aside to the effect that one could expect nothing more of an Ulsterman.

Impatient with Magnus's feigned gruffness—and it *was*

feigned, Andy was sure, for she had never known him to be the least bit narrow-minded in matters of faith—she had proceeded to invite St.Clare to services at her own church. She was almost surprised at how promptly he accepted. *Why* she should have been surprised, she couldn't quite say. Perhaps because he seemed such a solitary man, she would have expected him to seek out a place of worship on his own.

That St.Clare would be a churchgoing man was another assumption on her part, an accurate one this time. As it happened, he seemed genuinely pleased by the invitation and was already waiting at the front door when Andy followed Miss Snow and Miss Valentine downstairs on Sunday morning. His readiness to accompany them and his warm, almost courtly manners, especially toward the two older women, caused Andy a measure of guilt when she remembered her doubts about the man the night before.

Although she still puzzled over what he might have been doing, roaming around outside at such a late hour, she found it difficult if not impossible to imagine anything treacherous about St.Clare. This morning, especially, the transforming smile was quick and eager, his behavior that of a Christian gentleman with impeccable breeding and manners.

There was no time before the service to introduce him to anyone, even to those seated nearby. Andy found herself squeezed in between St.Clare and Miss Valentine in their usual pew halfway down the aisle. She was acutely aware of the whispers behind them and the sidelong glances from across the aisle before the service began. But when Pastor Galon approached the pulpit for the morning greeting, all eyes turned toward the front.

Throughout the singing of the worship hymns, Andy was keenly mindful of the photographer's considerable height; she felt annoyingly small and insignificant standing next to him. She was just as aware of his unexpectedly fine, strong singing voice as well. She didn't quite know what she had expected—a baritone perhaps, somber and subdued. Instead, she found herself singing harmony to a rich, full tenor that was nothing less than inspiring. In fact, in the wake of St.Clare's remarkable voice, Andy applied a little more gusto than usual to her own singing.

After the service, she lingered in the aisle as she usually did, anticipating the introduction of her new lodger to her friends and neighbors. To her surprise and chagrin, however, many squeezed by with no more than a mumbled "good morning" or a perfunctory nod. Others, even though they exchanged the usual pleasantries with Andy, raked St. Clare with suspicious eyes during the introductions, while some, to Andy's growing consternation, ignored him altogether.

She could not believe this was happening. To be sure, given the horrible events that had taken place over the past few months, everyone would be somewhat guarded around strangers these days. Even so, she would never have imagined that those fears would be carried into the church.

She *knew* these people, had known many of them her entire life. They were good people, *Christian* people who ordinarily would be quick to offer hospitality to the outsider, to welcome him not only into their church, but into their homes as well. Had things really come to such a pass that they would now shun a stranger in their midst—in God's own house—out of fear and suspicion?

As she stood there watching the parade of familiar faces pass by, Andy almost felt as if *they* were the strangers—these "good Christian people" who had sung the hymns and read the Scriptures and listened to the sermon—which, ironically enough, had dealt with the passage from Hebrews about "entertaining angels unawares." She might not have known them at all, so alien did their behavior strike her.

Roman St.Clare's voice jarred her back to awareness. She blinked and looked up at him. "I'm sorry?"

"I asked about your friend, Dr. Rutherford. Does he attend here also?" He was watching her with a questioning look. Was it possible he hadn't noticed the rudeness to which he'd been subjected?

Andy stepped back to make way for Ernestine Charleson, who seemed not to see her at all. "Niles? Oh, yes, he attends here, but he can't always make services," Andy said, distracted. "He often has to be at the clinic very early, even on Sundays." She paused, staring after the widow Charleson, who was elbowing her way up the aisle, flashing a huge, white-toothed smile at everyone she met. "I expect he'll join us for dinner, though. At least, he promised to try."

"Ah, then, I'll look forward to seeing him again. He seems an interesting fellow."

Andy studied him closely to see if he meant it, for she had never heard anyone call Niles "interesting" before. But the photographer's expression was inscrutable.

She was about to apologize for her congregation's poor manners when Jane Lowe and her husband, Donald, walked up.

Relieved, Andy greeted them with perhaps a little too much enthusiasm. She knew she could count on Jane. Jane Lowe had been one of her closest friends while growing up. Like Andy, Jane had been an inveterate tomboy when they were younger, her willowy blond good looks belying a puckish instinct for mischief. They often shared family holidays and outings, slept over on weekends, and pretended to study their lessons together. Andy had liked Jane because she always said just what she thought, yet at the same time could keep a secret better than any of the other girls in school.

Even though Jane was married now and the mother of two small boys, she still sported a capricious smile and a distinctly unladylike tendency toward frankness.

At the moment she was studying Roman St.Clare with unabashed curiosity. "You must be Andy's new lodger," she said at once, tugging Donald up alongside her as she offered her free hand to St.Clare. "Hello, I'm Jane Lowe, and this is my husband, Donald. Welcome to Staten Island. It's not always this cold, you know."

The two men shook hands, and Andy was pleased to see that Roman St.Clare responded easily to the Lowes almost at once. Jane continued to prattle on, as was her way, while Donald watched with an affectionate smile.

"I didn't see Niles," Jane observed after a moment, looking around at the few people left in the sanctuary. "He's working again, I suppose?"

Andy bit her lip. "He must have had an emergency at the clinic."

Jane's smile was skeptical. "Niles certainly has his share of emergencies."

"It's this awful influenza." Andy hadn't meant to be so abrupt. "Niles says if it gets any worse, we'll be in the middle of a full-scale epidemic." It was true, but she wished she didn't always feel the need to defend one friend to the other.

Jane had never really liked Niles very much and made no secret of the fact. She had always thought him deadly dull and perhaps even a little strange. Her opinion of him had only grown less forgiving as they grew older. She often insisted that Niles was obsessed. "Obsessed with his work—medicine is his idol, you know—and obsessed with you, Andy. Don't you dare let him talk you into marriage! You think he's a good friend, and maybe he is—but he'd be an insufferable husband."

Andy allowed for the drastic differences in her two friends and knew it would be pointless to hope that Jane would ever be sympathetic or understanding toward Niles. The truth was that there were times when she was almost afraid Jane might be right, at least about Niles's obsession with his work. But even if he were as driven as Jane accused him of being, Andy thought it must be because of his wretched family situation and his determination to better himself.

It was true that Niles often seemed absorbed in medicine to the exclusion of everything else. On the other hand, wasn't it entirely possible that what some might interpret as excessive ambition was actually a kind of selfless devotion? Not only did Niles spend hours every week treating the indigent ill at Bellevue, but he also volunteered his medical skills at the Negro clinic several times each month. In addition, he served on the board of one of the foundling hospitals in Manhattan.

As for his interest in *her*, Andy hardly thought it could be called an obsession. That she was uncomfortable with his affection had more to do with her inability to return his feelings. He was never heavy-handed with her when she refused to agree to a commitment. No, Niles's behavior toward her might be deemed persistent, but certainly not unnatural.

They stood talking with the Lowes for a few more minutes before Miss Snow and Miss Valentine finally returned from chatting with their own circle of friends. During that interval, no one else approached, nor did Andy make any further attempt to introduce Roman St.Clare. She wasn't willing to risk further embarrassment for either of them.

She could only hope the poor man hadn't expected very much

in the way of a welcome, although certainly most people *would* have expected more, especially from a Christian congregation. But, then, most people weren't living under the constant cloud of fear that had engulfed Staten Island for months now.

Andy cringed at the thought of what changes might yet lie in store for the Island if this siege of terror didn't end soon.

Fourteen

*A*ndy waited until they were nearly through dinner before attempting anything in the way of an apology to Roman St.Clare. She had no more begun to offer her rather lame excuses for the behavior of the congregation, however, when Niles jumped in to *defend* them—an unexpected turn of events, since he hadn't even been at church that morning and couldn't have known what went on.

"I don't think an apology is in order, Amanda," he said, frowning. "It's only natural that people are going to be suspicious of outsiders for the time being." Seated directly across from Roman St.Clare, Niles stared at the photographer with a look that invited the other to disagree.

His countenance was positively sullen, Andy decided. She would have kicked him under the table had she thought no one would notice. Instead, she merely glared at him. Niles pretended to ignore her.

"Well—" The short utterance and long pause from Miss Snow, at Andy's left, was almost certain to herald agreement with Niles. Miss Snow seldom *disagreed* with Niles, Andy had noticed, while Miss Valentine was more likely to keep her opinions to herself.

"Niles is absolutely right, of course." Miss Snow's tone suggested that everyone at the table had been waiting for her opinion. "We can hardly expect people to behave normally under circumstances that are anything *but* normal." She leaned across Andy to address Roman St.Clare directly. "The people on the Island are living in terror, Mr. St.Clare. If Amanda has told you of the trouble, then I'm sure you can imagine our state of mind."

Out of the corner of her eye, Andy watched Roman fiddle with his fork for a moment. "Perfectly understandable," his manner pleasantly casual as he went on. "I'm sure it's difficult to trust anyone, given the present circumstances. And of course," he added mildly, "we always suspect a stranger before one of our own."

Andy blinked, then looked quickly away. Could he possibly know she'd been watching him the night before? Staring fixedly at her plate, she tried to force down a large bite of pot roast, but the meat stuck in her throat. She took a drink, coughing as she studiously avoided St.Clare's gaze.

"You can't seriously think the lunatic behind these monstrous acts is one of the Islanders?" From his place at the head of the table Magnus glared at St.Clare as if the photographer had taken leave of his senses. "Impossible! I know most everyone on this island, and I can think of no one who has it in him to dig up graves or murder children!"

Roman St.Clare regarded him solemnly for a moment, then took a long sip of water. "It's been my experience that we can't always know what people are capable of, Mr. Doyle. Not even the people we think we know well."

"Is that an insight you've acquired through your extensive travels, Mr. St.Clare?" Niles's tone was so snide that Andy gaped at him in surprise.

The photographer, however, seemed not to notice, but merely gave a small shrug and went on eating. Niles flushed, as though he knew his rudeness had been rebuffed.

"No doubt you learned much about human nature during the War, Mr. St.Clare." Miss Valentine so deftly changed the subject that Andy could have hugged her. "It must have been a dreadful experience for you and all our fine young men," she went on. "My dear father survived the terrible War of 1812, you know. Poor Papa could never bear to speak of his experiences afterward. He was so very sensitive." She paused, then added, "I do admire that in a man. It shows true gentleness of spirit, I believe."

At Andy's left, Miss Snow uttered a small sound of disgust, though she said nothing. Roman St.Clare leaned slightly forward and smiled at Miss Valentine, across from him. "Permit me to observe that you obviously inherited that admirable trait from your father, Miss Valentine."

Miss Christabel, clearly charmed by this unexpected gallantry, practically cooed. "Why, how lovely of you, Mr. St.Clare! I take that as a great compliment. And if you don't mind my saying so, I do believe I detect the same sensitive spirit in *you*. But, then, the Irish are known to be extremely sentient by nature."

"Really, Christabel, what do you know about the Irish?" snapped Miss Snow.

"More than some, I'll wager," Magnus put in. His expression was inscrutable, but Andy knew by the twitch at one corner of his mouth that he was only trying to rile Miss Snow, his favorite sparring partner.

"Mr. Doyle certainly knows by now that I think very highly of the Irish," Miss Valentine replied, with a smile in his direction. "Such a romantic, valiant people."

A quick glance and Andy saw Roman St.Clare's smile break even wider.

Across the table, however, Niles seemed unamused. "You know, I almost forget that you *are* Irish, Mr. Doyle," he said. "You've been in the States for years, after all. Surely by now you think of yourself as an American."

For one of the few times Andy could recall, Magnus turned a disapproving eye on Niles. "Being Irish doesn't wear off like cheap paint," he snapped. "*Irish-American* is what I am, and I'm thinking that's better than being too much of one or the other."

Andy suppressed a grin at the exaggerated brogue, which Uncle Magnus tended to turn on and off at will. She saw that Roman was watching the exchange with a look of faint amusement.

"I meant nothing disparaging, sir," Niles said stiffly.

Magnus was still glaring. "I know what you meant, well enough," he grumbled. "There are plenty of bad feelings toward the Irish across the river. And small wonder, given the riffraff in that abomination they call the Five Points! I'll not argue that the city holds ten who shame the Irish for every one who makes us proud. But let's not be forgetting that those poor souls never set out to be ignorant and dirty and ill-used. Indeed, they can thank the British Crown in large measure for their misery."

Andy knew the story by heart. Uncle Magnus had seen to it that her education on the ancient enmity between Ireland and England had not been lacking. Most of the time, she let the frequently repeated story go in one ear and out the other. But Miss Snow was overly fond of reminding Magnus of her British ancestors whenever he started in on one of his tirades—any minute now the two of them would be at it—and since there was already quite enough tension in the dining room, she thought it wise to change the subject.

At that point, Niles partially redeemed himself by moving to do that very thing. "Andy says you're working on an assignment here, St.Clare. Is there really that much on Staten Island worthy of a journalist's attention?"

St.Clare pressed his napkin to his mouth before answering. "As a matter of fact, I find your island quite lovely," he said, and Andy wondered if he was merely being polite or was utterly sincere. "In any event, I'm not really a journalist, you see, merely a photographer. But to answer your question, yes, I think Staten Island has a great deal to offer."

"It's unfortunate you had to see the Island at its worst," Andy said, not wanting him to think November was typical. "Winter is rather dismal here, but we do tend to shine from May to October."

He smiled at her, but before he could respond, Niles—who seemed bent on being particularly exasperating this afternoon—also smiled, but thinly. "I'm sure Mr. St.Clare will be long gone before our best season is upon us, dear."

Andy glared at him, trying to suppress the sting of disappointment his remark had evoked. Niles knew she was counting on the extra funds Roman St.Clare's rent money represented. Why was he trying to discourage the man from staying longer?

And since when did he call her *dear*?

"Could hardly blame a body for *not* staying on, with things being what they are," Magnus put in, pouring even more cold water on Andy's hopes for a long-term boarding arrangement—and the accompanying income. "This bad business of late is enough to drive off even the old-timers. And it seems things are only getting worse."

"Just how long *do* you plan on staying, St.Clare?" Niles asked rather pointedly.

The photographer's hesitation was so slight as to be almost unnoticeable, and Andy found herself listening closely for his reply. "Actually, I may want to stay on longer than I'd originally thought, if Miss Fairchild can accommodate me. I've gotten a rather slow start on the assignment, you see. I wouldn't like to hurry it."

Andy felt a ridiculous lightening of her spirits at his words. But she was careful to keep her response perfectly businesslike. "I'm sure we can work out a suitable arrangement, Mr. St.Clare. You can see that things are somewhat slow at present." She was aware of Niles's disapproving gaze but deliberately avoided his eyes.

After a moment he turned his attention back to Roman St.Clare. "Well, let's hope there's no more trouble for the rest of your stay, then," he said tightly. "There's been more than enough since you arrived."

Andy shot him a murderous look. What *was* he thinking of?

Suddenly an ugly reminder of her own doubts of the previous night rushed in, and she felt her face flame at the memory. Still, Niles's deliberate rudeness wasn't to be tolerated. "I believe," she said, looking at him directly, "that most of the trouble on the Island happened *before* Mr. St.Clare's arrival."

Her words hung in the room for a tense moment. Andy wasn't sure whether anyone else noticed the strain between her and Niles, but she was fairly certain Roman St.Clare had. He suddenly seemed extremely interested in the dish of pudding in front of him.

"When, exactly, *did* you arrive, St.Clare?"

This was too much! Andy wouldn't have believed Niles capable of such insufferably bad manners. Furious with him, she pushed her chair back from the table with such a bang that Miss Snow jumped, her spoon clattering against her teacup.

"I'm sure Ibebe would like to clear," Andy snapped, not looking at anyone, especially not at Niles. "She deserves a few hours rest on the Sabbath, too."

———

At the front door only minutes later, Niles made an obvious attempt to win his way back into Andy's good graces before leaving. But she was far too vexed with him to be appeased.

"You were absolutely hostile, Niles!" she accused him. "What in the world got into you?"

"What are you talking about, Amanda? What exactly did I do?"

"You know perfectly well what you did, and I am *very* upset with you, Niles Rutherford! You were unforgivably rude to Roman St.Clare today." She paused to catch a breath. "Whatever were you thinking of, Niles, to behave as you did? And don't tell me how tired you are or that you had another emergency."

He frowned at her. "What is that supposed to mean?"

"It *means*," she said, "that you acted disgracefully at dinner today. You couldn't possibly have known what went on at church this morning, because you weren't even there—*again*."

"I often miss church, Amanda—"

"You do, indeed."

"—but not without good reason." He frowned, obviously considering his words before he spoke. "As for my being irritable, I might say the same for you. You certainly are touchy where your new lodger is concerned."

Now it was Andy's turn to frown. "And what is *that* supposed to mean?"

"Just that you're awfully concerned about St.Clare's feelings, it seems to me." His gaze didn't quite meet hers. "Lately, I almost get the impression that you care more about *his* feelings than mine."

Andy was growing more impatient with him by the minute. How *strangely* he was behaving today! She was beginning to wish he would just leave. She sighed and crossed her arms over herself. "Niles, what on earth are you talking about?"

His gaze swept her face. "Perhaps I'm a little jealous."

Andy stared at him in astonishment. "D-don't be ridiculous!" she stammered, dropping her arms and bracing her hands on her hips. "Why would you be *jealous* of Roman St.Clare?"

Even as the words left her lips, she felt a vague uneasiness beginning to stir inside her. His words had made her uncomfortable, had in some inexplicable way forced her to open a door she sensed would more wisely be kept closed.

"Oh, Amanda, I don't know." He suddenly looked so troubled and bewildered that Andy felt her anger wane. "I think I *am* a little jealous of St.Clare, whether you can understand it or not. He's the kind of fellow women seem to find attractive, after all.

He's a widower, not bad-looking—in a foreign sort of way—and he's something of a celebrity in his field, probably well-to-do at that. All things considered, why *wouldn't* I be jealous?" He paused. "It doesn't help that he's living here, right under your roof, either."

"Roman St.Clare is my *lodger*, Niles. He *pays* to stay under my roof." Andy was discomfited to realize that she couldn't actually deny anything Niles had said. "As for all the rest"—she made a dismissing gesture with her hand—"none of that is important. You're just being foolish."

For a long time Niles studied her. Finally, he attempted a small smile, though it failed miserably. "No doubt you're right," he said. "And I apologize for my behavior. But I hope you'll at least try to understand my side of this, Amanda. You know how I worry about you, out here by yourself, with only Magnus to defend you, if need be. And now you've taken in a perfect stranger—"

He broke off. One hand clutched his hat, the other fingered the buttons of his coat as he searched her eyes. "Amanda, please—try to understand that I sometimes act as I do because I care so much about you. I *love* you, Amanda!" he blurted out. "I've always loved you, that's no secret to you or anyone else. I only want you to care for me, too."

Her earlier pique with him entirely gone now, Andy softened. She lifted her hands to his shoulders and gave him a gentle shake. "Oh, Niles, of course, I care for you!"

His eyes brightened, instantly hopeful. So hopeful that Andy felt cruel for going on, but she was determined not to mislead him. She *did* care about Niles, cared too much to deceive him.

"You've always been very special to me, Niles," she said. "Why, you're my best friend in the world!" His face fell, but Andy hurried on. "Niles, I've never been less than honest with you about how I feel. I'm simply not ready to make any sort of commitment."

"Not ready?" he questioned, his face darkening. "Or . . . not willing?"

"Both, I suppose," Andy admitted, again feeling a tug of remorse. "But you must see that until I'm sure it's right, I can't promise you anything. I care too much for you to make promises

I might not be able to keep, Niles. That would be the worst sort of deceit, and I won't do that to you. Don't you see, it's because I *do* care for you that I can't say what you want to hear. At least not now, not yet. And I can't promise I ever will. Niles . . . you've asked me to try and understand *you*. Well, I'm asking *you* to understand *me*. I *need* you to understand, Niles, I really do."

Slowly, a small, rueful smile touched his lips, and he reached for her hand. "You know I could never refuse you anything."

Relieved, Andy squeezed his hand. "Good. Now, then, I want your word that you'll go along home and get some rest. You look exhausted, Niles, you really do."

He nodded, still smiling a little. "I *am* tired, I suppose." He hesitated, and Andy knew he was deliberating as to whether he ought to kiss her goodbye. She also knew she didn't want him to, not even a chaste, brotherly kiss on the cheek. Not tonight.

As if he had sensed her mood, he dropped his hand and reached for the doorknob, then turned back. "Andy? If you really think I was rude, I'll apologize to St.Clare."

"Well . . . it couldn't hurt."

He nodded unhappily. "Perhaps you're right."

After he had gone, Andy stood with her back against the door for a moment, then started for the stairway. Niles wasn't the only one who needed some rest, she thought. She was definitely beginning to feel the strain of the long days and late nights.

She trudged up the steps, anticipating a short nap to revive her. At the top, however, she met Roman St.Clare and the wolfhound. They were off to take some photographs while the light was still good, the photographer explained. Would she care to join them?

Though tempted, Andy remembered her need for rest—and Niles's hurt, bewildered eyes. "I'd like to," she said, "but I'd already planned to indulge myself in a nap. I think I'll just stay here."

"Ah, but the fresh air will do you more good than a nap," he encouraged. "Besides, I'll be taking the wagon. You won't need to walk a step. Actually," he said, watching her closely, "I could use an extra pair of hands for the work."

Andy gave him an dubious look.

"It's true," he insisted. "And we wouldn't be away very long.

There's not all that much light left."

"Well . . ."

"Your first assignment as my new assistant," he pressed. "Or had you forgotten that I offered the position?"

He smiled at her, waiting.

On the spur of the moment, Andy decided an outing *might* do her good, after all. Besides, Conor the wolfhound was grinning at her as if to implore her to come along, and he was hard to resist.

When they reached the bottom of the stairway, Roman St.Clare offered his arm, and she took it.

Fifteen

*D*espite the brisk chill of the afternoon, Roman St.Clare had exchanged his greatcoat for a well-worn, slightly baggy sweater. And after nearly an hour of hurrying to and from the wagon, trying to make herself useful, Andy had almost forgotten the cold altogether.

It hadn't taken her long to discover that there was a great deal more work involved in photography than she would have suspected. At the same time, she was beginning to understand why an experienced assistant might indeed prove invaluable, while a novice like herself might be more handicap than help. Even though Roman insisted that she was "most efficient," Andy was sure he was merely being polite. She only hoped he didn't regret asking her along, for she had enjoyed the afternoon immensely.

Had she thought about it before now, she would never have imagined that the process of making a photograph could be so complicated. Although Roman's expertise was perfectly obvious—so obvious that he made the entire procedure appear deceptively easy—Andy could see for herself that the work was anything but that. From the first step to the last, the operation was exacting, with a need for precise timing and relentless attention to detail.

After finally selecting a scene he wished to photograph, Roman would position one of the cameras on a tripod, then head back toward the wagon's darkroom, leaving Andy to follow. Inside, he would set about the painstaking task of retrieving a glass plate from a dustproof box and preparing it for exposure in the camera by dipping it into a tank of something called *collodion*, and, of all things, egg albumen! This caused a sticky kind of emulsion to form on the glass, which had to be protected, Roman explained, from any sort of disturbance, even drafts of air; otherwise, ripples would appear in the final negative to mar the photograph.

After the plate had been coated, and immediately before shooting the picture, he then "treated" the plate in a bath of silver nitrate. "You'll want to have a care when working with this stuff," he told Andy as she stood at his side, watching. "You can burn yourself badly, and it's poisonous as well."

Once the glass plate was finally ready, they had to go back outside, where Roman carefully placed the plate in the camera holder, shot the picture, then waited almost a full minute—the colder the day, the longer the wait, he explained—to make the exposure. After that, it was a rush back to the darkroom to develop the plate, which had to be completed and fixed within five minutes of exposure. Like other photography "correspondents," Roman performed the actual printing process in his Baltimore studio. His usual procedure while on the road was to develop and fix the negatives, then varnish and dry them, storing them carefully until he could return to Baltimore.

He had several cameras, Andy learned, each for a different function. The one he seemed to use most was the large box-shaped affair now resting on its tripod. But it was his smallest camera Andy found most fascinating, for this was the one employed for the "stereoview" cards that had become so popular as parlor entertainment during the War. She had spent many an evening with Jane and Donald Lowe viewing their collection of cards. To actually see the camera and the process that produced these delightful images was exhilarating.

The most fascinating part of the entire afternoon, however, was watching Roman work. Engrossed in what he was doing, he was almost like a different person—younger, more exuberant, surprisingly fluid and graceful, in spite of his bad leg. Now Andy saw not only the man, but the artist, an artist at ease with his own skill. He was everywhere at once, bending, pivoting, whipping around to check this angle or that, measuring the light—all with a boyish enthusiasm that made her smile. Gone, at least for the moment, were the pools of sorrow in his eyes, the taut features, the pallor of fatigue. He was suddenly youthful and animated, as if charged with energy.

Andy now realized that he had stopped for the moment and stood watching her. She looked around to see what had caught his attention.

"Now you," he said, gesturing to Andy's left. "Over there, with the hills behind you."

Andy stared at him, finally understanding his intent. "No," she said, shaking her head firmly. "Oh, no."

He started toward her, and she backed away.

"Yes," he said with equal firmness. "You've seen that it's all quite painless. Humor me."

"I won't. I . . . I don't want to . . . please," she stammered, laughing. "Roman, no—look at me! My hair must be standing on end, my face is probably dirty—"

"Your hair will do nicely," he said, catching her hand in his. "Over here. We'll do a contrast shot with those wretchedly dull hills behind the light of your face. A dancing flame among the embers."

Andy rolled her eyes, but with the wolfhound pressing her from behind and Roman pulling her along at his side, she really had no choice. She stood where he planted her, but when he went back to place the camera, she ducked her head and covered her face with her hands.

He turned and, seeing her, stood waiting, one dark brow lifted in feigned rebuke as she peeked out at him. "Is this really how you want to be remembered?" he chided her. "Hiding your face like a naughty child?"

Andy glared at him from between her fingers.

"Photographers have unlimited patience, you know. I can wait as long as it takes."

He left the camera and came to her, all business now as he positioned her here and there, lifting her chin a little, squaring her shoulders slightly, turning her this way and that as if she were merely a vase of flowers to be arranged. Self-conscious, she stood exactly as he placed her, except to try and smooth her hair.

Even this he disallowed, catching both her hands in his and holding them. "No," he said, his eyes going over her hair. "Leave it as it is. That's how I want it."

"But I'm a fright—"

His eyes locked on her face, and as she watched, his features underwent a sudden transformation. "On the contrary," he said, his voice soft. "You're really quite lovely."

His expression gentled still more. He no longer studied her with the skilled, professional eye of the cameraman, but with a peculiar intensity, almost as if he had seen something in her face that startled him. Andy drew in her breath, shaken and bewildered by the force of his gaze, yet unable to look away. He was still clutching her hands in his, and she wondered if he could feel her racing pulse.

Then he changed again, dropping her hands and reverting to the somewhat brusque, impersonal specialist. "Yes, that's it," he said shortly. "That's grand." He started for the camera, then turned back. Again Andy caught her breath, but his attention was now on the wolfhound. "That would make a splendid shot, the two of you. Would you mind?"

Andy looked at him, her head still swimming so that she could manage only to shake her head. "Yes . . . I mean, no, of course, I wouldn't mind."

He gave a small nod and returned to the camera. "Just put your hand on his head, why don't you?"

Conor, however, had turned his interest elsewhere. He kept testing the wind with his nose and barking at whatever scent it carried to him, even darting to and from Andy several times until Roman grew stern with him. By the time they finally completed the shots, Andy's heartbeat had almost returned to normal.

———

He had been watching them for nearly an hour now, his anger and indignation building by the minute.

He squinted from the dense stand of trees halfway up the hill, his gaze riveted on the clearing. Surely she could see what the Irish swine was up to, posturing in front of her with his cameras, feigning an interest in their surroundings . . . touching her.

He was trifling with her. She was nothing more than a diversion to him, a meaningless distraction from his real reason for coming here.

What was his reason for coming here?

At first Niles had thought St.Clare might be working for the police, that they had hired an outsider to do their spying for them. But the police weren't that clever. Bungling Irish peasants, most of them, scarcely able to make their mark on a piece of paper. Certainly not resourceful enough to plot some sort of secret investigation.

It was possible, he supposed, that the photographer was telling the truth—that he had come only for a brief vacation and to get a new assignment under way. Still, the man was an obvious meddler. Even if he were motivated by nothing more than idle curiosity, he could make trouble.

He couldn't have that, not now, when he was nearing the culmination of the work. There was a natural temptation to rush the final stages as it were, to hurry up and get it done before something happened to interfere. Yet haste might make him careless, and he couldn't afford carelessness. There was far too much at stake.

He saw them start toward the wagon now. The sky had changed from earlier in the day, becoming overcast and sullen as a sharp wind blew up. That should end the picture-taking. They would leave soon, no doubt.

Unexpectedly, the dog turned and stared in his direction, then barked. The ugly beast seemed to be looking directly at him. Heart pounding, he held his breath until the photographer called the animal back to the wagon.

He waited for a long time, but there was no further sign of them. Nor did the wagon leave the clearing.

He balled his fist and rammed it into the palm of his other hand, swallowing against the rancid swell of rage in his throat. What were they doing in there? Why would she go off this way with him, alone, out here in the middle of nowhere?

Of course, she wouldn't have an inkling what a man like that was capable of. She never saw anything but the best in others. She had always been that way.

St. Clare had her fooled, that was clear. And perhaps the others as well, with his sad-eyed looks and somber pretenses, his affectation of being the grief-stricken widower and war hero.

But *he* wasn't deceived. No, he had seen the cunning intelligence behind those hooded eyes, the watchful, measuring stare that belied the photographer's pretense of the sorrowful saint.

St.Clare couldn't be allowed to stay here. He would spoil everything.

He would have to get rid of him. And he thought he knew just the way to go about it.

———

As Andy stood beside Roman in the darkroom, watching him immerse the plate to "fix" the negative, she found herself newly fascinated by the smoothness of his movements, his calm precision, his absolute control at every stage of the process. She decided that much of his skill must be instinctive, for surely such precision could not be learned.

So absorbed was she in his movements that she hovered a little too close, accidentally bumping against his arm. Instantly, he froze, catching a sharp breath as he held the plate suspended above the dish.

Andy jumped back as if she'd been scalded. "Oh, I'm sorry! I didn't make you spoil it, did I? Oh, Roman, I *am* sorry!"

His hesitation was so slight as to be almost unnoticeable. He kept his eyes on the plate, smiling a little. "No damage done. I'm almost finished." He glanced at her then. "You've been a great help," he said, obviously trying to reassure her. "The job offer still stands."

Andy looked at him, puzzled.

"Photographer's assistant," he reminded her, securing the glass plate in its holder.

Andy made a sound of self-disparagement. "Just what you need," she said dryly. "A bumbling assistant who runs into you in the darkroom."

He shrugged out of his protective apron before turning to her. "I can think of worse things," he said, still smiling, "than bumping into a lovely girl in the dark."

Disarmed by this near flirtatious remark—so unlike him—Andy could only stare. She knew he had spoken lightly, perhaps even glibly, yet the comment seemed so at odds with his usual gravity that she found it difficult to discount his words altogether.

And what about the way he had looked at her earlier, when he was posing her for the photograph?

She felt unreasonably pleased, but also unsettled. Twice now he had referred to her as *lovely*. Did Roman really think of her that way?

She certainly wouldn't have guessed it by his behavior. Most of the time he treated her as if she were nothing more than a mildly amusing child, to be tolerated, even humored, but certainly not to be taken seriously.

Quickly, she reminded herself that *she* mustn't take *him* too seriously either. From the look of dismay lining his face, he had obviously spoken on impulse. No doubt he was already regretting his rash statement, wishing he could call it back.

Sixteen

*T*he moment the words were out of his mouth, Roman regretted them. He had obviously embarrassed her, perhaps even offended her. She wouldn't even look at him.

"Sorry," he muttered, avoiding her gaze with as much determination as she was obviously avoiding his. "I didn't mean to be forward."

It was the truth. But there was something about her that sometimes—when he least expected it—seemed to evoke an almost forgotten lightheartedness in him, a strain of youthful buoyancy he had thought to have died with Kathleen.

Often he would find himself watching for her smile, or tempted to coax one from her. Not that she needed coaxing; Andy's smiles were usually quick and spontaneous. Sometimes he even caught himself wishing he were a cleverer sort, entertaining enough to prompt the husky little laugh he found so charming.

He had been aware of her strange appeal for him, of course, had sensed it on a somewhat remote level. But he had deliberately refused to give that appeal anything more than a cursory examination, choosing instead to believe that he was more intrigued with her sprightliness, her quick, unselfconscious warmth and directness than with any manner of womanly attraction.

He knew he wasn't drawn to her because of any unhealthy sort of comparison with Kathleen. Indeed, in every way except the color of her hair, she was strikingly *unlike* his dead wife. Where Kathleen had been tall and almost elegantly graceful,

Andy was diminutive—and anything *but* graceful. Kathleen had been self-assured—quiet but confident of speech and mannerism—while Andy occasionally seemed ill at ease and unsure of herself. Whatever attraction this small, elfin creature held for him, it most definitely had nothing to do with any resemblance to his beloved Kathleen.

Andy was a child-woman. No doubt she would always look younger than her years, with those piquant, almost impish features—the droll little mouth, the too-large eyes, the band of freckles that danced like stardust across that saucy little nose. She had a keen, mercurial intelligence and a rather fierce kind of energy that seemed capable of all things and daunted by none.

Still, he had spoken the truth about her being a lovely girl. Not beautiful—at least not in the conventional sense—but with an allure all her own. Come to think of it, he wondered if *lovely* might not be too small a word to capture her unique charm.

Nevertheless, it had been altogether tactless of him to pay her such a direct compliment, although she probably wouldn't give it much thought one way or the other. More than likely, she considered him old and somewhat infirm—and perhaps wretchedly dull.

Not much comfort, that, he thought wryly.

How many years *did* lie between them, he wondered? At least ten, he would surmise, perhaps more. How did a girl of Andy's age view a man of thirty-four?

As well into his dotage, most likely.

With some irritation, he reminded himself that there were often as many as fifteen or twenty years difference in the ages of marriage partners. An appreciable age difference was the norm, not the exception, especially here in the States. It suddenly occurred to him that his present line of thought was so irrelevant as to be perfectly ludicrous. He gave himself a hard mental shake and turned back to her.

She still wouldn't look at him. Roman groped for something to say that wouldn't sound totally banal, but could think of nothing.

At last, she looked up, and he could see the uncertainty in her eyes. "Well—" she stopped, cleared her throat, then went on—"I suppose I should thank you for . . . the compliment."

Roman heard the question in her voice, but his mind seemed to have gone as thick as porridge. Because he could think of no response that wasn't utterly absurd, he simply smiled—rather foolishly no doubt—and stuck his hands in his pockets like a guilty schoolboy.

He was suddenly aware of her closeness, the fresh, warm scent of her hair and something else he had caught before, an elusive hint of something very like vanilla. The darkness about them was completely silent, the only sound the erratic drumming of his pulse.

How long had it been since his heart had hammered because of a woman's nearness?

Impatience suddenly rose up in him like an angry wave, and he reminded himself that he must not think of this girl as a woman. She was naive at best, almost adolescent at times. When it came to the coyness that seemed so natural to some women, she apparently had none. He hadn't the slightest interest in a meaningless flirtation, and he especially had no interest in making sport with a girl of Andy's youth and obvious naivete. She deserved better than that.

She deserved better than he . . . a man with a dark secret that even *he* could not fathom.

He was aware of her eyes on him, watching him intently. Unnerved by that searching green gaze, he struggled for a brisk, impersonal tone. "I expect we should be getting back, don't you? Your Uncle Magnus will have the authorities out for us."

She studied him for another moment, her expression still questioning. Then she dropped her gaze, and, in a voice as remote as his own, agreed. "Yes, we should probably go."

Roman started to take her arm, then stopped himself and commented casually, "I expect I've kept you far too long. Besides, we've lost the light for the rest of the day. But you *were* quite a help. I hope you didn't mind too much."

"Oh—no! I enjoyed it, really I did!"

The way her expression instantly brightened touched Roman. He sensed that, even if he had momentarily embarrassed her, she had forgiven him. And he was surprised to realize how much it mattered to him that she had.

He was equally surprised at how pleased he'd been to see her interest in his work. He had enjoyed having her at his side during the afternoon. Somehow the process that had become almost routine to him over the years had taken on more significance in her presence. For the first time in a very long time, he had recovered some of his own early pleasure in the work, but he was reluctant to delve too deeply into the reasons.

He followed her out of the wagon's darkroom into the living quarters, where she stopped to pat the dozing wolfhound's great head. Roman watched her, thinking how very small she really was; thinking, too, that he had not exaggerated her charm in the least: she *was* lovely.

"We'll do this again if you're willing," he said on impulse. "Actually, I had another site in mind I'd hoped to shoot today, but there isn't time for it."

She smiled at him, her earlier enthusiasm still evident. "I'd love to help. I really did enjoy today. This other place—is it nearby?"

Roman hesitated, calling up the image of the desolate, decaying house he'd happened upon a few days past. He had been intrigued enough with the place that he wanted to try to capture its essence on film. Yet somehow its corruption seemed starkly at odds with Andy's shining . . . *goodness*. He felt a strange reluctance to expose her to such ugliness, although as a native of the Island, she had probably seen the place any number of times, most likely even knew its history.

Finally, he went on to describe the house to her, including its disgraceful neglect, its dismal location, its apparent abandonment. He told her everything he remembered about it . . . everything, that is, but the dark feelings of foreboding the place had stirred in him.

———

As soon as he began, Andy knew he was describing the old Rutherford place.

She wasn't sure why she didn't come right out and tell him. It would hardly mean anything one way or the other to Roman that the hideously ugly old house had once been Niles's home. Yet, for some reason, she was loath to have him associate Niles with the place, even though he had abandoned it long ago.

Perhaps she had been more susceptible to the stories about

the Rutherford house than she'd thought. For years the rumors had grown up about the place, tales as wild as the weeds and brambles that surrounded it. Schoolchildren insisted that it was haunted, while some of the Island's adult residents suspected that vagrants and even hardened criminals sometimes used it as a temporary hideout in their efforts to escape the law.

Andy had never paid much attention to the stories. Even so, she'd always had her own share of bad feelings about Niles's boy-hood home, mostly because she knew how unhappy he had been there as a child.

The house held few good memories for Niles. With his moth-er's suicide and old Zachary's continual haranguing, her friend had known little but misery throughout his youth. Once his fa-ther was gone, however, Niles had wasted no time in taking rooms with Mrs. Conifer near the clinic and putting his home-place up for sale. Unfortunately, the house and grounds had been so badly neglected over the years that no one wanted to take on the labor and excessive expense of restoration.

Finally, Niles had given up all attempts to sell the property. One day he would have it leveled, he told Andy, and would build a new home on the same site. But not until he could afford the house he wanted.

And not until he had a wife who would live there with him, he occasionally hinted.

Roman's voice suddenly jarred her back to her surroundings. "I asked if you know the place?"

Andy nodded, but offered no explanation. "I'm surprised you'd want to photograph that ugly old house when there are so many truly beautiful places on the Island. I'd be glad to show you some of the more scenic spots, if you like."

He regarded her as if he'd been hoping for more in the way of explanation. "Of course," he said after a moment. "I'd like that."

He took her arm to help her onto the driver's bench of the wagon. "I expect it's nothing more than morbid curiosity, my in-terest in the place. Still, I'd like to take a few shots of it."

They talked about other things on the drive back, when they talked at all. Andy was learning that Roman was a man given to unpredictable silences, sometimes lengthy ones. She didn't mind, for she somehow sensed that his withdrawal had nothing to do with her. She suspected that he was a man who needed frequent periods of quiet the way others required rest, that he had over the years carved out deep and private sanctuaries within his own spirit. Rather than resenting his lack of loquacity or feeling strained by it, Andy found herself surprisingly comfortable with the silence between them, as though it were something to be shared, not merely endured.

But tonight Roman had been uncommonly quiet most of the way home, and as they drew near the house, she found herself growing uneasy. By the time they drove through the gates, dusk was settling in, and with the gloom came the fog, dank and chill. The mist clung to Andy's hands and stung her eyes. She glanced over at Roman to see the writhing tendrils of fog veil his dark head, obscuring his profile and making him appear even more distant and nebulous than ever.

The sense of comfort and familiarity she had known earlier in the afternoon suddenly vanished. She became chillingly aware that the man beside her was still a stranger, for all that he was staying under her roof and despite the fact she had just spent the afternoon with him. She reminded herself that, with the silent anguish and private demons that seemed to haunt him, he could just as easily be a threat to her as a friend. For the truth was, she really did not know Roman St.Clare at all.

There was always the possibility that he might not turn out to be what he seemed, and she didn't have to look very deeply within herself to realize that she would not be unaffected should this be the case. The potential for pain was undeniably present, should he disappoint her or, worse yet, prove treacherous.

The thought startled her, for until now she had not admitted to herself that he held the power to hurt her. That could only mean that he was more important to her than she had thought him to be . . . more important than she *wanted* him to be.

She found this realization far more frightening than any qualms she might have about his character.

Seventeen

S ometime in the night, Conor came up to the bed and dug a paw at Roman's shoulder to awaken him.

From the beginning, the wolfhound seemed to have sensed that even a short bark was unacceptable under the roof of this house, so on those occasions when he had to answer the call of nature in the night, he resorted to a quieter but equally effective method of getting his master's attention. Not relishing the idea of an accident in the bedroom, Roman seldom tried to put him off.

This had been one of those rare nights, however, when sleep had not only come almost at once, but had continued deep and unbroken. So when he felt the wolfhound's first tentative nudge, he didn't respond right away. Instead, he lay unmoving, feigning sleep to gauge the dog's seriousness. He knew from experience that sometimes Conor was merely in a playful mood, more interested in companionship than in attending to his bodily functions. At those times, if a ruse didn't work, the wolfhound would eventually give up and return to his pallet beside the bed, disappointed but resigned.

Apparently that wasn't to be the case tonight. A second, then a third insistent prod from a furry paw indicated that Conor would not be put off. Disgruntled, Roman poked his head out from under the bedding. Upon seeing him, the wolfhound gave a short, low growl and renewed his digging at Roman's shoulder.

The growl was a surprise and caught Roman off guard. Conor seldom growled, and never simply to make his presence known. It was a tactic he ordinarily employed as a warning or, even more infrequently, to take issue with a stranger who dared invade his domain.

Since there was no one else in the room, Roman could only assume that he was being warned. He had learned to take the wolfhound's warnings to heart. With no further delay, he propped himself up on one arm, waiting for his head to clear. "What is it, chum? What's got you fussed at this hour of the night?"

As if by design, the clock downstairs chimed once, then twice. Roman groaned, yawned, and swiped a hand down his beard. By this time the wolfhound had gone to the door and begun to circle, casting an impatient glance at Roman with each turn.

"Yes, all right, here we go." Roman hauled himself out of bed, wincing at the protest of his bad leg, which still stiffened considerably during the night hours. Once upright, he grappled for the cane hanging on the bedpost, then hobbled to the window to look out.

He could see nothing but the black of night. No moon, no stars to relieve the darkness. When he turned, Conor was pawing the floor and uttering a low, continuous growl.

A cold nudge of apprehension prompted Roman to move. "No more growling," he warned, stuffing his nightshirt into his trousers. "You'll have the uncle down on us like a wounded bear if he hears you."

The wolfhound obeyed, only to begin whipping back and forth from Roman to the door.

"All right, all right," Roman muttered, squeezing into his boots and throwing on his coat. "I'm coming. But not another sound from you, mind. Not a sound."

Conor wasted no time in the corridor, but headed straight for the stairway, glancing back only once to make sure Roman was behind him. "This had better be important," Roman said under his breath as he followed the wolfhound downstairs. "Nothing short of disaster will get you by. And if you're not being straight with me, old boy, you just may find yourself sleeping under the wagon for the rest of our stay."

The dog ignored him, bulleting from the steps toward the front door as if a banshee were at his back. Once there, he stood prancing and whining in frustration.

Roman stopped grumbling now. He knew this was more than a simple nocturnal whim on the part of the wolfhound. The uneasiness that had been lurking at the back of his mind now spread over him like a grave blanket as he followed Conor outside.

The wolfhound waited only long enough for Roman to light a lantern from the porch before tearing down the steps and around the side of the house as if he'd just broken jail. Only once did he gallop back to check on Roman before again charging off toward the wagon.

Roman took the path as quickly as he could manage, holding the lantern aloft with one hand, his cane with the other. From the direction of the barn, he could hear the whinny of horses, the restless stomping of hooves. He had a fleeting thought that he should have roused the uncle, rather than heading out here alone in the middle of the night. He quickly reminded himself that Conor was undoubtedly all the protection he might need, certainly more than a man Doyle's age could offer.

As he approached the wagon, he saw the wolfhound, head down, raking his nose along the ground. Suddenly the dog gave a vicious snarl and hurled himself at the side of the wagon as if to crash through the wall.

Roman stopped short, confounded by the sight of the normally mild-tempered wolfhound baring his teeth and ripping at the wagon. For a moment his courage threatened to fail him. His blood froze in his veins, and his heart began to slam wildly against his rib cage.

His mind raced. He had a gun in the wagon, but it was strictly for road travel. He never took it indoors with him unless he happened to be boarding at a particularly disreputable inn.

There was no time for wishing he had the pistol. He moved, giving a sharp warning to silence Conor, whose savage snarling had given way to hard, furious barks. At Roman's command, the dog backed off from the wagon, his body rigid, his head down and jutting forward, saliva rolling from his mouth.

The wolfhound had made it impossible to approach with any degree of caution, so Roman simply walked up and flung the wagon door open. As if he'd been given a signal, Conor jumped onto the wagon in one bound and streaked inside.

Roman held the lantern with an unsteady hand, his free hand gripping the cane like a weapon as he followed the wolfhound through the door.

Inside, he lifted the lantern to illumine the wagon's interior. Conor's fury suddenly gave way to a deadly calm. The dog stood in the center of the wagon, vigilant and alert, yet obviously bewildered. Finally, he turned to look at Roman, his great head cocked in an expression of bafflement.

The lantern swayed in Roman's trembling hand. He took a step forward, then stopped dead, staring in numb despair at what only hours before had been his snug, tidy studio and living quarters.

He was slow to comprehend the wanton destruction of his belongings, the shambles to which much of his equipment had been reduced. Little by little, his eyes took in the unthinkable. Books had been thrown from the shelves onto the floor. The upholstery had been savagely ripped from the chair, as if with a knife wielded by an angry hand. Two cameras were smashed beyond repair. Several photographs from his private collection were missing from the shelves.

Dread clamped his heart as he started into the darkroom, careful to avoid the shards of glass strewn across the floor. Broken bottles and smashed containers littered the counter and the floor, their spilled contents standing in pools. With sick incredulity, Roman found a number of his prized photographs doused with acid in the sink, utterly ruined.

He stood, his entire body wrenching with shock and despair at the unconscionable destruction all around him. The wolfhound came to him, pressing his great head against Roman's side, whining softly as if to console him.

What kind of madness was this?

It had taken him years to acquire much of his equipment. In the early days he had slept in the wagon, often going without food so he could pay for cameras and supplies. And his photographs—dozens of battlefield images of dead soldiers and fallen heroes that could never be replaced—months and months of work, now gone forever . . . so much loss, such waste. . . .

Why?

The crushing sense of loss would have drained his strength

entirely had it not been for the surge of anger that boiled up in him. The stench of spilled chemicals and acid assaulted him, followed by a wave of dizziness. The floor of the wagon seemed to tilt as he felt nausea crowd in on him, and he had to fight to get his breath.

Again the wolfhound barked, but this time the staccato sound came from a distance. The fog of confusion now lifted as Roman realized that Conor had bolted from the wagon and taken off.

He hesitated only an instant before limping to the door and scrambling to the ground in pursuit of the wolfhound and his prey.

————

Something had startled Andy awake. She sat bolt upright in bed, shaking her head and trying to focus her eyes in the dark room. The thud of Magnus's heavy footsteps charging down the hall set her heart to pounding, then sent her clambering out of bed. Hurriedly she yanked on her dressing gown and raced downstairs.

Magnus had already reached the front door, where he was struggling into his old mackinaw. Andy ran up to him. "What's wrong?"

"Some sort of fiendish commotion out to the barn!" he snapped, opening the door. "I mean to see what's going on. You stay here."

Andy ignored him, following him onto the porch. The dark was relentless, the air frigid, but a part of the chill inside her was fear. Magnus lighted a lantern, and in its glow Andy saw that his eyes were glinting with what could have been either anger . . . or alarm.

The idea of Magnus being afraid of *anything* was inconceivable to Andy. Even the possibility was enough to make her skin prickle.

"Go back inside now, and stay there," he ordered her again. He hurried down the steps, waving the lantern as he went. "I'll see to this."

Andy wasn't about to go back inside and leave him charging around in the darkness alone. She caught up with him as he started around the side of the house. "I'm going with you!" she said, tugging at his sleeve to slow him down.

"There's no telling what's going on out to that wagon! That infernal wolfhound will have raised the dead with his carrying-on!"

Andy had all she could do to keep up with his long-legged stride. "You heard Conor out here?" She listened but heard nothing other than the wind whipping through the trees.

"I told you you'd rue the day you ever let rooms to that Ulsterman!" Magnus jabbed his finger in the direction of the wagon, parked just outside the barn.

Andy scanned the wagon as they approached. "If Roman is out here at this time of night, something must be terribly wrong!" She suddenly realized that she had run out of the house in only her dressing gown; now she was shaking with cold.

Still dazed and clumsy from being awakened so sharply, she stubbed her toe on a stone. She yelped, but kept on going.

The door of the wagon was open, but there was no sign of Roman or Conor. Then she heard the wolfhound bark. The sound came from the hills behind the house.

At a sudden stirring of fear, Andy increased her pace. After a moment, heart pounding, she began to run, with Magnus right behind her.

They passed the wagon, heading for the bottoms where the rear of the property line merged with the hills. Even as they ran, they saw Roman and Conor coming toward them. With a lantern in one hand and his cane in the other, Roman seemed to be limping badly. Conor was loping along at his side. Instead of charging toward Andy, as had become his habit whenever he saw her, the wolfhound appeared to be heeling to his master's command, but with obvious reluctance.

Slowing her pace, Andy could see the hard, dangerous set to Roman's features. He was white-faced with fury. It was an unfamiliar—unnatural—expression for him. As he approached, she saw something even more terrible in his eyes—a heart-wrenching look of utter desolation.

"He's gone," he said, his tone hollow and without feeling. "There was no catching him. He was probably gone by the time we came outside."

In the glow from the lanterns, Andy could see the deeply edged white lines about his mouth, the unyielding set of his jaw that spoke of his struggle to control his emotions.

"Who's gone?" she questioned. "Roman, what happened?"

He looked at her. "Someone tossed the wagon," he said in a rough voice that seemed more terrible even than the livid mask of his features. He glanced back over his shoulder.

Andy felt sick. "Somebody vandalized your wagon? But *why*? What did they do?"

For a moment Roman said nothing. "You can see for yourself," he replied in the same strangled tone, his shoulders sagging as he passed by them and started in the direction of the wagon.

Eighteen

*T*wo days after the incident with Roman's wagon, Andy was still watching him for some sort of aftereffect. Instead, he remained surprisingly steady, at least so far as she could tell. If he was quieter than usual, his eyes shadowed, his features somewhat strained, it was surely to be expected. In fact, that he did not seem too severely shaken was, to Andy's thinking, nothing short of remarkable.

Perhaps it was true that trials tended to make one stronger. Miss Snow was fond of comparing the resiliency and strengthening effect of a mighty oak tree lashed repeatedly by the storms of nature with that of the soul, which undergoes its times of testing in the "storms of life." Certainly, Roman seemed to be a man of strength—spiritual strength, if not physical robustness. Even though he seldom spoke about matters of the spirit, Andy had sensed in him what would appear to be a deep, unshakable faith. This, then, must be what had sustained him in his own losses. What else would account for his calm?

He had also displayed a suprising resourcefulness over the past two days. Although some of the damage to his belongings was irreparable, he had still accomplished a great deal, restoring order almost right away by sweeping out the debris, returning books to their shelves, and repairing what equipment was still salvageable. He had even managed a crude restoration of his mangled chair with some batting and remnants of material donated by Miss Valentine.

Andy had offered to help and so had Ibebe. Even Magnus had volunteered a grudging assist. But Roman had declined each offer, politely but firmly.

147

It was as if he wouldn't allow himself to need anyone. He seemed to live his solitary life detached from everyone else. To all appearances, he was kind, always courteous, even thoughtful of others, if aloof from them. There was a separateness about him—whether unintentional or deliberate—that served to keep others at arm's length. Andy thought it wasn't so much that he guarded his privacy as that he had shut a door on the rest of the world and had chosen to live his life behind that door.

Despite his reticence to discuss his loss, however, it was obvious that the damage to his property had been extreme. Obviously, he faced a major expense in replacing the cameras and chemicals. He would also need to purchase a new supply of glass plates and other equipment.

The photographs from his private collection, of course, could not be replaced, and it was this loss that seemed to distress him most. All this was enough to completely dishearten even the strongest man, and Andy had begun to prepare herself for the likelihood that Roman St.Clare would leave the Island in the near future. She could hardly expect him to stay on after what had happened.

To her surprise and vast relief, however, Roman made no mention of going away. Instead, he continued to work doggedly on, refurbishing the wagon and its contents, laboring into the late hours of evening before coming inside. Andy had almost begun to hope that he wouldn't be leaving, after all.

Then today the *Gazette* had arrived, bearing the report of a woman murdered in the new state of West Virginia, and Andy had seen her hopes cruelly dashed. Had it not been for the hideous nature of the slaying and the fact that it involved another well-known photographer, the story would probably have never reached the out-of-town newspapers. For one thing, the crime had occurred in an obscure, small-town community, rather than in a major metropolitan area.

But as soon as she began to read, Andy knew that this was yet another murder Roman would feel compelled to investigate for its very similarity to his wife's slaying. With a sick clenching of her heart, she realized that even if the vandalism of his wagon hadn't impelled him to leave, this article surely would.

It was the middle of the afternoon and there was a roaring

fire in the library, but Andy was seized with a bone-numbing cold as she stood reading the newspaper account. The story sounded chillingly similar to what Roman had told her of his wife's murder. In a small town called Philippi in the new state that had been formed out of western Virginia, the wife of a photographer had been brutally assaulted and beaten to death. Although the house had been burglarized, the widower reported that few items of any real value had been stolen; he did, however, cite the unaccountable theft of some photographs he had made of his wife.

Andy went on reading, aware only on the vaguest level of those details incidental to the main story—that the town of Philippi had been the site of the first major land battle in the war between North and South; that the locale was primarily rural and somewhat remote; that the photographer and his slain wife had been newly settled in the community, having relocated to be closer to family. As she neared the end of the story, she suddenly froze, her eyes locking on the disclosure that the new widower was not only a photographer of some recognition—but that he had also been one of the many "camera men" employed by Mathew Brady to cover the War.

The newspaper rustled in her trembling hand as she read the words again, feeling a chill so deep within that no fire could reach it.

It could be coincidence. From what Roman had told her, the one connection between the murder victims seemed to be photography, but he had made no mention that any of the other photographers besides himself had been employed by Brady.

But Andy knew that even if this *was* a mere coincidence, he would go. He wouldn't be able to stop himself.

There was no accounting for the wrenching sense of loss that twisted through her. She had known all along that he was here for only a brief time. A hundred reasons bombarded her as to why she should not care whether he stayed or went. He was a virtual stranger, and a troubling one at that. She should have no interest in him, other than that for a casual friend. And hadn't she sensed that he could be difficult—given to dark moods and cryptic silences? He was also too familiar at times, and almost always far too direct.

Why should she care if he left sooner than she'd expected?

149

Why did it hurt so much?

For a moment she actually considered hiding the newspaper. If he didn't see the story, there was no telling how long it might be before he learned of it. By then perhaps the police would have found the killer, and Roman would no longer have to continue his pursuit.

Even as the thought flickered across her mind, Andy knew she couldn't go through with it. She had seen the depth of sorrow and loneliness in his eyes when he spoke of his wife, had felt his anguish when he told her about the night of the slaying. And she had heard the iron determination in his voice when he spoke of his quest to find the murderer.

How could she even consider not telling him? For all she knew, this might be the very case that would lead Roman to the man who had killed his wife.

Still holding the newspaper, she hugged her arms to herself, shivering. She was caught up in a tidal wave of conflicting emotions, not the least of which was her mind's frenzied insistence that she must not *care* if Roman left. She could not afford to feel anything for him except friendship. That much, at least, he had asked of her.

But nothing more.

Why did it no longer seem to be enough? she wondered, sick at heart. She reminded herself that even if she *should* come to care for him . . . too much . . . the shadow of his wife stood like an immovable barrier between her feelings and even the most remote possibility that Roman might ever care for *her*.

But even as she tried to deny the truth, Andy knew it was already too late. She had allowed him to fill her thoughts too much, too completely, had allowed him to take on an importance in her life that was disturbingly inappropriate. And now . . . now he had carved a place for himself in her heart that she couldn't imagine anyone else ever filling.

Foolish! How could she have been so foolish? She already had the love and devotion of a good man. A solid, decent man who utterly adored her, who wanted to spend his life with her. Niles would marry her tomorrow if she were willing. And with him, there would be nothing else—no memory of another love—to usurp her place in his affections. With Niles, she would always be first. Always.

So how could she have allowed herself to become caught up in what was at best a foolhardy infatuation with a total stranger?

In the same instant, Andy knew with a sudden, piercing clarity that, whatever else he might be, Roman was no stranger. Without understanding how such a thing could be, she knew with utter certainty that she had been waiting for Roman St.Clare for a very long time.

Her heart had recognized him at once. Perhaps that's why the thought of saying goodbye to him, even after so brief a time, brought such pain.

Nevertheless, she would show him the article in the paper. Earlier that afternoon he had gone to the police to report the vandalism to his wagon. When he returned she would tell him. She knew she dared not wait too long, for fear she would be tempted anew not to tell him at all.

He chose that moment to walk into the library.

Andy felt his presence as though it were a warm light. Her heart, aching at his gentle smile, turned over at the sound of his voice.

"Ah—so this is where you've been hiding," he said, coming to stand near her, by the fire. "I've been looking for you."

Absurd, how those few words, which he had probably meant only as idle conversation, arrowed right to her heart. "I . . . didn't know you were back," she choked out. "I was about to go and help Ibebe with dinner."

She should tell him now . . . right now. Instead, her hand clutched the paper even tighter. "Did you learn anything from the police?"

He shook his head and gave a wry smile. "Nothing. You were right, after all. I had the distinct impression that your Officer Riley and the rest of his men have far more important things to attend to than an isolated case of vandalism. I'm not sure they even took me seriously."

"I was afraid of that. It's this other trouble, Roman. There just aren't enough policemen."

"Ah, well," he said as if he wasn't all that perturbed, "I expected as much. I'll just have to do some investigating on my own." He looked at her and smiled. "First, however, there's something I want to give you, something—"

"Roman—" she interrupted him, her words spilling out in a rush, "there's something in the paper I think you'll want to know about."

"Yes, well, first let me give you this," he said, still smiling as he held up a stereoscopic viewer. "It turned up when I was cleaning the shelves. I thought you might like to have it."

Andy looked at him, then took note of the instrument he was holding out to her. "Oh, Roman! I couldn't take this! Why, it must be ever so expensive!"

"But I never use it," he said. "Besides, I have another back at the studio. You seemed so fascinated with the process the other day, I thought you'd enjoy a viewer of your own."

"Well, of course, I would!" Andy admitted, flustered. "But I couldn't possibly . . . I just couldn't."

He seemed genuinely puzzled. "Of course, you can. I *want* you to have it, don't you see? It's meant to be used, not gathering dust on a shelf." Again he held out the viewer to her. "Let's make it a token of my appreciation for your helping me the other day. Oh— I almost forgot—I also have some cards for it. I'll bring them in later."

Andy finally accepted the stereoscope, feeling a warm rush of pleasure that he wanted her to have it.

But when she glanced down at the newspaper she was still holding in her other hand, her happiness quickly fled. Reluctantly, she handed him the paper. "There's something—an article—you'll want to read," she said, unable to meet his eyes as she clasped the viewer tightly against herself. "I'm afraid there's been another murder."

His jaw tightened. "Not another child?"

"No." Andy swallowed against the knot in her throat. "A young woman. But not here."

He watched her as he reached for the paper. As soon as he began to read, he pulled in a sharp breath. Once, he glanced up at Andy, his expression as harsh as she had ever seen it. She waited in unhappy resignation for what she was sure would follow.

Before Roman could finish reading the article, however, Magnus appeared in the open doorway. His usually ruddy face was pale, his features taut. "Andy, you'd better come," he said without preamble. "It's Miss Valentine. Ibebe says she's taken ill."

For a second or two, Andy felt a peculiar, cold absence of understanding. She stared at Magnus, then glanced at Roman, who had suspended his reading and stood listening to the exchange. The only sound in the library was her own shallow breathing and the quiet ticking of the mantel clock.

Magnus stepped into the room, and now Andy saw the unmistakable lines of worry that creased his face. "I think it's the influenza, lass," he said, his voice low. "You'd best see to her while I go for Niles. She's upstairs in her room."

"Influenza?" For a moment Andy could only stare at him in bewilderment. She tried to think, but her mind was like a blank canvas. "All right—yes, you'd best get Niles." She glanced at the clock, saw that it was already half past four. "Oh, Magnus, you'll not find him now! He almost always goes across to Bellevue by four."

"There's Doc Summerville, then. He's not the doctor Niles is, but he's usually about."

After Magnus left, Andy turned to Roman. She glanced at the newspaper he was still holding, but there was no time for that now. "I have to go to Miss Christabel," she told him.

"Of course." He hesitated only an instant before asking, "What can I do?"

"I don't suppose there's anything." Her thoughts were still a tangle of confusion. "Perhaps Uncle Magnus is wrong. Perhaps it's not influenza at all."

She couldn't make herself feel nearly as hopeful as she tried to sound. With the way the dread sickness had been sweeping the Island over the past few weeks, it would have been foolish to think it might pass them by. Still, Andy had hoped it would do just that.

Still clutching the stereoscope, she started for the door, then turned back. "Dinner might be late. I may need Ibebe to help—"

Roman waved her on before she could finish. "Don't fret about dinner. We'll manage."

Andy watched a coal spark, then settle in the fireplace. "She's awfully fragile," she said, more to herself than to Roman.

"She'll be all right," he said gently. "Why don't you go along? Andy—"

She looked at him.

"I'll be here, if you should need me."

Andy left the library, Roman's words echoing at the back of her mind as she hurried up the stairs.

I'll be here, if you should need me. . . .

He had only meant to reassure her because of Miss Valentine, of course. But the certainty that he would *not* be here much longer made a painful mockery of his words. He was leaving, just as she'd known he would. She had seen it in his face as he read the article.

She couldn't dispel the aching disappointment that twisted through her at the thought, but this was no time to indulge her own feelings.

Andy reached the open doorway of Miss Valentine's room to find both Ibebe and Miss Snow already there. One stood on either side of Miss Christabel, who lay in the middle of the enormous poster bed, her tiny hands clutching the linens pulled snugly about her shoulders. She looked small and ever so fragile, her skin flushed with the angry crimson of fever.

Roman stood at the library door, watching Andy hurry up the stairs, then disappear down the hall, the small back and narrow shoulders hunched as if against a storm.

She hardly needed more trouble, he thought. And if this were the influenza, it would mean trouble indeed. He had seen what havoc the deadly disease could wreak upon the strongest of men in camp, much less a diminutive lady like Miss Valentine.

There was also the fact that it was virulently contagious.

He sighed and returned to the news article about the murder in West Virginia. Reading on, he shivered suddenly, as if someone had let in a cold blast of air from outdoors. It was *him*, of course. The animal who had killed Kathleen. Roman had known it the instant he'd begun to read the account of this latest slaying.

A blistering wave of anger roared through him, searing him with the old, familiar hatred.

He hadn't expected this, not now, not so soon. Obviously, the bloodlust was driving the killer with a vengeance. The murders were increasing in frequency, becoming even more savage with each new victim.

A coal popped, and Roman jumped. The fire hissed, then settled again. He should go *now*. No later than tomorrow. If he waited, the madman would simply slip away and go on to kill another.

But he wasn't ready to leave yet. He intended to talk with Samuel Harrington again, after the man had more fully recovered from his shock. He also meant to find out who had vandalized his wagon.

And why.

He scanned the article once more, then looked toward the upstairs hallway. It occurred to him that there might be another reason he was reluctant to leave just yet. A reason he wasn't willing to admit.

He suppressed the thought, refusing to analyze what lay behind it. Instead, he considered what it might mean if the influenza had actually entered the house. A stab of fear ripped through him. Fear, not for himself—after Gettysburg, there was little to frighten a man, apart from the threat of another blood-drenched battlefield—but rather, fear for Andy. She was such a wee thing, so slight, almost fragile in appearance. Even though she marched about the place like a tough little martinet with immeasurable energy, he hadn't missed those times when the slender shoulders slumped with unmistakable weariness and the green eyes took on the dark shadows of fatigue.

She would be no match for something as vicious as the influenza.

He looked at the paper again, then rolled it and tucked it under his arm. That he must go, he didn't question. But as to when—he couldn't decide that at the moment. In any event, another day or two couldn't make all that much difference.

He would wait until he saw what Andy might be up against here before leaving.

Nineteen

Within three days Miss Valentine's condition had taken such a turn that Andy was truly frightened for her. The fever raged day and night to such peaks the ailing spinster was frequently incoherent, and her lungs sounded full of rales. Niles had taken to stopping by twice a day to check on her. By Friday, he was insisting that she be hospitalized.

Although pitiful in her suffering, Miss Valentine remained adamant that she would *not* go to the hospital, and when Andy saw how distraught she became at the very suggestion, she couldn't bring herself to argue.

Niles grew daily more impatient with both of them. Andy supposed that, as a physician, he couldn't understand why a patient would refuse the professional care so obviously needed. But Andy thought she *did* understand. The Manor was home to Miss Christabel, its residents her only family. Her bedroom was her haven—a safe, secure place of her own in the midst of the few people in the world who cared about her. The hospital, on the other hand, evoked thoughts of impersonal hands, unfamiliar footsteps in the hall, and frightening cries in the night. Andy remembered her own fears during her mother's hospitalization and tried to help Niles understand Miss Valentine's resistance, but she could tell her efforts were to no avail.

Miss Snow, however, minced no words in giving him to understand that it was "Christabel's decision entirely. If she wishes to recover in the privacy of her own bedroom, that is exactly what she will do."

With the help of the resolute Miss Snow, Andy and Ibebe

157

worked out a schedule to provide round-the-clock care for Miss Valentine. Andy would have preferred that Miss Snow avoid the sickroom and not put herself at risk. But there was no dissuading her once she set her mind to something, so Andy could only hope that her constitution was as formidable as her will.

Unfortunately, even Miss Snow was no match for the vicious illness. She succumbed on Monday, three days after Miss Valentine took to her bed.

Now Andy felt the first stirrings of panic. How in the world was she ever going to manage? She was already suffering the effects of too little sleep and too much work.

Yet, there was nothing else to do *but* manage. With that in mind, she recalled the year when Ibebe had been abed with scarlet fever and Andy's father laid up with a broken arm, both at the same time. It had been utter chaos, and Andy had despaired of keeping everything under control. But with Magnus's help, she had managed.

As she would manage now.

Throughout this entire period, she was bothered, at least in a peripheral sense, by the awareness that she was sadly neglecting her other lodger. Roman, however, seemed not in the least concerned. In fact, he brushed off Andy's hasty apologies by pointing out that he had been on his own quite long enough to look after himself, that she should not concern herself on his behalf but instead devote her time and energy to her "patients."

In the meantime, however, Magnus also began to question the wisdom of Miss Snow and Miss Valentine remaining at the Manor. Like Niles, he thought both of them ought to be hospitalized. In addition, he seemed to think it would be advisable, "under the circumstances," for Roman to seek rooms elsewhere.

"The man's not getting what he paid for, after all," he reasoned with Andy. "It would be in his best interests, and ours as well, no doubt, if he were to go somewhere else."

It was early on Wednesday morning, and Andy had gone without sleep the entire night. She was cross and could have easily been goaded into an argument, but with some effort she kept her silence.

Magnus went on to point out that he had discussed all this with Niles, who agreed with him.

Niles *would* agree, Andy thought testily. She didn't doubt for a moment that Niles would like nothing better than to see Roman anywhere else but at the Manor. Besides, he almost always agreed with Magnus, just as Magnus usually agreed with *him*.

To Magnus, Niles embodied the best virtues of American manhood—strong character, intelligence, ambition, and common sense. He had long despaired that Andy didn't "haul the lad to the altar in a freight wagon before some other clever miss steals him out from under your nose."

Most of the time, Andy was pleased that the two got on so well. Sometimes she wondered if Magnus didn't represent a kind of father figure to Niles, whose own father had been such a disappointment. Lately, however, the two of them were beginning to get on her nerves. She was impatient with the way they'd joined forces against Miss Valentine's—and now Miss Snow's— wishes, equally impatient with their insistence on treating *her* as an adolescent rather than as an adult.

Perhaps the long days and short nights had simply strained her to the breaking point, but more and more Andy found herself biting back a sharp retort to their "advice," well intentioned as it undoubtedly was. This was still her boardinghouse, after all— her *home*. It seemed to her that she should be the one to make any decisions about its occupants.

In that regard, she had no intention of trying to coax Miss Valentine or Miss Snow into doing something against their will. Nor would she ask Roman to go elsewhere just to make things more convenient for everyone else.

What she didn't say to either Magnus or Niles was that there was really no reason to ask Roman to leave; he would almost certainly be gone soon enough of his own accord.

———

Later that same evening, as she kept her vigil in Miss Snow's spartan bedroom, Andy's thoughts were far removed from Magnus and Niles, and from Roman as well. In fact, she found it impossible to think of anything else but Miss Snow, whose condition had worsened with alarming speed. Her cough was violent and wracking, her breathing labored, her skin waxen and ablaze with the angry fire of fever. Even though she seemed to sleep, it was an unnatural rest, fraught with the moaning and thrashing of delirium and an increasingly difficult struggle to get her breath.

The only bright spot in the day had been Miss Valentine's obvious, if slight, improvement. Her temperature had finally broken the night before, and she had even taken a little broth at midday and again this evening.

An ongoing concern for Miss Snow, however, diminished what little relief Andy might have felt earlier. The longer she sat watching, the more anxious she became. She wished Niles had stopped by earlier, as had become his habit, but he'd sent word that he would be tied up at the clinic until late and most likely would not be by until tomorrow.

Guilt deepened her anxiety as she struggled with the thought that perhaps she'd been wrong in refusing to add her plea to Niles's urging that Miss Valentine and Miss Snow go to the hospital. The dread influenza had already caused a number of deaths on the Island; in fact, the newspapers indicated the situation was nearing epidemic proportions. Niles was an excellent doctor, after all, probably the finest on the Island. If he thought hospitalization would be best, who was *she* to disagree with him?

She knew that if anything were to happen to Miss Snow or Miss Valentine, she would never forgive herself. She loved them both like family.

For a moment she leaned back, resting her head against the wall. She tried to pray for both her ailing friends, and also for Roman, as she had every night for some time now. But her eyes soon grew heavy—almost as heavy as her heart—and in no time she began to drift off.

Twenty

*F*or days Roman had watched Andy struggle to keep everything under control, virtually by herself, except for the help of her stalwart housekeeper and the uncle.

She went between one sickroom to the other through the day, squeezing into the crowded hours as many of the household tasks as she possibly could before sitting up all night with one of the ailing women. She seemed to be everywhere at once, yet most of the time Roman managed little more than a hurried exchange of words with her in the hallway.

On Thursday morning after breakfast—from which Andy had again been absent—Roman met her racing down the hall toward the kitchen. She looked ghastly. Her eyes were bloodshot and darkly shadowed, her pallor a sickly gray. Her hair needed combing, and her shirtwaist was rumpled; obviously, she had not been to bed the night before. Probably not the night before *that* either.

He hesitated only an instant before catching her arm to detain her. "How is Miss Snow . . . and Miss Valentine?"

She blinked, staring at him almost as if she hadn't heard. Then her eyes cleared a little. "Miss Valentine seems to be improving. But Miss Snow"—she shook her head—"I'm awfully worried about her."

Roman heard the tremor in her voice. She rubbed a hand over her eyes in a gesture of exhaustion, and for a moment Roman feared she might fall where she stood.

He tightened his clasp on her arm to steady her. "Andy—you *must* get some rest. You simply can't go on like this."

She pulled away, frowning at him with obvious impatience. "I'm all right."

"I think not."

"Roman, you'll have to excuse me," she said, not looking at him. "I was on my way to make some more lemon tea for Miss Snow. I don't like leaving her alone for very long right now."

"How long has it been since you've sat down to a real meal, Andy?" he asked, his concern for her increasing. "Or slept more than an hour or two?"

Again the quick frown, the avoidance of his gaze.

Ignoring her pique, Roman again took her arm. "At least, tell me what I can do to help. There must be something."

She looked at him, and after a moment her expression softened. "You *are* helping. Don't you think I know who's been chopping the wood and stacking it? And Ibebe told me you've even been carrying your own hot water and changing your bed linens."

For just an instant, her features pinched, as if she'd just recalled something unpleasant. "Oh, Roman, I *am* sorry about all this! I know I've been negligent. All the confusion has completely spoiled your visit!"

"Don't be foolish," he said. "Nothing's been spoiled, not in the least. I told you, I'm used to managing on my own. I'm far more concerned for *you* at the moment, if you must know. You're going to drop from exhaustion."

Without giving her a chance to interrupt, he went on. "I want to help, if you'll only tell me how." Even as the words left his mouth, he knew a sense of surprise, for he found himself genuinely wanting, even *needing* to do whatever he could to make things easier for her.

Right on the heels of the thought came the more sensible reminder that he could not afford to become any more involved with this girl and her concerns than he already was. He had to separate himself from Andy and her problems if he was ever going to make any progress in dealing with his own.

As if she had read his thoughts, she lifted her chin and gave him a humorless smile. "Thank you, Roman, but that's really not necessary. And please don't fret about me. I'm young and disgustingly healthy, after all."

Roman smarted at the implication that he was neither. He forced himself to keep his face impassive. "Well, then—if you're quite sure," he said, letting his hand fall away.

"Roman—"

He looked at her, struggling to keep his feelings under wraps at the sight of her pallid skin, her red-rimmed eyes.

"I want to thank you for being so patient with us—with *me*," she said quietly. A look of uncertainty settled over her features before she went on. "I just . . . want to say that if you should decide to stay for a time, after all this is over, I'll do everything I can to make the rest of your visit more pleasant."

She left him standing in the middle of the hall, puzzling over what she'd said. Had she refused to admit her need simply because she feared imposing on him, or because she thought him inadequate? And had she said what she did about his staying on because she *wanted* him to stay, or had she merely been trying to placate a paying lodger?

Feeling restive and suddenly irritable, he told himself that, whatever she had meant, he couldn't afford to let it matter.

———

That afternoon Roman left the house to photograph a quaint old mill he had seen a few days past and to shoot some views of the bay.

A little over an hour later, he returned the equipment to the wagon and started back to the Manor. Halfway there, he turned on impulse and headed inland, in the direction of the abandoned old house he'd discovered during his first week on the Island.

The clearing in the woods stood in stark contrast to the sites he had left only moments before. Obscured by dense, overgrown foliage and a riot of brambles, the entire setting gave off the same air of desolation he remembered.

Conor also seemed to recall the place, for as soon as they got out of the wagon, the wolfhound bristled, suddenly alert and at the ready. Once inside the rusty gate, which clanged shut behind them, the dog gave a low growl, then another.

"I know, chum," Roman said, aware that he was keeping his voice low in deference to the silence all around them. "It's a ghastly old haunt, right enough. We'll just have ourselves a look, then take a shot or two and leave."

For a moment he stood considering the treacherous-looking steps that ascended to the front door. Finally, he decided against them. Instead, he started around the east wing of the house, Conor beside him. The footing was precarious, the ground rough and strewn with rocks and slippery leaves. Roman braced a hand on the wolfhound's back for added support as he tested the ground each step of the way with the cane.

The first window they came to was so covered with dust and grime he could see nothing, not even when he pressed as close as he could and cupped his hands to peer inside. After a moment he went on to the next window, and, finding a shard of glass missing from the pane, brought his face close, straining to see through the opening.

It was a disappointment, even as old, deserted houses went. Nothing to be seen but the dim lines of a dilapidated kitchen table, a chair with a broken back, and two or three rusty tins lined up on a sagging work counter. And cobwebs—everything appeared to be covered with cobwebs.

Again the wolfhound growled, then whimpered, but Roman moved on, toward the back of the house. "I know, fellow, I don't like it much either. But you know how it is. The place is here, so I can't resist having a peek."

A sharp wind had sprung up, and Roman hunched himself against it. With one hand, he pulled his greatcoat more tightly about his throat. He moved from one filthy window to another at the back of the house, but there was nothing to be seen except the shadowed tracings of furniture, concealed with dust covers.

Conor seemed to have taken a great interest in what appeared to be an old coal chute in the foundation, now boarded up. Roman had to order him away twice before the wolfhound returned to his side.

On the west side of the house, he found another broken window and crouched to squint through the opening. He found himself peering into a room that looked as if it might have once been a drawing room or a parlor. All the furniture was covered, but there were signs that once there had been life here. Candles still rested on the mantel. A threadbare rug lay in front of the fireplace, and a small pedestal table with an empty vase stood near the door.

Finally he straightened, putting a hand to his lower back against the dull ache that had begun there. The low, continuous growl with which Conor had greeted the house earlier still simmered in the dog's throat, and Roman moved to give him a reassuring pat on the head. The wolfhound looked up, chuffing as if to ask if he were quite finished with this foolishness, and if so, could they please leave the premises for a more cheerful setting.

"I expect you're right, chum," Roman said. "The place doesn't do very much for my mood either."

At the front of the house, he paused for a moment, his eyes scanning down from the center chimney, across the missing shingles and broken windowpanes. Again he decided it was undoubtedly the ugliest building he had ever seen, and he had seen a few.

The same dark sense of malevolence that had troubled him the first time he'd come upon the place now resurfaced, igniting a sudden desire to get away. Yet in spite of the growing urgency to get back to the wagon, he felt a vague stirring of restraint, an unaccountable reluctance to leave. For just an instant he had the fatuous notion that something about the hideous old place was reaching out to him.

At the same time Conor snarled and began to bark. Roman looked at him, saw that the wolfhound was barking at nothing but the house itself. He shuddered, suddenly as chilled as if someone had flung ice down the back of his coat.

With some effort, he shook off the oppressive pall of foreboding and turned away, taking the rough ground back to the wagon as quickly as he dared. The wolfhound required no urging, but ran along in front of him, as if blazing the trail.

By the time they reached the wagon, Roman had discarded all thought of photographing the house. The wind was blowing up in earnest now, the afternoon fast losing its earlier light. As he drove the wagon out of the clearing, he found himself wondering if light ever entered this part of the woods.

———

In his cell, the little black boy was dreaming. Jeeter lay on his straw-filled pallet, rubbing his head against the pain that was always there, even when he slept.

In his dream, giant claws seized his head on either side, raking the skin around his ears with their terrible knife-sharp edges. They scraped and squeezed—squeezed so hard he thought his head would surely burst wide open.

There was a noise somewhere at the back of his dream, a noise like a dog barking. It seemed to come from a long way off, from somewhere out in the woods maybe.

The boy tried to wake up. He shook his head to clear it, but the pain stopped him. He rolled over, then opened his eyes, listening. He was fully awake now, at least as awake as he ever was these days. His head always felt heavy, though, even when it wasn't hurting.

He lay without moving, listening. Had there really been a dog, or had he been dreaming again? Sometimes he couldn't tell anymore what was real and what wasn't.

He sure wished that dog was real. Maybe it was. Maybe it was still outside, just looking for a way to get in. He liked dogs a lot. He had had an old hound dog once, a stray that had come around. Ma had said he couldn't keep him, that there wasn't enough vittles for them all, but she'd finally given in, and the dog had stayed. Sometimes Jeeter still missed that old hound dog.

There was no sound now at all, except the muffled breathing noises on either side of him, in the other cells. He kept his eyes open, not wanting to sleep. He was afraid of the dream, afraid of the claws. He wished he could just go to sleep and not dream at all. Maybe if he didn't dream, his head wouldn't hurt so bad.

But when he woke up again, The Man might be back.

The Man always brought more pain with him. Sometimes the pain was for one of the others. Sometimes it was for *him*. He never knew when it would be his turn again.

Jeeter wished he could go home now. But he *had* no home. Not no more. Not since Granny had died at that clinic place. He wondered, if he ever got out of here, would the pain go with him? Or would he leave it here, in the dark, under the ground?

He turned onto his back and sat up, looking around. The thought of going home made him glance down at the chain around his foot, the chain that fastened to the wall.

The pain in his head pounded harder, and soon he sank down onto his pallet again. Eventually, he closed his eyes, shutting out the sight of the chain—and all thought of home.

Twenty-one

*L*ater that evening, Roman confined the wolfhound to the bedroom and then went back downstairs. Restless and somewhat bored, he wandered along the dimly lighted hallway, thinking he might come across some task that needed doing or even something that needed fixing.

He encountered a number of possibilities, all of which would seem to require materials that likely weren't available. He made a mental note about the hole in the plaster in the main library and another regarding missing bricks in the parlor fireplace. As long as he was here, he might just as well lend a hand, after all. He would pick up the necessary supplies in town in a day or so.

He went on then to the "music room," as Andy was wont to call it, but which in reality was little more than an extension of the parlor. He had eyed the fine-looking parlor piano before this evening, his fingers itching to try it. Now he gave in to the impulse.

Closing the heavy oak doors firmly behind him, he walked over to the massive instrument and touched the top of it. He wondered who played, smiling a little to himself at the thought of Andy sitting still long enough to make music.

Typically ornate, the piano was polished to a satin sheen and seemed to serve as a display for dried flowers and various small figurines. Roman glanced once toward the closed doors, then sat down on the velvet-cushioned stool and carefully raised the lid from the keyboard. The ivory keys bore the faint stains and impressions of much use at some time in the past, and Roman sat staring at them longingly. An ache came over him, for he had not played since leaving home in Baltimore. He missed the emotional release he had always found in the music. Finally, he allowed his fingers to roam over the keys, tracing their outline and savoring the cool touch of the ivory after so long a separation.

No longer able to resist, he sampled the midrange keys, then the treble. Next he tried the bass and found it rich and deepthroated, just as he liked. The instrument obviously had not been played for quite some time and could have used a good tuning. Yet the pitches were surprisingly true, the voice one of elegant timbre.

He hesitated only a moment before moving into a child's exercise, then another. Although he felt a little stiff and out of form, he was enjoying himself too much to mind. He played quietly and easily for several minutes, until at last he felt the familiar sense of freedom and lightness he craved, whereupon he danced his way through two of the Chopin *mazurkas*. At last, he sprang into another of his favorites by the Polish composer, the *Grande Valse Brillante*.

When he was younger, his taste had run to the more militant or frenzied Chopin. But the passion of the tempestuous *Revolutionary* and the fiery brilliance of the *F minor Fantasie* had held little allure for him since Kathleen's death. Now he mostly favored the haunting *nocturnes*, the stormy *ballades*, the graceful reflection of the *preludes*.

He had always loved a wide variety of operatic melodies as well, but he could no longer bring himself to play them. One of his favorite pastimes, when Kathleen had still been alive, was to adapt some of the more popular arias to piano. Kathleen had possessed a glorious voice, and the two of them had spent hours in the evening at the piano, Roman playing her favorites as she sang. Even now the memory brought him to tears.

Finally, he yielded to a steadily encroaching melancholy, seeking the solace of a Field *Nocturne*. He forgot his surroundings, instead allowed himself to drift off into the subtle mystery of an Irish twilight, a whispering hillside, a lonely valley so remote even the stars didn't know it was there.

Too exhausted to keep her eyes open any longer, Andy had fallen into a troubled sleep at Miss Snow's bedside. She awoke lightheaded, with the feeling that she was floating, drifting through a night filled with achingly lovely music.

She was also aware of feeling slightly unwell and wished she dared go to bed for at least an hour or two. But that was out of the question, so, after assuring herself that Miss Snow was sleeping comfortably, she rose from the chair and stepped out in the hallway to clear her head.

Still groggy, she stood at the balustrade, listening to music unlike anything she had ever heard before. The sound of her mother's piano after so many years wrenched her heart with memory. Emily Fairchild had loved to play, had often stolen precious moments from household tasks to indulge her love of music.

But she had never played like this. At once elegant and sorrowful, the tones were haunting, even mystical . . . and unbearably lovely. It was as if someone had given the piano a voice of its own. And what a voice it was—like the cry of the soul itself, giving vent to inexpressible things, feelings that defied description!

Even as she started down the stairway, Andy knew who was playing. She could hear his spirit, his very heart, sounding in the music, and she was drawn, compelled to go to him.

Roman seemed not to notice when she entered the room. Quietly, Andy closed the doors and stood just inside them, transfixed by the music and the sight of him at the piano. His dark head was bent low. His eyes were open, but Andy knew he was seeing something other than the keyboard. His hands, so large and slender, always so confident, so deft, coaxed sounds from the piano that broke her heart.

Andy's eyes stung to watch him, to hear what she knew to be the lament of his soul. Her mouth, suddenly dry, trembled, and her throat felt as if it had swollen shut. She had all she could do not to go to him, to put her arms around him and gather him close and somehow comfort him . . . heal him.

Instead, she stood, not moving, scarcely breathing. A vague sense of dizziness swept through her, and the heaviness in her chest tightened still more.

The piece drifted to its close, and Roman stopped playing and looked up, directly at her. His dark gray eyes were glazed with pain, and for a moment Andy didn't think he even recognized her.

Then she saw his features clear. At the same time, he rubbed his hands together and gave her an uncertain smile.

"I should have asked, I expect," he said. "I hope you don't mind?"

"Mind?" Still caught up in the enchantment of the music, Andy choked out the word, her tongue thick. "I . . . no. No, of course, I don't mind."

He sat watching her. "Who plays? You?"

Andy stared at him. "Me? Oh, goodness no! I can't play a note! It's my mother's piano. She played very well, I suppose, but not like you. Where did you ever learn to play like that?"

The familiar closed look settled over him. "Actually, I learned from *my* mother." He seemed to hesitate. "She's a musician. A very gifted one."

It was the first time Roman had volunteered even the slightest bit of information about one of his parents. Andy wanted to ask him more, but something in his eyes warned her to tread carefully. "And your father? Was he musical, too?"

His mouth tightened. "No. My father was an artist."

An artist for a father—a mother who was a musician. Small wonder Roman was so gifted in his own right!

"You must be very . . . proud of them," she said, trying for a light tone. "And very like them, obviously. Such talent . . ."

He looked at her as if he were searching for something in her eyes. "Actually," he said, his tone hard, "my mother is mentally . . . unstable, and my father was an almost entirely heartless, utterly selfish man. I've always rather hoped I wouldn't turn out much like them."

Again came the overwhelming desire to comfort him. Andy actually took a step toward him.

Abruptly, he rose from the stool and closed the lid on the piano, ending the moment. "I hope I didn't disturb the household," he said, turning toward her. "I was restless . . . just passing the time."

Something roared in Andy's head. She felt suddenly hot, then chilled and weak, overcome with the dizziness that earlier had been merely a threat.

She opened her mouth to assure him he was welcome to play whenever he liked. She thought she spoke, but was deaf to the sound of her own voice. The roar in her ears swelled until she thought her head would surely explode.

In that instant, she felt the floor rise to meet her.

Twenty-two

*R*oman's heart was a hammer as he stood watching Andy, looking so small and infinitely vulnerable in the enormous bed.

He wished he could have carried her up the stairs himself, instead of merely helping the uncle with her. He wished he could think of something more to do for her before he left to fetch the doctor.

And he wished he could convince her to leave off apologizing.

"I'm so sorry!" she kept murmuring, her head lolling from side to side. "I'm sure I'll be just fine in a few minutes. It's only that I'm tired, that's all."

Her skin was ashen and clammy. She seemed unable to focus her eyes for any length of time, even after she regained consciousness. Her breathing was shallow and uneven.

She was very, very ill, Roman knew with a sudden wrench of his heart.

The anxious uncle stood on one side of the bed, Ibebe on the other. Every now and then Andy would look at one or the other with stricken eyes, like a guilty child who wanted only to undo whatever inconvenience she might have brought about.

Roman stole one last look before leaving the room. The uncle followed him out. They had already decided that Roman should be the one to go for Rutherford, Doyle grudgingly admitting that he could not see well after dusk and could be a hazard in the buggy.

"You'll bring him as quickly as you can?" Doyle urged Roman again, out in the hallway.

Roman nodded. "You can be sure of it." He was anxious to get away, delaying only long enough to review Doyle's directions to the clinic and confine the wolfhound to the bedroom.

At the uncle's suggestion, to save time, he took the buggy instead of his own more ponderous wagon. Even so, it took him nearly an hour to find the clinic, located near Stapleton. An angry wind laced with snow pelted the buggy like needles of ice the entire distance, and by the time Roman finally arrived, he was chilled all through and shaking as if he had palsy.

According to Doyle, Rutherford and an associate maintained offices on the second floor, so he asked a white-haired nurse in the front entrance hall for directions to the stairway. When she heard whom he was seeking, however, she suggested he try the rear of the building on the main floor. "Dr. Rutherford isn't here this evening, but you'll find his associate, Dr. Meece, in the indigent ward. At least he was still there a few minutes ago."

Roman thanked her and, following her directions, started off down a dimly lighted, somewhat shabby corridor. The building was cold and damp, and he shivered all the way to the end of the hall, where a large dormitory-type room led off to the right.

Inside, the room was crowded with beds, probably twice the number for which it had been designed. Some of the patients were elderly. Some were children. A number were black.

On the other side of the room, standing over the bed of a small Negro boy, Roman spied a youthful-looking physician with rust-colored hair in a rumpled white laboratory coat. He appeared to be examining a child in the bed.

As Roman approached, the doctor looked up and frowned. He was probably in his mid-twenties, thickly built, of medium height. His glossy hair was full and badly mussed, his small mustache inexpertly trimmed. He had a perfectly round, childish face and wore spectacles of the same shape. As for the child, he appeared to be dangerously frail and ill.

"This ward is not open to visitors, sir." The voice was more that of a boy than a man.

"Would you be Dr. Meece?" Roman inquired, glancing at the child in the bed, whose face was wet with perspiration in spite of the chill in the room.

The physician made no attempt to hide his impatience. "I am. And I'm very busy just now, if you'll excuse me." Without a second glance, he went on listening to the child's chest.

Roman ignored his curtness. "Yes, of course," he said. "Perhaps you could just tell me where I might find Dr. Rutherford?"

"Dr. Rutherford is not here this evening." Meece didn't look up, but went on with his examination.

Roman hesitated, then asked, "Would I find him at home, do you think?"

The other man straightened, studying Roman more closely now. "No, Dr. Rutherford was going to be away tonight, I believe."

Roman found himself mildly curious about the young doctor. He had the features of a cherub, although without expression, yet something in his manner seemed slightly furtive.

"It's rather important that I find him," Roman persisted. "You might even say it's an emergency."

The round blue eyes behind the spectacles remained steady. "I'm afraid I can't help you, Mr.—?"

Suddenly annoyed with the man and begrudging the delay for Andy's sake, Roman bit down a testy reply. "St. Clare," he said, striving for a cordial note. "Roman St. Clare."

Something changed in the physician's face, something so subtle Roman couldn't be sure he hadn't imagined it. Still, hadn't there been a flicker in those guileless eyes, perhaps, or a slight tightening of the childish mouth?

"Well," Roman said after a moment, "I suppose there's nothing for it but to leave a message. If you should happen to see Dr. Rutherford anytime this evening, would you tell him that Miss Fairchild has been taken ill, that he's needed at the Manor? Her uncle sent me on her behalf."

At the mention of Andy's name, Meece's expression cleared. Suddenly he was civil, almost cordial. "Oh, dear—Miss Fairchild now? The influenza, I suppose." Without giving Roman time to reply, he hurried on. "Yes, of course, I'll get the message to Dr. Rutherford somehow. As quickly as possible."

Roman thanked him and went out, stopping in the entrance hall long enough to leave a similar message with the nurse he'd met on his way in. She eyed him rather strangely, then returned her attention to the charts she'd been reviewing.

"I'll be glad to tell Dr. Rutherford," she said with obvious indifference. "If he comes in, that is. He's seldom here in the evenings, though."

Roman nodded. "Yes, I understand he spends a great deal of his time at Bellevue after hours."

The nurse looked up. "Only on Wednesdays, I believe."

Surprised, Roman considered her reply. "Then perhaps I might find him at home, after all?"

She shrugged, again turning her attention to the charts in her hand. Roman was puzzled by the way her expression tightened. "I wouldn't know about that, sir. Dr. Rutherford doesn't usually leave word with us as to his whereabouts."

Roman thought that a rather peculiar practice for a physician, especially one as seemingly dedicated as Rutherford. "Do you think you could direct me to his residence?" he pressed. "It's really very important that I find him."

"He has rooms with Mrs. Conifer, just the next street down," she said with a shrug. "It's a private boardinghouse."

As Roman had feared, Rutherford wasn't at home.

The landlady was of little help, though she was a pleasant sort. Mrs. Conifer stood as tall as most men, with sturdy shoulders and a hearty smile. When Roman inquired after the doctor, she beamed, shaking her head, her double chin waggling. "No doubt he's calling on a patient *in extremis* somewhere. The dear man will work himself into an early grave, I'm always telling him. Dr. Rutherford never rests, never thinks of himself, only of his patients. I have no idea where you might find him."

Again Roman left word, thinking rather peevishly that surely even this paragon of medical science must sleep and eat *sometime.*

He spent most of the trip back to the Manor puzzling over what he'd learned about Rutherford, especially the fact that apparently he wasn't spending his evenings as he had led Andy to believe. Roman wondered, too, about the nurse's odd demeanor, the subtle hint of disapproval he thought he'd detected in her attitude about Rutherford.

There was also the matter of the physician's associate, Dr. Meece. Roman conceded that, for the most part, Meece had seemed perfectly ordinary. Perhaps the hostility he'd thought he sensed in the man had been nothing more than the harried behavior of a junior associate with too much to do—and a highly demanding superior for whom it was to be done. Yet Meece did seem an unlikely colleague for the austere, exacting Rutherford. Of course, if the latter was the despot Roman suspected he could be, perhaps young Meece wasn't such a strange choice after all. Certainly, he seemed malleable enough, a trait Rutherford might find desirable in an associate.

It occurred to Roman, fleetingly, that his dislike for Rutherford—and there was no other word for it, he did *dislike* the man—might be excessive. The physician was a virtual stranger to him, after all; they had exchanged a few tense words and nothing more.

Jealousy, perhaps?

The ugly, mocking whisper reared itself without warning, leaving Roman shaken even as he examined it.

All right, supposing he *had* allowed himself to become too emotionally attached to Andy? And he could scarcely deny that he resented Rutherford's domineering behavior toward her. But even given all that, he didn't think he was so petty as to dislike a man for no more reason than a misplaced sense of rivalry. There was something else, something more substantial, surely.

It struck him then that the vague, disturbing ambiguity Rutherford gave off was in essence an apparent *duality*. The man seemed constantly to send mixed, even conflicting messages. With Andy, he presented himself as gentle, devoted, and attentive, if somewhat overprotective. Yet he also displayed vestiges of intractability, heavy-handedness, and an intensity of such force it could be unnerving.

Roman suddenly realized how far astray his thoughts had roamed and shook his head at his own fatuousness. So Niles Rutherford was possessed of some rather stark contrasts. What man wasn't? The human nature was nothing if not a field of contrasts, an arena where darkness and light played out their ancient games of conflict and conquest, opposition and oppression.

For that matter, was he—Roman—any different from Rutherford? Certainly he had his own duplicities, his own ongoing battles constantly waging, his own factions warring against one another most of the time. Heaven help him, perhaps he was just like Niles Rutherford . . . or worse . . .

A particularly vicious blast of wind slammed him just then, jarring him back to his surroundings. He shivered and tugged his coat collar even tighter about his throat. He found himself almost dreading his return to the Manor, reluctant to face the uncle's disappointment when he learned that Rutherford hadn't been found.

For a moment he considered going back and trying to collect another doctor, but he knew that Doyle would almost certainly take exception. More discomfiting was the awareness that Andy would strongly prefer that Rutherford attend her.

Besides, he suspected that young Dr. Meece would find his superior. In spite of his professed ignorance of Rutherford's whereabouts, Roman was fairly sure Meece hadn't been entirely truthful.

Until then, he supposed all he could do was to stand by and be prepared to help.

———

Waiting for Rutherford to show up at the house, Roman had stayed with the uncle, standing vigil over Andy in the bedroom while Ibebe looked after the still-ailing spinsters.

For once, Doyle, who was understandably frantic, seemed not to take offense at Roman's presence. From time to time they took turns trying to coax a few sips of lemon tea into Andy, but she fought them both, seeming to want nothing other than sleep.

Roman remembered one of the army surgeons in camp preparing a restorative by stirring a small amount of camphor into a cup of boiling water and having the patient first inhale the steam, then sip the liquid after it cooled a bit. In fact, he had received that therapy himself, and it had proven quite effective. He was just on his way upstairs with a pan of the mixture when Rutherford finally arrived.

The flinty-eyed physician took one look at the pan Roman was holding and gave him to understand that they would be using no "quack remedies." Then he ordered him out of the sickroom.

Roman conceded to Rutherford's authority as a physician and remained outside Andy's room, but he had no intention of being banished altogether. Locating an extra chair from a spare guestroom, he pulled it up near the door to the bedroom, where he waited throughout the entire time Rutherford was examining her.

When Rutherford finally emerged, leaving the uncle ensconced with Andy, Roman had all he could do not to follow the physician downstairs and question him.

Instead, he waited for the sound of the front door closing before going back into the bedroom. He hesitated just inside, until Doyle gestured that he should enter.

Doyle glanced at him from across the bed. "'Tis not the influenza, after all," he said.

Roman looked up in surprise.

Doyle nodded. "She's simply worn out, Niles says. Exhausted entirely, 'til she's made herself ill."

Roman's initial relief that at least Andy had not fallen prey to the epidemic gave way to a different kind of concern. "And what's to be done for her then? Is there a treatment?"

The uncle's gaze returned to Andy, who seemed to be sleeping soundly. "We're to keep her abed, Niles says. She's a sick little lass, for all that it's not the influenza. Niles says she mustn't get up for days, else she risks more extreme complications, especially where her heart is concerned." He paused, meeting Roman's eyes across the bed. "That might not be the easiest thing to do. You've seen how strong-willed she is."

Roman thought for a moment. "It would seem that what we must do is keep things running so efficiently she'll not feel the *need* to leave her bed."

Doyle nodded slowly. "That would seem sensible. But with three of them down, I don't know that we can manage all that well."

Roman stood watching Andy, trying to ignore the anxiety tightening in his stomach. "I think we must," he said, a plan already beginning to form.

He felt Doyle's eyes on him and looked up. The older man was studying Roman as if he had something he was keen on saying. But after a moment his expression altered, his eyes narrowing. "Andy wouldn't approve of your pitching in, you know—you're a paying guest, after all. Besides, why would you offer?"

Why, indeed? Roman asked himself. Why, when he knew that he was only complicating his life by involving himself in hers?

Why, when it was all too plain that, with the possible exception of Andy, no one really wanted him here? And why, when the only sensible thing to do, obviously, was to leave as soon as possible, did he feel so compelled to stay?

He turned back to Andy, scrutinizing the small, appealing face, now so unnatural with the pallor of exhaustion and illness. Unexpectedly, the memory of their earlier conversation in the music room flashed through his mind. He had resented her assumption that he might be "very like" his parents, had just barely managed to suppress a caustic retort. But at almost the exact same instant, he had been shaken by the sickening possibility that he was, in fact, becoming more like his father all the time.

His refusal to get involved in the lives of others . . . his deliberate choice to lead a solitary life, to tend to his own affairs and leave everyone else to tend to theirs . . . his dogged determination to let nothing or no one stand in the way of bringing Kathleen's killer to justice—did all this point to the possibility that he was already more like his father than he could bring himself to admit?

What Andy couldn't have known was that at the very moment when she was questioning him about his likeness to his parents, a wave of aversion had washed over him. It had been that sense of self-digust that had caused him to be so curt with her only seconds before she fell to the floor, unconscious.

He was aware that Doyle was waiting for a reply. He answered with a question of his own. "Must I have a reason for wanting to help?"

Meeting the older man's skeptical gaze across the bed, Roman could see that he was indeed expected to have a reason. He attempted no explanation, however, for Roman could hardly expect Magnus Doyle to understand motives he himself couldn't comprehend.

Still, while he would do all in his power to lend a hand for Andy's sake, he would distance himself from her . . . for his *own* sake.

Twenty-three

*F*or more than an hour, Roman and Doyle worked side by side, splitting logs and stacking firewood.

Doyle insisted that the weather would soon turn from the almost mild temperatures they were enjoying to a more seasonal cold snap in a day or two. "Feel the sun on your back this time of year on the Island," he told Roman, "and you're sure to feel snow on your face shortly after. We're in for it by the end of the week, just see if we're not."

He was breathing hard as he unloaded another armload of splits, and Roman lowered the ax a moment to regard him anxiously. "When we finish here," Doyle went on, "we'd best see to the coal, if you've a mind to help. With Andy and the ladies abed, we'll be wanting to keep the house snug for as long as need be."

Roman nodded, lifting an arm to mop the perspiration on his brow with his shirtsleeve. He hadn't worked this hard for an age, and every muscle in his body was reminding him of the fact. But the sun felt grand, and the ache in his back was an almost pleasant reminder that at least he was fit enough to be doing something useful again.

At the sound of carriage wheels bumping up the lane, Doyle glanced up. "That'll be Niles, no doubt," he said, wiping his hands on his trousers. "I believe I will go inside to see what he has to say about Andy." He hesitated. "You might want to take a breather yourself, man. Don't want you dropping in the woodpile."

Roman grinned at him, then swiped his sleeve across his face again. "I'll keep on for a bit. Don't worry. I do know my limits."

The truth was he had no particular desire to encounter Rutherford. The man made no secret of his dislike. And even though Doyle seemed to be making a rare effort to be a bit more civil since Andy had fallen ill, Roman knew it was just that—an effort. He still felt very much the outsider with the prickly older man, would feel even more so with Rutherford on the scene.

He did take time out for a brief rest, laying down the ax and helping himself to a dipper of water from the outdoors pump. As he sipped the water, he looked around, thinking as he had before that both the house and grounds could do with some maintenance.

Andy was really in need of more business, that much was clear, and he had an idea that the appearance of the Manor didn't help. He thought he knew how she might improve her situation. Some proper advertising, for a start. He could make some photographs of the property and design them for advertisement, if she would allow it. A number of placements in selected newspapers and other publications would almost certainly bring more lodgers to the door than she could accommodate.

But a few essential improvements would have to be made first. Getting rid of that ivy climbing the outside walls like an invading horde of spiders, for one. Cutting back some of those old tree branches to let light onto the grounds and into the house. Clearing away some of the more scruffy shrubs in front. There were a number of things that could be done with only minimal expense to heighten the place's appeal and even restore some of its lost elegance. . . .

Abruptly, he checked himself. It was none of his business, of course. And Andy would probably be the first to tell him so. She wasn't exactly one to accept help graciously, after all. She seemed to think she could manage everything, and manage it on her own.

At least, that was the impression she gave. He felt a pang of sympathy for her, knowing how thoroughly difficult she was sure to find this sudden enforced rest. The thought of her not being able to bustle about the property, "managing," filled him with a kind of sadness. Andy was one for doing, not having things done *for* her. It wasn't going to be easy to keep her down.

———

Andy was floating on a warm sea of dreams, but she couldn't

seem to pause at any one of them. Every time she tried to linger at some particularly pleasant scene, a wave would rise and lift her away, on to another place, another time.

She knew she was dreaming, but the dreams seemed ever so real. They brought her a wonderful sense of contentment, a safe, warm feeling she had almost forgotten.

Now she was drifting on the tree swing out back. Her father was pushing her as a warm springtime breeze ruffled her hair, and she squealed with delight.

Drifting . . .

Next she visited her mother's sewing room, where Mama was making matching dresses for a little-girl Andy and her doll, Thomasina. Pink dresses with white pinafores and eyelet edging around the pockets.

Drifting . . .

A visit to the park now, with both her mother and her father. A picnic luncheon of fried chicken, potato rolls, and raisin cake. Mama had set out flowers along with the food on a blue-and-white checkered cloth.

Drifting . . .

Now she was back in her bed, but still dreaming. Dreaming that Roman was playing the piano. She wanted to follow the sounds rising up the wide staircase, beckoning to her. She tried to pull herself up . . . she would go downstairs, go to Roman and the music. . . .

But voices stopped her, warning her to stay quiet . . . to rest . . . not to move . . .

"Roman?"

The sound of her own voice startled her awake. But it was Niles, not Roman, leaning over her. Magnus was there, too, on the other side of the bed, his craggy face lined with concern. Magnus and Niles . . . not Roman.

Bewildered, Andy turned back to Niles, who seemed to be taking her pulse.

"What's wrong? Niles? What are you doing?"

"You don't remember fainting last night?" His voice sounded hard and short, not like Niles at all.

"Fainting?" Andy stared at him, her mind still fuzzy. "I never faint."

Magnus put a hand to her shoulder. "You did last night, lass. Dropped right to the floor in the music room, it seems. And you've been asleep ever since."

"I've never fainted in my life." She heard the uncertainty in her voice. She wasn't really speaking to Magnus, but to herself, trying to take in what he was telling her.

Now she remembered going to the music room, finding Roman there, listening to him play the piano . . . then nothing.

"At least that's St.Clare's story," Niles put in. "We've only his word, since you don't seem to remember." There was a question in his voice, along with a testiness Andy had heard before—the Sunday he'd behaved so abysmally to Roman at the dinner table.

She looked at him, unprepared for the cold stare of accusation fixed upon her.

"I warned you something like this might happen, Amanda, but you wouldn't listen." His voice was as hard as his eyes, again catching Andy off guard.

"Something like *what*?" Andy's head swam. "Do I have the influenza?" She wasn't so much frightened by the possibility of being ill as she was distressed at the thought of all the time she was wasting.

It was a relief when Niles shook his head.

"No, it's not influenza," he told her, but his next words dispelled her relief. "Still, it can be even more serious than influenza if you don't follow my instructions to the letter."

Why was he acting this way?

"I feel perfectly fine," she said, knowing it was a lie.

Niles let go of her wrist, but continued to lean over her, one hand braced on the bed beside her. "Now you listen to me, Amanda." He was all physician now, his tone professional, his features somber. "You are very ill. You're suffering from total exhaustion. I'm only surprised it didn't happen sooner. You are going to have to stay in bed until—"

Andy uttered a soft groan of protest, but when she struggled upright, he restrained her with a firm hand on her shoulder. His eyes searched her face. "St.Clare says you seemed all right one minute, then fainted the next. Amanda—is that the truth?"

Andy frowned at him. "The truth?"

Niles gave an impatient sigh. "Is that really what happened?

182

Are you sure St.Clare didn't do something to—upset you? Something that might have caused you to faint?"

Andy stared at him, momentarily baffled. "Roman was across the room from me . . . at the piano. I was listening to him play. How could that have caused me to faint?"

Niles didn't appear completely convinced, but finally he released his hold on her shoulder. "You *must* have absolute bed rest, or you're going to put yourself at terrible risk. Your heart is under severe strain as it is."

Andy's eyes stung with tears of dismay. She *couldn't* be ill now, she mustn't. "But Miss Snow! And Miss Valentine! I have to help take care of them—"

"No, you do not!"

Andy actually jumped at the sharpness of Niles's retort.

He stood glaring down at her. "Ibebe can take adequate care of the two women," he said, his tone still brusque. "They are recovering nicely . . . while *you*, on the other hand—"

Abruptly, his voice gentled slightly. "Amanda—you simply *must* take this seriously. Your heart is at risk. Your general *health* is at stake. You're going to have to stay in bed for as long as it takes to regain your strength." He glanced up at Magnus, across the bed. "Tell her, Mr. Doyle. Please, make her understand."

Magnus bent over her now, patting her hand. "Niles is right, lass. And I blame myself for not seeing what was happening long before now. I should have insisted you take better care of yourself. But now there's nothing for it but to do as Niles says."

He squeezed her hand, and Andy saw that his eyes were suspiciously red-rimmed. As she watched, he dug his large handkerchief from the pocket of his trousers and blew his nose.

"Hard as it may be for you, lass," he went on, "you're going to have to let others look after *you* for a change."

Discouragement washed over Andy in a torrent. "Oh, Uncle Magnus . . . how will we ever manage? You can't do all the work and take care of me, too! And there's Miss Snow to look after, and Miss Valentine—Ibebe can't handle anything more! What are we going to do?"

"Amanda, I'll come by twice a day from now on," Niles said, obviously trying to reassure her. "As for Miss Snow and Miss Valentine, they'll soon be up and about. And will you please stop fretting about Ibebe? She's only a *servant*, for goodness' sake!"

Andy stared at him in astonishment. She tried to push herself up from the bed, but her head spun so violently with the effort she immediately fell back, her heart pounding. "You know Ibebe is much more to me than just a *servant*! How could you say such a thing, Niles?"

For once, Niles made no attempt to placate her. His features seemed set in stone. "Amanda, you must consider *yourself*—your health is at stake. Do you understand that you really have no choice?"

Andy clenched her teeth. She was furious with him. But she also understood what he was telling her. Niles was nothing if not an excellent physician. Finally, she gave a grudging nod. "I understand," she said, turning away from him.

"Good." He hesitated, then went on. "I'm going to leave specific instructions with Ibebe, as well as a schedule for your medicine. Promise me you'll cooperate."

Andy slowly turned to look at him. She could still sense his anger vibrating in the air between them. But she merely nodded her acquiescence.

"That's fine then," he said. "You rest now. I'll stop by later this evening." Without a smile, without touching her again, he turned to leave the room.

At the same time, Andy heard footsteps in the hallway. As she watched, Niles and Roman met at the open door of the bedroom.

It was Roman who spoke first. "Doctor," he acknowledged the other, his tone guarded but cordial.

Niles eyed him for a long moment with an openly hostile expression. Then, to Andy's dismay, he shouldered by Roman and, without saying a word, went on down the hall.

Andy saw the slight flush that crept over Roman's face at the deliberate rebuff. But when he turned toward her, he was smiling. He rapped lightly on the doorframe, then stepped into the room. "Are you being a difficult patient, by any chance?" He grinned at her as if he would have expected as much.

"This is utterly ridiculous," Andy muttered. She didn't know who she was angriest with—Niles or herself.

"Now, Andy," Magnus warned from his station by the bed, "Niles only wants what's best for you."

"But Niles doesn't always *know* what's best for me," Andy shot back. "Although I'm sure that fact would come as a huge surprise to *him*."

Her voice sounded thin and weak, even to her. The truth was that she hadn't the strength to argue with Niles's heavy-handed edicts any longer. She could feel herself sinking rapidly into a cloud of drowsiness, the two men's voices distilling to a kind of incoherent buzz in her head. She decided that for now she would get some more sleep.

She would deal with Niles later, when she was stronger.

Twenty-four

*I*n the dank, silent basement, he stood in front of the empty cell, studying it with increasing impatience.

Almost spacious, it was easily twice the size of any of the other cells, its furnishings new and selected with an eye to her comfort.

He scowled. Tonight he didn't feel quite so inclined to cater to her comfort. Tonight he felt more like punishing her.

He knotted his fist, pressing it hard against the palm of his other hand over and over again.

It was ready. Everything was in place, waiting for her.

The *cell* was ready, but *he* wasn't ready to bring her here. There was still more to do. No risks, he had promised himself from the beginning. No risks where *she* was concerned. It didn't matter about the others; they were merely laboratory animals. Expendable, all. But he would take no chances on *her* being mortally injured or maimed. Even now, though thoroughly annoyed with her, he couldn't conceive of placing her in any real danger.

None of it was her fault, after all. She had simply been taken in by the photographer's deceit. The man had seduced her with his foreign mannerisms, appealed to her with his affectation of grief and physical infirmity.

That sort of thing always worked with her. She never could resist lending a helping hand, even if it meant *losing* that hand in the process. She had always been easy prey for those who would take advantage.

She had called his name. . . .

But it wasn't *her* fault! She was weak, ill, under duress. The

187

photographer had charmed her, like the viper he was.

Why hadn't the fool left after the incident with the wagon? Instead, he had merely replaced the damaged equipment and cleaned up the rubble as if it had been no more than an unfortunate accident.

Apparently, it was going to take something more violent—an attack on his person—to roust him. But there was no time for that now. Perhaps later he could hire one of the mindless brutes off the docks to deal with St.Clare.

For now, the work must go on. Once the final steps in the experiment were completed, he could bring Amanda here. Her illness, while unexpected, was proving a boon. All he had to do was accelerate the timetable, bring the work to its completion a little sooner than he had originally envisioned.

In the meantime, it was serendipitous that she was abed. And he had every intention of making sure she stayed there; if necessary, he would keep her sedated.

All in all, he felt a certain satisfaction about the way things were working out. It wasn't that he wanted her to be ill, though she *had* brought it on herself. The reality was that her illness should simplify his plans, and at the same time make her less susceptible to the photographer's influence.

He rubbed his hands together, feeling pleased.

———

Jeeter lay unmoving on his pallet, pretending to be sound asleep. He was cold, but he tried not to shiver. It wouldn't do for The Man to know he was awake.

He squinted through one eye, watching. The room was dungeon-dark except for the lanterns suspended over the table where The Man was working.

Earlier, Jeeter had been afraid it would be his turn tonight. The Man had paced up and down the row of cells, looking in, stopping in front of some, passing by others. When he came to Jeeter's, he paused for a long time, then went on as Jeeter released his breath.

But tonight The Man was working on one of the Dead Ones. He had gone through the narrow door to the dark place and come out later, dragging one of them behind him.

Most times he worked on one of the young'uns—one that was

still alive. There was never a sound out of them. The Dead Ones couldn't holler, of course, and the ones that weren't dead yet were asleep.

Like now. The only noise in the room was the occasional scratching of a rat in the corner or The Man's slow, even breathing.

Jeeter saw the needle in The Man's hand, so he squeezed his eyes shut. He tried not to think about the needle. It was more important to think about what to do, how to escape. Maybe that would help him stay awake. If he went on sleeping all the time, he'd *never* get out of here.

Maybe he wouldn't, nohow. So far, he hadn't seen a single soul leaving, except for the ones The Man carried out in a blanket or a flour sack.

Still, Jeeter ought to make a plan. When he felt scared or worried, he'd make up a plan in his head and keep adding to it more and more, until he finally stopped thinking about whatever was bothering him. And he prayed. He prayed most all the time he was awake, prayed for one of them angels his Granny had told him about—a "guardian angel," she'd called it.

But what kind of plan could he make when he was chained to a stone wall? And how could even *God* hear him way down here under the ground?

Jeeter was getting sleepy again, but he tried to fight it. He thought about the dog he'd heard the other day. Maybe the dog would come back again. . . .

Jeeter decided that if he heard the dog again when The Man wasn't around, he'd make a lot of noise. If the dog heard him, he might go for help. Some dogs were real smart like that.

But what kind of noise could a kid make down here that would be heard on the outside, even by a dog? Besides, he didn't even know if the dog was real, or if he'd just imagined him.

Jeeter was cold and scared again. He bit his lip hard so he wouldn't cry. He *couldn't* cry, or The Man would hear him and give him more medicine to make him sleep. He had to stay awake so he could make his plan.

But if he went to sleep, he wouldn't be scared or hungry, at least for a while. His belly wouldn't hurt, and he would forget about being cold . . . just for a little while. . . .

Twenty-five

*A*ndy had never felt so guilty, so slothful—so *worthless*—in her life. Lying in bed for three entire days and nights, doing absolutely nothing but sleeping for hours on end, eating the food Ibebe prepared for her, taking the medicine Niles prescribed for her—she felt about as useful as a loaf of stale bread.

She couldn't even read a book or the newspaper. After one or two paragraphs either the words would begin to fade in and out, or she would fall asleep. Even worse, she often drifted off to sleep in the middle of a conversation.

Most of the time she felt numb, almost removed from herself and the room. She seemed to drift aimlessly through the hours, never quite knowing whether it was day or night . . . and not really caring.

At some vague level, she knew that people came regularly to look in on her—Niles, Magnus, Ibebe. And Roman. She had the sense that he came more frequently than the others, and in spite of the stupor that held her captive, she looked forward to his visits.

On Sunday afternoon, she was determined to be awake and alert when he arrived. She even propped herself up in bed to inspect her appearance in the vanity mirror across the room. As it turned out, that was a mistake. Even from this distance, she could see that her hair hung as limp as an old workhorse's tail, and she had no color whatsoever, except for the deep shadows that bruised her eyes. She still looked utterly exhausted, frumpy, and ill. As Magnus would say, she was enough to scare the birds out of the berry patch.

She tried to run a brush halfheartedly through her hair. But when even that proved to be too much of an effort, she sank back against the pillows, refusing to look in the mirror again.

In spite of her resolve, she fell asleep almost immediately.

————

Roman found her sleeping when he looked in on her that afternoon.

He stood in the open doorway for a moment, deliberating on whether or not to go in. The need to see how she was faring won out. Instructing Conor to return to their bedroom down the hall, he walked into Andy's room.

As he stood beside the bed, studying her, he thought how childlike she looked in her sleep. She lay with her fist balled under her chin, her full lower lip pursed into a little girl's pout. Her burnished auburn hair had slipped free of its combs, and one tangled wave fell over the side of her face.

Her breathing was heavy, but rhythmic, her skin ashen.

Still watching her, Roman seated himself carefully on the chair beside the bed. The concern that had been nagging at him since he had stopped by earlier in the day now returned in force. It had been three days since she had fallen ill, yet he detected no sign of improvement in her condition.

He had seen countless cases of extreme exhaustion in the camps, and to the best of his recollection, most of these had shown at least a slight improvement after two or three days of rest and proper care. Yet Andy appeared to be no stronger than when she'd first collapsed.

His eyes swept the room, kept dark in accordance with Rutherford's instructions—a custom routinely followed in most sickrooms, Roman knew, but one he privately questioned. Perhaps it made sense in the presence of fevers and certain other diseases, especially those affecting the eyesight, but he couldn't help but wonder if the cheerfulness of daylight might not work to advantage in cases like Andy's, where lethargy and weakness were a part of the problem.

Still, Rutherford was the physician, and the consensus seemed to be that he was an exceptional one. Since he claimed to care deeply for Andy, it was unlikely he'd be anything but conscientious in her treatment.

After another moment, Roman loosened his tie and stretched. The room was warm, for a fire was kept going at all times. However, there was absolutely no ventilation, another practice he wondered about. The air was close and almost oppressively stale. He wished he dared crack a window, but no doubt Ibebe was merely following Rutherford's instructions to the letter. It wasn't his place to interfere; more to the point, he wouldn't want to risk doing anything that might hinder Andy's recovery.

He glanced at the table beside the bed. It was cluttered with medicine bottles, a pitcher and a matching water tumbler, a cup still half full of what looked to be beef tea, some clean towels, and a basin of water. He picked up one of the bottles; it was unlabeled and empty, although it retained a faint sweetish odor he couldn't quite identify. Another bottle was marked, but with an illegible scrawl which he took to be Rutherford's. Its fairly bitter, chemical odor was reminiscent of some sort of tonic.

Andy's eyes came open slowly as he was replacing the bottle. "Ah, the sleeping princess awakens at last," Roman teased, smiling at her attempt to focus her eyes.

"Roman?" Her voice was dusty with sleep. She tried to moisten her lips, which Roman noticed were cracked, as if she had suffered a fever.

"Some water?" He rose and poured her a drink, then put an arm around her to support her while she took it. A twinge of dismay jabbed at him when he realized how thin her shoulders felt to his touch.

"How are you feeling?" he asked, taking the glass from her as she sank down onto the pillows.

She blinked heavily, as if it were an enormous effort just to keep her eyes open. "So tired," she murmured. "I don't understand why I'm still so tired."

Roman didn't either, but he tried to mask his concern. "You were exhausted entirely," he reminded her. "Another day or two will make a real difference, I expect."

She nodded, but he could see that either she wasn't convinced or else she wasn't alert enough to care. She seemed uncommonly weak and, if not altogether oblivious to his presence, at least indifferent to him. Had he not been so worried about her, he might have been hurt. As it was, he could think of little else but the fact that she seemed even weaker than she had that morning.

"Andy?"

Her eyes were closed, but she murmured that she'd heard.

"Andy, tell me . . . are you in any pain? Is there anything you want? Anything I can do for you?"

A faint smile curved her lips, and she moved a hand to reach out to him, but it dropped away. Her eyes remained closed, as if she were too fatigued to open them.

Roman felt a sick clenching in his stomach. Gently, he touched the hand that had reached for him. Even her hand was almost childlike, small and fine-boned, with delicate nails. He smiled a little at the thought that it wasn't the soft, pampered hand of idleness, but rather one marked with the evidence of hard work.

As if his touch had revived her, Andy opened her eyes. She looked at him with a vague smile. "Roman . . ."

Her voice was weak, and he leaned closer so he could hear.

"Miss Snow . . . and Miss Valentine . . . how are they?"

It was so like her to be concerned with everyone but herself, even now. He could almost be impatient for her. Had she given a bit more attention to herself, she might not be lying here, ill and utterly depleted.

"Much better," he told her. "Truly," he insisted at her skeptical expression. "You're not to worry about them."

She frowned. "But, Roman—you *will* look in on them regularly? You'll make sure they have everything they need?"

He shook his head at her. "Andy . . . Andy . . . do you ever allow a single thought of *yourself* into that lovely head?"

"You did it again," she said, smiling a little.

"What's that?"

She turned her face toward him, and instinctively he moved closer. Evidently, the combination of fatigue and medication had diminished her usual awkwardness with him. She seemed warmer, more at ease with him. He rather liked the change.

But he could see that already her eyes were growing heavy again, her smile slack. When she answered him, her voice was thick and the words slightly slurred. "You called me 'lovely.' "

Roman looked at her, his throat tightening. "So I did." He paused, aware that she was struggling with no success to stay awake. "And so you are," he said more quietly.

"I'm not . . ." Her words trailed off.

Roman squeezed her hand gently. For one irrational moment, he felt an intense desire to press his lips to her forehead. He actually leaned closer. "Andy . . ."

But her eyes were already shut, the feathery lashes lying still against the pallor of her cheeks.

He didn't leave, but continued to watch her as her breathing leveled to the deep, steady rhythm of a sound sleep. *Andy . . . Andy, ma girsha . . . what are you doing to my head . . . my heart?*

And what was he doing, still here, courting disaster for both of them? Yet, he *couldn't* leave, not until he was sure she would be all right, not until she was well along the road to recovery.

With her hand in his, he could feel her pulse, and was certain it was far too sluggish. Renewed worry mixed with an aching tenderness for her. He wished he knew something more of medicine, enough, at least, to know whether she was improving or growing weaker. He couldn't shake the feeling that she was failing almost before his eyes.

"What do you think you're doing?"

Roman instinctively dropped Andy's hand, jerking himself to his feet as Niles rushed at him.

The physician's eyes were ablaze with fury. Roman felt a guilty flush heat his face, like a schoolboy caught up to no good. His own reaction irked him. He had done nothing wrong, after all, in spite of the accusation in Rutherford's gaze.

Roman straightened, his hand gripping the cane. "She fell asleep while we were visiting," he explained, annoyed that the muted words sounded so lame, even to his ears. "But perhaps we should step out into the hall so as not to awaken her."

Rutherford's long face was all angles and sharpness, the mouth hard and thin. "Yes . . . I doubt she'd appreciate a voyeur in the room while she sleeps."

Roman followed him out the door. "It was nothing of the sort!" he shot back, once out of range of Andy's hearing. He fiercely resented the suggestion of impropriety, especially since he was fairly certain that Rutherford's outrage was based more on personal dislike than on any real suspicion of wrongdoing on Roman's part.

"Amanda is very ill," the physician said waspishly, his pinched nostrils flaring. "I thought it was understood that she's to have complete rest."

"She *is* resting," Roman pointed out, "though I fail to see that it's helping her a great deal." Deliberately, he closed the distance between himself and Rutherford, taking a somewhat perverse satisfaction in facing down the physician from the vantage point of his own considerable height.

From the open doorway of his bedroom down the hallway came a low growl. Roman looked to see the wolfhound moving forward in a crouch, head thrust out, ears pricked, obviously ready to spring. Noting Rutherford's sudden pallor, Roman took his time in ordering the dog down.

On command, the wolfhound slid slowly to the floor. But he made it clear that this was no retreat. With his paws thrust out in front of him, he fixed a piercing, unwavering stare on Niles Rutherford.

"What sort of medication are you prescribing for Andy?" Roman asked on impulse.

Rutherford's eyes were chips of ice. "I hardly think that's any of your business. Now, if you don't mind, I'd like you to leave so I can examine *Amanda*." His emphasis of her name was quite obviously deliberate, a slap at Roman.

Roman knew an almost blinding flash of resentment at the awareness that Rutherford held all the power, at least for the moment. He was Andy's physician, a close friend—almost a member of the family, it seemed. He had her absolute trust and confidence, as well as Magnus Doyle's—and no doubt that of the others in the household as well.

Roman, on the other hand, was the outsider. He was suspect, if not by Andy, certainly by everyone else. He had no medical knowledge, could do nothing at all for her—and, in the face of Rutherford's hostility, was not even to be granted a civil accounting of her condition.

"I asked that you leave." The words were little more than a hiss from that tight, thin mouth. "And as Amanda's physician, I'll have to insist that you not intrude upon her privacy again."

Roman looked at him, wondering if jealousy alone could possibly account for the hot blast of hatred emanating from the other man. Or was there something else, something he had missed before now, something more treacherous?

"I will leave, for now . . . *Doctor*," he said evenly. "But it seems to me it's for Andy to decide who visits her, and who does not."

He gave a mockery of a stiff little bow and turned toward his room.

He could feel Rutherford's venomous gaze on him all the way down the hall, burning a hole between his shoulder blades. The wolfhound padded along beside him, but turned once to growl a warning over his shoulder.

Roman felt very much like doing the same.

Twenty-six

*T*hroughout the evening, Roman was edgy, almost as fidgety as the wolfhound.

Like Conor, he tended to be restless when the wind was up, which it was tonight, wailing like a banshee on the prowl through the old trees around the house. He ate a light supper, helped Doyle carry in more wood, and then walked the dog for a time.

Still unable to settle anywhere, he did some prowling of his own about the house, eventually ending up in the music room. But even the piano held no release for him tonight. He gave it up after a few minutes when he realized that he was only annoying himself—and possibly the rest of the household—with his agitated thumping.

He went upstairs with the intention of looking in on Andy before Rutherford made his nightly call, but when he found her sleeping, he went on down the corridor. Miss Snow's door was closed, but Miss Valentine's was wide open, and when she spotted him in the doorway, she eagerly beckoned him inside.

"Does the wind make you restless, too, Mr. St.Clare? I declare, I'm about to jump out of my skin!"

She looked anything but jumpy, Roman thought with a smile. Propped up with a book in her enormous bed, bedecked in pink lace and ribbons, her silver-blond hair as tidy as if she'd just had it dressed, Miss Valentine looked more like a wee faerie queen holding court.

"Odd, isn't it?" he said, walking in. "Neither the wolfhound nor I can seem to settle anywhere this evening."

"Where *is* your wonderful dog? I enjoy him, you know. He's so well-mannered—a real gentleman."

Roman grinned; as always, he found the lady delightful. "Conor is in the wagon just now," he said. "He tends to pace when the wind is up. I thought it best that he get some of the restlessness out of his system before bringing him in for the night."

She insisted then that he take a chair so they could "have a nice chat," and Roman accepted without hesitation. Almost from the time of his arrival at the Manor, he had enjoyed several "nice chats" with the merry spinster. Not only was she a most comfortable person to be with, but Miss Christabel Valentine had proved to be an intriguing conversationalist in her own right. She had a fascination with the Orient and was surprisingly well-read on the Chinese and Japanese cultures, with a seemingly endless supply of colorful minutiae about the countries and their people.

They paused in their exchange at the sound of footsteps on the stairs.

"That would be Dr. Rutherford," said Miss Valentine. "He comes every night about this time, doesn't he?"

Roman nodded, deliberately fixing his eyes on his hands atop the cane. "Indeed," he said evenly. "He's very punctual."

"Well, of course, he and Andy have been friends forever, you know. It's only natural that he would be exceedingly conscientious in her care."

Again, Roman gave a nod, but said nothing more.

As if she hadn't noticed his silence, Miss Valentine went on. "How *is* Andy, Mr. St.Clare? I do so miss seeing her. She's been so wonderful to Harriet—Miss Snow—and me." She sighed. "It's hard to imagine her ill. All that vitality and enthusiasm."

"Actually, I'm quite concerned for her." Roman chose his words carefully. He was reluctant to alarm Miss Valentine, since she was only now recovering from her own bout of illness, but neither did he think he ought to understate Andy's condition. "In truth, I can't say I've seen any real improvement as yet."

"Oh, my. The poor child. I suppose Dr. Rutherford is practically beside himself, what with his being so devoted to her."

For some reason, her words stabbed Roman, goading him into a renewed flurry of resentment. "No doubt," he said tightly.

He hesitated, then looked at her steady on. "Will she marry him, do you think?" he asked bluntly.

Miss Valentine's eyes widened. Obviously he had surprised her with his directness. But as he watched, she quickly recovered. "Well," she said, one small hand picking daintily at the pastel coverlet, "perhaps I shouldn't be quite so frank, Mr. St.Clare, but I'm not at all convinced that she will."

Roman eyed her curiously. "Why is that?"

When she hesitated, he leaned forward, gripping the head of the cane until his knuckles were white. "Miss Valentine?"

She regarded him with a distinctly speculative look. Indeed, Roman almost thought he detected a trace of something akin to mischief in those china doll eyes.

"If you don't mind my asking, Mr. St.Clare—why are you so interested in Andy's feelings toward Dr. Rutherford?"

Yes, he decided, those rather remarkable eyes were definitely twinkling as she continued to study him with unconcealed curiosity. Roman shook his head, feeling more than a little foolish, yet suddenly wanting to confide in her. "Perhaps because I'm struggling with my *own* feelings . . . for Andy."

She smiled and nodded. "Yes," she said softly. "Somehow I thought so." For another few seconds she scrutinized him. Then, as if she were finally satisfied with what she saw, she went on. "It is my observation, Mr. St.Clare, that Andy isn't in love with Dr. Rutherford. Not that she isn't fond of him, of course," she quickly added. "But I believe more than anything else, she feels . . . sorry for him."

Surprised, Roman frowned and leaned forward on the chair. "Sorry for him? I don't understand."

Miss Valentine glanced away. She made no reply for another moment, but Roman could sense that she was weighing her thoughts. "The poor doctor is a rather tragic figure, I think. You probably don't know about his family . . . his earlier life?"

Roman shook his head.

"Apparently, he had an absolutely dreadful childhood. His father was a terrible man, they say—I never met him—but Andy and her father were acquainted with him. His poor wife—Dr. Rutherford's mother—was a somewhat pathetic creature, too, according to those who knew the family. She killed herself, you know, when Dr. Rutherford was still a child."

Roman considered this new information, surprised to find himself feeling something akin to compassion for Rutherford. Certainly he could identify with the man, although his own father had not been a "terrible" parent so much as an absent one. As for his mother, she had never been strong—neither physically nor emotionally. But in her own way, she had loved her children, even if that love had been fraught with inconsistencies.

Roman was soon completely caught up in what Miss Valentine had to say. "I suppose that accounts for his rather . . . grim nature," she continued, "although I should think that with all he's accomplished—he's a very *fine* physician, you know—and with Andy and her father befriending him as they have, he would have managed to put the past behind him by now."

Roman thought *grim* might be too generous a description of Rutherford's decidedly unpleasant personality. But then Miss Valentine could doubtless be far more sympathetic toward the man than he.

Because he was jealous?

Probably.

He might just as well admit it, at least to himself. He resented Niles Rutherford for any number of reasons—and every one of them had to do with Andy. Rutherford had a claim on her affection that went all the way back to their childhood. He had known her "forever." Andy trusted him absolutely, and even though Rutherford did seem excessively proprietary toward her, even domineering, she allowed it, at least to some extent.

There was also the fact that at this moment, the physician virtually held her life in his hands.

All things considered, a certain amount of jealousy might be natural, Roman thought glumly. Unhealthy, but natural, especially taking into account the way he had come to feel about Andy.

And how had *he come to feel about Andy?*

"You have had a most difficult time of things, too, Mr. St.Clare." Miss Valentine's unsolicited observation broke into his reverie. "Yet I can't see that your trials have embittered you."

Roman made no reply. He had never been comfortable when others referred to his "difficulties" or his "trials." His usual response was a silent shrug.

But he had learned that, despite Miss Valentine's soft voice and genteel manners, the diminutive spinster was surprisingly tenacious. "Is that because you are a man of faith, I wonder?" Without giving Roman time to reply, she went on. "It has always intrigued me," she said thoughtfully, "how some people seem to grow through their circumstances, while others decline or even go to pieces altogether."

Roman merely regarded her politely as she went on.

"Dr. Rutherford, for example, seems to have become almost reclusive, perhaps even somewhat caustic in nature. Yet when I listen to Andy speak of him, I sense he's also a man of great ambition. Certainly he's a diligent, conscientious physician—if perhaps a little driven. I can't help but wonder if his finer qualities, as well as those less admirable, weren't born of the pain and rejection he must have suffered as a child."

"Because of his parents, do you mean?" Unknowingly, she had struck a nerve in Roman. He knew what it was to be ignored, rejected, by the very persons who were supposed to love you most of all. He remembered the pain of his own emotional abandonment all too vividly.

Before tonight, he would not have thought he could feel anything remotely like compassion for Niles Rutherford. Even now, he sensed the ugly serpent of jealousy coiling around his feelings for the man. But deep within him a vein of pity had been tapped, and he knew he would no longer be able to think of Rutherford without at least some measure of understanding and empathy.

The fact remained, however, that while Niles Rutherford might be deserving of his pity, he was *not* Roman's primary concern.

He heard Miss Valentine give a long sigh and feared he might have tired her. When he stated as much, she waved away his concern. "Not at all! I'm enjoying myself immensely. Please stay, Mr. St. Clare. With both Harriet—Miss Snow—and myself being ill for so long a time . . . and now Andy . . . I've been starved for companionship, I must confess. No, I was simply thinking of Dr. Rutherford, poor man."

"You truly don't believe Andy will marry him, after all?"

A pained expression very much like regret passed over Miss Valentine's fine features, but it was quickly gone. In its place was a clear-eyed, direct gaze that seemed to search Roman's heart. "Why, Mr. St.Clare, what *I* believe really doesn't count for very much, does it?"

"I value your opinion," Roman said, utterly sincere.

"Well, let me see, where was I? Oh, yes—about Dr. Rutherford and his family. I think he has been severely wounded, not only by the rejection of his parents, but by that of the Islanders as well. Whether it's largely his imagination or in fact has some basis, he seems to believe that the people here consider him something of an outsider. Unacceptable. As I told you, his father was really an awful man, of a disgraceful reputation. And with his mother's insanity—"

Roman's head snapped up. "Rutherford's mother was insane?"

Miss Valentine hesitated for a second or two. "Well . . . Andy's father always thought so. For that matter, Mr. Fairchild believed *both* Dr. Rutherford's parents might have been mentally . . . ill." She clutched the coverlet with one hand. "I don't mean to be a gossip—but I'm sure most of this is common knowledge, which, of course, has only made things more difficult for poor Dr. Rutherford."

Again, she paused to regard Roman with a thoughtful gaze. "Sad to say, I do sense a great deal of bitterness in the young doctor. Yet, in you—" she hesitated, then went on—"I see evidence that your grief and struggles have served to strengthen you. As I said before, your faith no doubt accounts for the difference. Faith and perseverance."

"Perseverance?"

She nodded. "The Chinese have a wonderful symbol for what I think of as 'godly perseverance.' Their language is pictorial, you know." She smiled, her fondness for the subject evident. "The Chinese picture for perseverance includes a knife and a heart. It means 'to continue with a knife in your heart.' "

She had glanced away for a moment in her reflections, but now turned back to Roman. "I believe that is what you've managed to do, Mr. St.Clare—you have continued on, with a knife in your heart."

She meant it as a compliment, Roman knew. But her assessment was painfully accurate. At times, that was exactly how he felt—as though he lived his life with a knife in his heart.

He realized then that she was again speaking of Andy and Rutherford. "If she *were* to marry the doctor," she said, her hand fluttering on the coverlet, "I fear it would be for the wrong reasons."

Roman watched her, sensing that she was of a mind to say more, yet uncertain as to whether she should.

"Perhaps, Mr. St.Clare," she said, now looking down at her hands rather than at Roman, "if Andy's future is really of interest to you, you might consider discussing her plans with *her*. I, for one, would hate to see all that wonderful zest for life and unselfish love for others confined to a lonely old house or a marriage founded on pity."

She looked up, locking her gaze with his, and Roman found himself squirming a little at the unmistakable look of challenge in those clear blue eyes.

—————— *Twenty-seven* ——————

*L*ong after midnight the man completed the most recent entry in the back of the journal. He wrote by the light of the oil lamp on the desk, its flame flickering crazily in the draft.

The old house above him shuddered in the night wind. The balmy temperatures of the past two days had been dealt a death blow by a fast-moving front, bringing in an unseasonable thunderstorm with dangerous lightning.

In spite of the storm, the basement laboratory was quiet, the subjects sleeping, the noise of the raging elements muffled by the thick stone walls deep underground. A deceptively still, calm atmosphere permeated the dark room.

But Niles Rutherford felt none of the stillness of his surroundings, only a churning anxiety and frustration. Nothing was happening as planned. All at once, at the most crucial stage of his work, everything seemed to be going wrong.

The last level of the experiment was at a standstill, and as yet he had been unable to identify the problem. He was going to have to run the entire last cycle again, isolating each unit for reevaluation. It was time he hadn't planned on, time he didn't want to spend.

And now there was another body to dispose of. He had hoped he was done with all that. It was getting more difficult to find new specimens and bury the old, now that the police had finally decided to concentrate on their investigation—an investigation that, up until recently, had been haphazard at best.

As if he didn't already have enough on his mind, it seemed that the skulking foreign photographer was becoming suspicious, even challenging him about Amanda's treatment! St.Clare couldn't possibly know anything for certain. Still, it was conceivable that the delay in Amanda's recovery had made him skeptical.

Both this afternoon and again tonight, St.Clare had been lurking near her room, watching through those hooded eyes of his, almost inviting an objection. Even after their confrontation earlier in the day, he had shown up again tonight, shoving that arrogant nose of his into matters that were none of his affair whatsoever.

The man was so annoyingly sly, snooping about the Manor as if he had a right to be there, all solemn concern and hawk-eyed watchfulness. Asking questions. Nosing around. Meddling into everyone else's business.

He tightened his grasp on the pen, brooding. The house above him groaned, seized by a bellow of thunder. One of the subjects whimpered in his sleep, then quieted.

Rutherford glanced up, then turned back to the journal. He had decreased the laudanum for Amanda tonight, would decrease it still more in the morning. Just for a day or so. That would mislead St.Clare, make him believe her condition was improving.

He added a note about the laudanum in the journal, then replaced the pen in its holder and closed the pages.

He still had much to do tonight. He would get rid of the body later. For now, it was crucial that the final stages be completed before bringing Amanda here. Nothing could be allowed to remain undone. Everything must be ready, waiting for her, so that she could not possibly misunderstand the scope of his achievement or what it would eventually mean to both of them.

Of course, once she had undergone the treatment, she would give him no argument. She would never argue with him again, but be completely amenable to his every wish, his every word and deed.

He leaned back in the chair and smiled, a musing smile of anticipation and longing. He was so close. Finally, he was going to see the fruits of his labor, the rewards of his genius. He would have everything he had ever dreamed of—the respect and recognition of his peers, the rewards of success . . . and Amanda.

Amanda as he had always wanted her to be—his adoring wife, ultimately destined for him, unquestioningly devoted to him.

And utterly dependent on him.

By one o'clock in the morning, Roman still had not closed his eyes. He had brought the wolfhound inside hours earlier, and for a time they had paced the bedroom together, eyeing each other uneasily with every new barrage of thunder, every blade of lightning that slashed through the room.

From his pallet beside the bed, the wolfhound now lay regarding him with an almost smug expression; he had exhausted his restiveness, a feat Roman had not yet accomplished.

Whatever was nagging at him, keeping him from sleep, it was more than the wind rattling the glass in the drafty old windows, more than the thunder rolling down from the hills.

It was Andy, of course.

Andy . . . and Niles Rutherford.

Andy . . . and what she had come to mean to him.

After encountering Rutherford again tonight in Andy's room, Roman had secluded himself, forcing himself to confront his feelings about the girl.

Whether or not he cared for her was no longer a question. He had never been one for lying to himself very successfully, at least not for any length of time. Long before tonight, he had recognized the fact that Andy meant more to him than he would have liked to admit, certainly more than he had ever intended. Although he still wasn't ready to analyze his feelings too closely, he confessed that he cared for her in a way he had cared for no other woman, save Kathleen.

Andy called forth feelings from deep inside himself that he had thought buried forever. Feelings of tenderness . . . warmth . . . the desire to protect and to cherish.

More and more he felt a need to simply be near her. He had come to crave her presence, look for her, long for her. Of late, he had felt compelled to come closer to her, to touch her. Not intimately . . . not yet. Just . . . touch her hair, her cheek . . . clasp her hand. Walk arm in arm with her. Laugh with her. Be with her.

She gladdened his heart, lightened his somber world. She made him feel alive again, almost made him feel young again, even made him believe he might eventually love again.

He had tried *not* to believe it was happening, had tried to suffocate the very thought—the idea of loving her. He had tried so hard not to care for her. But somehow, when he wasn't watching, when he had least expected it, she had come sweeping into his life, smiling her way into his heart, bringing him something incredibly beautiful and bright. Now he wasn't sure he could give her up.

And yet a part of him, a still-grieving, anguished, angry part of him fiercely resisted the idea of loving anyone else but Kathleen, denied even the possibility that he *could* love anyone else.

Still, it was Kathleen herself who had practically ordered him to love again, he mused, should the time ever come that they were too soon parted. Had that been merely a lighthearted gesture, a teasing remark made in the safe harbor of their early love? Surely, neither of them could have foreseen the tragedy of her death . . . or the annihilating pain and grief it would wield.

And there was the other business. Not even Kathleen, as close as he had been to her, had guessed the dark secret that at times had all but consumed him—the secret that had only grown more threatening after her death.

He had nothing to offer Andy. There was no place inside him for love, no energy to bring to it, no strength to nurture it, no right even to open the door to it.

Not yet. Perhaps later.

But Andy was *now*, not later. Andy might not wait. He was fairly certain Niles Rutherford would not wait.

He shuddered, at the same time wondered why the very thought of Andy with Rutherford struck him somehow as obscene. Something deep within him tightened into a sick knot at the idea of Rutherford's possessing her.

Possessing her . . .

He stopped his pacing, stood unmoving, scarcely breathing. That's exactly what Rutherford would do if he somehow convinced Andy to marry him. He would *possess* her. Without quite knowing how he knew this, Roman was suddenly dead certain that Rutherford's love for Andy was a killing thing, a destroyer. If he married her, he would *own* her. And eventually he would destroy her.

A cannonade of thunder shook the house, and at that instant every part of Roman's being seemed to rise up in outrage at the thought of Andy wed to Rutherford. Yet what could he do about it? The time was all wrong. It was too soon . . . too soon.

Why couldn't he have met her later, when he had successfully dealt with the struggles of his own soul? When he had exorcised his own demons? Why now, when he was little more than a dried husk of a man still struggling to deal with his own pain?

Why?

Going to his knees was not easy for him. It never had been, even before the injury to his leg. Before, it had been his pride that ached with the effort, now it was his leg, his spine. Yet, even though the physical discomfort was almost more than he could bear, he found himself on his knees more these days than he ever had before Gettysburg.

He went to his knees now, at first with the idea of soliciting some divine wisdom, some answer to the questions burning a hole in his heart. He had not expected the old, familiar anguish to wash over him again—the sense of loss and desolation, the intolerable loneliness and emptiness of a life bereft of love. When it struck him, he nearly hauled himself to his feet in protest.

But on the heels of the agonizing memory of the past came the soft reminder that he had moved past his yesterdays, that he had survived one loss, and that his emptiness had been filled with mercy and a measure of peace—at least where Kathleen was concerned.

He knew now, however, that there was much more—that he must at last confront the darkness, the unknown, that lay buried beneath the more obvious wounds inflicted by Kathleen's passing. Now it sprang at him from the depths of his soul like some primeval beast. He could no longer ignore its presence, evade its horror.

It was this near nameless dread for which he must beseech his Savior. Dare he voice it—even to the One who knew him better than he knew himself? For once it was acknowledged, there would be no turning back. He must either receive absolution . . . or he must admit that there was no hope for him—that he was a soul condemned to a lonely exile, if not in the next life, at least in this one.

For he could never inflict upon another human being—especially not on one so young and vulnerable as Andy—the heavy burden of his torment: *Was he capable—in the darkest caverns of his mind—of some unspeakable savagery?* Was he doomed to inherit the winds of his parents' legacy—the mental instability, even madness—that, compounded by the grim images of war, had left him with periods of blackness so deep he was unaware of where he had been, of what had transpired while he was "away"?

Could he—and the thought staggered him until he sank down, prostrating himself on the bare floor—could he have been responsible for the taking of a life? And not one life only, but many? *O merciful Father . . . help me . . . please, Lord, help me . . .*

Oh, yes, he could understand a man like Niles Rutherford, a man shadowed by his past. Why shouldn't he? He could *be* that man!

In that moment of searching clarity, Roman felt that in the matter of Amanda Fairchild, he must step aside once and for all. Even Rutherford, with all his faults, had something to offer her—the ability, the medical expertise, to help Andy in this crisis.

This loathsome darkness within himself must be expunged by the light of Truth. He must know the identity of the murderer . . . even if that murderer turned out to be himself! If so—and he almost retched at the thought—he would surrender to the authorities at once, lest he harm yet another innocent person.

He lay for endless moments. Or was it hours? He lay waiting, praying, listening. The night seemed to dim and fade away, the bedroom receded from his sight. He was alone, alone with his own tortured soul, waiting for either the condemnation . . . or the absolution . . . of his Lord.

Sometime later . . . much later, it seemed . . . he felt a stirring within him, almost as if infinitely gentle hands had shaken him awake. He thought someone whispered his name, then took his hand and sat beside him. Again came the quiet Voice, warming his soul, strengthening his heart, healing his spirit.

He sensed the nearness of a holy Presence and was overcome with a terrible awareness of his unworthiness, his fear, the darkness that had long dwelt in the recesses of his soul.

No answers came. No blaze of light dispelled his questions.

No thundering shout rent the silence of the night. But that still, quiet Voice spoke to his spirit, and Roman recognized the whisper of Divine Love.

Afterward, he slept. He dreamed of walking without limping and running without falling. He dreamed of lifting a slight young girl in strong arms and carrying her from a black, airless cavern where unspeakable things of the darkness lurked. He ran for her, and for himself, fleeing with her in his arms into a vast, sun-touched field where there were no shadows, no secret things . . . only clear, running streams and wildflowers growing tall and free.

Kathleen was there, with them. He neither saw her nor heard her voice, but she was there, in his dream. He felt her smile, sensed her presence, knew himself and the girl he was carrying in his arms to be completely enfolded in her love—Kathleen's love—while at the same time a greater Love draped them, the three of them together, in the veil of eternity.

The dream ended, but Roman went on sleeping. He awakened once in the night, only long enough to realize the storm had ended. He knew as well that the storm in his soul had ebbed. He felt peace he had not known since Kathleen had first led him to the Lord, an almost forgotten freedom of the spirit.

After a moment he felt a shadow move across that newly found peace as he recalled the still unanswered questions, the dark unknown with which he had lived for so long a time. But there was something else now. Like a flickering glow from a distant candle, it beckoned to him. Waiting at the end of what might well be a long and arduous road to the Truth was the light of hope. However far removed, however faint, it was there.

And so was Andy.

Twenty-eight

*T*he temperature plummeted, the rain changing to snow early the next morning. At first it was little more than icy puffs, swirling playfully against the windows. But by midmorning, the dancing flakes had turned wild and frantic, launched like invading battalions by a winter storm that now came roaring across the Island with a vengeance.

Roman stood at the study window, trying to see past the snow lashing the glass. The ground was already covered, the trees groaning and arching in the wind.

The snow was coming down as hard as he had ever seen it. Its ferocity called to mind the prediction Magnus Doyle had made at breakfast that morning, that a full-scale blizzard would soon be upon them.

It would have been beautiful to watch, had it not been for the mixed throng of potential problems it brought with it. Instead of the snug feeling of contentment he would normally have enjoyed during a snowstorm, Roman was growing increasingly uneasy at the idea of being snowbound in such a remote, isolated place, especially with three ailing women under roof. Miss Valentine was almost fully recovered, of course, and Miss Snow much improved. But Andy still had a long way to go—although Ibebe had brought the welcome news only minutes ago that, overnight, there had been a noticeable change for the better.

Roman was eager to see for himself, but not until Rutherford had gone. This wasn't the morning for another confrontation with the rancorous physician. He had something far more pressing on his mind—something that had occurred to him, born of his prayer vigil, in the wee small hours of the morning. A plan so daring, so radical that he was breathless with the audacity of it. There would be risk—he was sure of it—but he thought the risk would be worthwhile; that is, if things turned out as he hoped.

Relief swept over him like a wave when he walked into Andy's room later that morning and found her actually sitting up in bed, smiling at him.

The draperies had been opened, filling the room with light for the first time in days. In the natural light of day, made more stark by the snow blowing past the windows, she still looked exceedingly pale and thin. But considering her frightfully ill appearance of the past few days, she definitely appeared to be on the mend.

Roman stopped at the foot of the bed. "Well, now, this is more like it. I hope you're feeling as well as you look."

"You can't imagine! I feel ever so much better. I'm sure I'll be completely well soon."

Roman lifted a dubious brow at that. "Certainly, you're on the mend. But I should hope you won't push yourself just yet."

"I won't," she said, pulling a frown. "I *had* hoped to at least get up and walk around a little this afternoon, but Niles says I can't. He insists that I stay in bed for a few more days." She paused. "But that's simply impossible."

"If you're worried about the work, we're managing."

She rolled her eyes.

"Not to take anything away from your legendary efficiency," Roman said dryly, "but everything *is* under control. Can't you just pamper yourself a bit without this oppressive guilt?"

"I don't *need* pampering. I need to get out of this bed, and that's exactly what I plan to do, if not right away, then certainly before the end of the week!"

Roman clucked his tongue at her. "Sure, and you'd not be defying our Dr. Rutherford, would you? Such temerity."

She waved a hand. "Oh, feathers! If Niles had his way, he'd keep me locked in a cage . . . 'for my own good,' of course. I'll get up when I'm good and ready, whatever Niles says. And as for your sudden attack of Irish brogue, I think you could do with some brushing up. Uncle Magnus would be glad to help, I imagine."

Her flippant remark about Rutherford's possessiveness troubled Roman more than it should have. On the other hand, he was encouraged to see that her old feistiness had returned. "I can see we're going to have to find something to amuse you for the next few days," he said. "Perhaps you'll be happy to hear that your two special ladies down the hall will more than likely be up to visiting soon. At least, Miss Valentine will. She's feeling quite well again, I believe."

Andy beamed. "Niles told me. He said Miss Snow is recuperating nicely, too. I've missed them so much! I can't wait to see them." She paused, then asked him, rather slyly, "Is everything *really* under control?"

"They miss *you* as well," he said, ignoring her question. "Miss Valentine was just saying so last evening." Roman walked around to the window. "Can you see the snow? It's really been coming down. I think it's tapering off a bit now, though."

"You've no idea how frustrating this is for me, being cooped up in here when we're having our first real storm of the winter! Why, Miss Valentine and I won't get to build our snowman!"

He turned to look at her, smiling a little at the returning light in her eyes. "You and Miss Valentine are great builders of snowmen, are you?"

"Every winter! During the first snow, we always have the largest and the most handsome snowman on the Island."

He couldn't suppress a grin at her ingenuousness. "Handsome, too? I expect Miss Valentine supplies that particular touch?"

Andy nodded. "She's the artist, not I. She always manages to come up with a dashing hat of some sort and a perfectly elegant pipe."

"Souvenirs from her many admirers, no doubt."

Her smile faded. "I don't think Miss Valentine has ever had very many admirers."

"But she's absolutely charming," Roman said, surprised. "I should think the gentlemen callers would be breaking down the doors to court her, even now."

"She wouldn't allow it, I'm afraid," Andy said with a sigh. "She had only one great love, and he died during a missionary journey to the Orient before they could be married. There's never been anyone else for her since."

Roman knew an acute and heavy sadness at her words. That

perfectly delightful little woman, spending her life alone by
choice, with no husband, no family—it seemed so incredibly
tragic. "I'm so sorry to hear that," he said softly. "She's a grand
lady. I like her immensely."

Andy's features cleared a little. "And she's quite taken with
you as well," she told him, an impish glint appearing in her eyes.
"She thinks you're a 'splendid man.' "

"Does she now?" Roman shot her a roguish grin and shoved
his hands into his pockets. This whole conversation wasn't going
at all as he'd planned. He'd intended only to inquire after Andy's
health, then go about the business of the chores. But he was having the time of his life. Surely it wouldn't hurt anything to do
what he could to bolster her spirits while she was recovering.
"Well," he went on determinedly, "maiden ladies do tend to fall
at my feet, I confess. Is it the game leg, do you think?"

————

Andy suspected that it wasn't only *maiden* ladies who fell at
Roman's feet, though she wondered if he'd even notice the thud.

"I think it might be the wolfhound," she drawled. "He's a terrible charmer, you know."

He arched an eyebrow. "You *are* feeling better, aren't you? Are
you absolutely certain you're not Irish, *ma girsha*?" he said, dipping his head a little and eyeing her closely. "Irish women tend
to have tongues like knives."

"As a matter of self-preservation, no doubt." Andy narrowed
her eyes. "What does that mean . . . 'my geersha'?"

"*Ma girsha*?" He shrugged. "Nothing insulting, I promise. It
simply means 'my girl.' " He paused for just a beat, his eyes
searching hers. "It's a kind of endearment, actually."

Andy blinked. "I see."

"Do you?" He moved even closer to the bed.

Roman seated himself in the chair beside the bed, and for a
moment just sat there, watching her. "Do you object . . . to my
using the term, I mean?"

Andy struggled to answer. "Well . . . no, I . . . only a little surprised, perhaps."

She avoided looking at him, instead stared straight ahead at
the open doorway.

After another second or two, she glanced at him. He was all

seriousness now, his gray eyes intense as they met her gaze.

Flustered but unable to look away from him, Andy stayed very still.

"Andy . . . I want to talk with you," he said evenly, "if you're truly feeling well enough, that is."

He waited, watching her. Andy finally nodded, still unable to speak.

"There's something I must ask you first," he went on, his features even more solemn now. "We *are* friends, aren't we?"

Puzzled, Andy nodded. "Of course, we are."

"Andy, are you in love with Niles Rutherford?"

Andy stared at him in astonishment, not comprehending. But he was obviously intent upon a reply. "Why . . . why would you ask me such a thing?" she choked out.

"I'll explain," he said. "But please answer me first."

Andy's mind went spinning as the unpleasant realization dawned that the only response she could make . . . the only *truthful* response . . . was one she didn't want to face herself, much less voice to Roman.

"Please," he prompted quietly. "I'm not meaning to pry. I have a reason for asking."

Andy's eyes lingered on his face for another moment. "No," she said in a strangled voice, finally looking away. "I'm not in love with Niles. Though there are times when I hate it that I'm not."

Andy heard him draw a deep breath, which almost sounded like a sigh of relief. She turned back to him, her heart leaping to her throat when she saw how close his face was to hers. For the first time since he'd come into the room this morning, she realized how drawn he looked, how tired. His handsome features appeared almost gaunt, and his thick dark hair was slightly tousled. Not for the first time, she sensed that he had not slept well, if at all.

"Roman? Why did you ask me that? About Niles?"

Again he took a long breath. "I had to know," he said. "There's something I want to say to you . . . something more I want to ask you . . . but first I had to know about Rutherford." He stopped, his eyes searching her face as if he would reach her deepest thoughts, her heart.

"You've become very special to me, you see." His eyes

watched her closely as he spoke, his voice quiet and exceedingly gentle. "Even though the idea frankly terrifies me, I find that I care for you . . . very deeply."

Stunned, Andy could only stare at him in amazement. Something deep inside her, at the very center of her being, exploded into a blinding sunburst. A wild exultation roared through her, swelling and soaring up in her, until she thought she would surely shout with this new, uncontainable joy.

As she forced herself to think, to try and quiet the frenzied racing of her heart, she caught a sense of uncertainty in him, a kind of restraint. Andy suddenly knew that there was something he wasn't saying, knew in fact that what he *wasn't* saying might be of even more consequence than what he *had* said.

Reality came rushing in upon her like a cold, windswept rain. She felt an unexpected spike of dread. A moment ago she had been so sure her life was about to change. Something in his eyes, the tenderness of his words, had more than hinted of that change. She didn't want to lose that exquisite moment. But she had to know everything, not just what she wanted to hear.

With a great effort then, she managed a semblance of self-control. "I'm not sure I understand what you're trying to tell me, Roman."

He looked at her, and there was a reluctance in his eyes that told Andy her intuition had been right. There was more, and in all likelihood it was going to disappoint her.

Still he hesitated, and the slight trembling of his hand on the bed beside her, combined with the obvious uncertainty in his eyes, gave Andy the boldness to encourage him. She hesitated another second, then lightly touched his hand. "I think you had better tell me everything, Roman."

Something flickered in his eyes. Relief, perhaps, that she wanted the truth. And the same tender affection—for she recognized that it *was* affection—that had been there, looking out at her, from the time he'd first begun to speak.

"All right, now," she prompted, hoping she sounded more assured than she felt, "why don't you just tell me what this is all about?"

———

How? Roman wondered miserably. How did one go about

proposing to a girl—a woman—like Andy, what amounted almost to a marriage of convenience? And especially given the complications . . . and secrets . . . with which he lived. She was sure to be offended, perhaps even furious with him, that he would think her receptive to such an outrageous idea.

What on earth had ever possessed him to raise the subject in the first place? She would think him a lunatic, if not an outright scoundrel. She wasn't a girl—a *woman*, he reminded himself irritably—who had to stoop to such an arrangement. Certainly, she would have marriage offers aplenty before she settled on one man.

A man like Rutherford, for example?

Of course! And wasn't that what this was all about? While he had questioned the idea over and over again, he had finally been persuaded that the plan was of the Lord. For while it was true that he didn't quite trust himself—certainly, he trusted Niles Rutherford far less!

And he did care for Andy, after all, cared for her deeply. In fact, he wasn't sure he was willing to face just how *much* he cared. Still—and here his resolve faltered—he knew himself well enough to know that he was incapable of being a proper husband to Andy . . . to any woman . . . at this particular time in his life. If he were ever to love again, he would want it to be as he had loved Kathleen—wholeheartedly, a total commitment of his heart, his very life. But as yet, he was too empty for that kind of love, too self-consumed, too driven. Driven to find Kathleen's killer, to finally see justice done in her behalf.

Why, then, had he felt such an overpowering conviction as recently as last night that this was the direction his Lord would have him take? He felt himself vacillating and knew a moment of sheer exasperation with his own uncertainties.

Andy was watching him with an expression akin to fear, and Roman felt like the worst kind of wretch for leading her this far, only to turn away.

Yet wouldn't he feel even more the blackguard, insulting her with a proposition that no intelligent young woman would entertain for a moment?

Suddenly, what had seemed right and perfectly logical in the dead of night now, in the light of day, seemed almost absurd. He looked at her, found her studying him, waiting.

"Andy, forgive me. I may have been wrong . . . but I was so certain last night . . ." He knew he was making no sense at all. She was staring at him with a troubled frown, as if she feared he had fallen ill or was about to be taken by a seizure.

"Roman—what *are* you talking about?"

He had come this far, blurted out his idiotic prelude to an even more ludicrous proposal. It wasn't fair to simply walk off and leave her without some sort of an explanation, no matter how it might alter her opinion of him.

"You need to hear my idea in its entirety," he said, leaning toward her. "Otherwise you'll think me quite mad." He paused. "You may anyway. Just . . . give me the opportunity to explain it in detail before you slap my foolish face."

Her eyes widened. "Well," she said dryly, "you certainly have my full attention. I can't think—"

She stopped, both of them turning toward the open door at the sound of heavy footsteps on the stairs. Roman felt a crushing disappointment, almost instantly followed by relief.

After a second, they turned to each other and exchanged humorless smiles.

"Uncle Magnus," Andy said. "Coming for his morning visit."

"Yes," Roman replied. "I expect you're right."

"Roman—"

"Later today," he said quickly, as if anticipating her question. "I promise you, I'll explain later."

"Indeed you will," Andy warned him, lowering her voice. "I intend to see to it."

Twenty-nine

*N*iles hadn't planned to administer the sedative until tomorrow. That would have given him several more hours to work through the last stage of the experiment again, just to be sure he'd found the problem in its entirety. But with the snow setting in as it had in the last hour, he was reluctant to wait any longer. If the storm lasted through the night, by tomorrow the road might be impassable.

He would bring Amanda to the laboratory tonight.

He still had two patients he needed to see before leaving the hospital, but he had already decided that he wouldn't go to the clinic this evening. As soon as he was finished here, he would go directly to the Manor.

As he started down the corridor, he remembered that he would need the ambulance to transport her from the Manor to the laboratory. He stopped, whipped around, and headed back toward the children's ward, where he had left Meece. He was going to need him, too.

Roman had every intention of returning to Andy's room by midafternoon, but those intentions were thwarted when Magnus Doyle asked, in a somewhat apologetic tone of voice for the big, gruff Irishman, if Roman would be up to helping plow the lane from the Manor to the road.

"It'll take two of us to run the horses and the plow. I thought we'd best start on it now while the snow has slackened some," he explained. "If this storm turns back on us, we'll at least be caught up with it." He frowned, his concern evident. "With all the sickness in the house, it wouldn't do to have the lane blocked for any length of time."

Three hours later, both the lane and the path from the house to the barn were cleared to Doyle's satisfaction. As they trooped back to the house, Roman found himself a little amused at the thought of Andy fretting so about the uncle exerting himself. Doyle was puffing a little, it was true, but the man clearly had the stamina of a logger. If he would shed a few pounds, Roman thought wryly, he would probably shame most fellows half his age when it came to simple endurance.

They shook the snow from their coats and left their boots at the kitchen threshold before entering, then went to the woodstove to warm their hands. Ibebe, who was in the kitchen turning out bread, wiped her hands on her apron and poured each of them a cup of hot coffee.

"You two gentlemen look as though you're near frozen," she admonished, setting a plate of fresh cookies onto the table with the coffee.

"Thank you, Ibebe," Roman said with a smile. He sat down across the table from Doyle, thawing his fingers over the steaming cup. "I've wondered about Ibebe's name," he said to Doyle after the housekeeper had left the kitchen. "Andy said she's from the West Indies?"

Doyle nodded. "She was born in the Barbados, that's right. In truth, her family was freed while they were still in the Islands, but then got themselves captured by one of the slavers. They ended up on a plantation in Mississippi while they were still tykes." His smile was grim as he went on. "Apparently, the first English she learned was her name—the owner's little girl named her 'Baby.' What with her Island speech, if anyone asked her name . . ."

He shrugged, and Roman finished for him, smiling. "It would have sounded as if she were saying, 'I *Be-Be.'*"

"Exactly," said Doyle. "She and her brother eventually ran off. Came north with the help of some Quakers. But the name stuck."

They sat drinking their coffee in silence for a time. "You still believe we haven't seen the worst of the storm?" Roman finally said.

224

Doyle sipped his coffee and nodded. His white hair was still damp from the snow. "It's not done with us yet, I'm thinking. We'd best bring in more wood before nightfall."

Roman liked the brawny Irishman and knew a certain mild pleasure that Doyle was finally treating him like less of an outsider, even asking for his help. But how long would the cease-fire last once the man learned of his intentions toward Andy?

He was fairly sure he already knew the answer to that one. *If he keeps a musket in the house, I'd best have a care*, he thought, not entirely in jest. In Doyle's view, Rutherford was the only man for Andy.

Roman could only hope that in this case, at least, Andy and the uncle might not see things eye to eye.

———

Andy was browsing through some of the previous days' newspapers, pleased that for the first time since her collapse, she was actually able to read more than a few lines without falling asleep.

When Niles walked in late in the afternoon, some hours before he usually called, she had to mask her disappointment. She had been expecting Roman. Ever since he'd left her late that morning, she had been anticipating his return with an unseemly curiosity and growing impatience.

With an effort, she now turned her attention to Niles. Her first thought was that he looked positively haggard, even more worn and strained than he had that morning. Too many hours and too little sleep again, no doubt. With a stab of sympathy, she told herself she could at least act as if she were glad to see him.

"Back so soon?" she asked with a forced smile. "I wasn't expecting you yet."

He didn't return her smile but brusquely set his medicine case on the bed. "I left the hospital early," he said, lifting her hand to check her pulse. "The snow is starting up again, and I was concerned that I might have trouble getting through later this evening. I wanted to get you started on a new tonic yet today."

He was bending over her to listen to her heart now, and Andy tensed involuntarily. Niles was never anything but professional in his examinations, but the truth was she didn't like his hands on her. She couldn't help wishing that her physician were not also a friend. And, worse still, a suitor.

"What kind of new tonic?" she questioned. "I thought you said I was much better."

He straightened, and Andy was careful not to expel her sigh of relief all at once.

"You *are* better, but a long way from being completely well, Amanda. You surely know that without my telling you."

Obviously, his mood had not improved since his morning visit. He had been cranky then, too. When Andy questioned his churlishness, he had brushed her off with a muttered apology, his excuse being a difficult patient at the hospital and his concern over the storm.

His apology had seemed less than wholehearted, but Andy had said nothing more. Now, seeing the same dark hint of impatience in his eyes, she again kept her silence as he went on to explain, in a rather annoyed tone, she thought, the reason for the tonic. "It's primarily a restorative," he said, measuring the liquid into a small vial and holding it out to her. "To build the blood and restore the proper mineral and chemical balance to the bodily systems."

Andy tasted the tonic, and, finding it foul, made a face before tossing it down all at once. "Nasty stuff! How often do I have to take it?"

"Twice a day," he said, taking the vial from her and returning it and the bottle to his medical case. "Not for long," he added. "A few days at most."

Abruptly, his mood seemed to lighten a little. "Just remember that this will help to speed your recuperation, and you won't mind the bad taste so much."

Andy nodded and sighed, feeling a little tired for the first time that afternoon. "Whatever you say, Doctor."

He smiled at her. "That's better. I *do* know what I'm doing, you know."

"Will you stay for dinner?" she asked, barely able to stifle a huge yawn.

"I'm not sure I should, with this snow." He smoothed his tie and his cuffs. "Though if it would please you, I'll stay, dear."

Andy felt a peculiar heaviness settling over her, from her head down over her body. "Of course, Niles," she managed to say, though her tongue suddenly felt as leaden as her limbs.

"Then I shall," he said. "I'll have Ibebe bring up a tray for both of us."

It occurred to Andy that she'd actually rather have a long nap than dinner with Niles, but she didn't want to hurt his feelings. So she attempted a smile as he went on talking. But her mouth now felt frozen in place, and she seemed to have lost her voice.

Niles's words echoed strangely in her head, as if he were speaking to her from deep within a well. Andy wanted to tell him she couldn't quite make out what he was saying, but before she could force out even a word, a soft black veil fell over her, shutting out the sight of Niles and the late afternoon gloom of the bedroom.

By the time they had brought in the wood and Roman had cleaned himself up and donned dry clothes, it was going on to five—and he still hadn't made it back to Andy's room.

Finally, he left Conor in the bedroom—no point in having to compete with the wolfhound for her attention, after all—and started off down the corridor. To his great frustration, as he approached Andy's door, he heard her voice and Rutherford's coming from within. He stopped just before he reached the entrance, considering whether to turn back or to go ahead and beard the beast.

For his own part, he would just as soon face Rutherford's hostility now as at some later time. He and the acerbic physician had already acknowledged the strain between them, had more or less proceeded to draw their respective lines in the sand, facing off.

But for Andy's sake, he supposed the better way was retreat. He had seen her consternation during the few times he and Rutherford had given rein to their dislike for each other, and he knew an open confrontation would surely distress her. The last thing he wanted to do was cause her any further upset.

But he *must* talk with her this evening. He had to complete what he'd begun earlier today, or she would think him the worst sort of fool. Not to mention the possibility that every hour he delayed might well be bringing her that much closer to a permanent alliance with Rutherford.

At the moment, however, there seemed to be nothing for it but to wait, no matter how long it took. With bitter regret, he turned and started back toward his own room.

As the evening wore on, Roman's entire body was drawn tight with tension. A throbbing headache had begun a slow crawl up the back of his skull, and his insides felt tangled like so many lengths of rope.

Dinner was a fiasco. Somehow he managed to carry on polite conversation with Doyle, but he was far too agitated, too distracted, to be much aware of what they discussed.

To his dismay, Rutherford had stayed the evening. He was upstairs now, having dinner with Andy in her room, Ibebe explained. Outside, the snow was coming down thick and heavy, the wind howling and rattling the windows. The storm seemed to have settled in for the night. Roman stormed inwardly as he faced the possibility that Rutherford might have to stay over because of the weather. Certainly, that would crush any hopes he had of continuing his talk with Andy later.

It was with great relief that he looked up during his dessert to see Rutherford in the doorway, his coat slung over his arm. His relief was short-lived, however, as the physician came hurrying into the dining room.

He had seen Rutherford irritated, even angry, but he had never before caught him unnerved or distraught. So when the physician entered the room practically at a run, his hair falling over his forehead, his eyes slightly wild, Roman was astonished. The man was obviously in a state; perspiration beaded his face, and he emanated anxiety and distress.

He ignored Roman entirely, directing his words to Doyle. "I'm going for the ambulance! Amanda has taken a turn for the worse—she must be hospitalized as soon as possible."

Roman's heart gave a sudden lurch. He clutched the napkin in his hand until pain shot up through his wrist.

Magnus Doyle went white. "Surely not, Niles. Why, she seemed so well today, almost herself again!"

"I know. I felt optimistic about her improvement, too." Rutherford lifted a hand to sweep his hair back in place, still not acknowledging Roman's presence. "I'm not sure what's happened. She's had some sort of seizure, I'm afraid. She's virtually in a stupor."

"You mean she's unconscious?" Doyle balled his fist on top of the table, staring at Rutherford with incredulity.

The other nodded. "Her heartbeat is wildly irregular. She appeared to faint, and I couldn't bring her around." He paused. "I don't think I ought to try to move her alone. I'm going to go ahead to the hospital and send the ambulance wagon back for her."

Overlooking what he sensed to be deliberate rudeness on the physician's part, Roman offered, "I'll help you. We can take her in my wagon—it's sturdy enough."

Rutherford shot him a look of contempt. "I think not. You're in no condition to be of help," he said, darting a meaningful glance at Roman's bad leg. "I need the ambulance and the assistance of a trained professional, nothing less."

Infuriated by the man's arrogance, Roman held his tongue only with the greatest of effort.

Rutherford had already turned back to Magnus Doyle. "I'm leaving at once. I'd like Ibebe to stay with Amanda until I return. Tell her to dress her in warm clothing."

Roman felt as if he might be sick at any moment. As for Doyle, he appeared stricken where he sat.

"Must you, Niles?" said the older man, his voice trembling. "The lass hates the place so. And to take her out in this wretched weather . . . can't you treat her here at home just as well?"

A spark of impatience leaped to Rutherford's eyes. "Mr. Doyle, I wouldn't hospitalize her if I didn't think it was absolutely urgent. But quite frankly, I don't know what I'm dealing with here. I'm afraid something is going on with her heart, but I don't know what. I must run some tests before I can administer any sort of treatment." He stopped. "You know I'll do everything I possibly can for Amanda, sir," he said, his tone calming a little. "If I think it necessary, I'll summon one of the heart men from Manhattan. She'll have the very finest care, I promise you."

Doyle nodded and wiped a hand down his face. "Aye, I know you'll do your best for her, lad."

No longer able to contain himself, Roman scraped the chair back from the table and jerked himself to his feet. "If you don't mind my asking," he said to Rutherford, his voice more strident than he'd intended, "what could possibly account for such a sudden change in her condition? She was obviously on the mend this morning."

Rutherford turned a withering look on him. The implication of that icy stare was unmistakable: what right had Roman, an outsider, to question *him* about Andy's condition?

Rutherford's antagonism, however, was the least of Roman's concerns at the moment. Without another word, he tossed his napkin on the table and strode from the room, moving as quickly as he could with the help of the cane.

"If you have any thought of going to Amanda's room, sir, I'll have to ask you not to."

The caustic admonition stabbed Roman in the back, but he never hesitated. All the way upstairs his pulse pounded with rising fear and bewilderment, as he silently prayed that he hadn't waited too long to tell Andy what was in his heart.

───── *Thirty* ─────

*I*t was close on eight when Rutherford and his associate, Dr. Meece, arrived with the ambulance. According to Rutherford, the regular ambulance driver had been unable to make it to the hospital because of the storm, so Meece had volunteered to help.

It seemed to Roman that if the roads were all that bad, they were taking an excessive risk in trying to move Andy. His stomach knotted at the thought of her being stranded in the midst of such a snowstorm, in her condition.

But he kept his silence as he stood by the door with Magnus Doyle, watching Rutherford and his associate carry Andy from the house on a hospital litter. He wanted to call them back, indeed might have attempted to do just that had it not been for the fact that Andy did seem in urgent need of immediate treatment.

He had stayed with her while waiting for the ambulance, but, just as Rutherford had said, she remained completely unresponsive, as if she were in some sort of stupor. So it was with sick resignation that he held the door and watched the two men carry her from the house.

As they passed, he caught the eye of Rutherford's associate for an instant. Again, Roman puzzled at the slightly furtive look about the round-faced, bespectacled Dr. Meece. Despite the blast of cold wind that came hurtling through the open door, the young physician was perspiring heavily. He also seemed to suffer from an intermittent dry cough that appeared to be more a nervous habit than related to any sort of catarrh.

Doyle brought them to a halt by reaching out one large, trembling hand to touch Andy's blanketed shoulder. Roman ached to do the same. In that instant, he looked hard at Meece. The young physician flushed, then quickly glanced away.

After they were gone, Roman closed the door and turned to Magnus Doyle. If he had ever questioned the irascible Irishman's affection for Andy, the terrible combination of fear and helplessness he saw in the man's face at that moment would have laid any doubts to rest.

Doyle's eyes were red-rimmed, his voice tremulous as he said, "Well, then, it seems we can only wait. Wait and pray."

By now, the headache that had begun earlier was sinking its pincers full force into Roman's skull, and he longed to retreat into the quiet of his bedroom. But the despair in Doyle's face touched him so that on impulse he reached out to clasp the man's shoulder. "Would you like me to speak with Miss Valentine and Miss Snow, to explain things?"

The older man's face relaxed a little. "Ah, I'd be most grateful if you would. If you don't mind, that is. I'd not want to show my concern to the ladies. They do dote on the lass, you know. I might carry it off with Miss Snow, but that Miss Valentine . . . well, she has a way of making a man say more than he intended."

As he watched those strong, pugnacious features melt at the mention of Miss Valentine's name, Roman suddenly became aware of something he hadn't seen until that moment. So that was the way of it, then. The romantic in him silently applauded Doyle's good taste.

"I'll be glad to talk with the ladies," he said. Still, he hesitated, aware that Doyle was regarding him as if he had something more to say.

"You have feelings for our Andy, don't you, man?"

The question came like a thunderbolt, catching Roman completely by surprise, especially since he knew Doyle's words had been more statement than question.

He fumbled for a judicious reply, but Doyle gave him no time. "Aye, I've seen. These eyes may not be quite so keen as they once were, but only a blind man could miss the look in *yours* when the lass walks into a room."

Roman felt like a green *gorsoon*, caught in some mischief by the schoolmaster. Yet Doyle's bold appraisal held no reproach, only a curious understanding and perhaps a certain sadness.

"I care about Andy, I won't deny it," Roman said. "I'm sorry if that offends you, but I promise you I do hold her in the very highest esteem."

If he sounded as pompous to Magnus Doyle as he sounded to himself, the older man didn't seem to notice. Doyle simply nodded very slowly, putting one hand to the back of his neck in a gesture of extreme weariness. "I'd always hoped it would be Niles for her," he said, glancing about the entryway. "Those two, they've been friends forever, you know."

"Mr. Doyle—"

The other went on as if he hadn't heard, his expression changing subtly as he turned back to Roman. "She's fond of the lad, of course—as she might favor a brother. She has ever had this huge sorrow about Niles—a great pity for the boy. But then the lass has always been a soft one for the pain of others. Even a wounded bird will bring her to tears."

Roman thought Magnus Doyle was close to weeping himself, but he said nothing as the man went on.

"The truth is," Doyle said sadly, "that I'm not so sure she thinks of Niles the way he thinks of her. Now I'll not deny that's something of a disappointment to me, for the lad does cherish her. And he would seem to have a grand future before him. Andy would lack for nothing, 'tis certain."

Roman wasn't so sure of that, but in fairness to Rutherford, he knew his doubts, to some extent at least, were bred of rivalry.

Doyle gave a heavy sigh. At the moment, the man looked much older than his years. "Well, then, it's her choice and not mine, that's so. Seeing her so sick and helpless these past few days, it's made me realize that the lass has had no easy life, after all. Nor has she ever asked for anything more. But I have prayed for better things for her, and that's the truth. More than this"— he made a sweeping gesture with his hand—"though she does have a deep fondness for the old place. And certainly more than living out her days here, with no one for company but a sour old geezer like myself and two lonely ladies."

He looked at Roman, and the tired blue eyes suddenly narrowed. "What exactly are your intentions toward her, man? And don't be fencing with me."

Had Roman's own heart not been so heavy, he might have

smiled at this fierce display of paternal protectiveness. "I assure you my intentions are entirely honorable," he said, feeling inordinately awkward.

Doyle crossed his arms over his burly chest. "Sure, and they had better be. No man will treat the lass lightly while I have breath in my body."

Roman didn't doubt that for a minute. Uncertain as to just how much to tell Doyle, especially since he hadn't even spoken with *Andy* as yet, he hesitated.

Doyle's iron jaw jutted forward still more. "I have concerns about you, as you might expect."

That was hardly new information to Roman, but he said nothing.

"For one thing, you're years older than the lass."

Roman's head jerked up, but just as quickly he swallowed his words and gave a shrug of agreement. "True."

"You've lost a wife." Doyle's voice gentled slightly. "And a child as well, I'm told."

Again Roman gave an affirmative nod. "I expect I know the rest, Mr. Doyle," he said tightly. "Physically, I'm not altogether fit . . . yet. And you know little about me, almost nothing of my family and the like—"

"Aye, there are shadows on your past, man," Doyle interrupted. "A darkness. Whereas our Andy was made for the sunlight." He paused. "She deserves only the best."

"I couldn't agree more," Roman said quietly. "And you've every right to be concerned. But you said it yourself . . . it *is* her choice, after all. Not yours . . . and not mine."

Doyle's gaze was hard and steady, and Roman thought he could catch a glimpse of what a formidable opponent the man must have been in his younger years.

For that matter, he amended, Magnus Doyle would undoubtedly *still* be a formidable opponent.

"If you hurt her—" Doyle rocked back on his heels, glaring at Roman. He didn't finish whatever it was he meant to say.

He didn't have to. Roman took his meaning only too clearly.

———

Roman didn't sleep until nearly dawn. He paced the bedroom, his spirit as agitated as the wind hammering at the walls. He had

laid a fire, kept it going throughout the night against the relentless draft blowing through the room, but it did nothing to ease
the chill deep inside him.

From his pallet by the bed, the wolfhound watched him with
wary eyes, as if waiting for this disturbing behavior to either
cease or result in some unpleasant action. Occasionally, Roman
spoke to him in a quiet voice, to reassure him that all was well.

He wished he could convince himself. He felt as if things were
anything but well. Odd, that even in the dead of night, Andy's
absence would make such a difference in the house. It was as if
a great yawning emptiness had opened and swallowed the light
from the place, leaving little more than a cold, ominous silence.

A particularly vicious shriek of wind rattled the windows. The
wolfhound tensed and raised his head as if expecting the gale to
burst through the room. Roman stopped his pacing to pull the
drapery aside and look out. The window was glazed with ice, and
he could see nothing but the reflection of the firelight behind
him.

Branches from one of the towering old trees closest to the
house scratched at the window and against the walls, like a desperate old woman seeking entrance from the storm. Somewhere
on the other side of the house, a loose shutter banged against the
stone in angry protest.

There in the midst of the wild, forbidding night, Roman,
scarcely aware of the warm firelight or the hovering wolfhound,
knew the beginning of an acute and all-pervasive depression.
Something in the forlorn wail of the wind outside, the cold, en-
compassing silence inside this house so newly bereft of Andy's
light, the fire behind him hissing and snapping to stay alive,
caught him up in a comfortless, immobilizing despondency.

He had passed this way before, had in fact walked through
this same bleak, barren wasteland many times in the past, and
so was all too familiar with its pain and oppressive gloom . . . and
with the darkness that was sure to follow. In some arcane, incomprehensible way, his spirit was swept up in a vast, universal
anguish that filled him with a terrible sense of loss and a crushing despair, not only for himself and those he loved, but for all
humanity. He did not understand it, had never been able to name
either its cause or its source . . . it simply happened, and when it

came, it threatened to rip apart his very soul with hopelessness and dread.

A thought of Andy, her brightness strangely veiled and almost entirely concealed by something dark and malevolent, seized him and would not let him go. His spirit groaned within him, and he actually moaned aloud.

In that instant he felt himself sinking into the familiar cavern of blackness, and he knew no more. . . .

———

When it was over, as always, he was left shivering, drained, and badly disoriented. Panic gripped him, shaking him with the sickening awareness that it had happened . . . *again*. His gaze swept his surroundings. The wolfhound was on his feet, watching him with a steady but guarded gaze, as if he knew all about this strange behavior and, although accustomed to it, still found it unsettling.

Roman forced himself to breathe deeply and evenly as he checked his clothing, his shoes, the carpet. At last satisfied that he had not gone outdoors, he stepped quietly into the hallway, half expecting to see something different, something amiss, about the house itself.

Taking a candle and leaving the wolfhound in the bedroom, he made his way downstairs, shambling through the halls, his heart racing as he sought something, anything, that might help him to remember. Finally, after traipsing the lower floor and finding everything apparently in order, he went back to his room.

Upon entering, he felt engulfed by a numbing fatigue, so wrung out and depleted he wanted nothing more than to collapse onto the bed and sleep for hours. At the same time, he knew that sleep would not come so easily. It never did.

He knew what *would* come. And it did . . . the glacial fear, the self-suspicion, the questions, and at last the feverish, despairing cry of his heart that he had not, in his descent into darkness, brought harm to another . . . or to the name of his Lord.

So this was to be the way of it then? A glimmer of light, then a plunge into the abyss, until he was brought again to his knees. It occurred to him that some of the ancients had trod this path before him—Jeremiah, Solomon, even David the poet-king. . . .

Finally, he began to pray, at first a prayer that over the years had become a kind of despairing litany—a desperate cry for deliverance, for himself . . . and now for Andy . . . and at last, without knowing why, for a sea of unknown faces that seemed bowed beneath some deadly, malignant cloud of evil.

Thirty-one

When he first saw the men carry her into the room, Jeeter thought he must be dreaming. Dreaming of his angel. She was all covered up with white sheets, so he couldn't see anything but her face and her hair. Her eyes were closed, and she looked awful peaked, but he could see that she was sweet-faced and pretty enough to be an angel, for sure. Young, too. Not a little girl, but still a little woman who wasn't very old, from the looks of her.

After listening to the men talk back and forth as they put her in the big cell next to his, Jeeter began to realize that he wasn't dreaming, after all.

He could see them better now. It was The Man, and he looked and sounded mad. The other one was The Assistant. That one had red hair and eyeglasses and sometimes came to help, mostly late at night. Jeeter thought The Assistant sounded scared, or if not scared, at least awful jittery.

Jeeter felt jittery, too, but this was a *good* kind of nervous, not a *scary* kind. Because if he wasn't dreaming, then what he was seeing must be real. His guardian angel had come, after all, just like Granny had said she would!

He got so worked up he could hardly keep still. But he knew he had to be quiet so the men wouldn't notice him. He clamped his teeth together, clenched his fists as tight as he could, and bunched up on his belly, waiting for the men to go away.

They were outside her cell now, standing in the middle of the room. The red-haired one was talking in a shaky, high voice. "I can't do this anymore! You've gone too far this time! *This is wrong, all wrong!*"

239

"Oh, stop your sniveling! I'm losing my patience with you. You seem to have forgotten that I concealed nothing from you when you came into the project. Back then you thought it was— ah, what were your exact words now?—a 'brilliant idea,' 'a magnificent endeavor.' I explained in detail what might be involved right from the beginning. Now you're telling me I've gone too *far*?"

The Man wasn't shouting, but Jeeter could tell he was mad. *Real* mad. That one was always quiet, no matter what was going on in his head. In fact, it sometimes seemed that the quieter The Man got, the madder he was. He could be downright mean, without ever raising his voice, Jeeter knew.

Somehow his quietness scared Jeeter more than if The Man had just hollered or hauled off and caned him one. He was a bad man, all right. A *real* bad man. . . .

"You never told me you were going to murder anyone! *Children*, Rutherford! You never once told me you were going to kill *children*!"

The redheaded Assistant sure wasn't being quiet, Jeeter noticed. He was screeching almost like a woman.

"*Negro* children, Hayden. Laboratory animals and thereby completely disposable . . . for the sake of the project, of course. New York's gutters are filled with the filthy little rats. We're doing a service by exterminating them." The Man sounded as if he was getting all riled up for a minute, but it didn't last. Jeeter heard him clang something down on the table, then go on talking in that same scary, quiet voice. "What's gotten into you after all this time? I didn't know you were so sympathetic toward the coloreds. What was it you used to say? Oh, yes, I believe it was Cromwell you used to quote: 'Nits make lice.' "

Jeeter wasn't too sure what those *nits* were but thought they couldn't be no account if they had anything to do with lice.

"They're still children! And the girl—how can you possibly consider doing this to her? I thought you wanted to *marry* her!"

"Don't you dare question me about Amanda! Don't you dare! I know exactly what I'm doing, and it's in her best interests, you can be sure of it!"

"Oh, dear heaven . . . you're going to use the serum on her, aren't you? You're going to inject her!" The redheaded man sounded like he might choke to death any minute. "Rutherford, no! You can't! Why, she'll be little more than a vegetable—"

"She will be my *wife*—and none of your concern whatever. Now, get out of here. I'm tired of listening to your whining!"

"Rutherford, please—this is atrocious! You can't do this—"

Out of the corner of his eye, Jeeter saw The Man knot his fist and ram it into the palm of his other hand. He'd seen that gesture before and knew what it meant—The Man was about as mad as he ever got. He'd be shaking most any minute now.

"I said *get out!* And while you're at it, you can find yourself a new position. I won't be needing your questionable *services* any longer!"

Jeeter watched, biting his lip, as the redheaded man backed away, his eyes wide and afraid. Then he turned and practically ran out the door.

Jeeter looked at The Man, saw him grind his fist into his other hand, watched his eyes turn hot and mean, and wished with all his heart he was right behind the redheaded man.

————

At first, Andy thought it must be an hallucination, although the pain hammering at her temples seemed all too real. She felt herself fading in and out of consciousness, in and out of the dark, cold room, which smelled of coal ash and chemicals and mold.

Once she thought she heard voices, but they died away before she could identify them. The pain was something remembered . . . the same merciless throbbing, only more severe, that she had had during the first few days of her collapse, when she had gone without sleep and without food, taking in nothing but the medication Niles had given her.

Niles . . .

"Niles?"

His name fell from her lips. She was sure she had whispered it, but it seemed to rip through her skull, and she whimpered at the pain.

"I'm here, Amanda. Just lie still, dear. Everything is going to be all right now. You just rest."

Niles was here. Relief flooded Andy, and even the throbbing in her head seemed to subside a little. Still, her eyes wouldn't focus. She could see nothing but Niles bending over her, his face glowing eerily in the flickering light.

"Where am I, Niles?"

"In the hospital, dear. You had a relapse, but you're going to be just fine. You're not to worry about a thing. Just relax and go back to sleep."

"The hospital? Oh, Niles . . . I didn't want to come to the hospital. . . ."

Andy moved her head from side to side, testing the extent of the pain. The hammering increased, in her ears, at her temples, wreathing her forehead, dimming her vision. Niles blurred and swayed. She had to struggle to keep her eyes open.

Niles bent closer, pressed his hand over her arm. He was holding something. . . .

A needle . . .

"Niles? What's that?" Her head swam. Nausea rose up in her throat and she fought to choke it down.

"Nothing, dear . . . just some medicine to help you sleep. Lie very still now."

Andy felt something prick her arm . . . like a mild beesting. Dizziness whirled around her. Her mouth felt swollen, her tongue bloated. Niles went on holding her arm, murmuring encouragements that she couldn't quite hear.

Andy tried to force her eyes open wider, but Niles was fading. Another wave of nausea surged up in her, then ebbed.

Then everything went still and black. She was floating on dark water, drifting . . . then sinking. . . .

Niles Rutherford sat hunched over his journal, writing what would be, if not the final entry, at least one of the last.

The basement was utterly still. The remaining subject was sound asleep, as was Amanda. She would not wake up for hours, nor would the boy.

Tomorrow would see the culmination of years of study and grueling work and sacrifice. Endless hours of going without sleep, spending his earnings on equipment and chemicals, working late into the predawn hours, alone, unnoticed and unaided.

Except for Meece's paltry contributions—helping to transport and dispose of the subjects, and an occasional late-night assist at the surgical table—he had done it all alone. The ideas, the ef-

fort, the genius that had produced this unprecedented break-
through that would soon explode upon the scientific community
. . . and the world . . . had been entirely his doing. His alone.

Consequently, the benefits—the long overdue recognition of
his genius, the rewards of his labor, and, of course, Andy's absolute devotion from this time on—it would all be his at last. He
would be obliged to share the accolades, the financial dividends
with no one else. Except for Amanda, of course. He would share
everything with her, once they were married.

And that would be soon. Just as soon as her . . . *recovery* . . .
was complete, they would have the ceremony—small and private. No more delays. After tomorrow she would do whatever he
wanted, *whenever* he wanted. She would be what she was meant
to be, what she was born to be—his wife, his helpmate. Finally,
she would love him, completely and without reservation. She
would build a life with him, serve him, obey him—she would
never want anything or anyone *except* him.

Once he had injected the serum, he would never again have
to grovel to her or that lout Doyle, never again be in the position
of *begging* for her affection. Soon after they were married, he
would publish his findings. For the first time, civilization would
have a foolproof treatment for insanity; even the worst lunatics
would be treatable. Manageable.

And all would point to him as the one responsible.

He looked up from the journal page to glance across the room
at Amanda. Her breathing was even and blissfully peaceful, her
face lovely and placid in the candlelight.

He turned back, scratched the final notes for the day's events,
then closed the journal with a deep sigh of satisfaction and anticipation.

Thirty-two

*B*y midmorning it was still snowing, though not so furiously as the day before. But the wind was up, shrieking like a crazed beast as it battered the house and bent the trees. Standing at the dining room window, brooding, Roman could see nothing but white. Even the woods were lost behind the frothy clouds of snow.

"You'd best have a bite of breakfast," Magnus Doyle urged from his place at the table. Even though the older man had taken nothing himself, this was the third or fourth time he had insisted Roman should eat.

"Perhaps later," Roman said, distracted by the frenzied scene outside and the increasing sense of urgency that had been driving him throughout the morning. "I'm going to the hospital," he said, turning to address the uncle.

An odd mingling of emotions passed across the other's face. Relief, perhaps, at the prospect of firsthand information about Andy; but something else, something very much like concern. Roman thought he must be mistaken, for surely Doyle would not be concerned for *him*.

But apparently he was. "As much as I'd like word of the lass," Doyle said, frowning, "I wouldn't recommend you try to make it to the hospital in such a storm. It's the beginning of a blizzard that's upon us. You might not get through."

Roman had considered the weather, of course, but he had seen worse. "I can get through. But the sooner I go, the better."

Doyle still looked skeptical. "If you're determined to try, then I'll go with you."

Roman didn't like the idea of subjecting the older man to the elements. There was also something else to consider. "I understand your wanting to go," he said. "But are you sure that's wise? What if we *should* have trouble on the way and end up stranded? We'd be leaving three women alone here, in the storm. I believe I'd feel more comfortable if you stayed . . . for their sakes."

Doyle's mouth curled downward, but finally he nodded. "I expect you're right. You're certain you can make it?"

A muscle flexed in Roman's jaw. "I'll make it."

———————

In spite of the almost blinding whiteness blanketing the ground and swirling relentlessly about them, it could have been evening for all the natural light the morning offered. The road to the hospital cut through an eerie kind of twilight, slate-gray and ominous in its intensity.

Roman had wound two woolen scarves tightly about his head and throat. Still, the wind-driven snow slashed his skin and tore at his eyes, making it an agony to keep his face turned to the road so he could guide his mount.

Pulling along beside the bay, Conor gave a disgruntled chuff, occasionally glancing at Roman as if to say he'd have thought any master of *his* would have had more sense than to venture out in such a squall. "Don't be quarrelsome, chum," Roman told him. "You had your chance to stay snug inside at the Manor. I offered, you know."

The wolfhound regarded him with unmistakable disdain, then turned his attention back to their surroundings. In places, the drifts were so high he was fairly hopping over the snow, rather than trudging through it. Even so, the way wasn't quite so treacherous as Roman had feared it might be. There was evidence that a horse-drawn plow had come this way earlier, clearing at least two or three miles of the distance.

Still, it had taken him close on two hours to reach the hospital in Stapleton. By the time he tethered the bay and began to trudge up the snow-drifted walkway, he was fairly rigid with the cold, his face painfully raw in spite of his attempts to keep it covered.

Much larger than the clinic, the hospital was of stone with a columned portico and two flanking wings that looked several years newer than the original structure. The lower steps were piled so high with snow that Roman had to dig with his cane just to find them.

He left Conor beneath the shelter of the roof, ordering him to stay. Inside, he wiped his boots as much as possible on the floor mat, shook the snow from his coat, then approached the desk, where a stern-faced matron sat eyeing him with displeasure.

A tired-looking physician in a rumpled laboratory coat hurried by, passing between the matron and Roman, ignoring both. In the hallway to the right of the desk, two nurses stood conferring, so similar in appearance they might have been sisters.

The woman at the desk was lean and gray, with a face like carved granite and eyes like sharpened flint. Roman would warrant that every young nurse in the hospital—and probably a good number of the physicians—were mortally terrified of her.

No doubt the fierce glare she fixed on him was meant to intimidate him as well. But he returned her severe frown with what he hoped was a thawing smile. "Good morning," he ventured cheerfully. "I wonder if I might inquire about Miss Fairchild." He would, he decided, take one step at a time; it might be well to ease into a request for visitation.

"Visitors are restricted to early evening." The voice matched the eyes—hard and abrasive.

"Ah, I see," Roman said, still trying for a cordial tone. "I didn't realize. I'm new to the area, you see."

Her dour expression discouraged any further attempt at pleasantry, but Roman wasn't about to retreat so easily. "Would it be a terrible imposition just to inquire after her, do you think?"

The matron expelled an exaggerated long breath. "Who is her physician?"

"Dr. Rutherford," Roman said quickly, still trying to pierce her armor with a smile. "Dr. Niles Rutherford."

Did he imagine the slight tightening of her mouth as she ran her finger, line by line, down the ledger on the desk?

She glanced up. "What was the name again?"

"Fairchild," Roman said. "Miss Amanda Fairchild."

Once more she scanned the record book, then looked up to study Roman with a suspicious frown. "I have no listing of any patient by that name."

Taken aback, Roman stared at her blankly. "She was admitted last evening. Rather late."

The matron emphasized her impatience with a brisk tap of her fingers on the desk. But again she traced the entries in front of her, flipping the page forward, then back. "No," she said, the word ringing with finality. "We have no such patient. Perhaps you want St. Vincent's."

Roman shook his head. He was positive that Doyle had specified Doctors' Hospital in Stapleton. "Dr. Rutherford *does* have privileges here?"

The narrow mouth thinned even more. "He does."

Roman tried to think. The unease that had been lurking at the threshold of his mind began to squeeze in on him. Then he remembered Rutherford's associate. "What about Dr. Meece? Could Miss Fairchild have been admitted as *his* patient?"

The matron's scowl grew darker. "Hardly. Dr. Meece is no longer a staff physician at this hospital."

"But I thought he was Dr. Rutherford's associate," Roman said, gripping the cane more tightly.

"His *assistant*," she corrected. "But Dr. Meece no longer attends here."

Something flickered in the woman's eyes that made Roman think she knew more—a delicious secret to be had for the coaxing.

"I'm afraid I don't understand," he said, hoping she would see fit to enlighten him.

The hatchet jaw relaxed a little. "Dr. Meece had his privileges revoked some time ago," she said, divulging this bit of information with obvious relish.

"Revoked—" Roman stared at her, baffled. "But why?"

"It's not my place to discuss the situation."

In spite of the virtuous smirk that accompanied her words, Roman had the feeling she could be convinced otherwise. He leaned toward her, one hand pressed palm-down on the desk. He took care to conceal his growing anxiety, instead assumed a look of shared confidence. "This could be awfully important," he said, his voice deliberately low and urgent. "Naturally, anything you might choose to tell me will go no further than the two of us."

She looked from side to side, then edged forward on her chair, bringing her face closer to Roman's. "Patients were complaining," she said with a certain smugness. "I never did think he was much of a doctor, even though Dr. Rutherford seemed to approve of him."

Something tightened in Roman's throat. A chill seized him—a chill that had nothing to do with the storm outside. Forcing himself to reveal no more than a gossipy interest, he lifted his brows in a conspiratorial look. "Incompetent, was he?"

Again the matron darted a furtive glance about the waiting room. "Let's just say he wasn't as conscientious as he ought to have been."

"In diagnosis or in treatment?"

Her mouth pursed. "Both, from what I'm told. No one can understand why Dr. Rutherford has kept him on. He's so demanding of everyone else, you'd think he would have let Meece go long before now. But they still keep offices together at the clinic."

She shrugged as if to say there was no accounting for the strangeness of some.

Roman straightened. "Competent as you are," he said carefully, "I suppose there's no chance Miss Fairchild could have been admitted without your knowing it? Could someone else have been at the desk in your absence, for example?"

She shook her head. "Miss Arens, who assists with admissions in the evenings, has been ill with influenza for several days, and I've been working overtime in her absence. I was here last evening until nearly ten." Her indignant expression made it clear that she felt put upon, that his last insinuation chafed her unnecessarily.

Roman's mind raced as he groped for an explanation. "Is there any chance Miss Fairchild might have been taken to the clinic, instead of being admitted here?"

"Oh, goodness no! Not if you're talking about the Miss Fairchild who owns Graystone Manor, and I don't know of any other. Only the indigent and mentally ill are treated at the clinic. Dr. Rutherford would never take a patient of high standing there."

"But I saw children there," Roman said, more to himself.

"*Negro* children, perhaps, and orphans." She gave a faint sniff of disapproval. "They get plenty of those over there. But *decent* folks"—she shook her head emphatically—"do not go to that place for treatment. No, indeed."

The apprehension that had been creeping steadily closer during the last few minutes now leaped at Roman, hitting him hard. His hand trembled on the cane as he hurriedly murmured his thanks to the matron for her assistance. Then, his head hammering with confusion and fear, he swung around and made for the door.

He charged blindly into the storm, stumbling through the snow, fighting down a rising wave of panic as he went. *If Andy wasn't here or at the clinic, then where was she? Where had Rutherford taken her?*

Where was she?

The darkness was fading, the haze in Andy's mind thinning, letting the light seep in like a sharp blade. She tried to focus her eyes, but the light flashed crazily in front of her, piercing her brain. She eased a hand out beside her and touched a soft, plump mattress. The odor of chemicals—biting, caustic, compounded of mold and soot—assailed her. She found that she was covered with a fleecy blanket, but felt cold and stiff in spite of it.

She turned in an effort to take in her surroundings. Her head swam, and the throbbing at the base of her skull shot upward like lightning. Andy moaned and squeezed her eyes shut for a moment. When she finally opened them again, she saw that she was lying on a comfortable bed, made up with fresh linens. At first, she thought she was in her own bedroom, but as her head cleared, she saw the stone wall to the left, wet and dark green with lichen. The opposite wall was constructed of rough wood. The entire area resembled a large coal bin. A coal bin with a door of iron bars.

It was a cell! She was in a windowless, barred cell.

Andy cried out, or meant to, but it came out as little more than a pathetic whimper. She glanced down the length of herself. For a moment she thought she'd been injured and that was why her body felt so leaden. The irrational thought that she might be paralyzed seized her. She moved her legs, her feet. No. She could move freely except for the oppressive feeling of heaviness that seemed to engulf her, weighing her down.

Where was she? Her heart lurched, then began to race out of control. She struggled against panic, tried to push herself up from the bed. A wave of dizziness and nausea slammed into her, and she fell back with enough force to snap her neck. She groaned, lying still until the sickness passed.

On the other side of the wooden wall, to her right, something stirred and scraped the floor.

"Hello," Andy choked out, her tongue thick and heavy. "Is someone there?"

For a moment nothing followed but silence. Yet Andy had the definite feeling she wasn't alone. "Please . . . is anyone there?"

A tapping sound, at first hesitant, then stronger. Then a small voice, a child's voice. "Ma'am? Can you hear me?"

"Yes!" Andy lifted her head, trying to see who the voice belonged to. The dizziness swirled around her, but she swallowed down the nausea and fought to clear her head. "Who are you?"

Again her question was greeted with a long silence. But Andy was convinced that she could hear someone breathing on the other side of the wall. There was a scraping sound, like metal against stone. She pushed herself up on one arm, listening.

"It's Jeeter, Miss Angel-ma'am. I's the one you been lookin' for, I s'pect."

———

At the clinic, Roman met with the same dismaying impasse he had encountered at the hospital. By now he was close to panic. Despite the hospital matron's pessimism, and because he could not think of what else to do, he had gone on to the clinic, in the hope that, if he didn't find Andy, he might at least locate one of the two doctors. But he ended up roaming the dim, poorly lighted corridors for several minutes, only to find no one who had seen Rutherford or Meece. Or a young white female patient.

All the way back to the Manor, he told himself that by now there would certainly be some word from Rutherford as to Andy's whereabouts, some explanation. The man was a respectable physician, a trusted friend of the family, a lifelong resident of the area. It was preposterous to think he might have masterminded some sort of nefarious scheme, at least one as vile as what Roman was thinking. Only a madman would contrive anything as treacherous and outrageous as an . . . . abduction. Rutherford might be altogether peculiar, even a bit of a despot; certainly he seemed capable of duplicitous behavior, perhaps even aggression. But he was no madman.

Unless he had managed to deceive everyone around him . . . including Andy.

Thirty-three

"ho are you?" Little by little, Andy's head was beginning to clear. With the return of that clarity, however, came an increasing uneasiness.

"Name's 'Jeeter,' ma'am. Jeeter Johnson."

The voice on the other side of the wall was definitely that of a child—a little Negro boy, Andy conjectured, and probably not long out of the South. "Jeeter, where are we? What is this place?"

"Don't know, Miss Angel-ma'am. I never been here before now."

"What did you call me?" Andy strained to hear him better.

"Uh . . . Miss Angel-ma'am . . ."

"Why did you call me that?" He didn't answer for a long time. "Jeeter?"

"My Granny told me a long time ago 'bout guardian angels. She said they the ones the Lord sends to get us out of tight places and deliver us from evil. Granny said if I was ever in big trouble, I should pray for my guardian angel to come rescue me." He stopped. "Well, I did. And here you are."

"Oh, Jeeter, no . . . I'm not . . ." Dismayed that the boy had fixed his hope on her, who was as helpless as he, Andy could think of nothing comforting to say to him. "Jeeter—are we . . . locked in these rooms?"

"Yes'm. 'Leastways, I am, and all the other young'uns were, too."

"Others? There are others here besides us?"

There was a silence. His eventual reply was low and forlorn. "Not no more, ma'am. The others are all gone now. There's nobody left, 'cept you and me."

The idea of being trapped in this place with no one else but a child unnerved Andy beyond reason, even though as yet she had no idea where she was or why she was here. She had absolutely no memory of leaving home, no notion of how she might have ended up in this terrible place.

The last thing she remembered was Niles standing over her with a spoonful of the "new tonic" he had brought her. When was that? Today? Yesterday? Shaken, she realized that she didn't even know how long she'd been here.

"Jeeter?"

"Yes'm?"

"Do you know . . . what time it is?"

"No'm. I'm pretty sure it's Tuesday, but I don't know 'bout the time."

Tuesday . . . she had been here all night? But how . . . why?

Finally Andy was able to sit up, even though the effort made her head pound and her heart race.

Andy tried to think but her mind was a dark maze. Something, some vague sense of terror, balanced on the edge of her consciousness. She fought to keep it in check. "Jeeter . . . when you said you heard 'the man talking to his assistant' . . . who were you talking about? Who are these men?"

"I don't know exactly who they are, ma'am. But they're the ones who brung you here last night."

Only in the vaguest sense was Andy aware that the boy's voice was beginning to sound thick and heavy, as if he were about to drift off to sleep. "Who, Jeeter? Who brought me here?"

"The Man," he said. "The Man who works on me . . . with the needle. He's some kinda doctor, I reckon. The other one . . . The Assistant . . . calls him by a funny name, one I ain't never heard before—'Rudward' or 'Rugford'—something like that."

Andy's heart seemed to stop. For a moment she couldn't get her breath. " 'Rutherford?' Could his name be . . . 'Rutherford,' Jeeter?"

"Might be."

Andy began to tremble. She knew she dare not panic, she had to control herself, but she couldn't stop shivering. Something was wrong . . . terribly wrong. . . .

"Jeeter? What did you mean . . . about the needle? You said

254

this man used a needle on you and the others. What others, Jeeter? Who were they? Where . . . where are they now?"

The only reply was silence. Andy thought she could hear the sound of deep, even breathing on the other side of the wall. "Jeeter? Jeeter, are you still there?"

But there was no reply. Her trembling grew more violent. The cell seemed to darken still more. Even the faint ribbon of light that had been there earlier now began to fade, leaving only a damp gloom. The air grew close, oppressive. Some unnamed threat reached for Andy, clutched at her with brutal hands. She hugged her arms tightly about her body, as if to shield herself from whatever impending danger was arrowing in on her.

She was on the edge of blind panic, could almost *feel* herself slipping into terror. Calling up every bit of strength and sanity left to her, she *willed* her body to stop shaking, her heart to ease its clamoring.

"Dear Lord . . . what's happening?" she whispered desperately. "What *is* this place?"

Her choked words hung suspended in the silence, as if to mock her with the absence of a reply. On the heels of her unanswered question, the child's words came bearing down on her. . . .

"The man who works on me with the needle . . . some kinda doctor . . ."

Rutherford.

"Oh, Niles . . . Niles!" The cry that ripped from Andy's throat was born of the dreadful dawning of understanding, the terrible grief of betrayal and shattered trust.

Andy thought she now knew where she was. If she were right, she might just as well be trapped in a nightmare. Knowing *where* was horror enough. At the moment, she could not bring herself to ask *why*.

———

It took Roman nearly two hours to slug his way back through the storm to Graystone Manor. Disheartened and nearly sick with tension and fear, he arrived to find Magnus Doyle and all three women, Ibebe included, waiting for him.

Doyle descended on him in the entry. In another moment, the women appeared from the parlor. Exhausted and shivering with cold, Roman scraped his boots and tugged off his greatcoat before attempting to answer their questions. Then, lest they catch their death of cold in the drafty hallway, he shepherded them back into the parlor and drew the doors shut against the chill.

He was too weary and too anxious to ward off any grumblings about Conor's presence. No doubt the wolfhound was just as cold and as fatigued as *he* was; the faithful dog deserved the reward of a fire at his back, too. That no one seemed to object to the great hound's presence was a fair indication that everyone's mind was elsewhere.

Once he and Conor had stationed themselves in front of the fire, Roman wasted no time in telling them the truth: that Andy was not at the hospital, nor was she at the clinic. Furthermore, he had been unable to locate Rutherford and his inept assistant.

As he would have expected, Doyle and the women were stunned to the point of speechlessness. Miss Snow seemed to recover first. Roman noted the lady's uncharacteristic pallor, the evident weight loss that had somehow added years to her former robust appearance. When she spoke, however, her voice was as firm as ever, her manner just as compelling. "Impossible! She *must* be at the hospital! Where else could she be?"

Doyle immediately suggested the possibility of an accident en route. "No," Roman said, shaking his head. "I kept a careful eye out both ways. I would have seen some sign of them coming or going." His reply was short, perhaps *too* short. But he was as anxious as they were, and too weary for pretense.

"There's more," he said, going on to tell them about Meece's hospital privileges being revoked, the allusion to the man's incompetence, and the odd, troubling fact that apparently neither Meece nor Rutherford had been seen since the previous day.

Keenly aware of their worried gazes fixed upon him, Roman struggled to suppress his own growing sense of dread as he reiterated the fact that Andy was nowhere to be found. "I came back hoping you could give me direction as to some other place I might look."

"I don't understand this at all," said Magnus Doyle, his manner agitated. Roman eyed the older man with concern. The strapping Irishman had gone ashen, indeed seemed to age before his eyes. "They can't have disappeared! They must have met with an

256

accident . . . or some sort of foul play. There's no other explanation."

Roman studied him for a moment. Doyle had turned a look on him that seemed to hold both suspicion and appeal. That the older man still didn't quite trust him was apparent. But there was no one else but Roman to reassure him, to offer some word that would enable him to believe Andy was safe.

Again Roman found himself unable to dissemble. "As you suggest, Mr. Doyle, Andy may well have met with foul play. But it's my opinion that if she has, Niles Rutherford is directly responsible for it. For now, however, I'm not so much concerned about what part Rutherford may have played in her disappearance as I am about finding her. There must be something you can think of that would give me an idea as to where to begin."

"You *dare* to accuse Niles?" Doyle burst out, his eyes blazing with indignation. "Why, that's outrageous altogether! The boy adores Andy! And well you know it, jealous as you are of him."

Roman tightened his grip on the cane, clenching his other fist at his side. The fire was hot on his back, the flush creeping over his face hotter still. "Rutherford is no boy, Mr. Doyle. He's a man grown, and he has taken Andy away from this house to a place unknown to us. I can't think of any other answer but that he deceived us . . . deceived Andy most of all. But I emphasize again that Rutherford cannot be my first concern at the moment. I intend to find Andy—and I need your help in doing so!"

"Mr. St.Clare is absolutely right."

Miss Valentine's words were voiced quietly but with iron resolve. As Roman turned to look at her, she advanced toward them from her place near the window. Her eyes, however, seemed locked on Magnus Doyle. "Dr. Rutherford—Niles—has deceived us all unforgivably. It seems to me that he has much to answer for. I cannot help but think that he's behind whatever—" the woman's voice faltered, but only for a second—"whatever may have happened to Andy. But he shouldn't be our first concern at present. It's *Andy* we must think of now—her whereabouts, her safety. For all we know, her very life may be at stake."

"Preposterous!" Doyle growled.

But Miss Valentine would not be put off. Her small hands tightly clasped at her waist, she faced Doyle with worried eyes.

"Magnus—Mr. Doyle—I know you like Niles Rutherford and think of him almost as family. But there is no disputing the fact that he took Andy from her bed last night—took her while she was in an utterly helpless condition—on the pretext of admitting her to the hospital. Now it seems to me that if Andy is not where he claims to have taken her, then Niles Rutherford is quite possibly not the man we have *believed* him to be."

Doyle stared at her in stricken silence, his craggy face dissolving from anger to fear under her level gaze. After a long, tense moment, he shook his head and muttered, "I confess I do not like the looks of this. I don't know what to think, and that's the truth." He turned back to Roman. "I'll be going with you this time, if you're up to going out there again, that is."

"But *where*?" Roman shot back. He had never felt so helpless in his life. "We don't know where to look!"

"Perhaps we do." Again it was Miss Valentine's gentle voice that dispelled the tension with a note of calm. As the others turned to her, she put a hand to her throat, looking from Magnus Doyle to Roman. "There's a place he might have taken her . . . it's not likely . . . but it's possible."

Roman leaned on his cane, watching her. "Where, Miss Valentine?"

"Well, as I said, it's not likely . . . but since we can think of nowhere else, perhaps we ought to try . . ." She hesitated, looking at them with anxious eyes. "The old Rutherford place. The house where Niles grew up."

No one spoke for a moment. Then Miss Snow made a small sound of disgust. "Oh, Christabel, for heaven's sake! Niles wouldn't take *anyone* to that awful place? Certainly not Amanda!"

Miss Valentine blinked, but her voice never wavered. "I disagree, Harriet. If Niles has plotted something . . . deceitful, as I'm beginning to believe he has—wouldn't he need somewhere to take her? Somewhere . . . remote, where she wouldn't be easily found?" For a moment she went pale. "Andy has always had such a strong aversion to that awful place. . . . Oh, I do hope I'm wrong!"

Miss Snow glared at her friend as if she had surely taken leave of her senses. "Either the influenza or those silly novels you insist on reading have affected your reason, Christabel."

Roman had no patience for a woman's quarrel. "Where is this place?" he broke in shortly.

Doyle turned to him, his eyes despairing. "Near Tompkinsville, but farther inland."

"How long to reach it?"

"In this storm?" Doyle considered. "Hard to say. It'll depend on the state the roads are in." He paused. "You're thinking we should have a look there?"

"I'm thinking that *I* should," Roman said firmly, his eyes meeting Doyle's. "You're needed here, as we've already agreed. Besides," he added, trying to inject a positive note, "if Andy should return, you'll need to come for me."

The older man scowled, but finally gave a reluctant nod. "You'll be needing directions then."

"Just a rough idea. I know the general area. Perhaps you could jot down a few landmarks while I change into some dry clothes?" Roman started for the door, then turned back. "What does the house look like? I'll need a description."

"According to Amanda, it's absolutely hideous," Miss Snow volunteered, her mouth curling down in disgust. "A terrible place."

"Sure, you'll know it when you get there," Magnus Doyle put in. "Miss Snow is right—'tis the devil's own nightmare."

Something sparked a memory in Roman's mind. He stood staring at Doyle, waiting for him to go on.

"Hasn't been lived in for years, you see," Doyle continued. "Ramshackle old place . . . much as you'd expect after such neglect. Smashed windows, broken chimneys—it was probably ugly as sin when it was first built, but now it's a veritable disgrace. Only eyesore of its kind on the Island. You can't miss it."

The whole time Doyle was describing the place, a grim sense of recognition had begun to rise in Roman. It could not be anything else but the wretched old place in the woods that had struck him as so vile both times he'd gone near it. The one he had described to Andy. For some reason, she had been evasive. . . .

A strange sense of foreboding spread over him as he remembered that Conor, too, had reacted to the place with unusual hostility. *It had to be the same house. There couldn't possibly be two places on the Island that so perfectly fit Doyle's description.*

A terrible urgency swept over him. "Don't bother with the directions," he choked out, his body awash with dread. "I know the place. I've been there."

He swung around and started for the door, the wolfhound behind him. Doyle followed, and as Roman yanked his greatcoat off the hall tree, the older man put a restraining hand to his arm. "Your clothes, man! You must be drenched and chilled through. You meant to change, and you'd best do so."

Roman shook off Doyle's hand, pulled on his coat. "Not now. I don't want to waste any more time. If she's there"—he swallowed against the swelling knot of fear lodged in his throat—"if she's there, I fear she's in great danger. The place is—" He broke off, unwilling to give voice to the dread that even the thought of the place evoked in him.

But Magnus Doyle understood. "Evil," he said, his eyes locking with Roman's. "Andy insisted it was an evil place entirely, and I'll admit I've sensed the same more than once. Even so, I can't believe you're right about Niles. I simply can't imagine him doing anything . . . to hurt Andy."

Roman regarded him solemnly. "Believe me, Mr. Doyle, I pray that I am entirely wrong."

Leaving Conor to follow, he flung the door open and once again faced the storm, which by now had escalated to a raging, full-blown blizzard.

Thirty-four

*B*ecause he wanted to have the serum stabilized and bottled before Amanda fully regained consciousness, Niles Rutherford had spent most of the morning upstairs.

In the cobweb-draped room that had once been the kitchen, he bottled the last two containers, leaving one on the table while he placed the second in the wooden freight box, alongside the others. He had more than enough for Amanda's dosage over the coming weeks, plus a surplus, should he need to run any short-term experiments to complete the documentation.

Of course, once he had published his findings, there would be a stampede to obtain the rights for production. In the meantime, he would make a small amount available to the clinic, as a gesture of goodwill. He smiled to himself as he replaced the lid on the box and began to nail it down. The clinic board hadn't an inkling, of course, that their facility had provided most of the subjects for his project. Between the Negro orphans and the immigrant graveyard at Tompkinsville, he had had access to all the laboratory subjects he needed, and then some.

The thought of the forthcoming recognition, in conjunction with the wedding plans, made him tremble with anticipation. The beginning of his new life was right here, at his fingertips. After today, there would be no more tormenting memories, no more rejection, no more humiliation.

The serum was ready. He had done it. He had actually *done* it!

And at this moment, Amanda was downstairs, waiting for him. Later this evening, after he was certain her condition was stable, he would admit her to the hospital for an "extended period of rest and recuperation." With the storm and all, no one at the Manor need ever know of the slight . . . delay . . . in her arrival. And the nurses were sufficiently intimidated by him that he needn't worry about interference. As his private patient—and his fiancee—Amanda would receive only the most basic care and whatever treatment he prescribed.

His fiancee. For a moment he stopped, resting both hands on top of the wooden box that held the serum. After today, she would finally accept his proposal of marriage. In fact, she would agree to whatever he might suggest, not that he would ever propose anything less honorable than marriage. She would be too heavily sedated and lethargic for a few days to think clearly, but after that, they could concentrate on their plans for the future.

He expelled a deep breath of satisfaction. He had always known Amanda was a part of his future, one of the most important parts. Even though she had sometimes displayed a frustrating reluctance to commit to him, he had been patient with her. She was young, after all. And appallingly stubborn.

At least he would no longer have to endure her foolish notions about her "responsibilities." One of the first items of business he intended to take care of as soon as they were married was to sell that burdensome manor house. It had already consumed far too much of Amanda's time and strength over the years.

They would have no use for it anyway. With the profits he would soon realize from the serum, there would be more than enough money to build a fine new home. He would build it here, on his own land, for after today this accursed house would be no more. The new structure would be free of tormenting memories, free of the horror of the past. It would be new and clean, a place where madness had never dwelt, where devils like Zachary Rutherford had never walked. It would be his and Amanda's alone, and she would love it . . . and him . . . so deeply, so completely, she would never think of leaving.

As soon as he had her safely ensconced at the hospital later this evening, he would return only long enough to set fire to this abomination. An all-consuming blaze would purge even the ground itself of the place's corruption and madness.

He decided to take the box out to the barn and store it in the buggy before going downstairs to Amanda. He wanted everything ready for their departure later. As he threw on his coat, he remembered that there was still one subject left in the laboratory, the extra he had kept on hand in case a need should arise at the last minute.

The boy was of no use now, of course, but Niles couldn't let him go. He pondered for a moment, considering what must be done. Finally, he shrugged. The fire would take care of the boy . . . and everything else.

———

Even during the War, in the midst of winter camp with the attendant raw weather and miserable conditions, Roman had never been as cold as he was now. The baleful wind screamed all about him and Conor. The woolen muffler he'd wrapped about his face had become a brittle layer of ice beneath an outer coating of snow. His gloved hands were virtually numb, his boot-clad feet and legs like blocks of ice.

Even Hobbs, the stalwart bay horse that Roman often boasted of as "fearless," pressed on with noticeable reluctance. Slogging along beside them, the wolfhound was the only one of the trio who appeared relatively undaunted by the weather, though with his snow-glazed coat and frosty muzzle, he appeared more like an ice sculpture than a living beast.

An hour after leaving the house, Roman felt that he would never be warm again. His bad leg ached relentlessly, and the cold seemed to be driving nails through his skull. Only the thought of Andy, his fear for her, his determination to find her, kept him going.

It was impossible to make out where the ground ended and the hills began, for the area as far as the eye could see had become a vast winterscape of scalloped drifts and endless rolling waves of white. Roman was infinitely thankful for Hobbs's sure-footedness and rugged strength. The big bay trudged on with dogged persistence, finding and holding to the most level roads, the cleanest trails. When a particularly vicious blast of wind roared down upon them, the horse would simply pull ahead, as if to challenge the elements themselves.

Roman rode with his shoulders hunched, his head tucked down against the slashing wind. He reached to try to brush away the crusted ice and snow on his muffler. As he raised his head, he caught sight of the woods in which the Rutherford place sat, entrenched like a malevolent sentinel keeping watch over its evil domain. He thought of Andy, the possibility that she was somewhere inside that hideous shell of a house. The thought made him urge the bay on more furiously still, without regard for the safety of either the horse or himself.

"Not long now, chum," he told the wolfhound. But the screaming wind swept up his words and carried them off into the distant, snow-shrouded hills.

———

Andy was sure she had heard something upstairs, like someone hammering or a door banging open and shut. Holding her breath, she listened, but now heard nothing.

After another moment, she made an attempt to rouse the boy on the other side of the wall. "Jeeter? Jeeter, are you still there?" Instinctively, she kept her voice low.

She heard a scraping sound and tried again. "Jeeter, can you hear me?"

"Ma'am?"

Relieved, Andy forced herself to sit upright. After a minute she tried bringing her legs over the side of the bed, but pain gripped her head like a vise. Dazed, she fell back onto the pillows in defeat.

"Jeeter, are you all right?" she asked after a moment.

"Yes'm. I was just sleepin'. I get real tired these days."

His speech still sounded slurred, his voice thick, almost as if he had been drugged.

Drugged?

Andy's throat seemed to close as a terrible thought reared up in her. Maybe the child *had* been drugged.

And maybe she had been, too.

Niles was a doctor . . . he had access to every kind of drug imaginable. . . .

No! She was horrified that she could even think such a thing. Niles wouldn't do anything like that to a child, nor to her. He *loved* her. He had loved her for years. Niles had always looked out for her, protected her . . . he would never do anything to *hurt* her.

But Jeeter had heard his name. One of the two men who had brought her here, the boy avowed, had been named *Rutherford*.

"Miss Angel-ma'am? When you goin' to deliver me? Did the dog come with you?"

"What?" Her head still reeling, Andy fought down a swell of nausea. The sickness she was feeling now, however, was more from shock and revulsion than from any physical disorder.

"I heard a dog the other day, outside. Thought maybe he might have come with you last night, to help deliver me."

"Jeeter, I don't know what you mean." Andy hadn't intended to sound cross. But her head hurt so bad, and she felt so weak, so ill, that it was a monumental effort just to speak. "I'm sorry, but I don't know anything about a dog," she said, trying to gentle her tone. "And I'm afraid I can't very well 'deliver' you when I can't even sit up."

"Oh." A world of disappointment clung to that one word, but after a moment he spoke again. "I thought that's why you come. To deliver me. Ain't that what angels do?"

For some incomprehensible reason, the child still thought she was an angel! How he had gotten such a wild notion into his head, Andy couldn't imagine, though she wished with all her heart an angel *would* appear to deliver them.

She couldn't see any other way they were going to get out of here.

———

There was no sign of life as Roman approached the house. Still, because he didn't intend to risk being seen if someone *were* about, he tethered Hobbs at the edge of the woods, just beyond the clearing. Instead of approaching from the front, he started off to the right, slogging through the high drifts that rimmed the east wing of the house, moving as quickly as his leg would allow. Conor, as if alert to the potential for treachery, heeled to Roman's side, rather than trotting ahead as he normally did.

They reached the gentle swell of ground, now a sea of blinding white drifts, that rose behind the house. Hidden by the massive trunk of an old maple tree, Roman warned the wolfhound to silence, then stood watching. Any tracks from last night would have been buried by now. Still, he studied the white-blanketed ground before scanning the house, starting with the roof, also heavy with snow, on down. The ice-glazed windows made it impossible to see within, except for one with a shattered pane through which the darkness gaped.

No smoke rose from the broken chimney. No one moved behind the frosted windows. No sound broke the silence of the afternoon, as dark and desolate as an unbidden twilight, except for the shriek of the angry wind as it whipped sheets of snow against the house.

Conor bared his teeth and uttered a low growl. Roman silenced him, but his own nerves instantly tensed.

No sign of Andy. But she was in there. He knew it.

And Rutherford? He thought so. But what was he up to?

It was hard to believe Rutherford would actually *hurt* Andy, as obsessed as he obviously was with her. Yet, if the War had taught Roman nothing else, it had made him grimly aware that it was foolish entirely to underestimate the destruction one human being was capable of perpetrating on another, no matter the relationship.

For a long time he stood where he was, unmoving, wondering about Rutherford's state of mind, puzzling over whatever sick scheme he might have contrived. Suddenly, out of the corner of his eye he sensed movement. He looked to his right, saw Rutherford coming out of the dilapidated barn that sat back a short distance from the house. The man's coat was flapping open, and he was bareheaded. Apparently, he was making only a hasty trip to and from the house; otherwise, he would surely have been dressed more warmly.

Another low growl began in Conor's throat, but at a warning flick of Roman's wrist, the wolfhound quieted.

Rutherford appeared to be in a rush. After only a cursory look around, he hurried back inside the house, closing the door behind him.

No doubt he'd locked it as well.

He waited, uncertain as to what to do. He was convinced Andy was inside, but not knowing *where* inside, he couldn't simply go crashing into the house. A wrong move on his part might place her life in further jeopardy. But *no* move might put her at even greater risk. He had to do *something*.

He waited another two or three minutes. Then, again cautioning the wolfhound to absolute silence, he began the trek down the slope toward the house.

———————

The basement was dungeon-dark except for the lone oil lamp on the table across the room. With no windows, it was almost impossible to tell if it was night or day.

Inside the densely shadowed cell, Andy was growing more and more alert, although she wasn't so sure but what her earlier daze hadn't been a kind of blessing. As her mind cleared, panic threatened to overtake her. Had it not been for the stark reality that there was a child in the cell next to hers—a child who, incredibly, seemed convinced that Andy had come for the specific purpose of "delivering" him—she might have given in to hysteria.

Jeeter Johnson did not seem to realize as yet that she was a mere mortal, every bit as helpless as he to rescue them from this unthinkable predicament. Only minutes ago, she had made still another attempt to sit up, had almost gotten to her feet. But another wave of sickening dizziness—this one more violent yet— had slammed into her, forcing her backward onto the bed.

Lying there now, seething with anger and humiliation—and raw fear—Andy could only conjecture as to what sort of madness she was caught up in. The truth was, she was reluctant, even unwilling, to dig too deeply, for fear that what she might learn would drive her over the edge to total terror.

Looking around, she appraised her surroundings, searching for something . . . anything . . . that might provide a means of escape. The floor above was supported with precarious-looking rafters, many rotted or cracked. As for the walls, they were entirely of stone, with wooden partitions between the cells. There wasn't so much as an opening through which a rat could crawl.

Andy shuddered, quickly pushing out of her mind any thought of the ugly creatures.

With a strangely detached clarity, she faced the fact that there was no way out. She could do nothing but lie here and wait for whatever was to come. The only hope she had was that by now, Magnus or Roman was surely searching for her.

Just as quickly, she recognized that their chances of finding her were dismally slim, since they wouldn't even know where to look.

Thirty-five

*J*eeter had something on his mind that wouldn't give him any rest. Some of the talk he had heard last night between The Man and his Assistant hadn't made much sense at the time, but he'd understood enough to know they'd been talking about some bad stuff—*real* bad. He thought maybe he ought to be telling his angel what he'd heard. Even if she did keep on saying she *wasn't* no angel.

Jeeter knew better anyhow. She *had* to be. Leastways, she had to be part of The Promise. Her showing up here like she had couldn't mean nothing else.

Both his grandma and the Lord had given him The Promise when he wasn't no more than six or seven years old, before Granny passed on. Pure and simple, The Promise was that he would always be safe and "out of harm's way"—that's how his grandma put it—so long as he stayed close to the Lord, no matter where he went.

"You just stay so close by Him you're always walkin' in His shadow," Granny had cautioned. "The Lord say if we love Him and walk close to Him, then He'll deliver us from any harm. Why, He'll even command His angels to guard us. You just stay real close to the Lord, Jeeter, and that promise is yours to claim."

Jeeter had been mighty curious to know just how he would recognize this kind of heavenly intervention should he ever need it. "Why, boy," his grandma had said, "I 'spect there's any number of times He sends His heav'nly angels to deliver us and we don't even recognize them when we see them! The Holy Bible itself says that sometimes we entertain angels without knowing it!"

That had made such an impression on Jeeter he'd never forgotten it. Just imagine, meeting a real angel and not even knowing it! So even though the angel in the next cell didn't seem to want to admit she *was* one, he didn't pay that much mind. She probably just didn't want to be recognized, for fear a boy like him might be scared of her or something. Or maybe she liked to keep it a secret in case things didn't work out so well. That way, no one could blame the good Lord for sending the wrong angel for the job.

As far as Jeeter was concerned, she could just keep right on pretending if she was so inclined. He wouldn't let on he knew any different. But deep down inside him, he knew the Lord had sent her here, sent her to rescue him—Jeeter Johnson. He *knew* it!

He was thinking, though, that before they got to the deliverance part, maybe he ought to tell the angel what The Man had been up to down here. It seemed to him an angel would want to know that kind of stuff, so whoever was in charge could do something about it. Even though Jeeter didn't know exactly what The Man and his Assistant had been up to with the young'uns and the dead bodies, he knew for sure it wasn't anything good.

———

Andy had almost drifted off to sleep again when Jeeter's voice startled her awake.

"Miss Angel-ma'am?"

She was surprised that she could have actually relaxed enough to doze off. Then it occurred to her that if she had been drugged, as she now suspected, there might still be enough of the drug in her body to keep her in this dull, inert state. She made up her mind to fight it however she could. If she had ever needed to be in full control of her senses, it was now.

"I'm here, Jeeter."

"I been thinkin' about some of the talk I heard last night, between them two men when they brung you here," he said. "And it seems to me maybe I oughta tell you what I heard."

Andy scarcely drew a deep breath throughout the boy's narrative. The further he went with his incredible story, the more furiously her pulse hammered in her throat. "Jeeter"—her voice quavered—"are you absolutely certain they actually spoke of . . . killing children? You couldn't have misunderstood?"

"No, ma'am. I heard 'em clear as could be. I was wide awake, 'cause The Man hadn't give me my medicine yet."

"Your medicine?" Andy asked distractedly, her mind still spinning with what she'd learned.

"Uh-huh. Every night The Man gives us our medicine, so we'll be sure to get our sleep."

Andy felt sick. "You said . . . he referred to you . . . and the other children . . . as—laboratory rats?" She clenched her hands into tight fists, biting down on the revulsion rising up in her.

There was a slight hesitation. The boy's voice was somewhat less confident when he finally replied. "Yes'm. Said the gutters was full of us."

Oh, dear God, this can't be happening . . . this isn't real . . . it can't be real. . . .

"Jeeter . . . tell me again exactly what the other man—the one you called 'the assistant'—said about this . . . serum."

Jeeter's words came slowly and deliberately, as if he were taking great care to relay his answer as accurately as possible. "He say, 'You gonna use the serum on her. You gonna in-ject her'—" He paused, then added, "Then he say, 'She be a veg'table.' "

Andy wondered if she could bear to hear anything more and not go mad.

But Jeeter went on, his voice a little stronger now, "The Man got real upset. He say, 'She'll be my wife!' And then he tell the other one to get out."

Andy's mouth was so dry, her throat so swollen, she could barely force the words out. "You said he—Rutherford—mentioned a woman's name—" She faltered, then went on. "Do you remember the name?"

"Yes, ma'am. Sounded like 'Amelia,' No—'Amanda.' That was it. *Amanda.*"

Andy put a fist to her mouth to keep from retching. As if to shut out the horror, she squeezed her eyes shut. When she opened them again, Niles was standing at the door to the cell, watching her. For some reason, he looked surprised.

The same oppressive feeling of malevolence Roman had known upon his first look at the Rutherford place now revisited him, even more intensely this time. Conor was apparently having the same reaction. Two or three times Roman had to silence a low, threatening growl from the wolfhound, only to have those uncannily humanlike eyes turn on him in a look that plainly questioned his master's grasp of the situation.

It never failed to unnerve Roman a little when the dog took on so. At these times, it was as if the wolfhound heard things to which the human ear was deaf, sensed things too elusive for mortal understanding.

He was careful not to pass directly in front of any of the windows, instead hunched down as he edged his way from one to the other. He tried to look inside, but it was impossible to see anything past the thick coating of ice on the glass. Of the two windows off the kitchen, one had a shattered pane, but even with the missing shards of glass, nothing much could be made out, so dark and deeply shadowed was the room within. He caught a glimpse of the same battered kitchen table and broken chair he'd seen before, the same cobwebs, but not much else.

It took him a minute to realize that something was different. His gaze returned to the sagging counter on which some rusty tin containers and empty bottles had been pushed to one side. On the floor at the opposite end of the counter stood a large churn. Roman was positive that neither the empty bottles nor the churn had been there the first time he'd peered into the windows, only last week. Despite its shabby state, and for whatever reason, someone had used the kitchen in the meantime.

Almost instinctively he transferred the gun he'd earlier holstered under his coat to the pocket of the coat itself. Then he flattened himself against the wall of the house, trying to think. Given Conor's behavior and his own sense of impending danger, he might have felt an urge to turn and run. But he could not shake the conviction that Andy was somewhere on the other side of those unholy walls, and that she was in deadly danger; turning away now was out of the question.

The wolfhound had wandered round the corner to the west wing, and Roman now pushed away from the house to follow. He found the dog sniffing about the foundation. Ignoring Roman, Conor began to tunnel with his nose along the footing, chuffing and blowing snow as he went. Roman stopped him with a quick gesture of his hand. The dog shot him an indignant look, but obeyed.

Roman somehow managed to ignore the pounding of his heart and the tightening of his throat as he stood puzzling over what to do. That he had to go in was understood, but he could think of no way to pull it off unobserved. Whatever Rutherford was up to, he wasn't going to provide an unlocked door.

A broken window seemed the only solution, but without knowing which part of the house Andy might be in, there was no way to be sure he wouldn't jeopardize her by bursting in unawares. Yet the element of surprise might be his best offense. Indeed, it might be his *only* offense, aside from the Colt revolver in his pocket.

He knew now beyond any doubt that Rutherford was a part of the corruption of this place, whatever form the nature of that corruption might take. As he looked around the back of the house, the cold that had been gnawing into his bones all day sank even deeper at the bleak, stormy scene of desolation. A gust of icy snow slapped at his face, and he swallowed down a protest that was both angry and desperate. He felt himself caught up in the grip of something dark and menacing, something so far removed from his comprehension he couldn't fight it. And yet he knew he *must* fight it, for while he could only imagine the horror that lay waiting behind those baleful walls, Andy might well be *facing* that horror at this very moment.

———

As Niles turned the key in the lock and walked into the cell, Andy knew a split second of uncertainty. She had somehow expected him to look different, as if he might have donned a mask she had never seen before, a disguise to hide behind.

But he appeared the same as always. His initial look of surprise was gone now, and in its place was the fond smile he usually reserved for her. He wore the same gray suit he often wore to the hospital, carried the same medical case she had seen in his hand hundreds of times.

As she studied him more closely, however, Andy realized that something *was* different. It wasn't that he looked totally exhausted—although he did. She had grown used to the pallor of fatigue that was common to him of late. No, this was more. He was in need of a shave, his shirt collar was askew, and his hair needed grooming rather badly.

273

All this would have been enough to alert her to the fact that something was amiss, for Niles was usually neatness itself. But it wasn't until she looked into his eyes that Andy realized with a sharp, chilling clarity that something was horribly wrong. Though he kept the smile in place and spoke to her with the old affection, his eyes were devoid of all feeling.

Andy felt as if she had been struck a physical blow . . . by an utter stranger.

"I had hoped you'd still be asleep," he said evenly as he came to stand beside her. "You really need the rest, you know."

His voice was so horribly gentle. He sounded like he always sounded—kind, a little tired, but ever so solicitous of her well-being.

If she hadn't been so excruciatingly alert by now, Andy would have thought this was all an obscene, terrifying nightmare from which she would awaken at any moment.

But she wasn't dreaming. Suddenly the fear she had been struggling to suppress gave way to another emotion, this one stronger, more violent still. Anger roared through her, an anger she wouldn't have thought herself capable of before today. She pushed herself up on one arm, ignoring the painful pounding of her heart as she faced Niles.

"This is when you explain what exactly is going on, isn't it?" she spat out. "You'll have to speak very clearly, though. I'm still having a little trouble concentrating." She paused, then added caustically, "I seem to have been *drugged*."

Niles's expression underwent a subtle change at her outburst, as if he had been suddenly struck with uncertainty. But the moment was quickly gone, and now a thin smile played at his lips. Andy recognized the look as one he often wore when he was about to humor her.

"Of course, you haven't been drugged, Amanda. I would know if that were the case, and I can assure you there's been nothing of the sort."

"Don't you dare patronize me, Niles! I want to know what's going on, and I want to know *now*! You can start by telling me where I am—though I believe I already know. We're in the basement of your family home, aren't we? Why did you bring me here?"

He adopted a hurt expression. This, too, Andy had seen before, and it had seldom failed to move her.

Until now.

"It was never a home, Amanda. You of all people know that. But as to why I brought you here," he went on, "it was to ensure a measure of privacy and quiet that I could never have managed at the hospital." His voice was strangely flat, almost as if every word had been rehearsed. "I doubt that you remember very much about yesterday, Amanda, but you had a relapse, a most severe one. You required immediate treatment, and I knew you were going to need constant, round-the-clock attention. This seemed the best way to guarantee you would receive just that."

Amanda stared at him incredulously. "If I were that ill—and you're right, I don't remember what happened—then why didn't you just take me to the hospital?"

His composure seemed unshakable. "Amanda, if you'll just calm down, dear. . . ."

"Don't you dare call me that!" As soon as the words escaped her lips, it occurred to Andy that she should probably make an attempt to contain her anger, at least until she knew more about what he intended. But perhaps one of the pitfalls of knowing someone too well was the ease with which emotions were sometimes laid open. At the moment, she could have no more controlled her rage with Niles than she could have controlled the beating of her own heart.

He drew an exaggerated sigh. "I am well aware of your aversion to hospitals, Amanda. You made no secret of your feelings when I wanted to hospitalize Miss Valentine and Miss Snow. Because I only wanted to provide you with the best of care, I thought you would prefer this to the alternative. You have to know how concerned I was for you."

He moved closer, reaching for her hand.

Andy snatched it away as if his touch would maim her.

Again he sighed. "Amanda, surely after all this time, you don't question my competency as a physician?"

"It's not your competency I question, Niles," Andy shot back. "It's your *sanity!*"

As soon as the words left her tongue, Andy knew she had made a mistake. Niles's face went hard as she watched, his eyes taking on a dangerous glint, almost a feverish intensity.

Even then she could almost see him struggling for control. After a moment, he seemed to find a fresh reserve of self-restraint. "That was unkind, Amanda. But I know you're not yourself, so I'll ignore it. There are times, however, when I believe it would be a good thing for everyone if that sharp tongue of yours were not so quick to stab."

Andy almost strangled on the hot bile that rose up in her throat. "Niles—please—tell me the truth. What is all this about?"

He didn't answer right away, but set his medical case on the bed. Taking his time, he straightened and stood watching her for a moment. "It's about getting you well, Amanda. Nothing else. I brought you here because I honestly believed it would be best for you. I stayed with you all night, just to make sure your condition didn't worsen."

For an instant Andy's anger faltered. He seemed so sincere, his explanation so utterly plausible.

He must have seen her momentary hesitation. "You didn't know that, did you?" he said, still smiling. "Of course, you couldn't have. You were unconscious most of the night, poor dear. But you're *much* better now," he said cheerfully. "I assure you, you're doing very well. I think the worst is over."

Again, Andy looked at him, searching his eyes for some hint of duplicity. There was nothing, nothing but a chilling emptiness, as if Niles were no longer there, had vacated and been replaced by . . . something else.

Then she remembered Jeeter. "What about the little boy in the next *cell*?" she said, giving the word deliberate emphasis. "What has *he* done to earn your personal attention?"

He blanched, then recovered. "The Negro child?" He shrugged lightly. "He's just another runaway, using the house as a stopover. Good heavens, Amanda, you've surely heard the tales about vagrants and runaway children hiding out here? That's been going on for years!"

He was so convincing. So reasonable and altogether composed. Yet Andy knew he was lying. She *knew* it.

At the same time, she sensed it would be a mistake to challenge him, for she had begun to realize something else, something far more frightening, more threatening. She hadn't meant it earlier, what she'd said about questioning his sanity. It had simply been a remark thrown out without thinking, an impulsive jibe to try and shake him.

But now . . . now, she wasn't so sure but what she *didn't* question his sanity. There was something far more ominous going on here than deceit.

Without warning, he touched her cheek in a brief caress, then dropped his hand away when she flinched. "Oh, Amanda, I understand, dear. Truly, I do. It's only natural that you'd be confused, ill as you've been. And it has been necessary to medicate you rather heavily. But I didn't *drug* you. I gave you a light sedative, that's all, to slow your heartbeat slightly—it was far too quick and irregular. You're just feeling the combined effects of the illness and your own weakness. And, yes, the sedative and other medication have, no doubt, affected you somewhat, even caused you to become slightly disoriented. But you must trust me, everything is going to be all right. You'll be just fine in no time."

Trust him? She *had* trusted him! And it would be so easy to give in, even now. . . .

No! She had to remember what Jeeter had told her. About the children . . . murdered children. And about Niles admitting that he planned to . . . inject her with some sort of serum. . . .

Oh, dear Lord! What am I supposed to believe? I don't know what to think!

Andy forced herself to cling to what little reason she could dredge up. Whatever Niles had given her, it had been more than a light sedative. She wasn't so sure but that it hadn't almost killed her, given the adverse reactions she'd suffered.

And there was the fact that he had virtually abducted her.

Or had he?

"Does Magnus know where I am?" she blurted out. "Does anyone?"

"Of course," Niles said, his tone casual.

But something had flickered in his eyes, some hint of evasion that told Andy he was still lying. Now, instead of struggling to suppress the anger that had given her the courage to confront him, Andy groped to recall it. She sensed that *without* that anger, she might easily succumb to the cold, grasping panic that waited, lurking like a bird of prey at the back of her mind.

"He doesn't, does he? You lied to Magnus, too, didn't you?" Andy watched him, chilled by his total lack of emotion, the deadness in his gaze. "Who was the other man, Niles?"

"Other man?"

"The man who was with you when you brought me here. Your . . . partner in crime."

"Really, Amanda—aren't you being slightly childish?"

He lifted one eyebrow, as if amused, yet his face was white and strained and Andy thought his aplomb might have slipped just a fraction.

"What did you do to the children, Niles?" Andy voiced the question that had been plaguing her ever since Jeeter had told her about the others and their eventual disappearances. The boy had told her something else, too, something so hideous in its implication that Andy could scarcely bring herself to think of it. "And the . . . bodies . . . the bodies from the quarantine graveyard?"

If Niles was attempting to placate her, it wasn't working. Why was he so insistent on denying the truth?

"I can see you're more distraught than I'd first realized," he said now, his cold stare still unwavering. "Perhaps another sedative is in order, after all."

He bent over to open his medical case. Andy shrank from him, digging at the mattress with both hands. "I'll take nothing," she warned him in hot defiance. "Don't think you can make me! Don't even try, Niles!"

He raised his head and looked at her, and what she saw in his eyes made Andy's skin crawl. In that instant she knew that she should have pretended to go along with him, should have pretended to believe his lies.

For a moment she had to look away, had to remind herself that this was Niles, the same Niles who had been almost as close as a brother since her childhood. The same Niles who had helped her build her first dollhouse, who had threatened to take on the schoolyard bully in her behalf, and who had taught her the names of almost every wildflower and tree that grew on the Island. Andy could have wept for all that had been lost . . . lost to some unknown darkness within him.

She turned back to him now, met his gaze . . . and in that terrible moment of recognition, felt her soul recoil. For she knew now, with a devastating certainty, that the Niles she had known or *thought* she had known—was gone, and gone forever . . . if, indeed, he had ever existed.

Again he bent over his medical case. When he straightened, he was holding a small bottle and a long needle.

Thirty-six

*T*he faint scratching sounds outside the cell had caught Jeeter's attention right away, but what with straining to hear the conversation between The Man and The Angel, he didn't pay the noise much heed at first.

He had heard The Man's voice change, heard it grow rock-hard and cold, like water freezing up all at once. He knew that any second now The Man's eyes would go hard, too, would take on that wild, scary look.

Jeeter's stomach tightened at the thought. When The Man turned mean, then the least little thing would set him off. He would turn into a crazy person, ranting and raving, throwing things around the room, punching whichever of the young'uns happened to be the handiest. He'd gotten Jeeter more than once.

Jeeter worried that The Angel didn't know how fast The Man could change, and how crazy he could get when he did change. She sounded like she wasn't afraid of him—Jeeter supposed angels didn't scare very easy. But he wasn't so sure but what even an angel hadn't best be on guard around The Man when he was feeling mean. When he got that way, he didn't seem to have much sense about him.

They were still talking over there—The Man and The Angel—when the scratching sounds outside the wall started up again. Jeeter couldn't see a thing. The sounds seemed to be coming from the good-sized square of wood high up on the wall behind his pallet, the one that looked like a little door of some kind. It had a big iron hook on it, and Jeeter wondered if maybe it hadn't been a coal chute before somebody boarded it up, a chute like

Franklin Jones had coming into his basement.

Jeeter had gotten his hopes up over that little door his first night here. The Assistant had brought him from the clinic, after his grandma died from the influenza. That first night, they hadn't chained him to the wall, so after the men had left, he'd looped his belt around the hook on the wooden square and used it to help him shinny the wall—Granny always said he could climb like a monkey—hoping he could open the door and crawl through to the outside.

But the wood must have been boarded up on the outside, because it wouldn't budge.

Now, listening to the scratching sounds right above him, he eyed the square of wood again, wondering what was going on out there, on the other side of the basement wall. Glancing down over himself, he thought about taking his belt off and trying again. But now he had the iron band around his leg, with the length of chain that fastened it to the wall. He'd make too much racket with that chain dragging behind him.

The digging sounds were getting louder, though, and Jeeter couldn't stop staring up at the wooden door—it still looked like a door to him, even if it wouldn't open. He lay very still, listening. All at once he thought he knew what was making that noise outside. His first notion was that it was his own old hound dog come back to save him. Excited, Jeeter had to bite his tongue to keep from calling out to him. Then he remembered: his dog was still back in Georgia, most likely long dead by now, after all this time.

But it *might* be a dog, mightn't it? Some other dog, sniffing around, like the one he'd thought he heard some days past. A dog that could let his owner know there were folks trapped down here!

Excited, Jeeter glanced down at his foot, the one with the iron around it. Earlier this morning, he'd thought maybe something was different about the way the iron band felt. Now he studied it again. Curious, he wiggled his foot. Then again. There *was* a difference! The iron band looked and felt a lot looser than he remembered. Cautiously, Jeeter pushed at it with his other foot. Down, then around. Down and around again.

His ankle looked awful skinny, no meat on it at all. Maybe that's why the iron was slipping. Again he worked it with his other foot. To his amazement, the band slipped down—and slid right over his ankle.

He was free of the chain! Jeeter caught a sharp breath, then pushed himself up to his knees on the pallet and sat hunched, staring up at the wooden square in the wall.

After a moment he glanced toward the opposite cell, where The Angel and The Man were still arguing. Then, keeping as quiet as he could, Jeeter slipped his belt—which was also a ways too big for him now—through the loops of his trousers and pulled it off.

Now he would have to wait. Wait and hope for just the right chance to try and loop his belt over the hook, like he had before, and scale the wall.

"Wait for me," he whispered to the dog he hoped was out there. "You wait for me, you hear?"

———

When Andy saw Niles coming at her with the bottle and the needle, she froze. Stunned into immobility, she couldn't even scream, could only stare at the vial in his hand.

"What is that?" she finally choked out, terror spiraling through her, squeezing off what little was left of her reason.

Incredibly, he smiled at her. Andy noticed, however, that the smile didn't quite reach his eyes.

"This, Amanda," he said, standing over her, "is our future. Yours and mine."

Shrinking from the frenzied glint in his eyes, Andy stared at the bottle. "Our future?"

He gave a brief nod, his expression excited, even agitated. "I've wanted to tell you so many times, Amanda, to share everything with you. But I had to be absolutely certain there were no problems, no ill effects I hadn't anticipated. I had to wait until everything was perfected. I hope you understand. But I'll never keep anything from you again, dear."

He was so matter-of-fact, so normal. Andy shuddered.

For an instant he looked troubled. "I had wanted it to be a special time for us, when I told you. Not like this. I had planned that it would be just the two of us, alone together, somewhere private . . . just you and I. . . ."

He was beginning to ramble. His loose, disjointed speech and the wild look in his eyes only increased Andy's growing sense of panic.

Hoping to calm him, to lull him into trusting her, she realized that she must first calm herself. Slowly, she pushed herself up on one arm, forcing herself to take deep, steadying breaths, hoping her voice wouldn't betray her tenuous self-control. "Tell me *now*, Niles," she insisted. "I can't believe you've kept something so important from me all this time."

His gaze measured her. After two or three more seconds, he appeared to relax slightly. "This," he said, lifting the bottle in his hand as if it were the most precious of jewels, "is about to make medical history . . . throughout the world," he added with obvious pride.

"But what is it?" Andy didn't have to pretend interest. Frightened as she was, she couldn't help but puzzle over what was behind his alarming behavior.

"It is many things, Amanda," he said, sounding rather pompous. "You're looking at the first viable treatment for insanity. But that's just a start. It's much, much more. This serum is not simply another drug. It contains properties that will act as a control, a stabilizer, if you will, for those who suffer from obsessive, compulsive disorders. Finally, Amanda, there is real hope, not only for the lunatic, but the mentally unstable, the emotionally volatile—those who suffer a kind of hell on earth, through no fault of their own, and inflict their torment on everyone around them, even their loved ones."

A sense of overwhelming horror gripped Andy. Her earlier fear was overshadowed now by the awareness that Niles was totally, even dangerously, mad.

A fleeting thought of his mother and father—the old rumors about insanity in the family—flashed before her, quickly followed by a question she wasn't at all sure she wanted answered.

"But . . . why do you want to give it—the serum—to *me*, Niles?" she finally ventured. Her heart seemed to stop as she awaited his reply.

Niles was looking at her as if she should have known the answer without asking. "Why, to put an end to your destructive independence, Amanda. To eliminate once and for all your irrational resistance to our marriage. Our being together has always been inevitable. Can't you see that, even now?"

He paused, and his eyes took on a kind of distance, as if he had momentarily forgotten Andy's presence. "If there had only been something like the serum for my mother . . . her life would have been so much easier. It might have even helped my father, devil that he was."

"Oh, Niles . . ." The moan of anguish for his pain, the desolation of his life, slipped from Andy's lips. Her eyes filled as she watched him. "It was horrible for you, wasn't it?"

He looked at her and blinked. "Horrible?" he repeated. Without warning, he gave an ugly laugh. "You don't know what *horrible* is! You never knew what it was like for me! You couldn't possibly have known!"

"Niles—"

"Everyone else thought it was only *her*! My mother! She was emotionally . . . ill, they said. That's when they were being kind. But they weren't often kind, were they, Amanda? Most times they called her *crazy . . . touched in the head*."

He was right . . . some had said even worse—unspeakable things—about Niles's mother. . . .

"They didn't know *why* she was the way she was," he went on, standing over her, his voice higher than normal and oddly shrill. "They didn't know about *him*!"

That wasn't true. There had been those, her father for one, who had always suspected that Zachary Rutherford, Niles's father, was deranged. . . .

"They didn't know how he beat her . . . how he savaged her, like an animal . . . that's what he was, you know . . . an *animal*! A sick, disgusting, depraved animal! He beat her senseless, and when she couldn't bear it any longer, she killed herself—" Niles paused. Andy saw the bottle shaking in one hand, the needle trembling in the other. *"And then it was my turn!"*

Andy moaned aloud. She hadn't known . . . no one had known. . . .

"Niles . . . oh, Niles, I'm sorry! I'm so sorry!" she sobbed. It amazed her that, in the midst of this ugly, grotesque setting, with years of horror seemingly clinging to the walls around them and another kind of horror staring her in the face, she could still feel pity for him. In spite of her fear and revulsion, she almost reached for him.

"Over there!" Niles cried, whipping around and pointing toward the door behind the massive old coal furnace. "That's where he took me when I was bad! That's where he punished me! He beat me, and then he put me in there, in the dark, with the rats and the roaches and the filth"—he spun around to face Andy again—"and no one did anything about it! He almost beat me to death every night of my life—and nobody *knew*! Nobody *cared*! Nobody *stopped* him!" He broke off. "Until *I* finally stopped him."

Andy stared at him in horror. "*You* stopped him?" His meaning settled over her. "Niles?"

He twisted his mouth into an ugly grimace. "Oh, yes, Amanda. I stopped him. He didn't fall off the roof by accident."

Andy shuddered as the full implication of his words struck her. She broke into hard sobs, tears tracking her face like rivers of sorrow. She shook her head, trying to shake off the ugliness, the hideous enormity . . . and the awful sadness . . . of his words.

He suddenly quieted, his voice dropping almost to normal. "Don't you see? That's why the serum is so important," he said. "With the serum, we'll have no more maniacs beating their wives and children, making them suffer. We will control *them*, instead of them controlling others!" His mouth twisted. "And as one of the side benefits, Amanda . . . *dear* . . . your headstrong ways will cease. You will no longer mock me or make a fool out of me with your childish stubbornness!"

He stepped even closer to her, his eyes raking her face, then darting to her arm. Andy knew in that instant what he was about to do.

————

Jeeter had listened as the voices in the other cell grew louder and angrier. He looked up. The scratching sounds were louder now, too, and coming faster, as if whatever was out there was in an awful big hurry.

He eyed the small wooden door, tried to imagine what . . . or who . . . was on the other side. Then he studied the belt in his hand.

His heart was banging like a big old hammer inside his chest. He could hardly breathe.

"Please, Lord," he said under his breath, "this is Jeeter Johnson talkin'. . . . I'm in bad trouble, and what's more, Lord, your angel—the one You done sent to deliver me—I think she's in trouble, too. The Man, he don't care nothin' about nigra boys or angels . . . whatever he's up to over there, that angel sounds like she needs help . . . and so do I, Lord, so do I . . . and we need it right away, we surely do!

"So, please, Lord, could You just help me get up that wall again? Maybe this time You could help me get that little door open, and without The Man hearing me. I really need to find us a way out of here before he hurts us real bad. Please, Lord, You made a Promise . . . and Granny, she said You never broke a Promise yet, so please don't let this be the first time. . . ."

They were making an awful lot of noise now, and Jeeter knew he didn't have any time left to think about what to do, he just had to go ahead and do it. It took him three tries, but he finally got the belt to catch on the hook. He pulled one end down, took a deep breath, and started up the wall, his bare feet clawing the uneven, jutting stones.

"Stay there, please," he whispered. "Don't go 'way just yet. Wait for me . . . please wait for me. . . ."

———

Roman stared at the wolfhound as if the dog had taken leave of his wits. The great beast was practically dancing where he stood as he dug faster, more furiously, like something possessed.

Worried that the ruckus would alert someone inside, he commanded Conor to stop. The dog glanced back over his shoulder once, but went on pawing, growling as he dug and tossed, sending snow flying away from the foundation.

Caught off guard by this uncommon act of disobedience from the wolfhound—who before now had always proven unfailingly reliable—Roman stood frowning, as much in puzzlement as in disapproval. When he saw a block of wood emerge from its covering of snow, he still couldn't account for the wolfhound's behavior.

———

"*No!*" Andy screamed and reared up on the bed, lashing out and sending the bottle flying out of Niles's hand. It struck the stone floor, shattering and spilling its contents out into a puddle.
"*You little fool!*"

Niles slapped her face, hard, the needle still clutched in his
free hand. Andy reeled from the blow and sprawled backward
onto the bed. Her eyes burned with scalding tears. Pain
wrenched through her body, more from the anguish of his betrayal than the physical blow.

*"Now look what you've done! You bad, foolish child! Now I'll
have to punish you!"*

———

As Roman watched, the wolfhound pressed his nose to the
wood and began clawing and biting furiously at it, as if trying to
pry it open. Roman stepped closer to look, saw what looked to
be a boarded-up window, or perhaps a coal chute, nailed shut,
but with only a few rusty nails holding it in place.

"Stop it, you great eejit, you'll break every tooth in your
head!" He yanked Conor's chain to tug him away—the dog was
far too agitated by now to heed a command—then stopped at the
sounds he heard coming from within. Murmuring, like a child's
soft plea, then something else . . . scuffling, muffled voices . . .
and then a scream . . . a woman's scream!

———

Instinctively, Andy threw up her arms to hide her face, bracing herself for another blow. Instead, Niles caught her wrist and
began tugging her from the bed, all the while ranting and raving
like a man obsessed.

She screamed. "Niles! Stop it! You're hurting me!"

As if he didn't hear . . . or didn't care . . . he yanked her off the
bed, dragging her behind him. Andy fought, hitting at him, pum-
meling him with her free hand, kicking at his legs. But he was
deaf to her screams, impervious to her blows. It was as if he had
mustered a terrible strength, almost an inhuman force, as he
hauled her out of the cell.

"I'm out of patience with you!" he shouted at her as if she
were a rebellious child. "This time you'll learn your lesson! When
I'm through with you, you'll know how to behave! This time
you'll learn!" he shouted over and over at her. "You'll learn . . .
you'll learn . . . you'll learn!"

Andy fought down wave after wave of hysteria, at the same
time struggling to free herself from Niles's viselike grip. He had

her under the arms now, dragging her backward along the cold, crumbling stone floor.

She heard screaming, realized it was her own, and screamed even louder.

"Shut up. . . . shut up . . . shut up!" His shrieks were like some sort of deranged litany as he hauled her over the floor.

Andy knew she was on the verge of passing out. She struggled to ward off the fast encroaching darkness by continuing to fight Niles, twisting and tugging beneath his grasp, screaming out of terror as he went on shouting his obscene invective at her.

Andy saw now that he was dragging her toward the door behind the furnace. *"Oh, God, help me!"* She no longer knew if she were crying aloud or wailing inside her spirit. She only knew with a sickening, mind-shattering terror that what waited for her beyond that door could not be endured, would surely plunge her into the same madness that had engulfed its other victims.

─────── *Thirty-seven* ───────

With the support of the cane, Roman braced himself on his weak leg, kicking against the piece of wood as hard as he could. Twice, then three times he drove his booted foot against the wood before it splintered.

He stopped, his breath coming fast and heavy, as he worked to remove the wood. The wolfhound pushed his nose against his hand, trying to help.

Finally, Roman ripped the slab of wood free, only to find himself staring down into the small, thin face of a very young, apparently very frightened Negro boy.

The child was clinging to a ridge of stone just under the chute. Roman reached through the opening and pulled the boy free.

Immediately, the wolfhound began to lap the boy's face. At the same time the wide-eyed child flung his arms about the enormous neck of the dog and hugged him as if they were long lost friends finally reunited. "Good dog!" he crooned to the wolfhound, who was grinning from ear to ear. "And thank *you*, suh!" he said, turning to Roman.

Just then someone inside screamed again.

Andy! Grasping the boy's shoulder, Roman turned him around. "Who's down there?" he urged the youngster. "Quickly, boy! Who else besides yourself? *Tell me!*"

The child was obviously out of breath and badly shaken. "The Man—" he gulped out. "An' The Angel."

Roman stared at him, then heard Andy scream again. "Stay here!" he warned the boy as he hauled himself upright.

With the wolfhound leaping in front of him, taking the lead,

Roman headed for the back door, loping like a wounded stag. He tried the lock, found it secured, heaved his full weight against the door. Again he hurled himself at the door. This time the lock gave, the rotten wooden frame splintering under the impact.

Roman went in at as much of a run as he could manage, drawing the revolver as he went.

Andy's screams were coming from directly below. Spying a door just ahead, Roman flung it open. The stairway was narrow and dimly lighted by only an oil lantern on the wall at the base of the steps. Andy screamed again—this time a muffled sound—and the snarling wolfhound shot out in front, hurtling down the steps like a fury, leaving Roman to follow.

Downstairs, Roman caught only a glimpse of Rutherford—tie and jacket askew, hair falling over his forehead, eyes wild. He was standing near a narrow door, behind a massive iron furnace.

At the sight of Roman and the wolfhound, Rutherford thrust Andy from him with a hard shove, then began to fumble with the bolt on the door behind the furnace.

Too late. The wolfhound gave a terrible roar and, snarling savagely, jumped the man, driving him backward against the wall.

Rutherford was screaming like the madman he undoubtedly was. Roman knew he should call the dog off, yet just for an instant felt a perverse inclination to delay.

Finally, though, he ordered the wolfhound to cease. "Conor, no! Hold! *Conor*—hold!"

The dog obeyed, but with obvious reluctance. He eased back, but continued to pin Rutherford against the wall as commanded, both great paws holding the man captive as he pressed his enormous head only inches from Rutherford's ashen face.

––––––––

Even though the big man in the black coat had told him to stay put, Jeeter didn't think he ought to. He had seen that his rescuer was lame and thought he might not be much of a match for the crazy man in the basement.

Besides, Jeeter had a mind to stay close to that dog. He had never *seen* a dog like that! He was a *giant*! 'Course, he'd looked pretty funny, with his nose all frosted and his whiskers froze up. But his looks didn't matter. Not a bit! One look in that dog's eyes, and Jeeter had known he'd found himself a friend.

Besides, hadn't that big old dog saved his life? Seemed the least he could do was stay close to them—the dog and the man in black. Just in case they should happen to need his help.

He also wanted to make sure his angel was safe.

———

Andy watched in amazement as Roman burst into the basement with a gun in his hand. At the same time that Niles shoved her away from him, Conor the wolfhound exploded across the room, slamming Niles against the wall.

Sprawled on her knees, Andy thought she might faint with relief. Instead, she watched Roman call Conor off, then knock the needle out of Niles's hand with the butt of the gun.

The wolfhound glanced in her direction, whimpering as if to assure her that he cared but had more pressing business at the moment. Then he turned his attention back to the two men. Watching the powerful dog guard his master, Andy knew that, even without the gun, Roman would be fine.

Roman never took his eyes—or the gun—off Niles as he asked, "Andy? Are you all right?"

"Yes," Andy managed to choke out, rolling to her side to spare her bruised knees. She was shaking violently. Even her teeth felt as if they were rattling. Her hands appeared stricken with palsy, so fierce was their trembling.

But for the first time in days, she believed she really *was* all right.

———

Roman kept the gun trained on Rutherford, but let his eyes quickly scan the room. In one glance, he took in the table in the middle of the floor, equipped with rope restraints. He noted the oil lantern on the table, the empty cubicles that strongly resembled cells, the varied laboratory equipment.

All the while, he was sensing the aura of evil that seemed to leech the walls, the residue of unknown horrors and unspeakable secrets amassed by the years.

A sick, blinding rage roared through him that Rutherford had subjected Andy to these malignant surroundings. He swallowed down the sour taste of loathing, his finger tightening on the trigger of the gun involuntarily.

"You fiend," he bit out, his voice harsh and strangled. "You demented fiend."

Rutherford merely sneered at him. But his eyes were filled with a murderous look of hatred and something else . . . something Roman recognized as utter madness.

Only one time before tonight had Roman known the near paralyzing anger that now swept over him. The night of Kathleen's slaying, he had thought he would surely die from rage. He felt it again now—that boiling, crimson tide of fury seizing him, hammering at him, shaking all reason, all humanity from his soul as he stared into those wild, lunatic eyes.

Suddenly Roman thought of Kathleen and the madman who had taken her life . . . and the life of their unborn child. In that instant Niles Rutherford seemed to become two men—one his own poisoned, deranged self; the other, still faceless and nameless, but equally mad, surely, for who but a madman could do what he had done to Kathleen?

The hand holding the gun trembled slightly, his finger tightening still more on the trigger. Then, from somewhere in the depths of Roman's being, he sensed a quiet but imperious command: *"Stay your hand. Vengeance belongs to Me."*

Roman blinked, relaxing his finger on the trigger as his rage began to ebb. He was aware that Rutherford was watching him closely, as if waiting for an opportunity to break free.

Calmer now, Roman sent the wolfhound to stay with Andy, then stepped closer to Rutherford. *"Why?"* he grated out, studying the man with distaste.

Rutherford's eyes raked him with contempt. "You couldn't possibly understand." The words were laced with scorn.

"No doubt you're right," Roman said quietly. "And I trust that is to my credit."

Rutherford's mouth twisted still more.

"We'll be leaving," said Roman. "Is there a horse in that barn behind the house?"

Rutherford didn't answer. His eyes had taken on a remote glaze, as though he had retreated to some secret darkness within himself.

"Well, then," Roman said, "you can always walk. But the police quarters are some distance away."

Roman saw Rutherford's eyes narrow, then dart toward the table, and on instinct he half turned to follow the direction of the other's gaze. In that split second, Rutherford gave Roman a violent shove, hitting him hard enough to jar the gun out of his hand and send it clattering across the stone floor.

With relief, Roman saw Andy scramble to cover it with her hand, then pick it up.

At the same time, someone started down the steps at a run. Roman whirled around to see the little black boy trundling across the floor toward Andy and Conor. Distracted, the wolfhound barked happily as the child bounded up to him with a shout.

At that moment Rutherford lunged toward the table, seized the oil lantern, and raised it as if to hurl it at Andy and the boy.

His ruse worked. Roman shouted and broke toward Andy and the child, losing his balance as his injured leg buckled. He fell, and the impact shot a dizzying stab of pain knifing through his leg. Gnashing his teeth against the ensuing wave of nausea, he pushed himself up to one knee to see the lantern still dangling from Rutherford's hand. With a roar, he hauled himself upright and lunged toward the physician.

Rutherford gave a shriek and turned, flinging the lantern against the shelf of the sink. The globe shattered, allowing the oil to flame and ignite a pile of cloths lying on the shelf.

As Roman stared in horror, a bright burst of fire shot upward, lapping the wooden cabinets on a frenzied ascent to the rafters.

"Andy—run!" he shouted. "Take the boy and run!"

He turned to see Rutherford dart behind the furnace, throw the bolt on the door, and fling it open. "Rutherford!" he shouted. "Don't go in there! You'll be trapped!"

But even as he cried out his warning, the physician disappeared, slamming the door shut behind him.

Roman stared at the door for only an instant before turning to see that Andy and the boy had started up the stairway. Flames were spreading in deadly haste across the cabinets, groping for the steps like fiery tentacles.

He shouted a warning to Andy. She grabbed the boy's hand

and pushed him ahead of her on the stairway.

Watching until they were safe at the landing, Roman then limped back to the door behind which Rutherford had closeted himself. "Rutherford! There's little time! Save yourself!"

He tried the handle, yanked on it in an attempt to force the door open as he again called out to the man. But somehow Rutherford had jammed the door from the inside.

Behind him, the wolfhound gave a sharp bark, then another, as if to call Roman away.

Close to panic now, Roman glanced toward the stairway. Andy and the boy still stood at the top, both pleading with him to follow them, to get out.

Roman knew the steps were his only means of escape, and any minute now they would be cut off. Still he hesitated, unable to bring himself to leave Rutherford to the flames.

Incredibly, he heard the man mumbling behind the door.

Please, God, let him be praying. . . .

Dazed, choking on the hot smoke and ash, Roman stood staring at the closed door for another second or two. His eyes burned. His nostrils, his lungs, were filling with smoke. He felt a sharp pull on his coat sleeve and glanced down to see that the wolfhound had caught the material between his teeth and now stood tugging at him, trying to drag him away.

Roman tried one last time. *"Rutherford!"* he shouted. "You don't want to burn, man! Get out while you still can!"

His plea met only silence. Roman glanced down at the wolfhound, who was yanking even harder at his sleeve now. With one backward glance of genuine regret, he turned away and started for the steps, the dog practically dragging him.

———

Niles Rutherford sat alone in the darkness, his legs propped up, his head ducked down between his knees as he held the door shut with both hands.

He had been a bad boy again. He would be punished, of course. Father was on the way down the steps . . . he could hear his heavy, determined footfall, imagined he could hear him slapping the rope against the side of his leg . . . the rope with which he would tie Niles to keep him from escaping. . . .

Niles coughed, choking on the hot smoke that had begun to

creep under the door, around the flames, into his lungs. . . .

For a moment, he had the foolish notion that he wasn't in the black hole behind the furnace at all, but had been so wicked he had finally died and gone to hell. Father was always threatening him with hell, telling him that's where he would end up if he didn't mend his ways. He would beat the wickedness out of him, Father said, whip the demons out of him until there was no evil left in him, until he was a good boy. . . .

Squeezing his eyes shut, Niles gulped in the smoke, shivering as he waited for his father and the rope that would beat the badness out of him, drive the demons away from him . . . so he wouldn't burn in hell. . . .

Andy and the boy were standing at the top of the stairway.

Roman waved a hand to warn them off. "Get out of the house!" he shouted up at them. "Get out!"

"Not without you!" Andy's face, flushed and smudged with smoke, was a mask of terror. The boy, wide-eyed, stood watching Roman and the wolfhound.

Behind him, obviously agitated, Conor pressed at Roman with his great head. Still Roman hesitated, desperate to lure Rutherford from his hideaway behind the door.

"Rutherford—he won't come!" he yelled up at Andy. "I don't know what to do! He won't even answer me!"

As he watched, Andy's gaze snapped to the door behind the furnace, then back to him. Roman saw that she was weeping, great, sorrowful tears spilling over from her eyes.

For a long moment her gaze held his. Once she called Rutherford's name, then again. When he didn't answer, she turned a stricken look on Roman. "There's nothing more we can do," she said, her voice trembling. "Please, Roman—save yourself! For my sake!"

Roman stared up at her for an interminable moment. "Yes," he finally said, starting up the steps. With the help of the cane, and with the wolfhound pushing at him from behind, he dragged himself up the stairway, the flames crackling and hissing a fiery threat just below him.

At the top, he stood searching Andy's tear-glistening eyes for an instant before drawing her into a brief, hard embrace. Then, without looking back, the three of them allowed the wolfhound to herd them quickly out of the house.

———

Outside in the snow, they stood watching the house burn until, unable to bear the sight any longer, Andy buried her face against Roman.

"Are you okay, Miss Angel-ma'am?" she heard the little boy at her side ask.

Andy eased away from Roman to look at the child. "Oh, Jeeter! I told you, I'm no angel!"

The boy stared up at her, his dark, solemn eyes doubtful. "Maybe not, ma'am. But you're a part of the Lord's Promise, even so. That's for sure!"

Andy squeezed her eyes shut. Beside her, she heard Roman say quietly, "Indeed, she is, son. Indeed she is."

Thirty-eight

A week later, Roman sat in the rocking chair beside his bedroom window. Across the room, the wolfhound dozed peacefully in front of the fire.

It was late, and the house was quiet, most of the household
having retired by now. Roman was fairly well recovered from the
head cold brought on by his prolonged exposure to last week's
snowstorm. Even so, he still felt exceedingly weary. The week
had been a busy one, with much telling and retelling of Andy's
rescue and Rutherford's treachery; getting the little Johnson
boy—also stricken with a bad cold—settled in as a new resident
of the Manor, at least for the time being; and going back and forth
to the authorities until the entire dreadful business with Rutherford had finally been put to rest.

Andy seemed to be recovering nicely under Ibebe's solicitous
care. The new doctor who had been called in for consultation
had immediately ordered her to bed for nothing less than a full
week. Roman visited her every day, and though he found her understandably heavyhearted, she seemed for the most part to have
survived her harrowing ordeal with surprising fortitude—though
just why that should have surprised him, he couldn't say. Hadn't
he known almost from their first meeting that the girl had
enough pluck for two?

As for Jeeter Johnson, the boy had turned out to be a home-
less orphan, and so he also had promptly been placed under
Ibebe's wing. The stalwart housekeeper had wasted no time in
installing her new charge in the small room off her own, where,
as she put it, she could "keep an eye on that cold." The little fel-

low had already become a shadow to the woman, so closely did he follow after her through the day. Roman somehow suspected that Jeeter Johnson might have found himself a permanent home. He hoped so; surely the child deserved something better than the trouble and the terror he had known thus far in his young life.

Roman yawned, rubbed a hand over his beard, and leaned back in the chair. As was often the case, he found himself lonely for Andy. Earlier, he had donned a fresh change of clothes instead of his dressing gown, in hopes that she might still be awake and up to a visit. But when he looked in on her, she appeared to be sleeping, and so he'd come back to his own room, disappointed but relieved to know she was resting peacefully.

Her stunned sorrow during the first few days had wrung Roman's heart. Knowing that only time would heal the deep wounds of Rutherford's betrayal, he had deliberately avoided mention of the entire affair unless Andy herself raised the subject.

There still remained many questions about what, exactly, Rutherford had been up to. But from what Andy had related—and given the Johnson boy's depiction of his horrific confinement—it seemed to Roman the only possible explanation was that Rutherford had been experimenting with the fluids and tissue of the brain. Obviously, he had used live subjects, no doubt in an attempt to concoct some sort of mind-controlling drug, a drug that would render virtually useless that portion of the brain that determined free choice and individuality.

That his subjects for the experiment had consisted of helpless children and graveyard corpses made it all the more ghastly.

Rutherford's accomplice had been Meece, of course. The young, seemingly befuddled assistant had been apprehended in a disreputable hotel room in lower Manhattan, so badly frightened and riddled with guilt that he had fairly flung himself on the authorities once they found him.

Rutherford's journals and other records had almost certainly been destroyed in the fire; the police had searched his rooms at the boardinghouse but had found nothing. As for the infamous serum itself, Roman had silently sent the lot of it up in flames. After finding the cache of bottles in the barn and leading Rutherford's horse outside to safety, he had torched the building and watched it burn.

Thank the Lord, the cursed product of Rutherford's deranged efforts had been destroyed before it could claim the minds of countless unsuspecting victims. No doubt there would have been those who, if they had known, might well have condemned the wanton destruction of such a momentous medical "break-through." Roman, however, was at peace with what he had done. It seemed to him some secrets were meant to be kept.

He, for one, did not even want to know the gruesome details of Rutherford's efforts. It was bad enough that the man's lunatic obsession had taken the lives of helpless children and might well have ended up costing Andy her mind, if not her life as well. But to give any credence to the idea that some good might have eventually come about from that deviant genius seemed almost obscene.

When he heard the clock strike ten, Roman was surprised—and newly disappointed—for it was clearly too late to hope to see Andy tonight. He would have to wait until tomorrow.

Unprepared for the light rap on his door, he jerked in his chair, startling the wolfhound to his feet. Thinking it must be Doyle, Roman called out that he should enter. But the door remained closed, and after another moment, he heard Andy's voice. "Roman?"

She sounded small and uncertain. Quickly, Roman pushed himself up from the chair, reached for his cane, and went to open the door. "Andy?" He stared at her without comprehending. "Aren't you supposed to be in bed?"

"I couldn't sleep." She stood there, dwarfed in an enormous flannel dressing gown of soft blue, which might well have belonged to Magnus Doyle, so voluminous were its folds. Her face was pale, but scrubbed to a shine, and her eyes were unexpectedly bright and alert. Her hair had been twisted into two neat braids.

She looked, Roman observed, all of sixteen.

"I'm sorry to disturb you—" Her expression was one of uncharacteristic shyness. As if to avoid looking at Roman, she stooped to pat the wolfhound, who had appeared in the doorway at the sound of her voice.

Roman waved off her apology. "You're not disturbing me at all. In fact, I looked in on you earlier, but I thought you were sleeping. You *are* supposed to stay in bed, though, aren't you?"

"For a week. And it has *been* a week," she pointed out. "Besides, I . . . need to talk with you."

Pleased, Roman started to invite her in, then remembered the proprieties. Inviting her into his bedroom, especially this late at night, would be nothing short of scandalous. "Well—as it happens, I was hoping to visit with you, too. Are you strong enough to go downstairs?"

"Please, let's. I'm perfectly fine. In fact, I'm planning on getting back to work in the morning, if I can stay out of Ibebe's reach."

"That may not be easy, you know." Roman followed her down the hall, surprised at the eagerness he felt at the prospect of this impromptu late-night meeting, pleased that she had come to *him*—especially since he had arrived at a decision of his own earlier that night, one that would no doubt require quite an extended conversation.

———

Downstairs, the three of them—for the wolfhound *would* have his way and tag along—sat quietly before the fire in Matthew Fairchild's small study: Roman on the sofa; Andy, in a wingback chair opposite him. Conor settled himself between them, seemingly intent on taking up his dreams where he had left off.

By now, Roman was fiercely curious about what might be on Andy's mind, to bring her to his room at such an hour in search of conversation. But his interest also had to do with the fact that, depending on the direction their discussion happened to take, he had decided to broach the subject that had been weighing on his mind for days now.

For her part, Andy still seemed to be feeling awkward and somewhat timid with him. "It occurred to me that I haven't really thanked you properly for . . . everything. I wanted you to know that I *am* grateful to you." Her hands were clasped tightly on her lap, and she didn't quite meet his gaze. As Roman watched, she began to knot her handkerchief with some vigor.

"Andy," he said, wanting to put her at ease, "you've already thanked me. There's no need to say anything more."

She shook her head. "You saved my life."

Roman considered that for a moment. "I don't think Ruth-erford actually *intended* to harm you, Andy," he said carefully. "Certainly, I don't believe he would have . . . taken your life."

She blinked, and Roman could see that she was struggling to contain the tears glistening in those wonderful green eyes. "No," she said quietly. "I suppose he wouldn't have. He meant only to rob me of my mind."

Roman drew in a deep breath, looking away. There was no denying the truth of her words.

"I expect you can understand what I mean," she went on, "when I say that I would almost *rather* lose my life than the free-dom of will he meant to steal from me."

Roman turned back to her, nodding.

"I . . . there's more, Roman. I need to tell you how sorry I am that I put you through all that. Had I been more sensitive, more alert, to Niles's . . . problems . . . long before now, none of this might ever have happened. I put you in jeopardy, and I am so terribly sorry for that."

Roman frowned. "None of it was your fault, Andy."

She waved him off. "In a way, it was. I've even found myself wondering if those poor children might have been . . . spared . . . if I had only noticed how disturbed Niles was, years ago."

Roman saw her pain, and it took a real effort not to interrupt her.

"I can't stop thinking about the awful things he told me, there at the last," she went on. "I almost think the most dreadful part of all was learning that he had lived with all that torture and ug-liness . . . as a child . . . and no one had ever known. No one! There was no help for him, no one to intervene on his behalf. Oh, Roman—I was his best friend, and even *I* didn't know!"

She put her hands to her face in a gesture of dismay. Roman could not bear to see her in such distress. "Andy . . . you must stop this," he said softly. "You cannot blame yourself, *ma girsha.* Sick as he was, it's unlikely that anything you might have done would have made a difference. All you can do now is to put it behind you, in the past where it belongs." He leaned forward. "Andy, there is both darkness and light in each of us. Who can say why the darkness triumphs in one, the light in the other? Ultimately, I suspect it's a matter of that free will you mentioned—free will turning toward divine grace."

She was watching him closely.

Roman knew he was treading shaky ground on his own account as he continued. But perhaps he needed to voice this as much for himself as for Andy. "We choose, Andy. We choose the light, or we choose the darkness. While it's true that circumstances influence us, even mold us to some extent, the critical choice that determines what we will become is still ours to make. And when we choose God and His light, what we become is a child of God. But in Niles's case—" he stopped, shook his head, then went on—"perhaps his ability to choose was damaged by who he *was*."

"Because of his parents, you mean?" she said quietly. "The madness."

Roman nodded, his throat tightening. He felt a growing reluctance to go on with this. Who was he to judge a man like Niles Rutherford, when he had his own—*darkness*—to confront?

Yet she was obviously looking to him for more. "I don't think Niles's motives were entirely corrupt," he said slowly. "It's more likely that his mental illness impaired his judgment. Apparently, he'd been victimized for years by a kind of evil we can't really comprehend. In his own way, he was searching for redemption, I think. Perhaps in his quest to cure the torment of others, he hoped to find his own healing. What he apparently didn't realize was that the only cure for darkness—is light."

As he watched, her features seemed to clear slightly. The terrible sadness that had been there for days still gazed out at him, but he thought he saw a glimmer of understanding, and perhaps, finally, acceptance of what had been and could never be changed.

"I expect you're right," she said, momentarily glancing away. "But I still feel as if I failed Niles, if only by being blind to his torment. I know I'll always regret the fact that I failed to see his pain. If I had only known, I might have made a difference."

She turned those extraordinary eyes on him, and Roman felt as if she were looking into his heart . . . his very soul. For one fleeting instant he almost felt that her words were intended as much for him as for Rutherford's tragedy.

His voice was husky with emotion. He longed to take her in his arms, but restrained himself. After all, Niles's tragic end still haunted them both. "I believe, sweet Andy, that you would make a difference in any life you touch. Certainly, you've done so in mine."

Her eyes widened in obvious surprise.

"In that regard," Roman continued, "there's something I need to tell you . . . something I want to ask you."

She regarded him with an utterly solemn expression for a long time. Then, finally, just a hint of the smile he so often looked for touched her lips. "Yes," she said quietly. "I was beginning to think you might have forgotten . . . or changed your mind."

"I haven't forgotten," said Roman softly. "But perhaps I *have* changed my mind . . . in a way."

Thirty-nine

*R*oman couldn't recall exactly when he had decided to tell her everything, any more than he could pinpoint the precise moment when he had finally admitted to himself that he loved her. He only knew that if he dared confess his feelings to her, he would also be compelled to tell her everything, to bare his soul . . . even if it meant never seeing her again.

As for the idea he had previously contemplated—the possibility of a convenient "arrangement" that would allow them to be together without the necessity, on Andy's part, of any sort of permanent commitment—he had quickly come to realize that such a proposal bordered on the preposterous, indeed would all too likely offend her. In the first throes of his wild imaginings, he had actually considered asking her to marry him, to travel with him and work with him . . . but with none of the intimacies or obligations of a true marriage.

His motives hadn't been entirely selfish; such an arrangement would have extricated Andy from Rutherford's sick clutches. It would have also left her free for a future annulment, should the time come when she desired to separate from Roman. For his part, he could have continued his search for Kathleen's murderer, in hopes that he would eventually not only obtain the justice he felt his dead wife deserved but, assuming he *did* find the killer, he would at least know for certain that *he* had not been responsible for her death. That being the case, perhaps the missing hours for which he could never account might not seem to pose such a threat to Andy.

Rutherford was now out of the picture, of course. But even if he hadn't been, Roman had come to realize that the kind of arrangement he had so fatuously envisioned could never be enough now that he had confronted his true feelings for her. At least, it could never be enough for *him*. Finally, he had altogether dismissed the idea as outrageous.

Yet, because he could not bring himself to leave her without her knowing how he felt, he had decided to tell her—everything. There had been times when he had almost thought she sensed his feelings, even returned them. Wild speculation, no doubt. Still, he would have her know his heart.

But watching her now, seeing the sweet earnestness of her countenance and what he *thought* might be a genuine affection gazing out at him, he suddenly wondered if he could really go through with it. The idea of shattering her trust, or at the very least, implanting the ugliness of suspicion in her mind, was almost more than he could endure.

Only the reminder that she had already been deceived once, and with almost deadly consequences, gave him the strength to go through with his decision. So, before he could vacillate any longer, he blurted out the words he had been carrying so close to his heart for days, even weeks. "Andy," he said, feeling as if he would strangle, "that day in your room, before—everything happened, I was trying to tell you how much you've come to mean to me."

Her wide green eyes stared back at him with an inscrutable expression. Had she really not guessed? Apparently, he had hidden his emotions more successfully than he'd imagined.

He forced himself to remain on the sofa, across from her by the fire. "That morning when I came to your room—it seems an eternity ago, now, doesn't it?—I had intended to present you with a rather bold proposition, I'm afraid."

She looked startled, even a little embarrassed, and Roman hastened to explain. "Nothing improper, *ma girsha*, nothing of the sort. Indeed, I had every intention of asking you to marry me."

Her mouth went slack, and in spite of his near choking anxiety, Roman couldn't repress a small smile at her air of stunned bewilderment. "I had conceived what I considered to be a rather ideal . . . arrangement."

Roman winced as he saw her look of anticipation change to one of wariness. Desperate now to get on with it before she could break away from him and flee the room, he spilled out his words in a rush. "I thought I had worked things out rather tidily. You remember my telling you that I needed an assistant?"

She nodded, and he went on. "Well, it's true, you know, I do. There was also the fact that you had confided your desire to travel, to see more of the world. And I couldn't help but notice that any additional funds you might earn in wages could be put to good use. You see, I intended to offer compensation for your efforts if you would simply accompany me as my assistant, my companion—" He stopped, swallowing hard at the expression of pained disappointment that settled over her pert features. "Of course, we would have had to marry," he added lamely, "if for no other reason than to protect your reputation."

Her face had lost all its earlier sweetness, its expectation. Dismayed, Roman realized that what he now saw staring out at him was a kind of despair, very much like the expression of a child who has been bitterly betrayed.

He hurried to explain, fearful that at any moment she would break and run. "Ah, Andy, I can't expect you to understand, and you've every right to be furious with me, I admit. But at the time, it seemed the only way." Seeing her countenance darken still more, Roman struggled on, knowing that in his haste and desperation to *make* her understand, he was saying things badly, handling the entire situation poorly. "I can see now how absurd the notion was, but there were . . . reasons. For one thing, I thought it would be a way to keep from losing you . . . and to stop Rutherford from taking you over entirely. And there was something else, as well, something I couldn't bring myself to share with you at the time."

Roman looked away, no longer able to endure that relentless, wounded gaze. "I expect I was more willing to suffer your rejection, even your contempt, than to have you . . . fearful of me. You see, by then I knew what you had come to mean to me, how much I cared for you"—she blinked, and Roman saw a subtle change in her expression—"but I was simply too much of a coward to tell you the entire truth about myself and risk driving you away. There seemed to be so many obstacles, so many reasons for not allowing myself to love you—"

He saw the slight trembling of her mouth, the flash of surprise that again lighted her eyes. "Oh, yes, I do love you, *ma girsha*. I thought perhaps you knew. But in spite of my feelings for you, there was still my determination to find Kathleen's killer, not only to see justice done on her behalf, but—" He broke off. "Well . . . there was Rutherford, of course. I wasn't at all sure but what you cared for him more than you admitted."

She shook her head as if in denial, and Roman made a quick gesture with his hand. "I know. I know now that you didn't love him. But I wasn't altogether convinced of that then."

"Roman . . . don't do this."

Startled, Roman looked at her, not comprehending.

"Please don't do this," she repeated. "You're right, the idea you were going to suggest to me wouldn't have worked. I—could never have agreed to such a thing. But you don't have to make excuses. I've always known that you're still in love with Kathleen, and I understand. Truly, I do. Let's just . . . forget what you've told me. We'll not speak of it ever again."

Her look of brave acceptance broke his heart. What kind of struggle was taking place within her? "No, Andy," he said firmly, "you *don't* understand. Oh, yes, I love Kathleen. I expect I always will. Certainly, I'll always cherish her memory." He stopped, laced his hands together on his knee. "But that doesn't change the fact that I love *you*."

He smiled a little as he went on. "That's what Kathleen wanted for me, you know, to love again, should something ever happen to her. She even tried to make me promise that I would do just that." His eyes roamed her face, and a rush of tenderness welled up in him. "Kathleen would approve," he said softly. "She would have liked you very much."

He shifted uncomfortably on the sofa, suddenly aware of an uneasy twinge in his bad leg. "But there's something else, Andy. Something that even Kathleen didn't know. Something dark and terribly wrong about me, and that's what I've been so afraid of telling you. I hid it from Kathleen—and I would have hidden it from you, had it not been for the fact that I couldn't bring myself to deceive you. I saw your anguish when you realized how Rutherford had betrayed your trust—and I knew I couldn't live with myself unless I told you—everything."

Andy studied his lean profile, her heart wrenching as Roman confessed what he called the *darkness* in his life, those times of lost memory for which he had no explanation, no accounting of where he had been or what he had done.

"It began during the War," he said, staring into the fire, gripping his injured knee with both hands. "I would suddenly find myself standing somewhere on a battlefield and not remember how I got there—or when—or why. Or I would wake up outside the camp in the middle of the night, without the slightest idea of what I was doing there. After Kathleen died," he went on, "it got worse; it happened more frequently. Sometimes, afterward, I would shake in terror, for fear that I—" his voice faltered, and Andy leaned forward—"that I might have done something terrible, harmed someone . . . without knowing."

He turned to look at her, and the raw pain in his eyes hit Andy like a blow.

"God help me," he whispered hoarsely. "I still live in fear that I may have harmed someone, somehow . . . even—"

"Oh, Roman," Andy breathed, leaning toward him in an instinctive desire to comfort him. "You're not thinking . . . you can't for a moment believe . . . you might have hurt *Kathleen*?"

His stricken gaze was riveted on hers. "I can't bear to think I could have . . . I don't see how, but, yes, sometimes I can't help but wonder. . . ."

She left her chair then, impulsively going to kneel before him, looking up into his face as she grasped both his hands. "You mustn't ever think that, Roman! You mustn't *allow* yourself to think it for a moment! You would never have hurt Kathleen—you *couldn't* have! You loved her too much!"

He regarded her with a look of despair. "Do you remember what I said earlier, about each of us having both darkness and light within us, that there often seems no explanation for why one triumphs over the other?"

Andy nodded, frowning.

"Andy . . . how do I know what goes on in the darkest depths of my soul?" he groaned. "How can I *possibly* know, when I can't even remember where I've been or how I got there?"

Andy tightened her grasp on his hands to keep from drawing

him into her arms. "*I* know, Roman," she whispered. "*I* know you couldn't have hurt your Kathleen . . . or anyone else! It simply isn't in you!"

Just for an instant, he looked so vulnerable, so lost. Andy saw the doubt in his eyes, mingled with what might have been a cautious glimmer of hope. She could sense the conflict raging in him. It was almost as if he were struggling *not* to believe her, yet at the same time, wanting desperately to think she might be right.

He sighed, and the sound tore at her heart.

"You can't possibly know that, Andy. But thank you for *thinking* it, even so."

"I *do* know!" she insisted. "I know . . . because I know *you.* I know your heart, Roman! I do! You're kind, and you're gentle, and you're sensitive—I've seen for myself. And I've heard the very *voice* of your soul, in your music! I've heard your goodness and your nobility—and your honesty. There's nothing *dark* lurking in you! Perhaps there's something . . . wounded deep inside you, something that needs healing. But it's not *darkness*, Roman. It's *pain!*"

As she watched, his face contorted with the evidence of that pain. "Oh, Andy," he murmured, "do you really believe that? *Do* you?"

"With all my heart, Roman."

In that moment, Andy could almost believe she saw something fall away from him, something that had crippled him and injured him as surely as the minié ball that had shattered his leg. She felt his hands tremble in hers, and she squeezed them more tightly.

"My sweet Andy," he said, a raw ache in his voice, "you could almost help me to believe in myself again."

He leaned forward, tugging at her hands to bring her closer to him until his face—his beloved face—was so close to hers that she very nearly lost her breath.

"Ask me, Roman," Andy whispered.

He frowned, tilting his head as though he didn't understand. "What?"

"Ask me."

"Ask you *what*, Andy?" His hands still clinging to hers, he searched her eyes.

She freed one hand, lifted it and touched his bearded cheek. "Do you still want me to go with you, Roman?"

"Of course, I do! But I could never ask that of you *now*, Andy. It would never be enough. I *love* you, don't you see? I'd want you to be my wife . . . *truly* my wife, not just a . . . a companion."

"Roman," Andy pressed, ignoring the tremor in her voice, "just *ask* me."

It was as if he hadn't heard her. "How could I expect you to leave all this—the Manor, your loved ones—to go roaming about the country in a wagon with a lame photographer, years older than yourself?"

"How many years, Roman?"

He glanced up. "How many . . . well, ah, I don't expect there are *that* many. But there's still the matter of Kathleen's murderer. I can't give it up, you know. *I can't.* Then there's the other—the memory lapses. . . ."

Andy suspected that he didn't even realize he was drawing her closer as he spoke. "Still, you *could* ask me," she murmured, smiling into his eyes, suppressing the insane urge to throw herself into his arms.

He studied her face. "You wouldn't marry me . . . given all that? I mean, a *true* marriage, you understand."

Andy nodded, smiling into his eyes the answer to the question he had finally . . . well, he had *almost* asked.

Roman blinked, his expression momentarily blank. "What are you saying, Andy?"

"What are you *asking*, Roman?"

"I . . . I'm asking you to marry me, it would seem."

"Yes."

He rose from his chair, tugged her to her feet, and drew her at last into his arms. *"Yes?"*

Scarcely able to contain the fountain of happiness bubbling up in her, Andy laughed aloud. "Oh, yes, Roman! Yes . . . yes . . . *yes!*"

Her final words were muffled, stolen by his lips on hers as he kissed her . . . for the first time . . . then again.

But Andy's heart went on singing her reply to his proposal. For this time . . . for a lifetime . . . for *all* time . . . she knew her answer to Roman's love would always be . . . *yes.*

Epilogue

*T*hanksgiving Day had come and gone virtually unnoticed at Graystone Manor. There had been no time for a traditional observance of the day.

But two weeks later, those in residence gathered round the table for a more subdued, but no less heartfelt, occasion of feasting and giving thanks. All in attendance readily agreed that there were reasons aplenty to be thankful as they met around the banquet Ibebe had spread so generously and so graciously.

Magnus had paused at what everyone took to be the end of his traditional prayer of Thanksgiving—an uncommonly lengthy prayer, even for him. He seemed to be meditating over what, if anything, he should add.

Waiting, Andy couldn't keep from glancing about the table, her gaze lingering for a moment on each beloved face and offering a silent prayer of her own for the blessing of that person in her life. . . .

Dear Miss Valentine and Miss Snow. The two had not stopped showering her with love and attention since her return. More recently they had increased her happiness still more by adding their individual seals of approval to what would be a very brief engagement for Andy and Roman. Even Miss Snow, for once abandoning her customary restraint of emotion, had allowed a few tears to flow as she embraced Andy and wished her "and your Mr. St.Clare" a good life. Miss Valentine had pleaded to be in charge of the wedding—"with Ibebe's assistance, of course"—an arrangement to which Andy had readily agreed.

Uncle Magnus. How she loved him! And how truly grateful she was for his steadfast wisdom, his strength and protection throughout all the years she had been without a mother, and then a father. His shock and disillusionment upon learning of Niles's betrayal had been devastating to watch. Yet, as always, he had rallied to preside over the household—and over this special occasion—to offer his blessing on the meal, and on Andy and Roman's forthcoming marriage.

Andy's concern about all the work he would inherit in her absence had been considerably alleviated by Roman's proposal to turn most of the Manor's first floor into a new photography gallery. "Many photographers have more than one gallery in different parts of the country," he had explained to Andy. "I'd like to open my second one here, on Staten Island. I'll finance the remodeling and install a good assistant to manage the studio. That will free your uncle and Ibebe to occupy themselves mostly with running the household and renovating the upstairs floors. My flat in Baltimore is little more than a hidey-hole. Why not make the Manor our home? We'll come here often to rest from our travels, and, eventually no doubt, to stay."

When Andy had inquired about Miss Snow and Miss Valentine, Roman had quickly assured her he wanted them both to stay on. "This is their home," he had said emphatically. "I wouldn't have it any other way."

Andy's gaze now came to rest on Ibebe, a rare guest at the table. Today, at Andy's insistence, she would dine with them, as a valued and much-loved member of the family. In honor of the occasion, she had donned a frock of blue muslin she had made, and with her regal bearing, Andy thought she resembled an African princess.

Little Jeeter Johnson—the Manor's newest resident—insisted on sitting between Andy and his "new friend," Ibebe—his *two* guardian angels," he'd told them, his white teeth flashing against ebony skin. Jeeter had already won a place for himself in the hearts of all, and Andy suspected that the little boy would be permanently ensconced in the room adjoining Ibebe's, where she already kept a watchful, loving eye on him. Jeeter's own dark eyes were enormous as they took in the bounty spread before him.

And finally, on her other side, his large, strong hand clasping hers—was Roman. Andy's heart swelled to a fullness she could scarcely contain. He loved her. Roman truly *loved* her! In less than three weeks, they would be married! The Islanders would be scandalized, of course, but Andy had known that Roman was anxious to get on with his quest and his work. Besides, the notion of scandal had never bothered her very much before. She certainly wasn't going to fret over it now!

Soon she and Roman would be together—forever. He had promised her his love and his affection, his lifelong devotion. Andy could not imagine ever wanting more.

She felt his hand gently squeeze hers, and she knew he was thinking about her, too. She smiled to herself, surprised when she found it necessary to blink back a few tears that had welled up without her knowing . . . tears of gratitude and a vast, inexpressible joy for all God had given. . . .

"And to the Giver of all gifts, our Lord and precious Savior, we give all our thanks and all the glory, now and forever. Amen."

When Uncle Magnus looked up, his faint smile seemed to take in the entire group gathered around the table. But his words were directed specifically to Andy and Roman when, after tapping his spoon on the side of his teacup, he cleared his throat in an exaggerated fashion and declared: "Since there's no point in making a formal announcement of your betrothal—what with the lot of us having heard all the details of it repeatedly—I still feel compelled on this particular occasion to offer our congratulations and wish the both of you God's best."

Andy opened her mouth to acknowledge his blessing. But there was more.

"Further, I will reiterate what has already been pledged—that our prayers will follow you in your travels, and at the same time, we'll be taking good care of this old place until you've a mind to come home. For it *is* your home, you know. And wherever your journeys may lead, we'll be hoping to see you by the hearthfire often, until you're back to stay."

Magnus paused, and what Andy had come to think of as his leprechaun's grin broke across the broad features. "That said, lass, I will add my approval of your choice. Your man is an acceptable enough fellow, despite his Ulster ties. With a bit of patience and forbearance on your part, I believe he will do right by you."

Beside her, Roman laughed, sending an unexpected rush of rejoicing all through Andy's spirit. She realized that today was the first time she had ever heard Roman laugh—a sound so rich and warm and vibrant it fairly took her breath away.

In that moment, she vowed that from then on she would do whatever was necessary to evoke that sound—regularly and often.